THE BLACK MONASTERY

Ferenc K. Zoltan

A HellBound Books® LLC Publication

Printed in the United States of America

THE BLACK MONASTERY

Table of Contents

Chapter One

*A prudent man foreseeth the evil, and hideth himself:
but the simple pass on, and are punished.*

Proverbs 22:3

The darkness of the night settled on the city. Jonathan Dalton adjusted his hat and looked at his partner, whose eyes reflected bewilderment and terror. Jonathan stopped for a moment, then closed his eyes. Cold, salty air flowed through his lungs, and he exhaled a long breath. He enjoyed the moment, the joy of liberation, and wanted to savour it.

"Calm down, Nick!" he said. "We'll go in, take the money, the gold, and leave!"

Nick shook his head in alarm, then took hesitant steps backwards.

"This is not allowed! This is God's house! It is forbidden to steal from here!"

Jonathan moved to his friend, then showed his revolver. "We have permission!" he hissed angrily. "Now put the cloth over your face and let's go!" Jonathan turned around, walked up the church steps to the main entrance and opened the door. The interior of the tiny Corpus Christi church lay before him, now empty. The parishioners rested in their homes, and the church's two priests were probably already asleep. He looked back, then nodded to his partner to come in.

Nick took out his gun and walked between the rows of pews with small steps. His eyes caught the friendly expression of the Virgin Mary's statue, and he felt the accusing gaze of the saint on him. He felt ashamed that they were trying to steal from a church. He and Jonathan had been looting and plundering in the southern states since the end of the Civil War. No one stopped them, and he knew this would certainly not change in the near future. They'd ended the war on the winning side, as soldiers of the northern army. He and Jonathan had then started to raid the land of former slaveholders. He looked at his partner as he walked greedily towards the altar, picked up a gold chalice, examined it closely, then put it in a canvas bag and continued to search for valuable things. Nick walked beside the statues, trying to find loot, but a strange smell hit his nose. He tried to find its source, but it was too dark, so he went towards the direction it seemed stronger.

"What are you doing?" Jonathan asked.

"Can't you smell it?" Nick replied. "Something really stinks here!"

"It's probably just a rat! Have you found anything valuable yet? If not, then find out where they keep the money and bring it here!"

Nick nodded, then moved forward, but stepped into something sticky. He lifted his foot, but couldn't determine what it was. Scared now, he took out a lamp from his bag and lit it. In the faint light, he tried to find out what he had stepped into. He squinted, then gasped as he saw the pool of blood in front of him. "Jonathan!" he shouted. "Let's get out of here!"

The man angrily threw his bag to the ground and was about to rush to his companion, but he stumbled on something and almost fell. Both men stared in shock at the dead body lying in front of them illuminated by Nick's lantern. The corpse's abdomen had been opened all the way up to the chest, and the entrails were scattered around the body.

Nick's eyes bulged with shock, and he was overcome with nausea. He placed the lamp on the ground and leaned against the wall, then began to vomit.

Jonathan crouched beside the corpse. He had never seen anything like it before. The sound of distant footsteps caught his ear, and he knew that the perpetrator was still here. *Perhaps another thief had beaten us to it?* The answer to his question arrived quickly.

Nick and Jonathan turned towards a creaking sound. A hooded, cloaked man had just closed the door of the church, cutting off their escape route. Nick dropped his bag in shock and lowered his pistol. The hooded man had a rifle slung over his shoulder, which he picked up and aimed at the thieves. Jonathan wasted no time. He aimed his revolver and fired. The sound of the shot filled the church, and the bullet hit the wall. The hooded man lifted his repeating rifle to his shoulder and fired. Jonathan crouched down and crawled behind the altar for cover. He looked up at the towering crucifix before him and saw with horror that a priest had been nailed to it. His head was tilted to the side, and he was groaning in agony, blood dripping from his mouth onto the stone. The lamp remained on the bench, so Jonathan couldn't tell where his partner was. The hooded man's shots rained down around him or hit the altar; Jonathan knew their only chance was to fight back and make a run for it. He cocked his revolver, took a deep breath, closed his eyes, and let the familiar calm he always imposed on himself before battle wash over him. He exhaled, turned to the side of the altar, and stepped out of cover. He held his weapon in front of him and fired blindly, two shots in quick succession. The hooded man hesitated, then sought refuge behind one of the benches.

"Nick! Are you still alive?" Jonathan called.

Nick was hiding behind one of the statues depicting Christ. He peered out from behind it and fired a shot at their attacker before sneaking along the wall towards the exit. "I'm alive! I'll take down this scum!" he shouted.

Jonathan cursed under his breath as he searched in vain for the gunman. A shot rang out, accompanied by a bright flash. Jonathan jumped out from behind the pew and ran towards the exit. He grabbed hold of the heavy door, exerting all his strength to pull it open. The door opened, and the moon's shining light gave him hope of escape. He turned around and blindly fired shots. "Come on, you fool!"

Beside the wall, he caught sight of his companion sneaking towards him. He strained to focus, trying to notice any movement.

Nick darted towards the door, turning at the last row of pews, but a new blast filled the church.

Jonathan instinctively recoiled, then searched for the source of the gunshot. His partner collapsed, screaming. Jonathan rushed to the wounded man, keeping his gun in front of him as he tried to grab his friend. Another shot echoed, whistling by his head; he lost his balance and tumbled. As he looked up, he saw not one, but several hooded figures approaching him. He glanced at his friend, his comrade. From the injured man's eyes, fear and desperation radiated.

Nick grabbed Jonathan's leg. "Help me!" he roared. "Don't leave me here!"

"I'm sorry," Jonathan said, then shook Nick off, jumped to his feet, and ran through the door into the open air. Bullets rained down around him as he ran to his horse and mounted it. He spurred the frightened animal on, then galloped away as fast as he could, gasping for breath, his heart pounding fiercely in his chest. The prey no longer interested him, only his life. Once he deemed himself to be at a safe distance from the church, he stopped and dismounted from his horse. He looked around, but saw no sign of pursuers. He buried his face in his hands. He had seen many forms of human cruelty in his lifetime, and had committed his fair share, but what he had witnessed in the temple had horrified even him.

The lights of the small town of Corpus Christi could be seen in the distance, and he decided to make camp where he was for the night. He removed his cavalry cape, belt, and holster, and approached a nearby tree to dig in the ground with his bare hands. He knew it would not be wise to ride alone into the revengeful southern town at night, dressed in his northern uniform. He dug as much as he could, and when he was done, he filled the small hole, dusted off his hands, and mounted his horse again. He stroked the head of his black stallion and rode toward the small town.

***

Unnoticed by him, an elderly man had been watching the events from a few meters away.

On the veranda of his office, Wratiszlaw Arisztid leaned against a column, smoking after the long and tiring day. Refugees from Mexico had flooded the port and city; women, children, and old people fled by sea and land to the United States. The southern states were not prepared for this influx of refugees. Only a year ago, they had emerged from the civil war as losers, and now a new challenge had been thrust upon them. The French imperial troops and the soldiers of the Austro-Hungarian monarchy had occupied Mexico, and Benito Juarez and the republicans fought bloody battles against them. Miksa, the Mexican emperor and heir to the Hungarian throne, proved to be a tough man who led his troops into battle, forcing Juarez to retreat. However, people who only wanted to live their lives found themselves in unprecedented chaos.

Arisztid sighed and crushed his cigarette butt underfoot, then turned around and entered his office. He was tired and wanted nothing more than a good night's sleep. He sat down, rubbed his face, and poured himself some hot tea. Slowly sipping it, he twirled his mustache. His life had not turned out the way he had planned. He had only been fourteen years old when he took up arms with his father at Petőfi's call and fought against the Austrian oppressors. He'd had to grow up quickly and become a man. He'd seen fierce battles and painful gunfights. His father first smuggled him to London, then went on to the United States from there. At the age of eighteen, he had become a State Marshall and traveled from town to town fulfilling his duty. Over the years, he had made his home in Texas, but the war had caught up with him here, too. He'd volunteered for the Confederate army and fought almost the entire war. Once again, he'd had nothing but disappointment, pain, and defeat. The agonizing cries of the wounded still echoed in his dreams; he saw severed legs, severed fingers, and the tears of the widowed. The sound of horse hooves brought him back from his reverie. He snorted angrily and walked to the door. The old man, Anthony, dismounted wearily from his horse. What was this old fool doing here at this time? The old man wore worn-out, butter-colored pants, a yellowed white shirt, and a gray vest. His beard had turned gray, and he wore thick-framed glasses. Wratiszlaw opened the door as the old man waved at him. "Deputy Reserve!" Arisztid nodded. "What brings you here so late?"

"I'm sorry to bother you at this late hour, sheriff! May I come in?"

"Come in, Anthony..."

The Deputy Reserve entered the office and collapsed onto one of the chairs, letting out a huge sigh.

Wratiszlaw closed the door, then went to the pot and put it over the fire. "Bet you haven't eaten anything today, my friend," he said.

"Indeed," replied the old man. "I'm about to collapse from hunger."

Arisztid heated up some food for him, poured it onto a small metal plate, and gave it to Anthony.

The old man took a dirty spoon out of his boot, then began to eat greedily. After swallowing a few bites, he grimaced and said to Arisztid: "Forgive my rudeness, sir, but this beef stew is terrible!"

"That's tomato soup, Anthony!"

"Well, it's divine then!" smiled the old man, and continued eating.

Wratiszlaw took out a cigarette and lit it. His eyes grew heavy with fatigue, and he had neither the desire nor the time to deal with the old man. "Why did you come here tonight?" Arisztid asked.

"Sheriff, tonight I saw something extremely strange! Outside the city limits, there was a black man digging in the ground!"

"That's not an unusual sight down here in the south."

"But, my lord, this nigger was burying something! I think he's up to some kind of trouble. I was on patrol duty when I heard the sound of hooves. He was galloping like a bandit fleeing from someone!"

The sheriff rubbed his eyes again, knowing that his much-needed sleep was not going to happen anytime soon. "And, incidentally, you know exactly where this negro is now. Am I right?"

"Yes, sheriff!" He straightened up. "I followed him into town. He went to the inn!"

Wratiszlaw got up from his chair, then fastened his gun holster to his belt, put on his hat, and said to Anthony, "Then let's go to the inn and find out what this guy is up to!"

The old deputy hauled himself up from his chair, then hurried after the sheriff as fast as he could.

Thanks to the sea, the night air was colder in Corpus Christi than in other cities in Texas, and Arisztid already regretted leaving his coat in his office. He walked down the main street, which was almost deserted. The only noise came from Solomon's shady inn. Wratiszlaw stepped onto the porch, wooden boards creaking unpleasantly, and entered through the swinging door, followed by Anthony. He exchanged nods with the bartender, looking for the newcomer, whom he soon found.

Jonathan Dalton leaned against the counter, avoiding curious glances. As in other cities in Texas, blacks were not welcome in Corpus Christi. However, because of the northern occupiers, no one dared to act violently against them publicly. The black man gestured to the bartender, who poured him another whiskey.

Arisztid also stepped up to the counter and the bartender, with his experienced movements, placed two glasses in front of him and poured into both. The sheriff drank his drink, and the other glass he pulled towards himself. Jonathan avoided the sheriff's gaze. The sheriff smiled, dancing his fingers on the counter.

Anthony had circled around and now stood on the other side of the black man.

"Good evening, sir!" nodded the sheriff. "My name is Arisztid Wratiszlaw."

Jonathan continued to avoid the probing glances, but felt he had been cornered. He drank his whisky and slammed two coins on the counter, signaling for another round.

"I'll pay for this one," said Wratiszlaw. "So, sir, what brings you to our little town?"

"I'm just passing through," he replied.

"Really?" the sheriff was surprised. "Without any traveling gear? I saw your horse outside, and apart from a canteen and a blanket, there's nothing else on it. It must be tough surviving the Texas heat like that!"

Jonathan rubbed his face. "I haven't done anything, Sheriff! Please, let me finish my drink and I'll be on my way!"

"Did I say you did something?"

Jonathan got fed up with the game and turned to face Arisztid. "I just arrived in town, and the sheriff and his deputy are already on my back. I can see that he has his gun ready, and I can feel that everyone in this dive wants my blood!"

The sheriff smiled, then visibly raised his hands to show that he meant no harm. "Come on, friend! Why would it be suspicious if a black man rides into town at night, alone, unarmed, after burying something on the edge of the forest? So tell me, what brings you to our town?"

"I'm not up to any mischief!"

"Did I say you were?" asked Wratiszlaw, then drew his gun and aimed it at the man. "I'll ask you one last time. Why did you come to town?"

The black man grinned, then locked eyes with the sheriff for a brief moment.

The inn fell silent as everyone watched the tense situation unfold. Arisztid didn't want to start shooting, but he could sense that the man in front of him was not just a passing traveler as he claimed to be.

Jonathan's eyebrow twitched, and with a sudden movement, he darted towards the swinging door.

The sheriff didn't hesitate, aiming his gun at the man's feet and firing. Jonathan jumped in surprise, and his momentum was broken. Arisztid quickly caught up to him, and struck the man in the face with the handle of his pistol, causing him to collapse. "Anthony!" he called out. "Take this man and put him in the cell! Let me know when he wakes up."

The old man stepped next to the unconscious stranger and tied his hands together, then signaled to one of the onlookers to help him pick the prisoner up and take him away from there.

The sheriff, as if he didn't notice, continued to gaze at the black-haired guy's unconscious body being carried out. He didn't want to get into another argument with the innkeeper, but deep down he knew that what was coming next was somewhat justified.

"Look at me when I'm talking to you!" Solomon shouted.

Arisztid turned his gaze to the innkeeper, then spread his arms and responded in a somewhat apologetic tone: "I'm sorry, friend."

Solomon angrily wiped his mouth and briefly turned away, then faced the sheriff and raised his finger to begin his explanation. "How many times have I told you not to shoot in my inn?!"

Everyone was watching the argument between the two men. The inn girls stopped dancing, the poker games stopped, and the drinks stopped being served. The innkeeper looked at the people inside in disbelief, then let out a roar: "What the hell is wrong with you? You there!" He pointed to two girls. "If some goddamn drunken pig isn't panting on you within five minutes, then you can go to the harbor to be a sailor's whore! And you, Timothy!" He looked pointedly at the bartender. "Start selling the whiskey very urgently because I'll cut off your fucking finger!" Solomon looked around the saloon again, but nobody moved. He sighed, rubbed his eyes, and then his voice softened. "Half-price pussy and booze for the next half-hour!"

The people in the saloon shouted for joy. Men stood up from their tables and rushed to the bar, or approached the girls with clear intentions. Wratiszlaw's mouth curled up in a faint smile, then he looked up at Solomon standing behind the bar. The man gestured to him, and the sheriff hurried up the stairs and found himself in the office. Solomon closed the door tightly and offered the man a seat. He took a bottle and two glasses out of his desk drawer, poured them, and pushed one in front of Arisztid.

The sheriff sat down, took a sip of his drink, and pulled out a cigarette. Smoke filled the spacious room. "I'm sorry," said Arisztid. "I didn't want to shoot, but I had no choice!"

The saloonkeeper pulled a cigar from his coat pocket and lit it. "I don't care if you're the sheriff!" he began in an uncompromising tone. "I won't let you ruin my business! What did that unfortunate man do out there?"

"He was seen burying something in the forest by the reserve deputy, then he rode into town."

"And for that you have to start shooting? So if I go out and bury my handkerchief, you'll start shooting in the town? Do you know how many throats I had to cut to teach those worthless wretches the rules? Mexicans, Yankees, Hungarians, Austrians, French... God knows what kind of people are wandering around here nowadays, but everyone knows the rule! We don't shoot in Solomon's Inn!"

"I'm sorry! I..."

"Fuck your apologies!" he interrupted. "I care about one thing! Money! And you're causing me a big loss! I had to take one of the girls out for a while because she's got the pox, and the doctor can't give her any pussy cream because he can't examine her because of you!"

"Why not?" Arisztid was surprised.

"Because you shot him in the leg!" Solomon shouted.

"He was trying to run away!"

"Maybe you shouldn't have threatened him with your gun while waving it around!" "Alright!" The sheriff gave up. "Alright, I understand! Is that why you called me here again, to scold me?"

Solomon poured himself another whiskey, then stood up and walked to the balcony, stared out into nothingness through the window.

Arisztid followed the man's gaze and knew there was more to it than just a simple reprimand. Solomon Golding, the Jewish innkeeper, never spoke unnecessarily. Every action, every word that left his mouth had a purpose.

"I got a tip from New York," the barman said.

"What kind of tip?"

"The White brothers are on their way here, to Corpus Christi."

"You mean Jeremiah and Anton White? Lee's wild boys? Why would they come here?"

"Someone hired them," he said, and turned halfway towards the sheriff. "Do you know what that means?"

"That someone is going to die, miserably, and in agony."

"A black fugitive appears in the middle of the night at our place, and before that, I heard that those two bounty hunters are heading this way. I want you to find out if there's any connection between them. And if there isn't, then find out what the hell those damn bastards want in my town!"

"Your town?"

Solomon turned to him with an apologetic but half-smiling expression on his face. "I mean, your town, sheriff!"

***

Anton lay in his brother's carriage, attempting to sleep with little success, with a folded blanket under his head. However, the early morning cold, the noise of the harbor, and the alcohol consumed the previous day prevented him from finding rest. He felt dizzy, nauseous, and cold. In the past two days, they had driven their horses almost to exhaustion to reach New York. Their uncle had visited them earlier with a promising offer. Anton, though young, knew that such a large sum of money was not usually offered for a simple job. The sound of his brother Jeremiah's boots grew louder and closer, and he groaned as his brother lifted his hat from his face and looked directly into his eyes. Anton groaned and sat up. "Has that goddamn ship docked yet?" he asked.

"Indeed, my brother. Those two goddamn fellows will be here soon. Pull yourself together! Let's find them before someone puts a bullet in their heads!"

Anton jumped off the carriage, dusted off his blue denim pants, adjusted his lemon-yellow shirt, and buttoned up his black leather vest. His brother always dressed better than him.

Jeremiah wore black leather trousers, a black shirt, and a long dark coat that reached his knees. His head was adorned with a snakeskin hat, and his belt buckle displayed their family crest animal: a white scorpion. Jeremiah patted his brother's shoulder, lit a cigarette, and watched as people disembarked from the ship. Women in hoop skirts with parasols, men in tailcoats and top hats strolled down, casting curious glances at the wonders of the new world.

Anton could only think of present-day America as nothing but pigshit. Over the past years, he and his brother had fought their way through the Civil War, from the siege of Fort Sumter to the bitter Battle of Palmito Ranch. After the Confederacy laid down their arms, he and his brother returned to the town of Blackstone in Louisiana, but they were not greeted with a carnival or tears of joy from parents or lovers. The Union Army had invaded the southern states, looting and pillaging. Former slaves had risen up, burning everything around them. The image of their once-beautiful state reduced to ashes was etched into Anton's soul. In their family villa near Blackstone, they'd found nothing but corpses. The black workers who had played with the two brothers as children had slaughtered the family and taken the jewelry and cash stored in the safe. Anton longed for his old comfortable life more than anything, but he knew it had become a victim of the flames.

Jeremiah, on the day he found his violated sisters, was forever changed. Together with his younger brother, they'd salvaged what little value remained and used the proceeds to buy weapons. Since then, they had lived as bounty hunters, roaming the country.

At the harbor, two figures dressed in black caught their attention, casting shadows over their faces as they searched for them. Jeremiah signaled to them, and the two men approached the brothers, extending a handshake to one of them.

"Greetings! My name is Cristofano Bianchi, and this is my companion, Agustíno Guasparre. We come directly from Rome. On behalf of His Holiness, I would like to thank you for coming to our aid so promptly!"

Jeremiah looked at the two priests and still couldn't believe that they would receive five thousand dollars for such a simple task. He wasn't fond of playing games, so he had to gather all his strength not to ask questions. He looked at the two priests again. They were surprisingly well-groomed and well-dressed. Cristofano, the younger priest, combed his thick brown hair back, his green eyes sparkled with intelligence, and his skin shone pale white. The red cingulum adorned his impeccable black cassock. On the other hand, Agustíno wore nothing but a cassock, with a white collar around his neck. His face revealed more horrors. His hair had turned gray and his face was lined with wrinkles, but the older brother was certain that Agustíno couldn't have been older than fifty. Jeremiah could sense that the stern-faced priest standing in front of him had witnessed too many things that most people couldn't bear. "Gentlemen! " Jeremiah pointed towards the carriage. "If you wish, we can depart right away!"

Anton took Cristofano's suitcase and placed it on the carriage, then put Agustíno's on the coach as well.

As he reached for the bag, the priest stepped back. "This stays with me," he said in a colorless tone.

Anton was taken aback, but jumped onto the carriage.

Agustíno also climbed onto the wagon and placed his cylindrical leather bag on his lap.

Jeremiah took hold of the reins of the horses and they set off. "So, we're heading to Corpus Christi?"

"Yes, please!" Cristofano replied. "How dangerous is the journey?"

Jeremiah grimaced before answering, "Gentlemen, the war has barely ended! The lands of the South have been burned and looted, the president was shot last year, and now there is an influx of invaders from Mexico. It's no longer safe outside the city. Bandits, looters, robbers, violent men, and Indians who refuse to stay in reservations. You picked a bad time to come and see the new world."

"We're not here for amusement!" Agustíno said. "We are carrying out the holy task of the Lord, so no harm can befall us."

"Well then, why do you need armed escorts?" Anton asked.

"Forgive us, Father Guasparre!" Cristofano interjected. "His Holiness insisted on having armed guards accompany us on our journey."

"Did the Pope really send you?" Anton exclaimed in surprise.

"Yes," Cristofano replied. "As I said, we come directly from Rome."

"And what is so important to His Holiness that he sends priests from Rome?"

"We are heading to Corpus Christi, to the Abbey of Saint Lucia. We need to escort one of our young sisters back to foggy Albion!"

Jeremiah stopped the horses, unable to hold back his concerns any longer. "Gentlemen! Answer me honestly! What should we expect on the journey? Five thousand measly dollars for a nun!"

"Watch your tongue!" Agustíno reprimanded him.

"Calm down!" Cristofano retorted. "His Holiness deemed our mission of utmost importance! There shouldn't be anything extraordinary on the road, at least as far as we know, no threat of attack! Consider the offered sum of money as the generosity of the Church. We will find Sister Gareth, you will bring us back to New York, and we will pay the other half of the money."

Jeremiah locked eyes with Cristofano, who showed no sign of fear and didn't avert his gaze. He didn't like what the priest had said at all, but their reputation hadn't been gained through cowardice. "Alright! I'll trust you. We'll take you to Corpus Christi, even if it costs us our lives! If we stop every second day for our horses to rest, we should arrive within a week."

"Excellent! " Cristofano nodded. "I hope we can stop along the way for a bathroom break. Father Agustíno's bladder is not what it used to be!"

The two brothers chuckled, while the older priest looked at his companion with an angry expression. He didn't appreciate humor.

"We'll reach Chester by evening! We can get food there and replenish our water supplies. If anyone smokes or is an alcoholic, they can also stock up there!"

Jeremiah gave his younger brother a meaningful look, and he turned his gaze away.

The two oxen pulled the carriage at a steady pace, and the road passed in silence. Cristofano leaned against the side of the wagon, observing the endless fields, the riders hurrying about their business, and the small settlements they passed through. He had been preparing to become a priest since childhood, despite his father's hopes for him to pursue a medical career. He no longer spoke to his family, except for occasional correspondence with his sister. Although he was aware of the difficulties of the priestly vocation, he believed that serving God was the noblest task. In these challenging times, the Catholic Church carried an even greater burden in its fight against spreading evil and blasphemy. They were traveling along the base of a steep mountainside when Cristofano noticed a horseman on the rocky hilltop ahead of them. The rider cast a shadow over his face, causing Cristofano to squint as he tried to make out the figure.

"Iroquois. If there's one, the others will be here, too," Jeremiah informed the priest.

"Are they dangerous? I've never seen an Indian before!" Cristofano replied.

"No, they are fur traders, and they do business with them. As long as you don't take their prey, they won't harm you. Although they don't particularly like priests..."

"And why is that?" Agustíno asked.

"Have you ever heard of James Hopkins?" Agustíno responded.

"If you're referring to the inquisitor among the first settlers, then yes!" Agustíno replied.

"Well..." Jeremiah began his story, and his audience listened intently. "This man, James Hopkins, firmly believed that the religion of the Native Americans—their gods, rituals, and customs,—were all the work of the devil. It didn't take much persuasion to convince the Governor of New York, the good old Willem Kieft, to grant Hopkins permission to establish a small armed group. They called themselves the 'Holy Inquisitorial League.' They sought the mark of the devil on the Native Americans, who initially welcomed them with friendliness. You know, the Iroquois are not like the Comanches. The latter would have sent arrows flying at their heads pretty quickly! So, at first, they simply conversed with them, observed their customs, and the Natives showed them where they could find silver and how much fur they had. Poor fools! Hopkins and his team attacked at night. They slaughtered the men, sold the women, and sent the children to work in Europe. Hopkins, the governor, and the other bastards then mined the silver, sold the fur, and the church blessed their actions."

"Rome ordered the arrest of this man!" Agustino interjected.

"Well, of course!" Jeremiah retorted. "After he forgot to send the church its share to Rome! His Holiness didn't appreciate that! The Inquisition burned Hopkins not far from here! He was condemned on charges of witchcraft."

"Why did he tell this story?" asked the younger priest.

"Well, Father, because I don't want to end up like the Native Americans!" Jeremiah looked at the younger priest, then at the older one. Neither of them could withstand his gaze now. "You can't fool me! Five thousand dollars just for a simple escort? Come on, boys... I didn't start lying yesterday, either!"

***

The sheriff woke up to the sound of pounding. His eyes felt heavy, and he could only move his limbs slowly. He had consumed too much alcohol again. He could feel his body struggling hard, but it was an impossible task. The pounding came again, louder this time. Arisztid looked out of the window, and it was already daylight. Had the negro regained consciousness? He couldn't see any other reason why someone would be looking for him. With sluggish movements, he sat up in his bed and put on his boots. He tried to wipe the drool from his face, then hurried down the stairs to the door. Outside the door stood Solomon, the innkeeper, with a worried expression on his face. "Good morning, Solomon! How can I help you?"

"Are you deaf?! " he asked angrily. "Can't you hear people shouting in the streets, desperately searching for their children?"

"The children?" Arisztid was taken aback. "What happened?" He looked out the door. Indeed, men and women were hurrying on the main road, calling out names and clearly searching for someone.

"The altar boys disappeared, along with the organist and the sexton. The stable boy rode to the church, but luckily, he ran to me first. I have my men there now, not letting anyone in." Solomon looked at the stunned sheriff and clapped his hands twice in front of his face. "Come on! Wake up! Head to your office, I'll go with you!"

Arisztid continued to observe the chaos spreading through the streets. People watched from the windows of wooden houses, forming queues in front of shops and stalls, gazing at the scene. Wratiszlaw rubbed his face, then put on his holster and stepped out onto the street with Solomon. Arisztid walked with his head down, trying to avoid eye contact, but a weeping woman startled him.

"Sheriff! Sheriff! My son! He's gone!" she sobbed.

"Calm down!" he said. "Everyone calm down!" he shouted to the people on the street. "I have no idea what's happening right now, but I kindly ask all of you to return to your homes and carry on with your usual tasks! I will thoroughly investigate what happened, and tonight, at Solomon's inn, I will tell everyone what's going on!"

The people listened silently to the sheriff's monologue, nodded, and most of them continued with their own business.

Solomon grabbed his arm, and they headed towards the office, but the weeping woman approached them again.

"Please, Sheriff!" she pleaded. "Find my dear son! My husband passed away, and he's all I have left!"

Arisztid could only stammer, as he had no clue about what was happening in his otherwise quiet little town.

"We'll find your son, but for now, please leave! " Solomon told her. "The sheriff needs to work! Go now!" He pushed the woman away.

Entering his office, the sheriff found his equally stunned deputy, Frederick. Solomon closed the door behind them, then pushed a chair to the center of the room and sat down. Arisztid took his place behind his desk, and that was when he noticed the black man locked in the cell, leaning against the bars, observing the events. Though it was early morning and he hadn't eaten anything yet, the sheriff took out a bottle of whiskey from his desk drawer and poured himself a drink, offering one to Solomon as well. He proffered the bottle to his deputy, but he declined. Wratiszlaw drank the whiskey and poured himself another. "What the hell is going on out there? Why didn't anyone wake me up? When did our guest regain consciousness?"

The innkeeper took out a cigar from his jacket pocket and lit it. The sun shone harshly through the office windows, and the summer heat had become unbearable even in the morning hours.

The deputy took over the conversation: "I apologize, sir, but chaos has erupted. It never occurred to me to wake you up. In the early hours, I became aware of the women looking for the altar boys. More and more people started searching. The blacksmith rode out with his sons, as did the stable boy. Solomon informed me about what happened at the church."

"What happened? Why are your men there?"

"Well, because the stable boy discovered a ransacked church with several dead bodies. He claims that our dear Joseph was nailed to the cross, and Frank was disemboweled. In addition, he found a dead black man with a sack containing the church's valuables."

"Oh my God!" Arisztid exclaimed. "But why didn't the stable boy inform me?"

"I believe, Sheriff, it's because you're an alcoholic, opium addict, hotheaded cowboy who shoots first and asks questions later. As the true ruler of our town, I have enough sense to see what's happening, so that's why he came to me! And he did the right thing! My men won't let anyone in, but you should go to the scene with the deputy. And that foolish reserve deputy should start patrolling the town and try to reassure the people. I'll assist you in that."

"And tell me, Solomon, if you're so clever, then in your opinion, what the hell happened? " the sheriff asked.

"Well, I think this black man in the cell is one of the robbers. Nowadays, since the Confederacy fell, lawless blacks have been plundering our lands, as you well know. I think they broke into the church, got into a shootout with the priests, killed them, and this guy got away. But Sheriff, go to the scene and find out for yourself! In the meantime, I'll ensure there's peace in town!" The innkeeper slapped his thighs and stood up, smoke swirling from his cigar as he took big puffs. Then he walked towards the door, nodded, and departed.

Arisztid leaned back in his chair and let out a deep sigh. He took out a cigarette and looked at his companion. "Another beautiful day in the new world, huh?"

Frederick chuckled awkwardly.

"Do you still have your eight-shot rifle?" Wratiszlaw asked.

"Of course!" The deputy nodded.

"Good! Because I think we'll need it!" The sheriff stood up and approached the door of the cell.

Jonathan Dalton locked eyes with the Hungarian, but he could see in his gaze that this foreign man wouldn't be scared of anyone. "Am I not getting breakfast?" Jonathan asked.

"Of course you are!" Arisztid replied, blowing smoke into the man's face. "As soon as you reveal your name and tell us what you're doing here!"

"What I'm doing here?" The black man laughed. "Well, you arrested me!"

"Indeed!" Wratiszlaw smiled. "Did you hear that, Fred? I brought him in! Who would've believed it?"

Fred laughed and took out his eight-shot rifle from the gun crate in the corner of the office. He pulled out a rag and began cleaning it while directing a question to the prisoner. "Sir, it would be nice if you could tell us your name because we don't really like your kind down here! You could end up on the gallows quickly if you don't give us a good reason to think otherwise!"

"Shall we start with your name then?" Arisztid suggested.

"My name is Nick" he lied. "And as I said, I'm just passing through!"

"Oh, of course! " The sheriff smiled. "Then we'll ride out of town now, be gone for hours, and when we come back, we'll have a hearty lunch at the inn, washed down with fine beer! Sound good, Fred?"

"Sounds good indeed!" His smiling partner nodded.

"In the meantime, we'll leave you here, hungry and thirsty, in the hot cell. We won't even cover the windows with curtains, so that the upstanding citizens of the town will surely notice you! Eventually, the questions will turn into accusations, after a robbery attack and a strange-looking stranger in the cell... and they'll call for the gallows. Have a nice day!" Arisztid nodded towards the prisoner, then shrugged off his coat and headed towards the horses. As they reached the church, Frederick and Arisztid noticed Solomon's gunmen. Their faces radiated shock and disgust. Most of them were hardened, experienced veterans who had served in the Confederate army. Like almost every man in Corpus Christi, Arisztid had returned to the town broken and plagued by nightmares. The town, after the surrender, was nothing more than a burned-out heap of rubble. Over the past year, the survivors had rebuilt the houses and breathed new life into the settlement.

Wratiszlaw knew that the task he had taken on was far from safe. Smugglers from the sea, former slave traders, flooded the town, while Indians, robbers, or bandits attacked from the mainland. However, he always managed to maintain order and security with the upstanding citizens of the town. He took a bite of bread from his saddlebag and quickly finished it. The alcohol burned his stomach, but he felt he needed another drink. He adjusted his coat and gestured to the gunmen. He hurried up the steps of the church and immediately began examining the gunshot marks.

One of the gunmen stood beside him and started to explain. "Welcome, Sheriff! " he said. "There must have been a terrible brawl here yesterday. These damn looters..."

Arisztid entered the church, where bullet holes adorned the walls. A few meters to his right lay the lifeless body of a black man. He squatted beside him and rummaged through his pockets, finding nothing but chewing tobacco, matches, and a comb. He began examining the dead man's shoulder strap. The victim was a northern soldier. He looked up, straightened himself, and started walking along the rows of pews near the wall, his eyes scanning between the wall and the ground. Gunshot marks, wood debris, and blood. Then he spotted the second body. Frank, the local priest, lay there, frozen in his own blood. Arisztid was shocked by what he saw. The middle-aged man's body had been opened from the abdomen upward, with his entrails spread around him. The dead Frank's eyes reflected fear and pain.

"Look at this, Sheriff! " Fred said.

Arisztid looked up and saw the body of Joseph, the elderly priest, nailed to the cross in the church.

"Who could commit such an atrocity? " the deputy asked. "May the devil take these pieces of filth!"

Wratiszlaw touched the blood pooled on the floor. It was dry, with the imprint of a boot sole in the middle. He rushed over to the lifeless body of the black soldier, pulled off his right boot, and examined the sole. He found dried blood in two places. He looked up and spoke to Fred: "It wasn't the black men! Come here, Fred!"

The deputy slung his rifle over his shoulder and hurried between the pews to join Arisztid. "Why do you think so?"

"Look at the sole of the boot! " He pointed. "The blood stains are barely present in a few places, but now look at the pool of blood! The footprint matches this footwear perfectly!"

"So...?" – Fred asked, puzzled.

"This unfortunate thief stepped into the coagulated blood, which only stained the sole in a few places. If it were fresh blood, it would have covered the entire sole. So, someone had already attacked the priests earlier!" The sheriff looked around the church again, examining the gunshot marks. "These likely come from rifles, see! No shotgun pellets, and the bullet holes from pistols are too small. These were Winchester rifles!" Arisztid frowned thoughtfully. "But who could these thieves have shot at? Rivals?"

"I don't think so, boss! " The deputy shook his head. "The donations are intact, and the dead man's sack still contains gold and silver reserves."

"So, they didn't come to steal," the sheriff declared. "What on earth is happening here?"

Fred stroked his mustache, tipped his hat, and started fanning himself. "Perhaps we should dig through the prisoner's belongings. I'll notify the boys outside!"

"Great idea, my friend!" Arisztid nodded. Fred was about to leave, but the sheriff grabbed his arm, causing him to turn back in surprise to his superior. "Fred, I didn't have time to tell you. But Solomon mentioned something last night. So... do you know the White brothers?"

"The henchmen of General Lee? Of course! But you don't think they're involved in this, do you?"

"No, not at all!" the sheriff replied. "But someone hired them, and they are heading to the town! In light of this, the two dead priests, the shot Unionist sergeant..."

"Jenki?!" Fred exclaimed.

"And I'd bet my neck that our prisoner is one of them! So, if we don't want a bunch of blue-coated Northern fools on our tail, we won't let him go for a while!"

Back in town, Arisztid and his deputy tied their horses at the watering troughs and headed towards Solomon's inn. The scorching summer day was eased by a gentle breeze, but Arisztid's stomach growled with emptiness. His hand trembled slightly from the lack of alcohol, and his face turned pale. Entering through the swinging door, he approached the bartender. "What's for lunch today?" he asked.

"I can offer you a beef steak, sheriff."

"I'll take it! And a large mug of beer with it!"

"Then you'll have to bring it up!" a voice from above said.

Arisztid took a step back to see who had spoken, although he already knew.

Solomon looked down at him, leaning against the railing. "Bring it up for him, and you and your deputy come to my office immediately!"

The sheriff and his deputy ascended the stairs and took their seats in the room.

Solomon buttoned his gray coat, sat down, and poured himself a whiskey. He looked at the sheriff, who showed a desire for alcohol, his gaze wandering between the bottle and the innkeeper. Solomon smirked sarcastically and took a sip of his drink. "You're not getting any today! You look like shit! It's time for you to sober up, although, as I've noticed, you don't disdain opium or whores either!"

"Everyone has their own demons... "

"Indeed, although you've got a whole legion of them! Pull yourself together because you won't be of any use to me like this! I put you in this position to make my dealings easier! So, what have you found out?"

"The black folks didn't kill the priests. The sacristan, the organist, and the altar boys were not there; we checked the place. However!" He brought out the buried items. "We found a Northern officer's coat. The guy was a captain in the cavalry judging by the insignia. Also, a Colt regularly used by the Northerners with nearly a hundred rounds."

"So they wanted to rob the church, but someone beat them to it?" Solomon asked

"Nothing went missing!" the deputy said. "Robbers didn't finish off the priests."

"So who and why, then?" The innkeeper raised his eyebrow.

"That's the tricky question," Arisztid interjected. "Who did the Yanks run into? I hope hunger, thirst, and the heat have tortured this Nick enough to make him spill the truth."

"So his name is Nick?"

"I don't think so, Solomon! Once I finish my lunch, I'll interrogate him."

"No!" the innkeeper insisted. "I'll go over and talk to him! You just focus on your job! Find the missing ones so that the town's people can spend money at my place again!"

Jonathan Dalton had not planned the robbery this way. He was disoriented, and the heat had become unbearable. Hunger and thirst tormented him, and he felt infinitely pathetic. The only place where he could find a bit of shade was under the bed. He took off his shirt and hid under there, just like a thief. After all, that's what he was. He was saddened by the death of his partner, guilt creeping in for being unable to save his friend. However, his own life was the most important to him. For the first time in his life, he gave orders to others, and he was not willing to give that up. He still considered that April day five years ago, when he and his comrades had rebelled upon hearing about the war, as the happiest day of his life. A smile appeared on Jonathan's face as he remembered how he first raised the rifle to his shoulder. By then, in the Battle of the Hemp Bales, he no longer killed impulsively but poured out the blood of the Southerners he hated with premeditated, purposeful intent. His hands had trembled that day, not out of fear, as he had always experienced in his previous life, but from the almost ecstatic excitement. The manual labor he had been forced into from childhood made him incredibly strong, and his endurance became above average. Thanks to the whip lashes he had suffered from his former owner, he could endure pain that was considered exceptional even among his fellow slaves. As the war progressed, he climbed the ranks, and finally, he could feel that his skin color did not hinder him in anything. He became proud, strong, and free. Free... He reluctantly smiled as he looked at himself lying half-naked under the bed in the cell. *Well, you messed this up, Jon...*

The door swung open, and a man in a gray pinstripe suit entered, scanning the room for the prisoner, not finding him at first. The man twirled his mustache, adjusted his hair with his hand, then stepped in front of the cell door and crouched down. A mocking smile appeared on his face, then he pulled a chair over and sat down. "Don't you want to come out from under the bed, Nick?" Solomon asked.

Jonathan didn't respond. He didn't know what to say to this. He felt ashamed for ending up in this situation.

"Don't play games, Nick! Be a man and tell me what happened! I know you're a damn Yankee!"

Dalton crawled out from under the bed and took a seat on the floor. "Could I have a little water, please?"

"That won't get you far with me! I won't pity you! So, I offer you a chance, with which, if you take it, I can make your time here a bit easier. I ask, and you honestly answer! If I believe what you say, then I'll give you water. Deal?"

"Deal." Jonathan nodded.

"Is your name Nick?"

"No."

"The dead nigger in the church, is he Nick?"

"Yes."

"Good!" grumbled Solomon. "Looks like hunger and thirst have been effective." He stood up from his chair, poured water into a bowl, and slid it under the bars.

Jonathan eagerly reached for the water and drank it all. He sighed deeply and leaned back. He could feel his dehydrated body gaining strength again, though he knew it was only temporary. "My name is Jonathan," he said to Solomon.

"So, Jonathan, I see. We found a cavalry coat, lots of ammunition, and a revolver. I assume you're a soldier for the North. Is that right?"

"There are no Northerners and Southerners anymore!" he spoke up. "There's only one army! The United States Army! You and those dirty white-faced bastards will pay for everything you've done against the blacks!"

"Dirty white-faced! Me!" Solomon raised his voice mockingly. "My boy, I'm Jewish, I couldn't care less about what the whites did to your soot-faced friends! I'm interested in criminals like you! You know why? Because you cause losses, and I don't allow that, be it black or white! You wanted to rob our church, but something went wrong. Tell me what happened!"

"Nothing."

Solomon angrily stood up, then grabbed the bars. Anger emanated from his voice. "Listen here, boy! You're hungry, right? Answer my damn questions! What happened in the church? Where are the kids?! Where is the organist, the sacristan, what happened to the priests?!"

"I don't know!" Jonathan replied.

Solomon slammed the iron bars and continued threateningly, almost whispering: "We'll see about that, my boy! Is your stomach growling? Well, we'll fill it up soon enough!"

The innkeeper stormed out of the sheriff's office with a face contorted in anger. After a few minutes, he returned with the sheriff and his deputy. Solomon held a wooden bucket in his hands, its top sealed, yet he could still hear rattling sounds, the ominous murmurs emanating from within. The sheriff had a bunch of keys, and his deputy aimed a rifle at Jonathan. Arisztid opened the cell and signaled for the prisoner to come out. Jonathan stepped out of the cell, and the sheriff forcibly sat him down. His hands were tied behind the chair. Solomon placed the bucket down and took out a long metal clamp from his pocket. Carefully lifting the lid of the bucket, Jonathan was horrified by its contents. A multitude of scorpions clashed and trampled each other inside. The clicking of the scorpions' pincers seemed like an endless, eerie symphony. Jonathan's heart pounded, he began to sweat, and his lips trembled. He hated scorpions. The deputy stepped behind him, holding his head, and the sheriff stretched his mouth wide open. Using the clamp, Solomon picked up a scorpion. A strange, blackish liquid dripped from the creature onto the floor. "I'll ask you one last time, Jonathan!" he hissed. "What happened in the church?"

Jonathan trembled, but refused to answer. Solomon placed the scorpion on the man's face, still holding its stinger with the clamp. Jonathan felt the insect's hard, piercing legs slipping into his mouth, the pincers catching on his nose. "I DON'T KNOW!" he screamed in terror. "PLEASE DON'T DO THIS!"

Solomon looked at the sheriff, who this time shoved a funnel into Jonathan's mouth. He began to retch, shaking all over, kicking his legs, but it was all in vain.

"Do you know what I learned during the war, my boy?" the innkeeper asked. "I learned to interrogate quite well! What you see is a Texas Emperor Scorpion, soaked in oil! Quite a tasty dish, isn't it? The oil slightly intoxicates it and makes it pleasantly slippery. It easily slips into your stomach without any problems. Thanks to its armor, it might take up to two days before it dissolves in stomach acid and only reaches your intestines on the third day."

The innkeeper placed the scorpion into the funnel, then pressed it deeper with the clamp. Jonathan thrashed wildly, tried to scream, but the two men held him firmly. He felt the creature smoothly slide down his throat without any obstruction. Tears welled up in his eyes. He knew that excruciating torment awaited him.

Fred and Arisztid let go of the prisoner and stepped back. Solomon took the funnel out of Jonathan's mouth, who gagged, tried to vomit, but the innkeeper chuckled maliciously. "Well, buddy! It will only come out from the bottom! Now, off to the cell to carefully consider what you answer next time!"

Chapter Two

"And I will send upon you famine and evil beasts, and they shall bereave thee; and pestilence and blood shall pass through thee; and I will bring the sword upon thee. I, the Lord, have spoken."

Book of Ezekiel 5:17

Father Agustíno jumped off the wagon, stretching his tired limbs. They had been on the road for a long time, and he was finding the exhausting journey increasingly challenging. They were only a day's ride away from their destination, but he knew they couldn't linger in the town for long. They would rest for a day or two, replenish their supplies, and then leave this wild and dangerous country with Miss Gareth. The skepticism and constant mockery of the elder White brother, Jeremiah, annoyed the priest, but he was aware that they wouldn't last long without the two men. He considered it a minor miracle that no one had attacked them in the past six days.

Behind him, Anton threw a log onto the campfire, then took a hearty swig from his flask. Cristofano and the younger White brother had become quite friendly during the journey. Agustíno turned around and sat on the spread-out blanket on the ground.

Jeremiah, who had hunted several rabbits during the journey, dished out a portion of fresh game onto the elder priest's plate, who ate lost in thought. The sun had already set, and Jeremiah performed the usual security measures. He stretched a rope at ankle height in a square around their camp, placing several tin cans along its length. This way, if anyone tried to sneak up on them at night, they would be immediately alerted.

Anton rolled a cigarette and lit it. "Father Guasparre!" Anton called. "Since we've become so well acquainted, can I address you as Agustíno?"

"Call me whatever you want," replied Agustíno nonchalantly.

"Tell me, Agustíno, why can't you be as friendly and straightforward as Cristofano?"

"Because Cristofano is still young and believes in the goodness of people. I haven't done that for a long time..."

"Why not?" Anton inquired.

"Do I have to explain this to you? I understand that you Southerners declared your independence after Kansas and Nebraska chose the Southern model, not the Northern liberal one."

"You mean the Missouri Compromise?" Jeremiah asked in a raspy voice.

"Exactly," Agustíno replied. "So after Abraham Lincoln came to power, you decided to break away from the industrially more advanced North, creating an independent system to ensure your own development. Isn't that right?"

"True." The two brothers nodded.

"They drafted their own constitution, democratically elected Jefferson Davis as president, who only requested the withdrawal of the Northern army from Confederate territory. Lincoln refused this demand and was unwilling to recognize the confederation created by your free will; he could not be persuaded to take part in any negotiations. He seized the Confederacy's diplomats on international waters and didn't hesitate to get into a conflict with the British over it. He sent thousands of people to slaughter, all because he wasn't willing to give up Southern taxes and tariffs! The will of his own people didn't matter a bit! This story is just one of many reasons why I am no longer capable of believing in human goodness. Man is flawed, and every day reinforces the downfall of God in me."

"Agustíno!" Cristofano exclaimed.

The elder priest looked disapprovingly at his younger companion and continued: "Man is inherently sinful, imperfect, and infinitely selfish. Instead of creating the perfect being, God created the greatest pest. Believe me, Cristofano, I have seen evil. And the devil no longer needs to tempt people, as they willingly rush into damnation. Our task would be to lead them onto the right path through the word, but the church has long deviated from that path." He looked at the young priest. "Only a few follow the right path and work for the salvation of the human soul."

"I agree with you, Father!" Jeremiah spoke up. "We have all seen the devil, human wickedness. We Southerners didn't want anything else but to live in our own country, under our own laws!"

"But slavery is inhumane and sinful," Cristofano replied.

"Oh, come on!" Jeremiah retorted. "President Davis wasn't pro-slavery! Our war wasn't about that! General Lee liberated his own slaves, and what did he get in return? They started looting our lands and biting the hand that fed them! And up north, what happened? There's no one left to accommodate them, give them food, drink, or work. They work in Northern factories for thirty cents a week! They fought hard for their freedom! I say, Booth did well to shoot that scoundrel Lincoln! I wish I had been there when he fired that bullet into that bastard's head! He leaped from the balcony, straight onto the stage, held his pistol high, and you know what he shouted? 'Sic semper tyrannis!' That's what happens to tyrants! He was the true patriot!"

"You say it well, brother!" nodded Anton. "We spilled our blood for our country! Our comrades, our brothers died in the battles, and what did we get? The people I grew up with slaughtered our family, burned our land, and destroyed our house! They stole our family fortune!"

"But you're alive!" said Father Cristofano. "I'm sure the Creator intentionally led you down this path! Every wound, all the pain that torments us, is part of God's mighty plan, and in the end, it will all make sense! Your sacrifice will not be in vain."

"Forgive me, Father…" Jeremiah stood up, dusted off his pants. "But I've outgrown this. Now I'll make another round around our camp, wouldn't want an unexpected attack!" Jeremiah threw his repeating rifle over his shoulder, then pulled his coat tight around him. The pale light of the moon filled the night, and the stars shone perfectly in the clear sky. Jeremiah reached the hilltop, lit a cigarette, and stared into the distance. Gravel crunched under his feet; he kicked larger stones out of his way. The tough battles of the past years had toughened him and his brother, so he no longer feared bandits attacking at night. There were few things that scared him, and among them was loneliness. Although he never told his brother, he loved and protected his younger sibling. After losing his family, he'd vowed to take care of him, and he did just that. He turned back towards the camp where the others had already gone to sleep. They would reach Corpus Christi within a day, and Jeremiah hoped the return journey would be as simple and smooth. Doubts still haunted him; it was hard to believe they would receive so much money for such a simple job, but the priest might be right. The Catholic Church was still the most influential institution, and Jeremiah was starting to believe it was just an act of generosity. Before discarding his cigarette, he took one last drag, then flicked the butt, crushed it underfoot, and turned around.

He had barely taken a few steps forward when the sound of footsteps caught his ears. He halted, slowly turning towards the direction of the noise. His hand gripped the pistol, knowing that if someone had sneaked up so close without him noticing, he wouldn't stand a chance to grab his rifle. He caught a glimpse of a fleeting shadow from the corner of his eye, and Jeremiah immediately turned and fired. A painful groan followed by a dull thud accompanied the shadow. More shadows stirred at the foot of the hill, and Jeremiah turned back towards the camp, then started running. "ANTON!" he yelled. "Wake up, everyone, let's go, let's go!" The older White brother took his rifle and sought refuge behind their wagon. Bullets rained down on the camp, hitting the ground or slamming into the wagon. The tethered horses neighed desperately, leaping and struggling, but they had no chance of breaking free.

Anton White sheltered the two terrified priests behind the wagon, then peered out. It was dark; he could barely see anything, just the muzzle flashes emerging from the darkness. He aimed and fired.

Jeremiah also shot blindly. "There he is!" shouted the older brother.

A man in black emerged from behind a bush, holding a revolver, and fired a few shots towards them. His face was covered with a black mask, and a dark hat adorned his head.

"We need to spread out!" Jeremiah shouted. "Anton, run to the right, and I'll take down whoever aims at you!" The older brother handed his pistol to Agustíno and said to the priest, "Shoot at everything that moves, Father!"

The priest nodded, then aimed at one of the attackers in black and fired. Surprisingly, he hit the man, who collapsed, screaming in pain.

Anton began running to the right of the wagon, bullets whizzing past his head; he could almost feel the force of the shots. His brother aimed and fired. Another attacker fell, and the shots ceased. Jeremiah stepped out from behind the wagon, focusing all his nerves on potential further assailants, but he saw none. The injured attacker continued to scream in pain, and Anton approached the man. "Bandits, huh? You couldn't take down the White brothers, you cursed bastards!"

The injured man looked at Anton and spoke in a pained voice: "Va au Diable!"

"What?" Anton was surprised. The injured man pulled down his mask and coughed blood onto the ground. Anton aimed at his head and fired.

"No!" Cristofano yelled. "You shouldn't have shot him!"

"There's another one on the hill!" Jeremiah shouted. The older brother shot, but the man in black didn't flinch.

The attacker raised his arm and pointed accusingly at the two priests. "Vous êtes les serviteurs du diable!"

Anton and Jeremiah fired more shots, but the man simply lowered his arm, turned around, and walked away. Jeremiah ran to the hill and was astonished to find that the mysterious attacker had vanished. "What in God's name?! I hit him multiple times! Just like you did, my brother! Father! Did you understand what he shouted?"

"He shouted it after pointing at us," said Agustíno, looking into Jeremiah's eyes as he approached "You are the servant of the devil!"

"Why did he shout that, and in what language?"

"French," said Cristofano. "The 'why' is a very good question."

The two priests' eyes met, and then Agustíno turned his face away and walked over to one of the corpses. He felt through its pockets but found nothing. The cuff of the man's right sleeve slipped up, and Agustíno noticed a tattoo. He grabbed the dead man's arm and rolled up the sleeve, revealing a coat of arms. Three stars, a holy cross with angel wings. A bird with a rose in its beak, an all-seeing eye, a flaming heart. It was the coat of arms of the Archbishop of

Esztergom, he realized, astonished. But why would they attack them, and why with the French?

"We leave the bodies here!" Jeremiah told everyone. "Gather your gear; we're heading to the town immediately! If we drive the cattle, we'll arrive shortly after midday!"

Frederick, the deputy sheriff, was peacefully dozing off in the office. He couldn't bear the heat any longer, so he darkened the room and placed his hat over his eyes, with his feet on the table, sinking into sweet relaxation. A faint breeze stirred the dusty floor from outside, and a fly landed on Fred's nose. The man grumbled and tried to swat it away, but the annoyance pulled him out of his slumber. The buzzing insect circled around him, but despite his attempts, the deputy couldn't manage to crush it. "Damn it! " he snarled angrily and jumped up from his chair. He wiped his eyes, yawned, and walked over to the coffee maker to put it on the fire. Long and unpleasant days awaited him, so he knew they would consume plenty of coffee, whiskey, and tobacco.

Fred became aware of a painful groan and turned towards the cells. Jonathan Dalton sat on the metal bucket with a pained expression, his pants pulled down. He gripped the iron bars with his hands, his face contorted, eyes bulging, and let out a painful scream. The bucket echoed with a hard thud, and Jonathan leaned to the side, leaving a bloody streak behind.

The deputy walked up to the cell, pushed his hat up on his head, and leaned nonchalantly on the bars. "What's up, pal?" he said mockingly. "Did the venom come out, or was it the scissors?"

"Rot in hell!" Dalton whimpered. "May you all die!"

"Oh!" Fred said. "Well, that might happen sooner than you think, buddy! But you won't see it... Because tomorrow at noon, you'll be on the gallows. This is Texas! Here, lawless niggers can't plunder freely!"

The door of the sheriff's office swung open, revealing Solomon, curiosity reflected on his face. He looked at Fred and nodded. Fred reciprocated, and the innkeeper approached the cells, covering his nose with a handkerchief. A foul stench pervaded the office. Solomon grimaced as he walked to the window and opened it. Curious onlookers outside tried to peek in, but Solomon shouted at them sharply. "Stop gawking, you miserable folks!" he yelled. "Go find your kids! At least then you'll have some use! And if you have no one to look for, spend your money at my place, but get away from the sheriff's office!"

The curious townsfolk shook their heads and walked away, going about their business.

"How can you stand this damn shitty smell, Fred?"

"In the war, I saw quite a few corpses. Every dead body is covered in shit. I got used to it," replied the deputy impassively.

"Well, indeed. " Solomon shook his head. "The hymns and romantic war stories don't tell you about the smell. If God wanted to give us dignity, we wouldn't shit ourselves before lifting our feet! I say, the good old Creator has a grotesque sense of humor!"

"That's for sure!" Fred nodded with a smile. "But our prisoner is not in good shape. If he keeps it up, he won't even make it to his own hanging!"

Solomon leaned on the bars, then pursed his lips. He looked at the man lying on the ground, groaning. The deputy spoke the truth. The red blood dripping from his buttocks didn't bode well. "We need to call the doc," announced the innkeeper. "The smoky one will die soon. He can't until we know what happened. This applies to the hanging, too!"

"If you say so, Sol..."

"I'll go get Dr. Samuel. Thanks to the sheriff, he can only walk with a cane and someone's help. Pay attention to this Hungarian before he shoots someone else in the leg!"The innkeeper turned around and quickly left.

Fred approached the stove, poured fresh black coffee into his metal mug, then sat at his desk and watched the dying prisoner. Poor guy. No one deserved such cruel torments. Fred knew, or at least suspected, that the black guy was innocent; certainly innocent of killing the priests. The dry, makeshift floor creaked loudly under his foot, and the jingle of his spurs echoed metallically. He lifted the mug to his mouth, blew on the drink, and consumed it in small sips. Fred didn't desire anything else, just peace and quiet. He was tired of war, of cruelty. But the America he loved was lost in a senseless war, where his fellow countrymen died by the thousands, all because of the words of a president who didn't live to see the end of the bloodshed. The man smiled uncomfortably, painfully. The black guy lying across from him, almost lifeless from pain, could be him. If he hadn't escaped from Northern captivity, by now he'd either be dead or a servant to some bloodthirsty Negro regiment. *I'd prefer a bullet in my head than to kneel in front of anyone.*

Fred noticed a curse, then turned towards the door. Samuel, the aging, grumpy doctor, limped in, followed by Solomon. The doctor's wavy gray hair, turned into shades of silver, reached down to his shoulders. He wore a black coat, a red vest, and a bow tie. Leaning on his cane, he shuffled forward, cursing with every step. "Just don't let me see that wretched Arisztid!" He raised his gaze to the deputy and gruffly inquired, "Well, what are you standing around and gawking for? Open that damn gate already!"

A small smile appeared at the corner of Fred's mouth as he pulled out his keys. The cluster jingled metallically, then with a sharp click, the lock turned, revealing the small cell. Jonathan Dalton still lay on the ground, his eyes radiating not reason but pain.

Samuel carefully examined the injured man, then turned to Solomon. "Bring my stick from the bag. And you, Fred, boil water and disinfect!"

The doctor squatted next to Jonathan amidst painful groans, then began examining his bleeding buttocks. "Can you hear me?" he asked the man.

"Yes," Jonathan replied in a choked voice.

"I'll be inserting my stick into your rectum. Would you like some whiskey before that? I'm out of opium, so it will be a dreadful experience. I apologize for that."

"Give me whiskey! These bastards fed me scorpion! If my comrades get here, then for sure..."

"Your comrades?" Fred interrupted. "So, he has comrades... Damn it!"

"We don't have time for this now! Someone give me a bottle of whiskey!"

Solomon skillfully took out the sheriff's bottle and helped the man sit up. Jonathan grabbed it and eagerly started drinking the alcohol in large gulps. He handed back the bottle, then looked at the doctor, terror reflected in his eyes.

"I have a suspicion, sir," the doctor began, "that the bleeding is not caused by the scorpion. I need to make sure. Now, I ask you to get on all fours, and turn your buttocks toward me."

Jonathan did as the doctor requested, and Solomon handed the sterilized stick to the doctor, who adjusted his glasses on his nose.

"Jonathan, is that right? As much as it hurts, don't jump around, or I may cause damage to your insides. Shout your lungs out if you need to, cry like a little girl, but don't resist. The best would be if you faint. Do you understand what I'm saying?"

"Yes."

"Great! I will count to three, then insert the stick. One... two... three!"

With a quick and decisive motion, Samuel thrust the stick into Jonathan, who experienced a burning pain. He felt the doctor probing inside, each tiny movement felt like a thousand stabs. Jonathan couldn't bear the pain and started screaming. Water poured from his face, his arms trembled, but he tried to remain motionless. His screams echoed in the street; his voice completely changed. He feared his vocal cords might snap.

Samuel pulled out the stick, and the black man collapsed to the ground again, pulsating with pain. "You have proctitis," Samuel declared dryly. "I'll prescribe medication for you, which you must take every day, or there will be severe complications. I'll try to get some opium from the Chinese for the pain." Samuel turned to the two men. "And you, don't feed anyone scorpions, understand?! The war is over, and there's no need for more bloodshed or torture! The United States should be a civilized country!"

Fred spat on the ground. "Screw the United States! This is Texas!"

Samuel pointed his index finger at Fred's nose, then replied with fiery eyes, "Say that even when you need ointment on your privates!"

The doctor turned away, then, leaning on his cane once again, muttered obscenities as he left.

Solomon adjusted his gray coat, smoothed his hair back with his palm, then spoke to Fred: "It's time for me to find out who this scoundrel's comrades were. The Indians probably know something about the Yankees nearby. What's your plan?"

"I'll feed this bastard, then ride out of town. The tracks led towards Kingsville; maybe the local farmers saw something."

Adjusting his vest, Arisztid walked towards the port. The sun was nearing its zenith, making the heat unbearable. The once deserted port of the town had grown into an increasingly important trade route in recent years. Although the boards creaked and cracked under the sheriff's boots, the town's taxes had still allowed for expansion. Arisztid had made deals with the ship captains, which both parties upheld. The sheriff and his deputy turned a blind eye to smuggled goods, and in return, the crews refrained from violence against the town's residents. Arisztid loved peaceful days when he strolled along the shore during idle evenings, which often turned into poker games and unrestrained revelry at night. He took off his hat and began fanning himself. Sweat droplets rolled down his mustache, down his chin to his neck. He grimaced while looking up at the cloudless sky, and the sails of the ships hung weakly on their masts.

"Well, isn't it a sailor's day, my friend?" asked a familiar voice.

"Indeed," grumbled the sheriff in his raspy voice. "My throat is parched."

A short man emerged from behind the crates covered with fishing nets. His sun-kissed skin seemed almost unnatural under the scorching sun. His black shirt was completely open, revealing his wrinkled stomach and chest to Arisztid. He wore a worn-out straw hat on his head and cream-colored trousers with patches.

Arisztid's eyes caught the man's bare feet. "Where's your boots, sailor?"

"It's a long story, sir!" he replied with a smile. "But let it be enough to say that not every corner of the Caribbean Sea looks favorably upon you when you sleep with a married woman."

"Just one?" The sheriff looked disapproving, but with a sly grin.

"Alright!" The sailor spread his arms. "Four. But I'll tell you, I haven't experienced such a ruckus in a long time!"

"Which way did the wind take you, my friend? Panama? Bumped into a few Gringos?"

The sailor grinned widely, revealing his incomplete, yellow-black set of teeth. "Nicaragua, believe me, these bastards were the filth of the conquistadors!"

Arisztid just smiled and leaned against one of the crates. He took out tobacco leaves from his pocket and offered them to the man. However, before he could take them, Wratiszlaw snatched the leaves away. "Before we start reveling, Pedro..."

"No!" the man snapped, his face contorting into a grimace.

"You don't even know what I want to say!"

"Because I don't care!" Pedro retorted, then turned back towards his ship and started walking. "The last time you looked at me like that, the natives almost ate me, and then they shot my ship to pieces!"

"I wouldn't have thought we'd run into Yankees!"

"Well, the cannibals bothered me more!"

"Pedro!" Arisztid raised his voice, and the man stopped, turned around, and scrutinized the sheriff.

His gaze reflected fear, surprising Pedro. "Tell me, Sheriff... After all, you're the law here. And I am a law-abiding citizen." Pedro dramatically took off his worn straw hat and bowed.

"That's enough! Our priests are dead, and the altar boys have disappeared."

A momentary shock crossed Pedro's face. He turned his face towards the sea, sweat glistening on his skin. "Do you want to know if I heard anything true?"

"Exactly," Arisztid said, nodding.

Pedro approached the sheriff, then snatched the tobacco leaves from his hands, stuffed one greedily into his mouth, and started chewing. The man spat, then bit into another leaf, all the while speaking to the sheriff: "I have no idea who they could have been, but I heard something from one of the captains. It was a strange story that immediately crawled into my ear," Pedro pointed to his ear, "like when you hear a sweet melody in the midst of noise, and you can't concentrate on anything else. I'm an old sailor, I've heard and seen a lot, so if something seems strange to me, it's definitely not ordinary. The captain was drinking with his buddies…" Pedro gesticulated vigorously, spitting small bits of tobacco onto Arisztid's vest as he spoke, "and suddenly he said something in that idiotic grumbling voice of his: 'And then those hooded guys came, wanting to get into Mexico!'"

"Into Mexico?! What the hell are you talking about?"

"Wait, Sheriff, listen to me!" Pedro again began to imitate the captain, with broad gestures. "The hooded one said he wants to get into Mexico! He even said he'll pay with gold! Well, easy money doesn't fall from the tree every day!"

"Someone paid to smuggle them into Mexico?"

"Strange, isn't it?" Pedro chuckled. "But that's not all! It turns out another captain smuggled them into the country earlier, with weapons, horses, and all."

"Who was this captain? I want to talk to him now!"

Pedro turned his gaze away, and the sheriff felt he was hiding something from him. "Pedro...?" He raised an eyebrow. "Who brought these people here? Who was that captain?"

An uncomfortable smile appeared on the man's face, his eyes danced around, avoiding Arisztid's gaze. "Well... I..."

The sheriff's pupils widened, and suddenly, in his anger, he slapped Pedro hard. The slap echoed sharply, and the man staggered, grabbing his face.

"Hé, hey!" the sailor snapped. "We agreed you wouldn't hit me again!"

"Who were those people?"

"I don't know!" Pedro yelled in a desperate tone. "All I know is they were taken out last night."

The sheriff put his hand over his mouth, then started pacing back and forth. His thoughts were racing wildly in his head. He had to find out who these people were and why they came here. Hooded ones, as that captain had said. "Who is the captain who took them out?"

"Well..." Pedro laughed awkwardly.

Arisztid stepped up to the man, their noses almost touching. "Who is the captain that took them out?"

"My brother..."

As soon as the sheriff grasped what the man had said, he once again erupted into sudden anger. His eyes momentarily widened in disbelief, then he shoved Pedro hard. The man staggered and, with a splash, fell into the ocean. The sheriff took out his pistol and waited. Bubbles rose in the deep blue water, and Pedro emerged, gasping for air amid the foam.

Once his eyes cleared, they stared directly into the barrel of the sheriff's gun. In fear, he screamed and tried to shield his head with his hands. "Don't shoot, Sheriff, we're friends!" he shouted.

"Where did they go?! Answer, or I'll send you to a watery grave!"

"Oh, Jesus!" Pedro yelled. "I don't know! Uh... I think that..."

Arisztid cocked the gun, and the sound made Pedro panic again.

"No, no, no, no! I remember now! The captain took them to Santa Isabel! They paid with gold, lots of gold."

"And where did you meet them?"

"In Matamoros! Arisztid, let me come out of the water!"

"You stay there! What did they look like?"

"Well... Uh... They were in hoods. Several of them. At least six, but maybe more. One of them spoke only, wore a sombrero, and a poncho. He had two Colts with him. Distinctive long gold barrels, pure white handles. His right eye was white."

"So, partially blind?"

"Yes! And a massive scar under his eye, running all the way down his face!"

Arisztid looked incredulously at the sky, then holstered his pistol. "I can't believe it, Pedro, that you had to bring a damn amigo here." The sheriff grabbed the man and pulled him out of the water. Pedro coughed and sprawled on the ground, groaning. "That's the value of your gold, buddy. Two dead priests and missing kids. I hope it was worth it."

The sheriff turned on his heel and hurried to his horse. He adjusted the saddle on his mount and mounted the animal. Pedro discarded his dirty clothes and wrung out the water. Arisztid observed the naked man's emaciated body. He didn't like sailors, but they undeniably proved useful. Pedro, glancing at the sheriff, cursed loudly while spreading his soaked clothes on a crate.

"Pedro, I want you ready by dawn tomorrow. We need to go after the boys into Mexico."

Pedro spat, blocked one nostril, and blew a massive snot onto the boards. "My dear sheriff! I never said they were kids! I only brought three men through for my brother to Mexico."

"You said there were six!"

"That's right. I brought at least six. But I don't think your concern is about them. They didn't come for kids. They came for brides. At least that's what they rambled about."

Arisztid's horse nervously snorted and paced back and forth. The sheriff patted the animal's back, calming it down. He didn't understand Pedro's words. "What brides are you talking about, Pedro?"

"They were talking about craving Christ's brides. I don't know what they meant by that, probably whores...," Pedro spread his arms, still naked.

"Christ's brides," Arisztid whispered to himself, lost in thought. Suddenly, his eyebrows shot up in amazement. "The Saint Lucia Nunnery!" He spurred his horse, and the animal neighed, reared, and started galloping back to town.

"Alright!" Pedro shouted. "I'll be waiting for you from dawn tomorrow, Sheriff!"

Father Cristofano placed his black hat on his head and glanced at his companion. Elderly Agustíno also struggled with the long journey, the terrible heat, and dryness. Both were accustomed to comfort, prosperity, and luxury in Rome, but God's holy mission did not always call them to beautiful places. "When will we arrive?" Cristofano asked.

"A few minutes, and we'll be in town," Jeremiah replied.

The young priest surveyed the distance, and indeed, the silhouette of a town emerged before him. He desperately wanted to sleep in a bed for at least one night, have a proper meal, and drink fresh water. He watched the two draft horses in front of the wagon, their heads bowed as they trod forward, silently pulling their passengers. He admired the animals' patience and endurance. They were undisturbed by the heat, hunger, and thirst, only fulfilling their owners' wishes until the end of their lives. A gust of wind blew an eerie creak through the dusty road, outlining the view of Corpus Christi. Wooden houses, verandas, market stalls, and people hurrying about their business. Next to a cactus as tall as a man, the post office and inn came into view. *At last, we can stay somewhere*, he thought. Arriving in the town, the father noticed the worried, frightened looks of the people. Eyes stared at them from all directions, and whispers circulated as they were being observed. "It seems, dear Jeremiah, your reputation precedes you," remarked the father.

"I highly doubt that," he replied in a monotone. "There's something else going on here. I'll tie up the horses, then we'll inquire at the inn."

"Perhaps it would be better to ride straight to St. Lucia's."

"Not a good idea, Father Agustíno," Anton intervened.

"Why not?"

"Our supplies are running out, we're all exhausted. We're not heading into battle or a rescue mission. Sister will be there in a few hours. The horses need to rest as well."

"My brother is right. You also need to rest. Meanwhile, I'll find out what's going on in this town," Jeremiah said, turning a piercing gaze toward the two priests. "I sincerely hope, gentlemen, that it's not about our attackers! About whom, of course, you have no idea who they might be!"

The two priests remained silent, continuing to survey the town. Jeremiah stopped his horses in front of the inn. The man sitting against the wall next to the swinging door observed the newcomers. Pulling up his upper lip, he grimaced, squinting behind his glasses. Sweat drops clung to the aging, balding skin, which he tried to wipe away with a handkerchief. The old man stood up, thoroughly scrutinized the priests, then hurried into the inn with brisk steps, considering his age.

"We got company!" Anton said.

Jeremiah nodded, then looked at the priests: "If they shoot, hide under the wagon."

"I doubt they would attack us without asking questions," Agustíno retorted.

Jeremiah snorted. "Maybe they don't shoot without questions at the Vatican, but they do in Texas."

The two brothers entered the inn with the priests, where behind the counter, a guy wearing a gray jacket, with black hair and a catfish mustache, observed them with keen interest. The old man they had just seen whispered something in his ear, emphasizing his words with gestures. People in the inn glanced at the newcomers, but everyone was more concerned with their own affairs.

At the poker table, a drunken man called out to them: "Have the new priests arrived? Just make sure you don't end up with your guts hanging out too, hahaha!"

"Shut your trap, Frank!" shouted the catfish-mustached man standing at the counter, then hastily approached Jeremiah as the old man left the inn. "Welcome to Corpus Christi!" Solomon began kindly. "What brings you here? Perhaps you'd like to buy some land? Real estate?"

"We're escorting these two gentlemen to the convent!" Anton replied.

"Anton!" his brother sharply scolded him.

Solomon raised his eyebrows across his forehead, then responded with a feigned surprise in his voice: "Could it be Anton White, the famous Confederate sharpshooter?" The innkeeper covered his mouth with disbelief. "Then you must be Jeremiah White! Good heavens! Timothy!" he yelled to the bartender. "Get beer and hot food to this table immediately!" Solomon turned back to the company. "I apologize for interrupting you; please feel at home in our town!"

Solomon turned around, about to walk away, but Father Cristofano stopped him. "Please!" he said. "What did the gentleman at the poker table mean by hanging out with guts?"

Solomon's face showed a half-smile, and he first glanced at the poker table, signaling to the man that he had done the right thing by asking him. "Oh, don't take that drunken fool seriously. Due to an unfortunate event, we lost two priests in our community. But I am confident," he said, as he looked over at the two priests, "that the Church will soon address our issue."

"We need to go to the convent immediately!" Agustíno stood up abruptly. "What news is there about Saint Lucia?!"

"News?" Solomon was surprised. "Oh yes, the nuns. I have no idea, as far as I know, nothing happened in that direction." Thoughts pierced Solomon's mind. "Saint Lucia... I didn't even think about that."

"I demand that you take us to the convent right away!"

"Father, be silent!" Jeremiah ordered firmly.

"Is there something our community should worry about?" Solomon asked.

Jeremiah raised his hand, wanting to answer, but the young priest intervened. "Absolutely nothing is wrong, and the residents of Corpus Christi have nothing to worry about! Divine duty calls for our sister, and we came to safely take her from here so she can continue her mission in these difficult and perilous times. Please forgive Father Agustíno's intense concern, but we have also heard about the recent bestial and cruel anti-church acts. Your community's loss surprised us as well, and I assure you that the Holy Church will provide you with the path to spiritual purification. There is no need to worry! We are merely passing through."

The priest adjusted his clothes, then glanced over the guests of the inn. People listened quietly to the priest's words and then turned back to their tasks. Cristofano sat down and looked around. For the first time in a long time, he sat quietly, desiring nothing more than a moment of peace and tranquility. He observed the wooden bar. Simple, yet a mirror covering the entire wall with shelves and bottles adorned it. Above the counter, a deer antler was displayed, with a hunting rifle resting among the antlers. The bartender calmly wiped the dusty glasses with his yellowed cloth, seemingly unaware of the earlier events. Cristofano looked at his companion, whose eyes radiated concern. "Calm down, Agustíno," he said, taking his companion's arm. "I am sure Sister Gareth is fine. We need to rest. The Lord would not want us to fail due to our own fault."

The older priest didn't respond; he just turned his gaze away. Solomon appeared before them with a large tray. He brought them food, drinks, and kind words. Anton politely thanked him and began to eat. They were all hungry and exhausted.

Jeremiah noticed the sound of horse hooves and, pushing his food away, looked out the window. A man was riding hastily into town. He wore a black hat, a black vest, a white shirt, and blue pants. The sun reflected off his black boots. The man dismounted and immediately stood next to the elderly man they had seen earlier. The old balding man explained something to the stranger, pointing vigorously towards the inn. The man turned momentarily towards Jeremiah, revealing his badge. So, he was the sheriff. Authoritatively, the town's guardian pointed towards the inn and the old man lowered his head and left the sheriff behind.

"Anton!" Jeremiah called to his brother. "I have a little business. I'll visit the town's sheriff. Stay here with the priests." Jeremiah stood up, adjusted his shirt, and left through the swinging door.

Arisztid nervously walked along the dusty dirt road towards his office. The southern sun was scorching, tormenting him with thirst and hunger, but he had neither the time nor the opportunity to stop. He scanned the town, but saw nothing unusual, except for a few worried looks. It seemed as if their town hadn't descended into chaos in the short time he was away. Arisztid was stunned by the indifference of the people. *Damn the kids*! he thought to himself, then entered the office. Jonathan was sitting shirtless on the sunburnt mattress. Intelligence sparked in his eyes again, but the slightest movement painted painful grimaces on his face. "I'm glad you're feeling better, Jonathan," said Arisztid, then approached his desk, retrieving a keychain from his drawer. "I have good news, my boy! You are free to go." The sheriff walked to the cell and inserted the key in the lock.

"Will I get my clothes and weapons back?"

Wratiszlaw stopped moving and looked at the black man. "Of course. However, it would be nice if you could tell me exactly what you were doing in our church, and I'd appreciate it if you could share what you saw."

"So you can lock me up again?"

"That would only happen if you were involved in something serious. But you know what, my friend? Today is a busy day for me, and I don't have time to argue with wandering niggers."

Jonathan opened his mouth to respond, but the office door swung open, and, panting from the heat, sighing heavily, Anthony, the deputy reserve, walked in.

The elderly man hunched over and let out a loud exhale. Leaning against the wall, a yellowed paper trembled in his shaky hands. He lifted the paper, barely audible as he spoke to the sheriff: "You can't do this, Arisztid! This..." His breath caught again, but he took a deep breath, wiped the sweat from his forehead, and continued, "This common bandit, sir, doesn't deserve mercy! Look!" He handed the trembling paper to Arisztid.

Furrowing his brow, the sheriff took the document, then pulled a dusty magnifying glass from his vest pocket and held it up to his eyes. Arisztid's gaze reflected astonishment for a moment, then he looked at Jonathan and back at the paper. "Well... This indeed changes the course of things, I believe. Thank you, Anthony!"

The deputy reserve straightened up, wiped his sweaty forehead with a browned cloth, and said, "I found it in my drawer. I've been keeping it since Secretary Breckinridge sent it to us."

Wratiszlaw raised the poster high, then approached the cell. He carefully examined the man sitting across from him. Pain clearly tortured him, but determination had not left him. Arisztid reached out the paper to the man through the bars. "Take it, Jonathan. Tell me, is this really you?"

Jonathan stood up, and with a pained expression, he walked to the bars and took the poster. He squinted, then smiled. "This is the worst picture ever taken of me."

"But it's good enough to hang you. What do you say, Anthony? Shall we hang this arrogant bandit?"

"The official position of the deputy reserve, sir, is that this filthy swine cannot leave Corpus Christi alive!"

Wratiszlaw smiled and looked back at the black prisoner. "So, Jonathan, it seems I cannot set you free after all."

Anger reflected in the prisoner's eyes, and in his rage, he slammed the bars with all his might. The deputy reserve stepped back in fear, and Arisztid curiously observed the prisoner.

Jonathan snarled like a wild beast caught in a deadly trap. "Give me back my weapon, Sheriff, and let's settle this with a duel! If you win, your justice prevails. But if I win, I can go free!"

Arisztid's gaze showed determination, and he approached the bars, lowering his voice to a whisper. "Do you swear that if you win, you will leave the town and never return?"

"I swear, Sheriff." nodded Jonathan.

"So be it! To the duel! Anthony, bring Jonathan's clothes and weapon. We'll settle this with a showdown on the main street!"

"You wouldn't win that duel," declared a deep voice.

Wratiszlaw turned toward the source of the voice. He saw a man dressed entirely in black, leaning against the door frame, staring directly at the prisoner.

"Well, strike me with lightning and make me bow if this isn't Jonathan Dalton!" applauded Jeremiah. "It's hard to believe, Sheriff, that you managed to capture him."

Jeremiah moved slowly and deliberately towards the cell, the boards creaking ominously under his boots. He stopped in front of the cell and tapped on the bars. "This here, Sheriff, is Captain Jonathan Dalton, a cavalry officer of the Northern Army. The hero of the Battle of Bull Run, the legendary marksman who charged into the midst of battle on his black steed, dealing headshots like playing cards on a poker table. Or should I just call you the butcher of the whites? Or perhaps you prefer the Vicksburg terror?"

Jonathan Dalton remained silent, but Jeremiah's presence disturbed him, throwing him off his previous role. Arisztid was no longer focused on him but on the recently arrived White brother.

"This here... This... This..." stammered Deputy Reserve Anthony in a trembling voice.

"My name is Jeremiah White!" The man tipped his hat and nodded. "Whom do I have the pleasure of addressing, Sheriff?"

"Arisztid Wratiszlaw."

"What kind of name is that?" Jeremiah wondered.

"Hungarian. But that's not important now! It would be a long story, and time is running out. Anthony!" Arisztid shouted, startling the deputy reserve. "Fetch Mr. Dalton's gear; we'll proceed with the duel immediately, then off to the nunnery!"

"If you duel this man, you might as well head to the afterlife. Believe me," Jeremiah said and then glanced at Jonathan. "I already know... Is it true, Mr. Dalton?"

Wratiszlaw rubbed his eyes, exhausted, but he didn't have time to rest. The old man urged them; every minute spent talking hindered his mission. If this was indeed Jonathan Dalton, then he could truly only reach the afterlife. "Look, Mr. White!" Wratiszlaw stepped forward. "I agree with you! I wouldn't stand a chance in this duel, but I need your help. A terrible murder occurred in town, and I've traced the culprits. I believe they will strike at the St. Lucia nunnery, so I need to get there as soon as possible. My partner rode towards Kingsville. I need an armed man like you."

Jeremiah rubbed his face and surveyed the sheriff. He seemed like a simple but honest man, not the type to trap others. Anyone foolish enough to duel Jonathan Dalton couldn't be a coward, he thought. "Alright, Sheriff. Our path leads that way anyway. I'll inform my brother, and we can get going."

"No!" Arisztid retorted. "Until we know if he has accomplices and if so, where they are waiting, I'd like to have at least one capable warrior in town, like your brother."

Jeremiah turned his head, lost in thought for a moment. "Alright, Mr. Wratiszlaw." He nodded. "I'll stay with you. On the way, you can fill me in on what's happening in your town because I feel the two priests we're escorting are hiding something from me."

"You arrived with two priests?" he sighed deeply. "We need to leave immediately, and there's much to discuss!"

Frederick pulled his hat down over his face, riding with a lowered head. He moved at a measured, slower pace, observing the hoof prints and boot imprints sunken into the dusty ground. To most people, these would go unnoticed, but to him, they were a peculiar puzzle, revealing many details about the other party. Three riders had passed through here, closely following each other, like soldiers on parade. Frederick was certain that these riders had received military training. The tracks led to Liam Benjamin's family farm.

The deputy stopped and patted the head of his black steed. The animal gazed back at its owner, loyalty and courage reflected in its eyes. They were old friends and comrades in arms. During the war, the Confederacy had assigned him the horse as a cavalry mount, but Fred didn't see it as a mere tool; it was his companion. They fought, suffered, froze, starved, cried tears of joy and sorrow together, and finally, they returned to their hometown to witness their beloved country being looted and desecrated.

The dry heat took a toll on the deputy, and the years had not spared him either. He took out his canteen, took a big gulp of uncomfortably warm water, and surveyed the farmstead at the end of the distant clearing. Fred squinted, shading his eyes with his hand, trying to make out any movement. The barn looked abandoned, and the flock of sheep seemed too scattered across the green field. The wooden door of the farmhouse ominously stood ajar.

The deputy sighed, then took his revolver in hand, checking the cartridges. He rotated the cylinder one by one, each metallic click echoing, before cocking and decocking the hammer. He looked up again, hoping his intuition had failed this time, but he saw no signs of movement. "Let's go, buddy," he said to his horse.

The horse neighed almost painfully. Fred was sure that it already knew what awaited them. Animals instinctively sense the proximity of death. They galloped straight across the field, the high grass and vegetation brushing against the horse's belly. As they approached, the deputy's pulse quickened, then his horse slowed down and began to walk. Fred held his silver Colt ready for action. The farmhouse porch showcased Liam's empty rocking chair, and the laundry strewn across the ground. The deputy stopped, dismounted, and examined the ground. The three riders had been here. They had approached from three different directions, strategically diverting the owner's attention. The deputy glanced at the window with a wooden frame, shattered in multiple places. The house beams bore the marks of gunfire. "This is Frederick William, Deputy Sheriff of Corpus Christi! If anyone is inside, come out with your hands up!"

No response came, only the rustling of wind-blown leaves could be heard. The deputy cursed to himself, then cautiously, with slow steps, holding his gun in front of him, he stepped onto the porch. The dry wood painfully creaked, and Frederick could only hope that if there was someone inside, they wouldn't shoot him as soon as he entered the door. Behind Fred, his horse snorted, pacing back and forth impatiently. The deputy stepped inside, then peeked into the house through the partially open door. The table lay overturned on the floor, surrounded by debris, glass, and shards of plates. Fred looked behind the door, where he saw Liam Benjamin's lifeless body. The man lay on his back with open eyes, still clutching a rifle in his hand. Fear and terror were etched into his gaze. Fred averted his eyes from the dead man, then headed towards the bedroom. He took a deep breath, kicked the door open, and entered. It was empty. Besides the single bed, there was only a wardrobe, illuminated by the faint sunlight. There was no one left in the house. Fred slid his pistol back into its holster, then returned to the living room, heading straight to the fireplace. Leaning on it, he pulled a flat bottle from his pocket and took a big swig. A framed photograph adorned the fireplace. In the picture, Liam, his wife, and two daughters smiled proudly and happily. Fred hummed to himself, then put the photo back and headed towards the back exit of the house. As he stepped outside, he once again examined the ground. The tracks clearly showed that the wife had fought, resisted, but was abducted. Fred squinted, then noticed a red and white feather on the ground. He knelt down and thoroughly examined it. "Comanche feather adornment?" he asked himself aloud.

The situation was becoming increasingly strange for the deputy. Since when did skilled Indians attack farmers? The deputy began to examine the tracks again. Footprints of various sizes lined up around each other. He could almost see the picture in front of him, Liam's wife being dragged by her hair, the woman fighting fiercely, kicking and struggling every inch of the way. Fred couldn't imagine what kind of horror the two little girls had had to go through and maybe still had to endure... The sound of boot steps caught his attention, coming from behind him. He immediately reached for his pistol and took cover just inside the half-open door. He tried to listen, but there was silence. Perhaps it was just a trick of the wind. He cautiously peered out, then moved slowly and quietly across the living room. He tightly gripped his revolver, stepping towards the front door, attentive to every sound, noise, shadow, and movement. He heard another step, this time from the right side of the door. Now he was sure he wasn't alone. He took a deep breath, then stepped through the door, aiming his gun to the right, but as he left the safety of the house, the cold metal of a revolver barrel pressed against his face from the left side. Fred saw in front of him a man wearing a blue coat, brown trousers, a faded yellow hat on his head, holding a hunting rifle aimed straight at him. He couldn't see clearly who was pointing the gun at him from the corner of his eye, but the man had his revolver unholstered. The unknown man emanated the smell of alcohol and an unwashed stench

"Well, well, who did the wind blow in here?" said the stranger in his high, mocking voice.

"My name is Frederick William, deputy sheriff! Put down the gun, and let's talk about this!"

"I know exactly who you are, deputy! Don't you remember me?" he asked irritably.

Fred tried to dig up the owner of the familiar voice from his memories, but he had to admit that he had no idea who the person was. "Considering that I can't see your face, unfortunately, I have no idea who you are!

"Owen Grayson!" he shouted. "And this here is my brother, Isaac! Remember now? You cheated me out of a hundred dollars at cards! Now you're going to give it all back!"

"Oh!" Recognition hit Fred. "So, you're Owen? As clever as you are, I didn't have to cheat..."

Owen delivered a massive slap with the handle of his pistol to Fred, causing him to stagger, and he had to lean his back against the wall.

The younger Grayson quickly appeared next to him and took Fred's gun out of its holster. "You won't need this anymore!" he said, laughing. "I told you, brother, God will smile upon us! And here it is!"

"Indeed, brother!" agreed the older one. "In the past few days, only misfortune laughed at us! We barely made it out of Kingsville!"

"What happened in Kingsville?" asked Fred with sincere surprise.

"You have nothing to do with that!" Owen shouted again, pressing the gun deeper into Fred's face.

Fred squinted and raised his hands in submission. "Since I'm going to die anyway, could you at least tell me?"

Owen licked the corner of his mouth, blinked significantly. Fred could look at him with one eye. He wore a yellowed white and burgundy striped shirt, his face covered with a thick, long beard, and his greasy hair hung in clumps down to his shoulders. "Well... Dirty, smoke-faced Yankees came into town and shot everything! They didn't ask anything, just rode in, shot everyone, looted the town, and headed towards Corpus Christi!"

"When did this happen?" Fred asked, astonished.

"Yesterday," the older one cut in. "We fled through the forest here, where we stumbled upon those miserable Indians. We were damn lucky they didn't notice us!"

"Comanches," Fred said.

"Damn right! They were all dressed in black and shooting with rifles! Now, off to the garden outhouse!" Owen grabbed the deputy's shoulder and shoved him hard.

Fred looked up and saw the privy next to the house. "I'm not going there!"

"You're going there, or I'll blow your brains out!"

"Even if I go there, you'll blow my brains out. So, I'll stay here."

Owen hissed, then nervously paced back and forth, scratching his head. He smeared the brown dirt under his fingernails onto his worn-out brown pants while constantly aiming at the deputy. "Fine!" he said in an annoyingly whiny voice. "Say your goodbyes, deputy!" Owen half-closed one eye and aimed at Fred's head.

"Wait! Wait!" pleaded the deputy. "And what about the last wish? Everyone is entitled to that!"

The younger man grabbed his head in disbelief and then looked at his brother. Bewilderment reflected in the older brother's eyes. He shrugged and answered. "Why not? After all, he's unarmed, and we're two!"

Owen nodded and asked determinedly, "So, what's your last wish?"

Fred had a half-smile on his face. "Would you like to see a real card trick? Since we got to know each other through cards, let the farewell be similar, shall we? Now, slowly, I'll take my deck from my vest pocket, alright?"

Fred reached towards his pocket, but Owen snapped at him. "But absolutely no tricks! Otherwise..."

"Otherwise, you'll blow my brains out. I know, you've said that. So, let me take out my deck now." Fred took out the deck of cards, and the two brothers watched with interest, wondering what would happen next. The deputy spread the deck, then extended it towards Owen. "Draw a card, look at it, but don't show it to me!

"Can I show it to my brother?" Owen asked, puzzled.

"You can show it to him without any worries," Fred replied condescendingly. "Draw a card!"

Owen licked his lips again, then slowly and cautiously lifted one card with his left hand, looked at it, and showed it to his brother. The older brother squinted, then announced that the card was the nine of clubs. "Now what? If you try anything..."

"I know, I know!" Fred reassured him. "Put the card back in the deck."

The younger brother returned the card to the deck, watching closely as the deputy thoroughly shuffled the cards.

Confidently, Fred then drew a card with a wide grin. "Was this your card?" Fred displayed the two of spades.

Owen, incredulous, slapped his thigh and responded angrily, "What a pathetic magician you are! This is not..."

Exploiting Owen's momentary distraction, Fred lunged at him, twisted his wrist, took his gun, and pulled him in front.

The brother immediately fired, hitting his younger brother, who groaned in pain before collapsing with a bleeding chest.

The deputy aimed and shot the older brother in the thigh. He screamed in agony, dropping his rifle. "You damned scumbag!" he screamed in pain, "You killed my brother!"

"Actually, you killed him!" Fred smiled.

Isaac groaned, tears falling like a child's. "You scoundrel! You're not a real magician; you just tricked us!"

The deputy chuckled, confidently approached the injured man, and aimed his gun. "I'm not really a magician, and I hate it when people touch my gun!" Fred didn't wait any longer; he shot. With a dull thud, the older Grayson brother fell. The deputy twirled his gun around his finger and holstered it. He walked to his horse and galloped towards Corpus Christi.

Arisztid and Jeremiah were galloping at a brisk pace on the road leading to the Saint Lucia nunnery. The rhythmic beat of the horses' hooves echoed around them like a war anthem. The cloudless blue sky shone brightly, and the treetops swayed gently in the mild breeze. The sheriff and his temporary companion urged their horses up the hill in front of them. They stopped at its summit, and Arisztid, walking his horse in a circle around Jeremiah, observed the nunnery in the distance on the barren, dry ground. It stood in solitary grayness, its stark construction giving it a forbidding air. The sheriff's horse snorted and growled. Nervously, Jeremiah paced alongside him. Arisztid squinted, shading his eyes with his hand, focusing on the monastery in the distance. A foreboding silence and grayness cast shadows upon him. A sense of unease crept over him, and every fiber of his being wished to escape from there. "I don't like this. Something's not right," said Wratiszlaw.

Jeremiah took off his snakeskin hat and began fanning himself. His horse stood calmly, looking ahead, waiting for its master's instructions. Every inch of the animal exuded pride and strength, just like its owner. The older White brother's black shirt shimmered in the sunlight. He adjusted his hair and then turned his gaze towards the sheriff. "How many nunneries have you seen?" he asked in a monotone.

"Well, actually," stammered Arisztid, "I haven't seen any."

"So, what makes you think something is wrong?" Jeremiah inquired.

Wratiszlaw sighed, then took a deep breath. He briefly looked up at the sky before responding. "Mr. White... You fought on the Confederate side, right?"

"Indeed, I did," replied Jeremiah. "I laid down my weapons at Palmito Ranch."

Arisztid snorted and spat on the ground. "The damn Yankees attacked for no reason! I was there that day too! I sent a filthy bluecoat to his death with my last bullet! And you know what, Mr. White? Before they attacked... I felt the same as I do now."

Jeremiah scrutinized the man opposite him, then responded with genuine curiosity in his voice. "What exactly do you feel, Sheriff?"

"The closeness of death."

White raised an eyebrow, thinking of the black-clad figures attacking them on the road. Perhaps Arisztid was right. Maybe death was indeed lurking nearby, waiting for the right moment to snatch these two lost souls. Jeremiah rubbed his face, took a sip, and looked at the distant monastery. He saw nothing but a stone building with a large cross on top. "What did you say, Sheriff? What awaits us inside?"

"Mr. White, you know very well that I didn't tell you anything. We were riding at a brisk pace, and I didn't have time for chit-chat. But now, I feel you need to know a few things. Our town's priest and sexton were murdered recently, and the altar boys have gone missing. We found the dead in a horrific state. I've never seen anything like it, even after fighting in two wars. In the port, I learned that hooded figures were smuggled into the country, who came 'for the brides of Christ.'"

"I assume there's no other nunnery nearby, right?" Jeremiah replied. He reached for his rifle without hesitation and checked the cartridges. His black repeating rifle gleamed immaculately in the radiant sunshine. "So, friend, it's time to check these scoundrels, isn't it?"

Arisztid shook his head, then blocked Jeremiah's path with his horse. The two men's eyes met for a moment, but Wratiszlaw did not look away. Suspicion lingered in the older White brother's gaze; he kept his rifle ready to fire, knowing the sheriff had the upper hand. "Don't worry, Mr. White, I don't intend to take your life. But there's something you must tell me. Why did you come to our town, and what's your connection to those two priests?"

Jeremiah's face revealed a sly half-smile. He adjusted his snakeskin hat and answered, "Look, Mr. Wratiszlaw! My brother and I are bounty hunters. We don't ask questions; we just grab the money, take down whoever needs to be taken down, and then move on to the next unfortunate soul. But about a month ago, we received a peculiar job. We got a sealed envelope addressed directly to us. They promised five thousand dollars for us to meet two priests in New York and bring them here!" He pointed towards the nunnery. "Waiting for us is a nun who needs to be safely taken back to New York."

"Hmm... Five thousand dollars for a nun seems like a lot of money to me. Didn't that raise any suspicions for you?"

"I rejected it immediately. But my brother and uncle insisted. They thought it was easy money, but I'm sure there's something else going on. On the road, unknown armed men attacked us."

"Bandits?"

"No!" Jeremiah retorted. "They were dressed in black, with their faces covered in black rags. And I swear, one of them..." He hesitated, not believing what he had seen himself. "I'm sure I shot him... but his body wasn't there."

"Do you swear that...?"

"I think one of them spoke French."

Arisztid cursed loudly, swore, then looked at Jeremiah. "French? Do you know who's south of us a few kilometers?"

"Napoleon's army..."

"And the Austro-Hungarian Empire's soldiers," concluded the sheriff, then raised his gaze to the monastery. "How the hell did we get mixed up in this, Mr. White?"

Jeremiah swung his rifle over his shoulder, spurred his horse, and began to gallop. Looking back over his shoulder at Arisztid, he shouted: "Let's find out, Sheriff! Let's find out..."

"A daring Southern fool," muttered the sheriff to himself, then spurred his horse towards the monastery. Barren, lifeless soil embraced the gray stone structure, yellowed tufts of grass dotted the black ground, reaching all the way to the forest behind the monastery. Wratiszlaw was not pleased with what he saw. This was not how he imagined the Lord's house. It was not the faded, lifeless, and desolate place he envisioned, exuding only the stench of death. Where was mercy, where was grace?

Jeremiah stopped in front of the massive wooden entrance of the monastery. The double doors were adorned with iron hinges and had a wrought-iron handle in the middle. Carved into the stone above the ancient entrance was a message for visitors: *Sin is lurking at the door, and its desire is for you*!

"Do you see this, Mr. White? This could be the greeting on a Christmas card, don't you think?"

Jeremiah laughed, not caring about Arisztid's comment. "You're right, Wratiszlaw, you're right!" he nodded, then dismounted. He swayed his long black coat in the strengthening wind, raised his gaze to the cross on top of the monastery, and watched it for a few moments. All the windows of the building were covered with curtains, as if they wanted to hide everything that happened inside.

Arisztid also dismounted and began to walk along the wall next to the main entrance, carefully observing any signs of possible attack.

Jeremiah approached the door and knocked. The sound echoed dully, but no response came. He stepped back and began examining the windows once again. "How are we going to get in if the door is locked?".

"Just look!" Wratiszlaw pointed towards a window. "That one's open!"

The bounty hunter took a few steps back and headed towards the sheriff, where he noticed the open window, but it was too high for them to climb through. "Sheriff... Are you planning to crawl through that window?"

"Why the hell wouldn't I want to crawl through it? After all, we came here to find out something, didn't we?" he replied completely naturally. "Although, Mr. White, I must admit it won't work alone! Please, lend me a hand!"

Jeremiah sighed, feeling in every fiber of his being what a bad idea this was.

The sheriff advanced thoughtlessly, solely focused on the goal, losing all sense of danger, shutting out even the spark of possibility of failure. Wratiszlaw rolled up his sleeves and stood under the window, impatiently waiting for the bounty hunter, gesturing for him to come closer.

White took only a small step forward, then extended his arm, pointing his index finger straight at Arisztid. "Mr. Wratiszlaw, are you aware that if you go in alone, I won't be able to help you?"

"Yes," Arisztid replied, slightly surprised.

"And are you aware that if those hooded figures are inside, they might shoot you full of holes and probably scalp you?"

"Of course!" said Wratiszlaw. "I understand the risks, but whatever awaits me inside, I have to go in. I get it if you're scared and don't want to take the risk, but I'm the sheriff! I don't have a choice!"

Jeremiah understood the hint, acknowledging it with a simple smile. He stepped beside the sheriff, providing a boost for Arisztid. The sheriff stepped onto the man's palms, using them as support to leverage himself upward. With a sudden push, he propelled himself and grasped the edge of the open window. In the momentum, he lost balance but managed to pass through the window. A muted thud resonated as he landed on a table, causing it to topple along with metal plates and utensils, creating a loud clatter on the hard stone floor. Arisztid cursed and looked around, finding himself in a small dining area. The room featured stone walls and plain wooden cabinets along the sides. Two chairs accompanied an overturned table. A stone archway led to a long corridor illuminated by torches. Wratiszlaw got up, dusted himself off, kicked the overturned table aside, and peered out of the window to see Jeremiah looking up at him with a curious expression. Arisztid leaned out of the window and extended his arm towards the man.

White approached, caught Arisztid's hand, and pulled himself up. Jeremiah surveyed the room, then approached a fallen crucifix on the ground and picked it up.

"Did you knock this down?" asked the sheriff.

"I don't know, I... I fell over the table, and the crucifix was far from there. Do you think it's normal for believers not to pick up a fallen crucifix among them? Look!" He traced his finger over the crucifix, covered in a thick layer of dust. "And the fruits on the ground, all brown and decaying... This is not a good sign, Sheriff."

Wratiszlaw quickly scanned the surroundings; the bounty hunter was right. No one had been here for days. He reached for his pistol, cocked it, and signaled to White before heading down the torchlit corridor. His boots echoed loudly with each step, resonating through the narrow passage lined with wooden doors.

Jeremiah, keeping his gun at the ready, walked backward slowly behind Wratiszlaw, his senses heightened, and the familiar hunting instincts rekindled within him. The scent of cruelty and bloodshed hung in the air.

The sheriff reached a spiral staircase and descended slowly. The air reeked of decay, and the stench of rot surrounded them. Arisztid felt the alcohol churning in his stomach, an uncomfortable, burning sensation filled his body. Tremors ran through his legs, and claustrophobia gripped his mind, an overwhelming fear of confinement. He wanted to get out, but there was no choice. He had to face everything that happened, and deep down, he suspected they were nowhere near the worst of it. Upon reaching the bottom of the stairs, they found themselves in a crypt. Their steps stirred up the dust that had settled over the years. Stone monuments of deceased nuns surrounded them, and in alcoves carved into the walls, the dead rested for all eternity. The flickering light of torches and the rhythmic crackling of the fire froze Wratiszlaw's blood. He looked back and saw the same horror on Mr. White's face. The bounty hunter's gaze briefly met his, then Arisztid turned forward again, holding his pistol in front of him, ready to move on. In the darkness, a lavish throne came into view, occupied by a woman dressed entirely in black. Her hair was covered by a black and white scarf, her face concealed by a black veil. Her aged fingers, adorned with rings, rested on the armrests. Arisztid squinted, then lowered his pistol. His soul calmed as he saw a living person. Behind him, Jeremiah let out an audible sigh of relief, then stepped beside the sheriff. Wratiszlaw holstered his gun, raised his hands, and addressed the woman. "Please forgive us for trespassing into the convent! I assume you are the Mother Superior, right?" The woman remained silent. Arisztid tried to discern something from the mysterious Mother Superior in the dim light, but the black veil completely covered her face, concealing every feature. "Mother Superior, please help us! Have you experienced anything in the past few days? We have good reason to believe there is danger. "

A chilly silence enveloped the crypt, sparsely lit by the torches. The dust cloud swirling with each step, the woman dressed in black, and her grotesque throne filled Wratiszlaw with terror once again. Arisztid began to lose patience. He stepped closer to the woman and spoke louder. "Please, Mother Superior! Tell us, please..." Wratiszlaw grabbed the woman's shoulder, but her head dropped forward and fell into his lap. From there, with a dull thud on the stone floor between her legs, it rolled among the tombstones. In his horror, Arisztid screamed. The lifeless body of the Mother Superior leaned to the side, and from the red wound on her neck, a red chunk of flesh was expelled with a slick, squelching sound, landing on the ground.

Jeremiah approached the headless corpse, inserting his finger into the gaping wound. His fingers delved into the slimy, cold flesh, progressing through the dead skin and decaying tissues with an unpleasant, mushy sound. "The blood has coagulated." announced Jeremiah. "Are you okay? "

Wratiszlaw stood hunched over, leaning on one of the tombstones. He retched, his hat fell to the ground, and amidst surprising groans, vomit erupted from the Sheriff of Corpus Christi. The sound emanating from Arisztid reminded him of pouring a bucket of water onto hot stones in the summer. Wratiszlaw coughed, spat a few times, then knelt down, retching a few more times before sitting down. He leaned against the stone, groaning.

Jeremiah, placing his gun in the lap of the deceased woman, squatted beside the man. From a small leather pouch strapped to his right thigh, he retrieved an opium-alcohol tincture and handed it to Arisztid. "Drink it!" he declared in an uncompromising tone. "Drink it, Sheriff, and get your wits back, or I'll leave you here!"

Arisztid gasped, his eyes wide open, starting to lose consciousness.

Jeremiah grabbed the man's chin, opened his mouth, and poured the contents of the bottle inside. "Swallow it, you fool, don't vomit!"

The sheriff rested his head against the tombstone, waiting for the opium solution to take effect. Slowly but surely, reason returned to his eyes, and the fear seemed to dissipate. He looked up at the bounty hunter. "Forgive me, Mr. White..." he whispered. "I can guess what you might think of me now, but believe me, I am not a coward!"

"You are not a coward, Mr. Wratiszlaw, but an opium addict. Since when has the drug held you captive?"

"Since '64."

"War injury?"

"Shot in the shoulder."

"Be glad you survived. But now we have to go. We have to leave this accursed place!"

"It's not possible!" Arisztid grabbed his arm. "I need to find out what happened here! Please help me!"

"I'm not a detective! I won't be of any use!"

"But I will! Do as I say, and we will unravel the story of this dreadful place!"

White pursed his lips, then looked over his shoulder at the headless corpse. What he had seen horrified him as well. He wanted to leave the convent as quickly as possible, find his brother, and ride so far away that he could forget the memory of this cursed place. He rubbed his eyes, his face twisted into a desperate grimace, then stood up. For a moment, he locked eyes with Arisztid, seeing a mixture of fear and determination in the sheriff's gaze. "Come on, Sheriff!" He extended his hand. "I'll help you, but only as long as we're here. Once we step out of this unholy convent, my brother and I will leave the town!"

Wratiszlaw grabbed the bounty hunter's hand and successfully stood up. He dusted himself off, picked up his hat from the dusty ground, and placed it on his head. He looked for the exit and found a staircase behind the throne, leading upwards. Arisztid started walking, then spoke to White, who quietly walked beside him: "Come with us to Mexico, please!" he pleaded. "I could use someone armed like you!"

"No way, Mr. Wratiszlaw!" declared White firmly. "I'm not a hero, and you couldn't pay enough to make me come with you."

The Hungarian paused, then looked back directly into Jeremiah's eyes. In his gaze, there was iron will and burning determination. "Perhaps it's time for you to do something noble, don't you think, Mr. White?"

"The last time I did something noble, I received my sisters' and parents' blood as payment..."

"We both have lost a lot." He continued to look into Jeremiah's eyes. "But if there's even the slightest chance of finding our children alive, I'll take it. For free." He emphasized the word. "Not because it's my job, but because honor dictates it! I suggest you think about this before taking someone else's life for good money, Mr. White!"

The bounty hunter was not used to being lectured. Over the past years, wherever he'd gone with his brother, they only received fearful glances, trembling voices, and gunshots. After his momentary shock passed, a smile appeared on his face. The sheriff was audacious, but Jeremiah quite liked this behavior. He adjusted his coat and, rushing up the stairs, found himself in a small room. The walls were adorned with paintings depicting the crucifixion of Christ and the Virgin Mary kneeling beside him. In the middle of the room, a door stood wide open, emitting an ominous reddish light. Arisztid and Jeremiah entered, finding themselves in a chapel. Stained glass windows displayed images of saints, and rows of wooden pews lined the sides of the sanctuary. The sunlight streaming through the painted windows cast a reddish hue over the chapel. Above the altar, the crucified Savior gazed upwards with a pained expression, tears of blood flowing from his eyes.

Wratiszlaw slowly walked between the pews, his heart pounding intensely at the sight before him. He squinted, genuinely hoping that his eyes deceived him, but as they approached, he became certain of what he saw.

"What the hell is going on here?" exclaimed the bounty hunter.

"What the hell is happening here?" Arisztid asked, his pupils dilated.

Jeremiah and Wratiszlaw stood side by side in front of the steps to the podium, staring in horror at the dead nun lying on the altar. The Hungarian approached the lifeless body. Her head had fallen backward over the edge of the altar, and her throat was cut from ear to ear. The sheriff covered his mouth with his hand in shock. The nun's clothing was torn apart, revealing her breasts and upper body. Her legs were spread apart forcibly, and her eyes were filled with torment.

"Sheriff..." Jeremiah pointed to the wall. "I think this is meant for us."

Wratiszlaw glanced at White, then turned and pointed to the wall. Stepping aside to get a clearer view, his blood froze in his veins. A message was painted on the wall, and Arisztid was certain it had been done with the nun's blood. Slowly and quietly, he read aloud the words written on the wall. "Without shedding blood, there is no forgiveness!" Arisztid whispered to himself.   He buried his face in his hands and rubbed his eyes. First the town's church, then the nunnery, blood, death, kidnapping... Thoughts raced through his mind like lightning, and for the first time, he looked at the bounty hunter standing beside him with suspicion.

"Tell me, Mr. White... Why should I believe you, exactly?" he asked skeptically. "Who are these priests, and why did they want to come here? Why did they need two experienced killers?"

"You're making a mistake, Arisztid, by turning against me! " The bounty hunter looked at the sheriff meaningfully.

"And I've already told you. We came for a nun named Kassandra Gareth."

"Who is this nun, and why is she so important? "

"I don't know; I only know as much as they told me. She's likely very important, as the two priests came on papal orders. Probably she's the one paying us."

"Papal orders..." Arisztid's words caught in his throat. "What the hell..."

"I have no idea, Sheriff!" Jeremiah approached Wratiszlaw, placing his hand on the sheriff's shoulder. "But believe me, we are not behind this!"

White looked at the wall, then closed his eyes for a moment, sighed, and continued: "The truth is, Sheriff, that I understand exactly as much as you do about what's happening. And it seems we've both plunged into the same shit. So, I suggest we both leave this place alive and not turn against each other."

"I apologize, Mr. White. Anger and fear got the better of me. You know..." He raised his gaze to the mutilated nun. "I'm not a God-fearing man, I could even say that I wade knee-deep in sinful pleasures, but this sight makes my soul plead for mercy."

Jeremiah glanced behind the altar, then signaled Arisztid to pay attention. Behind the massive crucifix, they saw a half-open door emitting the flickering light of a fire. Jeremiah raised his index finger to his mouth, drew his pistol, and silently approached the door.

Wratiszlaw followed suit. With each step, the sheriff heard a dull echo beneath his boot on the cold stone floor, and each tiny sound seemed as loud as a trumpet. His revolver's grip felt cold in his whitening fingers, and his heart pounded in his throat. Slowly, he approached the door, then opened it with his free hand. They found themselves in a small room, likely the office of the deceased head nun they'd found in the crypt. The opposite wall held a massive bookshelf filled with old leather-bound volumes. On the simple, unadorned table lay only a quill and ink, next to an ashtray. Arisztid examined the ash. "Something was burned here. Look. It's paper."

Jeremiah stepped forward and examined it too. It was almost entirely burnt; no writing was discernible. "We won't find out anything from this. Let's go, Sheriff! There's nothing here, just the dead."

Wratiszlaw grinned mischievously, then reached for the kerosene lamp beside the table. "Do you think it's unreadable? " He smiled. "Then watch and learn!" The Hungarian carefully took the tiny piece of paper from the ashtray and placed it on top of the kerosene lamp. The paper flared up, and in a brief moment, the ink on it also ignited, revealing a fragment of text.

Jeremiah read the words with a stunned expression, then looked at Arisztid. "'This is an unholy betrayal, Your Holiness, born from my own blood. K. Garreth.' What could this mean? Do you understand?"

"I certainly don't. But K. Garreth... Wasn't that the nun they came for?"

"Yes. So you think..."

"The girl figured something out and wanted to warn someone... But the hooded men might have arrived here before she could send the letter."

Wratiszlaw straightened up, dusted himself off, and then walked resolutely towards the exit. "Come, Mr. White! It's time to visit a few cantinas in Mexico!"

Chapter Three

"This is what the Lord says: 'In the place where dogs licked up Naboth's blood, dogs will lick up your blood— yes, yours!'"

1 Kings 21:19

Anton reached into his vest pocket for the flat bottle resting there, then took a big gulp from it. The journey had exhausted him, and the heavy lunch he'd had in town weighed heavily on his stomach. He felt a slight stabbing pain at his left temple, the familiar feeling of a hangover, which a sip of whiskey immediately cured. "The healing sip," as he called it. He leaned back in his chair, his fingers dancing on the table. He could feel people's eyes sticking to him, the curious looks as they scrutinized him. A faint smile crept onto his face. Over the years, he had grown accustomed to people staring at him. The noise of footsteps coming up the stairs from the inn's upper floor pulled him out of his reverie. Father Cristofano strode confidently towards him, exuding strength and trust. Anton didn't share his brother's opinion of priests. He was sure they were hiding something, but after all, this was the Catholic Church, with its centuries-old secrets and the mystique surrounding them. The young priest was clutching a wooden pipe in his hand, something Anton hadn't seen him with during the entire journey. The priest nodded towards the swinging door with his pipe. Anton nodded back, then pulled out a rolled cigarette from his pocket and, stepping through the swinging door, they sat down. "I didn't know you smoke, Father. Is it allowed for priests?"

"The Lord does not forbid smoking, and actually, the Bible doesn't say anything about it either," replied Cristofano, as he took out a match and quickly struck it on the sole of his shoe. After taking a big puff from his pipe, he leaned back and let out a sigh. "It's good to relax a bit. Where is your brother?"

"Well..." Anton pondered. "Now that you mention it, I have no idea! I should look around."

The younger White brother was about to jump up hurriedly, but Cristofano grabbed his arm. "There's no need to rush," reassured the priest. "After all, we're talking about your brother. He can take care of himself. But please, answer me one question. You see..." he said softly, but in a more confidential tone. "My colleague, Father Agustíno, is terribly worried. The thing is, I had no idea that the priests of Corpus Christi were murdered. It's a dreadful tragedy..."

"But...?" The bounty hunter asked suspiciously.

The priest leaned in closer. "Several priests have died in the area in the last seven or eight months."

"Were they gutted too?"

"No!" he snapped. "That's not the case. The Lord called them in various ways. Accident, illness, old age... But you know, I also feel that something is not right here. I need to investigate whether this vast area where these things happened is still sacred at all. I feel like evil has started to erase the presence of our holy men around here. So, may I ask you, dear Anton, would you like to join our holy mission?"

The young bounty hunter chuckled, then blew smoke out of his nose. "I doubt, Father, that the holy mission pays as well. And celibacy is not my thing, either."

Cristofano took a puff from his pipe, then after a short silence, replied, "I suppose you are aware that the church is willing to overlook certain things in exchange for the right services."

"So the church is just like the whores and their pimps. Forgive me, Father, but I believe the path I'm on is just right for me. And somehow, by some coincidence, we're still here, right? On a mission 'by the will of the Lord, he emphasized.

The young priest smiled, then blew out the smoke. "You're smarter than we've heard." He stood up, dusted himself off, stretched a bit, then reached out his hand to Anton. "We'll meet again soon, but for now, I'll fold my hands in prayer." Cristofano nodded in farewell.

"And I'd soon like to fold my hands on a pair of breasts, Father. Oh," Anton caught himself, "you've never... so you understand."

"I understand, my son..." The priest smiled. "But serving the Lord means more to me than any earthly pleasure."

Anton tipped his hat, nodded, and then set off to find his brother.

The younger White brother adjusted his vest, and from the cartridge belt strapped around his waist, he retrieved a bullet. The heated metal almost sizzled in his palm as he twirled it between his fingers while walking on the town's dusty road. A gentle breeze chased devil's carriages in front of the sheriff's office. The headhunter's boots clicked on the office's hard and dry wooden steps. His steps echoed with a mournful creak, and the door swung open with a sharp squeak. Behind the bars of the cell sat a familiar face. A sardonic smile spread across Anton's face as he spotted their old enemy, the killer of their comrades and family; Jonathan Dalton. The younger White brother stood in front of the bars with his hands on his hips, observing the black man. Jonathan slowly lifted his gaze, as if sensing who stood before him. The younger White brother continued to twirl the bullet between his fingers. "Captain Dalton." Anton nodded.

Jonathan's smile turned into a grimace of pain in an instant, the torment still evident. "Mr. White," he replied. "I've already had the pleasure of meeting your brother. I see you've brought me a gift as well." He gestured to the bullet. "How the world has turned, hasn't it? Such a noble white man bringing a gift to a dirty black slave. I suppose this isn't your perfect world anymore, Mr. White. By the way, how is your dear sister?"

Anton angrily slammed his hand against the bars, hatred burning on his face. "This bullet here." He lifted it up. "I reserve for you. It's from the rifle I found next to my father's body. Remember this, Dalton." He emphasized the words. "I will chase you through hell for what you did to my family. You will pay with your life."

Jonathan, as if he hadn't heard the threat, glanced towards the window. From outside came the sound of hammering, the creak of dry wood, and the shouts of working men. "If you truly reserved that bullet for me, you'd better hurry, because they'll hang me soon. A miserable end, isn't it?" Dalton smirked. "Well, I've only made it this far from your father's slave farm. To a Texas gallows."

"You'll get what you deserve."

Dalton disregarded the pain and leaped up to the bars, locking eyes with Anton, who held his gaze without flinching. Sweat dripped down Jonathan's face, his lips trembling with anger. "Perhaps I should have asked to be born a slave, huh? Do you think I willingly accepted the lashings, the humiliations?"

"What are you talking about, Captain?" the bounty hunter asked with a threatening tone. "We played together as children, you ate from our table, my father treated you well. He was a good man, but you killed him, along with my family, while we fought for our freedom."

"Your father was a filthy pig! Did he ever tell you how many times he beat my parents just for fun? How many times he forced violence upon his slaves? Or how he forced adult men into bloody fights at night with his slaveholding friends? Didn't he tell you? Oh." He lifted his gaze mockingly. "Your dear father had plenty to tell. But there is one thing I can be grateful to him for; without his teachings, I wouldn't be the country's best duelist."

"The hunts..." Anton whispered to himself. "You were there with us."

"Indeed." Dalton nodded. "I loaded your guns, polished them, adjusted the sights. I sneaked and crept with you. I watched your every move, and I soaked in every word of your father as if he were teaching only me. He was sure of our loyalty. Oh, that old fool! When the first slave uprisings broke out, your dear father gave us weapons and we had to patrol. He trusted us so much that he didn't even check the bullets, so I practiced. Once I realized how good I was, I started training the others, and then I escaped. And your family…"

"They thought you were dead," Anton concluded.

"Exactly. My father convinced your family that during one of our patrols, we got into a shootout with rebellious slaves, who wounded and kidnapped me. But I fled north to join the Union army."

"But that didn't go as planned either, did it?" asked the younger White with a mocking smile. "If I understand correctly, you were also sentenced to death and dismissed from the army in the north."

Jonathan flashed his yellowish teeth, crossed his arms, then nodded towards the window. "My own fate is not important to me, but victory is! And it seems, my dear friend, that luck is smiling on me once again."

Confusion reflected on Anton's face, then he turned towards the window. In the main street of the town, soldiers of the Northern Army appeared. Mounted on horseback, they moved slowly, casting accusing glances at every passerby and resident. The bounty hunter stepped closer to the window. The Union's black soldiers were outside, armed with rifles, dressed impeccably in uniform. He turned to Dalton: "The rescue squad has arrived, it seems... Deserters, thugs, looters, and bandits. Quite a group, I must say, Captain..."

"And they'll be very angry once they find out that one of our comrades is dead."

The man leading the cavalry halted on the dusty dirt road, then raised his fist, signaling to the others. Everyone stopped. The man's gaze swept over the terrified villagers, then after a short pause, he addressed them loudly: "Southerners! Confederates! We've heard that in recent days, in violation of United States laws, you attacked and seriously harmed an officer and an enlisted man. I want the sheriff of this town to hand over Captain Jonathan Dalton and Private Nick Lloyd to us immediately! If you surrender them now, unharmed, we will overlook this transgression and leave without bloodshed!"

Curious glances from the inn's windows were directed at the strangers, while armed men from the town gathered in doorways, on rooftops, and on verandas, eagerly awaiting the escalation of the situation.

Anthony, the deputy reserve, hurriedly emerged from the inn's swinging door. The blazing sun gleamed on his bald, sweaty head as he squinted at the men before him. Slowly, almost stumbling, he approached the horseman, shading his eyes with his hand. "Your comrade, that certain Nick Lloyd, broke into our church and, together with Jonathan Dalton, attempted a robbery! Our brave and true-hearted sheriff dealt with the nigger, and Dalton was locked up in the jail!" he lied with an uncompromising, offended tone.

The man's face reflected anger, his eyes radiated hatred, then he delivered a powerful kick to Anthony's face, causing the deputy to groan and fall to the ground. The horseman spat on Anthony. "Dalton's ours, you Southern dog!" He picked up his rifle and aimed it at the groaning man on the ground. The men waiting for the shootout put their hands on their pistol grips. The Union officer looked up and addressed the townsfolk again: "United States laws prohibit carrying firearms in states fighting on the Confederate side! Surrender Captain Jonathan Dalton immediately, or this man dies here! In the name of the law, I demand..."

"But you're not the law here!" Anton White shouted back. Walking down the veranda of the sheriff's office, he stepped onto the dirt road, confronting the Union soldiers. "You're nothing but dirty deserters, bandits. Cowardly men who, posing as officers and soldiers, loot, rape, and kill on the land of the defeated! So your word here is not law, but an offense to every decent person!"

The officer, in his rage, took a deep breath, then loaded his rifle. Anthony pleaded for mercy with groans. "We'll see about that! " he bellowed, then aimed and tried to shoot. The sound of gunfire filled the air, then more and more shots rang out. The horseman clutched his chest, his eyes widened and he toppled from the horse. Three shots had torn through his chest, leaving his bleeding body lying lifeless on the ground.

Smoke rose from Anton's revolver as he turned his gaze towards the terrified soldiers. Silence fell over the town, no one dared to speak a word, the air almost crackling with tension. A half-smile played on his face, knowing that alone, without his brother, he wouldn't last long against more armed soldiers.

"Shoot them all!" yelled one of the northerners, then fired into the crowd of people in front of the inn.

A bone-chilling scream erupted from the woman hit, and she fell to the ground with a dull thud. Hell broke loose. The men of the town collectively roared and drew their weapons. Beside Anton, bullets slammed into the ground, tearing it apart. Seeking cover, he pressed himself against the side of a building, then fired off more shots. Dalton's comrades scattered through the street, riding their horses into the midst of the crowd and shooting at anyone they saw. Men groaned and fell dead. The silence of the street was replaced by the agonizing screams of women and the cries of children.

Anton loaded more bullets into his revolver, then cocked the hammer and stepped out from his cover. He came face to face with a horseman, who was dragging a woman by her hair. Anton whistled, causing the man to raise his head. Terror and disbelief reflected in his eyes as he glanced into the barrel of the gun. Another gunshot rang out, and the man fell dead from the saddle. The horse panicked and began to gallop, dragging the soldier's lifeless body along the ground. The younger White approached the sobbing woman, who was crawling on all fours, seeking refuge on the ground. Anton ushered her into the sheriff's office while blindly firing. He relished the fight. Fear had long dissipated, leaving only the adrenaline coursing through his body, the instinct and enjoyment of the hunt. He glanced at the terrified woman. He tried to smile kindly at her, but he wasn't sure if he succeeded. Bullets slammed into the office, the window almost exploded. Shards flew everywhere, one hitting Anton at the shoulder. He winced, then darted out of the door, firing his gun. His first shot hit a northerner charging towards him, who cried out and fell forward on his horse. Anton took a deep breath and continued towards the inn. Around him, the town's men, Solomon's gunmen, were shooting at the intruders, but more and more were falling dead. The younger White heard a whinny and turned around. Behind him, a soldier reared up on his horse, raising his pistol at him. He knew he had made a mistake; they had gotten behind him, and he would pay for it. He didn't have time to aim his weapon, just waited for the sharp pain.. The bounty hunter closed his eyes for the first time during the battle, his heart pounding. Instead of a gunshot, he heard the sound of a sharp whoosh, followed by a painful groan. He opened his eyes and watched, astonished, as the soldier dropped his revolver and clutched at his throat. Blood flowed thickly between his fingers onto his blue coat, his eyes bulging with fear and shock. A gurgling sound escaped him, then he collapsed to the ground. His body convulsed for a moment, then became still.

"Come in!" Solomon, the innkeeper, shouted.

Overcoming his astonishment, Anton rushed into the inn, checking his pistol, then looked at the man standing beside him. "Thank you!" he blurted out awkwardly.

Solomon Golding nodded, then pulled another throwing knife from his pocket, squinted with one eye, and hurled it. It struck a northerner in the chest, who promptly dropped dead. The innkeeper shook himself, then glanced at Anton. "My skills have dulled a bit over the years. I was aiming for the head... Another dirty one!"

Anton smiled, then peered out the window. Despite neutralizing several intruders, it seemed they were gaining the upper hand. The northerners still outnumbered them. "Your gunmen aren't really equipped to stop the Yankees," the younger White remarked.

"My gunmen are mostly farmers, ordinary folk who've been through the war, but they're not trained killers like those over there! Or me..." Solomon turned a piercing gaze towards White. "If we survive this, I hope you know you owe me your life! And I will collect my debts!"

"Let's focus on surviving first, then we can talk about payment."

Outside, the battle raged on relentlessly, and the bodies continued to pile up. Anton was aware that if his brother and the sheriff didn't return soon, they would only find corpses.

He stepped to the window, then used his elbow to break it and fired a few shots. The northern soldiers were now solely targeting the inn. Solomon and White threw themselves to the ground and waited for the barrage of shots to end. The gunfire ceased, and the town fell silent for a few moments. The air was filled with the smell of blood and gunpowder. The bounty hunter sat up, then cautiously made his way to the window. Seven more riders stood in front of the inn, all of them poised with their weapons ready to fire. Dead bodies littered the street, reminding Anton of the worst battles he had witnessed. He leaned against the wall and waited.

"Your comrades are dead!" one of the riders shouted. "If you so much as move, we'll shoot the inn to pieces and burn the whole town down. Save yourselves while you still can, and surrender! We've won! A few of us will find Captain Dalton and leave you here!" The rider spoke quietly to one of his companions, who dismounted and headed towards the sheriff's office.

The younger White exhaled heavily, then moved to shoot decisively, but Solomon stopped him. The riders raised their rifles and unleashed several shots at the inn. One shot hit a man lying on the ground, causing him to cry out in pain.

"Enough!" shouted the innkeeper. "I'll go out!"

Anton looked at him angrily. "What do you think you're doing?" he snapped. "These are bandits! And with Dalton on their side, you can be sure they'll come back to slaughter everyone in town!"

"Trust me!" Solomon reassured him. "The deputy sheriff will be back soon, along with your brother and Wratiszlaw! They're not far from town and they've been on their way for hours! We need to buy time, or else we'll die!" He winked at Anton, then raised his hands and stepped out of the inn through the swinging door. "Gentlemen..." he said, spreading his hands in surrender. "The war has long been over. Why don't we discuss this civilly? We don't want anything else but to live in peace here! You want Captain

Dalton? I have the key to the jail! I'll set him free if you promise to leave the town and everyone remains unharmed!"

The rider hesitated, then looked at the others. Fearful yet determined gazes met, and almost imperceptibly, each of them nodded. "Agreed! Go to the sheriff's office. Once you hand over Captain Dalton, we'll leave the town, and you can continue living your lives in safety."

Solomon nodded. "Sounds like a fair deal to me!" The innkeeper continued to walk across the street with his hands raised. His gaze swept over the fallen, a sense of anguish washing over him. The main street of Corpus Christi was strewn with lifeless bodies frozen in pools of blood among the shattered windowpanes. Solomon knew that the town would struggle to recover from this bloodshed. One of the northerners was already inside the sheriff's office, conversing with Dalton. The innkeeper slowly approached the door, then opened it. The door creaked open slowly, the ominous sound of the bell filling the small space. The eyes of the northern man and the innkeeper met for a moment. Solomon nodded, then stepped up to the cell. "It seems Captain Dalton will be the one to go free after all," he said.

The northerner behind him chuckled, then replied, "You southern rats really thought you could stop us? You couldn't even do it in the war."

A mocking smirk appeared on the innkeeper's face, and Dalton immediately exclaimed, "Trap!"

But his companion couldn't react anymore. Solomon swiftly and silently sliced the man's throat with a quick motion. The northerner's eyes bulged, he clutched his throat, dropped his rifle, and collapsed to the ground. The innkeeper grabbed the rifle, secured it, and then aimed it at Dalton. "Stay quiet! Captain..."

"You fool!" Jonathan erupted. "You won't survive this!"

"But neither will you!" Solomon winked at him.

From outside came murmurs of protest, and then the surviving soldiers' leader cautiously peered into the office.

Astonishment spread across his face, and immediately he aimed his weapon at Solomon.

The innkeeper just laughed, then shouted loudly towards the street: "Now this is a Mexican standoff, isn't it?"

The northerner didn't respond, just signaled to his remaining men, who took up defensive positions against those trapped inside the inn. "If you don't drop your weapon, we'll slaughter everyone inside! Is that worth it to you?"

"Absolutely," Solomon replied calmly.

"Very well! Fire!"

A single shot rang out, prompting the leader of the soldiers to turn towards the sound. At the end of the main street appeared Wratiszlaw Arisztid, his badge gleaming in the sunlight. The sheriff cocked his revolver and fired another shot, but that missed its mark as well. The soldier laughed and taunted him: "You're the clumsiest sheriff I've ever seen!"

More shots rang out, this time from the rooftops. The northern officer turned around and was astonished to see his remaining men falling to the ground, motionless. He looked up and spotted a man in a black coat on the rooftop, holding his pistol ready to fire. He reached for his rifle, but before he could aim, he heard the sound of galloping hooves. Suddenly, he felt a rope wrapping around his upper body.

Deputy Frederick rode past him, throwing a lasso. As the horse raced by, the rope tightened, and the officer was yanked out of the saddle. He tried to scream, but the fall knocked the air out of his lungs. Frederick held onto the rope tightly and then turned back towards the fallen soldier. "But I'm much better at aiming!" A final shot rang out, and the soldier didn't move anymore.

"I couldn't care less about those damn priests getting into trouble!" Solomon snapped. "Can't you see what's happening out there?" The innkeeper grabbed Wratiszlaw's shoulder and pulled him to the window. "Look!" He pointed to the street. "The remaining people of the town are picking up their husbands and wives from the ground! Compared to this, the problems of two strangers don't matter! How do you think we'll get out of this?"

"I have no idea..." Arisztid sighed. "But this is about much more than just the problems of two strangers." He stepped away from the window, scratched his chin, then turned back to the innkeeper. "For our town to have a future, we have to look after our children. There's no doubt about that."

"But what the hell did you find in the convent?!"

"I'm honestly curious about that too." Fred remarked.

Solomon walked to his desk and took out three glasses and whiskey from the drawer. He filled them all, then handed them to the two men.

Wratiszlaw sniffed it, loving the intoxicating scent of alcohol. He took a sip, sighed, then spoke up: "Actually just blood and two dead bodies."

"Who are the victims?" the deputy asked.

"Presumably the head nun, and a nun we found with Mr. White at the chapel altar. She was lying half-naked, her throat cut ear to ear."

"Good God..." Fred gasped. "And the head nun?"

"We found her in the crypt. Someone left her sitting in a pose, and when I touched her, her head fell into her lap."

The room fell silent. Everyone was affected by what had been said. Arisztid continued: "But that's not all. They painted 'no forgiveness without shedding of blood' on the wall with the nun's blood. And we also found a torn piece of paper with Mr. White. It said, 'This godless betrayal, Holy Father, springs from my own blood. ' It was signed by someone named K. Gareth, who we assume is the same woman the priests came for."

"Do you think Dalton's appearance could be related to this?" the innkeeper asked with genuine curiosity.

"I consider it entirely unlikely." Arisztid shook his head. "Those hooded figures are frighteningly efficient. They struck quickly at the convent and our church. Swiftly, and lethally."

"And silently," Fred added. "We saw or sensed nothing of it."

"And the niggers rode in and shot... No... The two incidents are just unfortunate coincidences," the sheriff declared. "In fact, I believe Captain Dalton is also a victim of all this. If it weren't for those hooded figures, they would have simply looted our church and moved on, but he and his companion stumbled into it."

The deputy crossed his arms, then paced nervously around the room. "What I don't understand, though, is if Dalton is as good as they say, then why did he run? Straight into our arms, unarmed. Damn it all! We're talking about one of the best shooters in the country!"

The innkeeper and the sheriff's gaze met for a moment, then concern settled on both of their faces.

"But what, or who, is so terrifying that even Jonathan Dalton himself skedaddled with his tail between his legs? " Solomon asked.

"People against whom both of us, me and Fred, are nothing. We need a team."

"Look around, Arisztid!" his companion interjected. "There are barely any living men left... There won't be a team from this."

Wratiszlaw's face bore a significant smile. "The situation is that we have three legendary gunslingers in our town."

The innkeeper and Fred were left speechless.

Solomon approached the window, then spoke up after a few seconds of silence: "Are you really planning to recruit the two bounty hunters into a team when one of the members is inherently hated?"

"We have no other choice," the sheriff declared unequivocally. "Our only chance lies with them, and even then, I'm not entirely sure."

"I agree with Arisztid." Fred nodded. "I found tracks leading towards Kingsville. But... These were trained. They marched and struck purposefully. Probably some kind of Comanche group." He pulled out an Indian feather from his pocket. "Only they use these. They hit the farmhouse, but I only found the husband's body, the woman and the child were missing."

"Which family?" asked the innkeeper.

"Liam Benjamin's farm."

"Liam is dead?" the sheriff asked sadly.

The deputy nodded. "He fought bravely, to the last of his strength, but he didn't stand a chance."

Sweat trickled down Solomon's temple, his mustache quivered, and he wiped his sweaty forehead with a yellowed rag. He poured another round of whisky for everyone, and they drank it in one gulp. The man lit a cigar and exhaled a long puff of smoke, filling the room.

"By evening, I'll arrange a meeting with the bounty hunters and the mayor. The townsfolk need to be informed. We have to tell them what happened and what we're going to do," declared the innkeeper. "But that's my job. You two should handle the tasks that are necessary. Sheriff, did you find any leads to follow?"

"The tracks lead towards Matamoros."

"So Mexico..." Solomon remarked.

"Mexico." Arisztid nodded. "Pedro will take us across, I've already spoken with him."

"Excellent," replied the innkeeper. "Then we'll meet tonight! Until then, get ready and sort things out!"

The sheriff and his deputy nodded, then tipped their hats and left.

"We're leaving, Anton! Get ready!" Jeremiah declared in an uncompromising tone.

His brother took off his hat and threw it onto the bed. He approached the window, watching the people outside. The sound of sobbing women and children pierced deep into his soul. Although he hadn't been a child for a long time when he lost his parents, he understood and felt their profound pain. The sight of orphaned children deeply disturbed him. Behind him, he heard his brother throwing his travel bag onto the bed, then packing his knives, spare ammunition, and other gear. He sighed, then turned to his brother. "I'm staying."

Jeremiah stopped in his tracks, then slowly raised his fiery gaze to his brother. He hated it when he defied him. "You're not staying. And that's not up for debate! Now, pack your things. We're leaving!"

"And what about the priests?" Anton asked angrily. "They paid us! It's our duty to fulfill our task, otherwise they'll call us dirty cheats!"

"We fulfilled our duty and brought them this far. The deal was to escort them there and back. There was no mention of a fight."

"It was agreed that we would bring the nun. Where is she?"

"She's dead." His brother's voice was cold and emotionless. "Just like that foolish sheriff will soon be, along with his deputy." He turned to his brother, who still stared at him motionlessly, with bewilderment and disappointment reflected on his face. He lifted his hat, wiped his sweaty forehead, then put the hat back on. He sighed, then slowly approached his brother and placed his hand on his shoulder. "This is no longer our fight." He tried to speak in a softer tone. "And what about Dalton? We could just shoot him dead in his cell! We'll never have a better chance than this!" Jeremiah shook his head. "There would be no honor in that."

"As if you ever cared about honor. If you had seen..." Anton felt a massive blow to the right side of his face, causing him to stagger, his back hitting the wall. Stars danced before his eyes, dizziness overcoming him. He hadn't expected a slap. Once his vision cleared, he saw his brother's enraged gaze staring back at him.

"I won't tolerate you questioning my honor! We'll deal with Jonathan Dalton when we have the opportunity for a fair duel, until then, we'll continue on our own path. You and me. It's my duty to watch over you. And as for the priests, they can eat what they've cooked. There's much more going on here than they've said, and what I saw in the convent..." He grimaced, then continued, with a hint of unsettling fear in his voice, "What I saw in the convent, it even frightened me. And considering that we were attacked on the road, and what happened here in Corpus Christi... No. I won't subject us to that."

The anger faded from Jeremiah's face, replaced by shame; he regretted striking his brother. After their parents' death, he had vowed to always protect his only remaining sibling, even if it meant bringing shame upon himself.

This time, it was Anton who stepped closer to his brother, then scrutinized his gaze. "What did you see in the convent?"

Elder White grumbled softly, then turned away from his brother. He approached the table and lit a cigarette. Briefly, he recounted the entire journey and what had happened.

Anton was horrified, but his determination only grew stronger. He took a deep breath, then defied his brother's will and declared: "I'm staying, regardless."

Jeremiah looked at him incredulously. "And what good would that do you? Money?"

The younger brother spread his arms and replied in a raised voice: "I'm tired of killing for money, we've been doing it ever since we left home! I'm just sick of it! This isn't life! In the war, we had a purpose and a common will that gave us strength! But now what do we have? Nothing! We feed on people's blood so we can kill someone tomorrow! Look at me and tell me to my face that this satisfies you! Tell me you don't feel the gaping emptiness in your soul that nothing can fill! It's time for us to finally do something good, selflessly, to do something that finally ends this dreadful emptiness!"

In his anger, he slammed his hat against the wall, then tried to leave hastily, but Jeremiah stepped in front of him. "I feel it too, brother," he said resignedly. "If this is what you want, then I'll stand by you, because someone has to protect..."

Sharp pain pierced Father Cristofano's shoulder as his companion removed a shard of glass embedded in his flesh with a pair of tweezers. The young priest hissed, and the leather strap fell from his mouth.

Agustíno cast a disapproving glance at him and pressed the strap back into his mouth. "You're still young, my friend, and you struggle to understand that God's ways often lead to suffering. This wound is nothing. Bear it with dignity."

The young priest bit down on the strap again, his gaze lifted to the sky as he waited for another shard to be extracted from him. His heart no longer pounded fiercely; calm settled over him once more. He had yet to experience battle, he'd only heard stories. Stories of glory and dignity, but he had come to realize that there was no glory or dignity in falling in battle, only raw pain and agony. He pondered whether the grace of the Lord was truly infinite, and why humanity was cursed with suffering.

Agustíno extracted another shard and placed it on the table with the others, removed the strap from the young priest's mouth, and set it aside.

"Father," Cristofano began thoughtfully. "Have you ever wondered what God's intention is with all this death and cruelty?" He pursed his lips and continued in a tone filled with sadness. "Down there, when they were shooting, there was a boy beside me. I tried to pull him towards me, but a bullet hit him... He didn't die right away, but suffered slowly, in agony. What could be the purpose of such cruel torture for such a young soul?"

"Our mortal minds can never reach the glory of the Lord and understand His will," his companion declared sternly. "Think of him as a young soul who didn't have to endure the mortal and bitter existence of man. The Lord called him to Himself, and now he sings with the choir of Archangels by God's throne."

"And if he wasn't baptized?"

"Then he is damned..."

Cristofano turned his gaze away, then rose and approached the window. He wasn't watching the street; he was lost in thought. He pondered on good and evil, life and death, wickedness and human goodness. Yet bitterness crept back into his soul as he remembered Sister Gareth. Bowing his head, he asked Agustíno: "Will the Lord forgive us for lying? And we will lie again."

"We are doing the Lord's will, in the name of the Holy Father," the elder priest replied. "The locals need not know what is happening. We need them until they fulfill their duty."

"But they are already becoming suspicious. The elder White sees through us and doesn't hesitate to confront us. And what happened with our companions here... it's disgraceful! Those black-clad strangers who attacked us as well. A multitude of questions to which we have no answers! I feel, Father, that His Holiness made a mistake sending the two of us... We simply aren't enough for this. We arrived too late."

Agustíno grasped both of his companion's shoulders and looked deeply into his eyes. "The Lord guides us! So we could not have arrived too late, but precisely when we needed to be here! Yes... it's dreadful and disgraceful what happened to the people here, but never forget! We are carrying out a mission that no one must know about! That's why only the two of us came! We need to speak with the sheriff about what they found at the convent."

"Sister Gareth..." Cristofano paled.

Agustíno nodded grimly. "Jeremiah and the sheriff returned without her..."

"Do you think they got to the..."

"Silence!" the old priest interrupted. "The Holy Father forbade us from voicing these thoughts aloud! We need to know exactly what happened, then pursue them, no matter how dangerous it may be." The older priest reached for his leather bag and opened it. Metallic clicks were heard, and to Cristofano's greatest astonishment, a revolver emerged.

"Father..." the younger priest said. "I didn't even know you had... Where did you get it?"

Agustíno looked at his companion with steely eyes, then replied in a hoarse, gravelly voice: "I haven't always been a priest and follower of the Lord. Once, I walked the path of sin and did things for which I must atone one day. Under the guidance of our Creator, I brought this piece with me now. I felt we would need it. And so we will." Agustíno extended the weapon towards the younger priest, then addressed his companion again: "You are still young! Strengthen your heart and fulfill the will of our Creator! What will happen next may raise doubts within you, but believe me! I always fight for the Lord, and I want to know if you are with me!"

Beads of sweat ran down Cristofano's face. His throat felt parched, his heart beat fiercely. With trembling hands, he grasped the cold metal, then hesitantly rotated the revolver in his hands. "I am with you, Father. Until my last breath."

Agustíno patted the man's shoulder. "Good" he smiled. "Very good."

Someone knocked on the door, and both turned towards the sound. The old priest opened the door, facing the still stunned sheriff.

"Father." Arisztid tipped his hat. "I came to inform you of what we found at St. Lucia's."   Wratiszlaw's grim expression revealed everything to the two priests. Agustíno gestured for him to come closer, and Arisztid recounted everything he had learned.

Father Cristofano paled, then walked towards the window with a bewildered look. He tightly grasped the cross hanging around his neck, praying aloud with trembling hands.

The sheriff briefed the elder priest on the plan to travel to Mexico and organize a team for this purpose, with the meeting scheduled for that evening at Solomon's inn.

Agustíno thanked him for his efforts and invaluable assistance, then ushered him out of the room. He closed the door, resting his hands on the dry wood for a moment. His gaze lingered on his wrinkled hands. He was beginning to tire. He felt the grip of time in every fiber of his being. His spirit remained strong, but he knew his body would soon start to fail him. He prayed earnestly to the Lord that these days would not begin now. He turned and looked at his companion, whose fear was almost palpable.

Cristofano clutched his cross with trembling hands, praying with a faltering voice. "...Melt me, Lord, mold me, fill me with yourself, order me..."

Agustíno folded his hands in prayer and stepped beside him, continuing the prayer together: "Drive away from me all demonic afflictions, witchcraft, black magic, black masses, spells, bindings, curses, evil eye, demonic harassment, demonic possession, demonic nightmares, all that is evil, sinful, envy, jealousy, deceit, physical, mental, moral, spiritual, demonic diseases—with the power of Almighty God, in the name of the Savior Jesus Christ, through the intercession of the Immaculate Virgin, let every unclean spirit, every presence harassing me, be ordered and commanded to leave immediately, depart and go to eternal hell! Amen!" Both men made the sign of the cross, then instinctively looked at each other. "Are you ready, brother?" asked the elder priest.

Fear disappeared from Cristofano's eyes, replaced by the tranquility and determination of prayer and his companion's resolve. He kissed the cross hanging around his neck and replied: "Even though I walk through the valley of the shadow of death, I will fear no evil..."

"Are you sure about this?" Jeremiah asked with a skeptical tone.

Anton White nodded decisively, with a stern look. "I'm staying. I feel like we're not here by accident, that something or someone is guiding us."

His brother skeptically tossed the cigarette box he held, which landed with a dull thud against the wall before falling to the ground. "You can't seriously believe that God is guiding us... Only superstitious fools believe in that!" he burst out. The elder White brother leaned against the windowsill, gazing at the darkening sky. The oil lamps burning between the houses cast a reassuring light onto the street. Jeremiah had been to many American towns where with the nightfall, evil emerged as well. Robbers, assailants, murderers, and perverts. This was the man created "in the image of God" to him. He closed his eyes, sighed, and looked back at his brother. "Don't force me to reconsider! I'll go with you if you want to ease your conscience, but I won't let religious fanatics and all sorts of superstitious people cloud your judgment! I hope I've made myself clear enough!"

Anton walked to the cigarette box, took out a cigarette, and lit it. "It feels different now anyway, brother. Don't you sense it?"

"I sense that this is a very bad idea."

There was a knock on the door, but neither of them answered. Whoever it was knocked again, and then the sheriff's deputy spoke up: "I'm Deputy Frederick William.

I'd like to inform you that the sheriff's waiting for you at the inn."

"And in what matter exactly?" Jeremiah asked.

"He wants to speak with you about Jonathan Dalton, and about what they found in the convent."

The two brothers' gaze met for a brief moment, then Anton stepped to the door and opened it. "We're ready to go" he declared.

The deputy nodded. "Please follow me. There are still a lot of glass shards in the inn, and it's quite windy, but we've managed to fix things up as much as the situation allowed."

The two brothers stepped out of the door, then followed Frederick. Grief and astonishment reflected on the deputy's face. Jeremiah understood the situation perfectly; small-town lawmen were not accustomed to this; it would be a challenging task even for the sheriff's offices in Washington and Los Angeles. They quickly reached the inn. The swinging door had been removed, broken windows covered with curtains. The inn was no longer a place filled with life and joy, but stood quiet, wounded, and empty. Several relatively intact tables had been pushed together in the middle of the room to form a larger one. Sitting around it were the innkeeper Solomon, Wratiszlaw Arisztid the sheriff, Agustíno, and Father Cristofano. Their gaze conveyed shock and incomprehension, grief and pain. The town had received wounds over the past weeks that would take a very long time to heal, and elders would still be telling their grandchildren about it years from now. Behind the counter, the bartender filled glasses with whisky, beer, and accompanying water. There was no toast this time; everyone reached for their drink individually.

Arisztid cleared his throat, stood up, and looked at the others. "Gentlemen," he began. "Evil has arrived in our beloved town. This may not be an exaggeration to say. We have gone through events that we could not even imagine in our worst nightmares, despite the fact that this city has already been devastated and ruined by war." He paused for a moment, then continued: "However, the shadow of war had barely receded from us when their war broke out in Mexico. Thousands of refugees flooded our county, trampling, stealing, or consuming our crops, slaughtering our livestock, looting our pantries, in the worst cases, our families. Then came the murder in our church, the kidnapping of our children, and the street shootings, in which many fathers and mothers lost their lives." Arisztid's gaze swept over those present. "I believe it is time for us to finally emerge victorious from this seemingly impossible situation. I firmly believe that the altar boys are still alive, and the clues lead to Mexico. My deputy and I are organizing a team to go after them."

The sheriff took off his badge and threw it on the table. "This will not be an official operation, Mexico is no longer within our jurisdiction, so I think we don't necessarily have to solve this task in accordance with the law. Mr. White!" He pointed to the older brother. "You have seen what we are up against. You have seen the horror in the convent perpetrated by these barbarians. I would like you and your brother to join us. I know," he spread his arms in resignation, "that you are not detectives, but that wouldn't be your task. Leave the investigation to us with Fred. We can't pay much, but whatever we have, we'll give it to you."

"Please, sheriff, let me!" interrupted Father Cristofano. "As it turns out, the church is also involved in this matter, so naturally, it will pay any reward. Please, Mr. White, just name the price, and you'll get it! Of course, this applies to you too, sheriff."

"We don't ask for money," declared Arisztid. "This is our job! If you weren't here, Fred and I would go to Mexico alone."

"That's a noble gesture from you, sheriff. We won't forget it" replied the elder priest. "Well, Mr. White. Are you willing to join us?"

Anton nodded, but Jeremiah still didn't respond. He pulled his hat over his eyes, his black shirt ominously gleaming. He scratched his chin, then looked around at those present. "This is all fine and good" he began in a hoarse voice. "But look around! No matter how much money they can pay, what good is it if we die trying? Based on what we saw in the convent, and what they did to their priests... A small-town sheriff and his deputy, with two priests by their side, aren't exactly the kind of guarantee I'd stake my life on... Even if we're here." He sighed, then continued. "My brother is firmly determined to help you. So, I'm with him... But I still think it's a terrible idea."

"Thank you, Jeremiah!" nodded Arisztid. "This is quite surprising, but still joyful news. And yes! Mr. White is right! Indeed, we would be few. But in Mexico, near the border, lives a good friend of mine; his name is Bruce. He's a legendary Indian hunter, a war veteran, ever since the government stopped paying for Indian scalps, he's been working as a bounty hunter. He would surely join us for my sake."

"Bruce?" Jeremiah asked, surprised. "Bearslayer Bruce? Don't joke! He's just a legend they used to scare Indian kids with before bedtime..." "Oh!" The sheriff smiled. "Bruce is very much alive, and he'll find joy in hunting Indians."

"Alright," Anton replied. "But that's still just one person, and I don't know how useful a hunter would be against enemies who shoot back."

"If it's really Bearslayer Bruce, then don't worry, little brother," Jeremiah retorted, then scrutinized Arisztid's face. "But is there something else true here?"

The sheriff smiled, then briefly lifted his hat, revealing his sweaty head. "Actually, yes... There is something else. We should also bring Captain Dalton with us."

An uncomfortable and tense silence fell over the inn. Solomon, Arisztid, and Fred all looked at the White brothers as one, disbelief, shock, and anger radiating from their faces.

"You've lost your mind!" Jeremiah shouted.

"After what his gang did in town today, you'd leave him alive and take him on a rescue mission?!" Anton asked, outraged.

"We don't stand a chance without a gunfighter like Captain Dalton!" the sheriff replied, trying to shout over the brothers.

"We're not even here anymore! You're insane! Just rub the money on your hair and stop preaching morals to me!"

The two White brothers got up from the table and headed towards the door, but the innkeeper called after them: "Mr. White!" he called loudly, and the brothers turned back. "As far as I know, you've sworn vengeance against Mr. Dalton! Think about it! You'd leave the United States, be in the Mexican desert where anything can happen. War is raging, foreign soldiers are trampling the country... A little murder wouldn't even raise an eyebrow."

"That's right! You don't know Captain Dalton!" Jeremiah emphasized. "He'd shoot you at the first opportunity. And you, sheriff... You wouldn't be a match for him, just like your deputy. Neither would the Bearslayer."

"We had to retreat, too, when we attacked them in the mountains..."

Jeremiah silenced his brother, who immediately fell quiet.

"I've heard this rumor," Deputy Frederick interjected. "But I thought it was just a legend. You really took on Dalton with a tenth of your force, and he hunted down your entire squad? That's hard to believe."

"But it's true. We could barely escape..."

"Quiet, Anton! " the elder White burst out.

"If I were in your shoes, Mr. White, I'd seize such an opportunity," said the sheriff. "We'll shackle Dalton, and he'll only get a weapon if it comes to a fight. If the captain refuses, he'll be hanged tomorrow. What do you say? I have to be honest with you, Jeremiah. I don't think we'll all survive this operation."

"And if it's God's will, then you can serve justice," concluded Father Cristofano.

The two brothers glanced at each other, then Jeremiah buried his face in his hands, while Anton smiled. "I accept these conditions."

Those sitting at the table smiled.

"If he's in, then I have no choice either. Count me in," declared the elder White.

"Excellent! We'll leave at dawn!" The sheriff clapped his hands together. "Pedro will smuggle us into Mexico, and from there, we'll head towards Matamoros. Bring only the essentials. Don't worry about medicines; we'll take care of that."

"And I'll prepare a week's worth of food for you by dawn," Solomon announced. "If you haven't returned in a week, we'll bury you with a proper ceremony."

"Agreed," nodded the sheriff, as did the others. "Then let's get to work, gentlemen! It's time to pay a visit to Mexico!"

Chapter Four

"Then another sign appeared in heaven: an enormous red dragon with seven heads and ten horns and seven crowns on its heads. Its tail swept a third of the stars out of the sky and flung them to the earth. The dragon stood in front of the woman who was about to give birth, so that it might devour her child the moment he was born."

Revelation 12:3-4

A small, cold drop of water fell on Kassandra's forehead, instantly waking her up. She pulled her legs up in alarm, curling into a fetal position. As her fear subsided, she realized that the horrors of recent times were not just nightmares, but reality. She wiped her face. Once again, the urge to cry overcame her, but she feared retribution. *They'll beat me again*, she thought to herself. *I mustn't cry, I mustn't make noise.*

She tried to sit up, but sharp, stabbing pain shot from her groin, causing her to grab it immediately. With another slight movement, the thought dawned on her… *There's something inside me*. Her fingers reached for her genitalia, which had blistered as if burned. She emitted painful groans as the sharp pain overwhelmed her, while she pulled out the long, still warm object from inside her. She sighed with relief and tossed aside the metal object, which landed with a hard clang on the cold, moldy stone floor. Her throat was scratchy, her mouth dry, her lips chapped, her hair disheveled, and the only piece of clothing she wore was a nightgown. At least it had been. Now it was nothing more than a torn, yellowed, filthy rag, barely covering her body enough for the men who visited her to easily access any part of it. Her head throbbed, her hands trembled. Crawling on all fours towards the small table next to the blankets, she tried to reach for it, but she couldn't control her movements and lost her balance. She fell onto her side, and the hard stone scraped her skin. A metallic click sounded from the direction of the door, and she knew what that meant. "No..." she whimpered, but it was too late.

With a loud, metallic click, the iron cover of the peephole swung open, revealing the dreaded pair of eyes behind it. Dark brown eyes glared at her angrily.

Kassandra instinctively curled up, her legs trembling, as the last of her strength faded away. She tried to cover her body with her dirty clothes, but to no avail. The door slowly creaked open, the light from the torches outside blinding her.

A robust figure stood in the doorway, wearing a dark blue, tattered shirt, brown trousers, and a pair of worn-out boots. His skin was brown, his unkempt greasy hair falling in clumps onto his shoulders. With a sinister grin, he stepped into the room. "You made noise... again," he said ominously. "Do you know what happens when you break the rules?"

The woman started to cry, shaking all over. She crawled onto the blankets, then into the corner. Facing the wall, she began to scratch at it with her nails, causing her skin to tear and bits of her nails to remain embedded in the rough surface. The man approached, then grabbed her hair tightly and pulled her towards him. Kassandra screamed as her head was forced backward.

Her torturer stared directly into her eyes, stuck out his tongue, and slowly licked the crying woman's face "Why are you crying, my child?" The man tightened his grip on her hair, pulling her head closer, and whispered in her ear. "I thought you enjoyed it when men pampered you." He grabbed both of Kassandra's shoulders, pulled her up with a swift motion, then slammed her forcefully against the wall. "Or perhaps we misjudged you?" he asked, his yellowed, incomplete teeth flashing. "Perhaps you didn't throw yourself at that Austrian officer like a whore, knowing that you are the bride of Christ?" The man let go, took a step back, and delivered a powerful slap to the woman's face.

Kassandra fell to the ground like a puppet. Lying there, she felt her hot blood trickle down the corner of her mouth, onto her face. She could no longer cry, only sob and whimper. She knew that pleading with her tormentor would be futile; he would only become more savage.

The stranger noticed the metal rod lying on the ground, picked it up, and knelt beside Kassandra. "I see you've taken out my little plaything" he smirked, then spat. "How about I warm it up again, but place it somewhere entirely different?" With pity but also enjoyment, he looked at the suffering woman. Now she was his toy, for as long as he wanted. *As long as the Father allows it*, he corrected himself. *The woman still had a task and a purpose. I couldn't let her die.* He took a step back, danced his dirty fingers on the wall, then took out a small vial from his pocket, grinning. "Would you like your medicine?"

Summoning all her strength, Kassandra looked at the man. She longed for the bliss, the peaceful sleep that would momentarily take her away from this dreadful place.

"Crawl here for it, like the serpent that God commanded to crawl on the ground forever."

The woman slid on her belly to his feet, then looked up at him with tear-filled eyes. She knew they were humiliating her. Again and again. She had no idea how long her martyrdom would last, but she was certain she wouldn't be free anytime soon. "Please," she pleaded. "I need my medicine."

Her torturer smiled almost kindly, sympathetically. He squatted beside her, then opened her mouth and poured the alcoholic opium tincture down her throat.

Kassandra's eyes widened, then frothy saliva dripped from the corners of her mouth, giving her already bloody face a grotesque appearance.

The man leaned her against the wall, then sniffed her hair. "Señorita, you smell very bad." He wrinkled his nose. "You'll need to bathe tonight," he told her, but he knew Kassandra was already somewhere else. "Tonight, you'll have to assist us in bringing forth a holy generation of newborn."

Kassandra emerged from the sweet, empty void, slowly, surely, accompanied by a torturous sensation. A voice called out to her. Her subconscious hoped it was the Virgin Mary calling, but her mind quickly recognized it was Sister Judith. She blinked painfully, her eyes burning and stinging. She wiped them with her dirty hands, but the sensation only worsened. She pressed her head into the dirty blanket, waiting for her dizziness and pain to subside.

"Kassandra, look at me," the voice called. "Sit up and look at me."

The woman struggled to sit up, then crawled on all fours to the stone wall on the left side of the cell.

Amidst the broken stones, a kind, almost innocent pair of eyes watched her. "You must not drink the opium. It's not medicine, it's poison. It will rob you of your mind, body, and spirit. You'll become a slave."

The pain crept back into her soul. She knew Sister Judith was right, but the drug had already ensnared her. "I'm sorry... I can't... live like this." She leaned her head against the stone, then began to cry softly.

"Kassandra, look at me. Come on, lift your head. I want to see your eyes."

The woman looked up, their gazes meeting. Deep down in her soul, she wished she could resist temptation as Sister Judith did. She felt ashamed of what she had done before. She had broken every oath she made to the Lord. She lied, fornicated, took lives, and stole. "How do you stay so strong, Judith? Aren't you afraid?"

"Not of death, for the Kingdom of God awaits us. The pain of the body is temporary. Christ our Lord is the remedy for the torment of the soul. If your faith is true, no matter where they take you, no matter how terrible the place, you will remain strong."

"But I betrayed God."

"Listen to me, Kassandra," Judith began firmly. "I don't know where you came from, who sent you, and for what purpose, but I do know that these people wanted you and came for you. You have a task with them. It's the will of the Lord, so you have no choice, either. Strengthen your soul and face them, for they come for us today. The Creator is with you."

"Why are they coming for us? What do you know?"

"Sister Evelyn was taken away."

Kassandra covered her mouth with her hand.

"She's giving birth today. The monks are already preparing," Judith said. "I heard them from my cell door."

They heard the sound of footsteps. Kassandra turned towards the door as it opened, and her torturer stood in front of her in a gray robe, tied around his waist with a rope. A wooden cross hung around his neck, covered by a hood. She looked up, and her blood froze in her veins. The lascivious, longing, evil smile was replaced this time by fanatical hatred and zeal. The man said nothing, just stepped towards her and grabbed her forcefully. Kassandra screamed. She would have called for Judith, but she couldn't risk being caught, having this taken from her; the last spark of humanity, not just an animal they could torture at their pleasure. The monk pushed her forward in the underground passages. The light of torches illuminated the narrow corridors, lined with closed doors. Kassandra looked around in circles. She saw nothing but the barren corridors illuminated by the torchlight, filled with the sounds of bitter crying and painful screams. The sisters had been tortured almost constantly with who knows what and how.

The monk pushed her again, then ordered a halt. "Take off your rags, and hands on the wall!" he ordered.

Kassandra hesitated to comply. Her torturer stepped closer, then repeated: "I said take off your rags and hands on the wall."

Another monk approached them, holding buckets of water in both hands. The woman took off her nightgown, then closed her legs and covered her breasts with her hands.

"I said hands to the wall!" the man shouted, then hit her.

Kassandra staggered and fell against the wall. There was no time to comprehend the blow, as icy cold water was immediately poured over her, feeling like knives stabbing her.

"Don't cry, just wash! Water is precious, but we have to waste it on you!" her torturer yelled.

She started to wash. She had almost forgotten what it felt like to be clean, or at least what she could call clean. They poured water over her again, but this time she wasn't surprised. She didn't hiss, didn't gasp for air, just mechanically washed herself, ignoring how the two monks stared at every inch of her body. One of them handed her a choir robe, which she quickly put on. Once again, she could feel like a nun. "Don't I get a cross?" she asked.

"That's not for you. Let's go! " The man pushed her and led her down the stairs, straight into the chapel. Nuns sat in wooden pews, heads bowed, hands clasped in prayer. Fear and vulnerability radiated from each of them.

Kassandra looked up at the altar, her gaze resting on the crucified body of Christ. She knew her own suffering was nothing compared to what Jesus had to endure. *Give me strength, Lord, to fulfill your will, give me faith to resist evil, and give me patience to understand your plan.* She looked up again. On either side of the altar stood armed Indians, crosses hanging around their necks. She had seen them before, but she still didn't understand who they were and what purpose they served. The monks seated her. She looked for Judith, who was sitting a few rows behind her. She nodded slightly, and the nun nodded back.

"Our Father, who art in heaven, hallowed be thy name..." prayed the nun sitting next to her, struggling with her tears, clutching a rosary in her trembling hands. Kassandra placed her hand encouragingly on her shoulder, and the nun's trembling seemed to ease. Their gazes locked onto each other's. Without words, they understood each other's pain.

She saw movement from the podium and heard some commotion when a man wearing a gray poncho appeared at the altar. Kassandra froze.

His black hair reached his shoulders, a huge scar adorned his right cheek, and his left eye gleamed white and glassy. He wore a cartridge belt and carried white-handled revolvers on his hips. His gaze swept over the nuns, then he turned back and spoke almost inaudibly: "Bring her forth."

Kassandra craned her neck, trying to make out what was happening, and was shocked to see Sister Evelyn's naked body being carried in the arms of a tall, dark-haired Native American, then placed upon the altar. She looked unwell. Her hair was matted, her body covered in sweat, and she seemed to be in immense pain. The other nuns looked around, bewildered, considering what they were witnessing sacrilegious.

"Brides of Christ! You holy women! " began the scarred-faced man. "Perhaps some of you have heard of me, my name is Father Ramirez. Diego Ramirez. Perhaps many of you wonder why we brought you here, why we treat you as we do, and why we don't let you go. Well... Look deep into yourselves, examine your hearts, and you will find the answer."

A mournful cry came from the direction of the altar; the birth had begun.

"For God's sake, let us help her!" screamed one of the nuns.

"For God's sake!" replied Ramirez. "Are you trying to help for the love of God, or out of Christian goodwill? You see, sister, I brought you here today so that you might witness a miracle, a true miracle! One that you can only read about in the Bible, or hear about in tales told by travelers from distant lands! But you weep, you tremble, and even here, YOU BREAK THE LORD'S COMMANDMENTS!" he yelled fervently. "Do you see? Do you all see what we are? This is the problem with humanity! So answer me, my children, what is God's second commandment?"

He swept his gaze around and, losing his patience, he growled at the nun sitting beside Kassandra.

"Thou shalt not take the name of the Lord thy God in vain!" the woman replied in a trembling voice.

"Thou shalt not take the name of the Lord thy God in vain!" Ramirez reiterated firmly, raising his index finger. "And what do we do about it? We call upon God for things!" The Mexican spread his arms and stepped onto the podium stairs. "God payeth my debts! Is that how the saying goes? The world is a big zoo, and God helps those who help themselves! Do you know, ladies, what is written on the belt buckles of the Austro-Hungarian soldiers who tread upon our land?"

"We are in Mexico," Kassandra whispered to the nun next to her. "At least we know that."

"Gott mit uns! God is with us!" Ramirez continued. "But is God truly with them? Is God truly on the battlefields with the soldiers? I do not believe so!"

A wretched cry, a painful scream, filled the small chapel, yet no help arrived.

"And why is God not there with the soldiers on the battlefields? Because God does not ask you to fight for Him! God does not expect anyone to launch a final assault, to slaughter the men of other countries, to rape their women, or enslave their children! Ye are not children of the Lord, no! The LORD merely asks that ye believe and obey! And then ye shall be saved! And for this, ye need do nothing else but obey His clear instructions!"

Ramirez held up all ten fingers visibly towards the nuns. "The Lord asked for ten things! Ten things! Would it be too much of a burden to uphold ten habits throughout one's life? I think not! After all, many of us drink coffee, shave, and bathe every morning. These are not essential to life, merely habits! And we can uphold them. But you!" He gestured to the nuns. "You could not uphold these, even though you should be showing the way for humanity in these troubled, sinful times! Sister Katelyn, please answer! What is God's seventh commandment?"

All eyes turned to the woman, who stood up and answered in a trembling, uncertain voice: "Thou shalt not steal."

"Thou shalt not steal!" Ramirez repeated. "Did you remember God's command when you stole an apple from the Corpus Christi town market? No! Yet it would have only taken a short walk from the city to Saint Lucia! Our Lord and Savior, Jesus Christ, spent forty days in the desert while being tempted by the devil, yet did not sin! So, would it have been such a great feat to endure the barely one-hour walk?" He paused briefly, then continued. "Sister Charlotte, what is God's fifth commandment?" "Thou shalt not kill." came the answer.

"Thou shalt not kill! Did you think of God when, under cover of night, you snuck out of the convent to seek out the Corpus Christi physician and abort your fetus?" Ramirez turned to the suffering woman on the altar. "And what is God's sixth commandment?"

"Thou shalt not commit adultery," Kassandra replied loudly and firmly.

The man nodded, then two Indians grabbed a nun each and took them to the altar. They immediately began assisting in ensuring the child's birth in the safest possible manner. The priest turned back to his audience, speaking with a solemn tone: "The thirty-eighth verse of the first book of Moses, the twenty-fourth paragraph: "*And it came to pass about three months after, that it was told Judah, saying, Tamar thy daughter-in-law hath played the harlot; and also, behold, she is with child by whoredom. And Judah said, Bring her forth, and let her be burnt.*"

A frosty silence fell over the chapel. Dazed gazes stared ahead, with only Sister Evelyn's agony audible.

"You cannot do this!" Sister Judith screamed. "I can already see its head, the baby is coming out!"

A massive, bone-chilling scream erupted from Evelyn.

"Its head is out!" one of the nuns exclaimed.

The woman screamed, then stepped beside Ramirez, who lifted her head. "You will witness a true miracle, my child" he whispered ominously.

The sound of a baby's cry filled the air, and among the nuns, everyone gave thanks to the Lord for the healthy birth of the child.

"It's a boy," said the nun with a smile as one of the Indians severed the umbilical cord.

Ramirez took the crying newborn in his arms and stepped to the side of the podium. The faces of the nuns displayed bewilderment and horror.

"My son," Evelyn called. "Give me my baby."

Ramirez glanced at the Indians, who nodded before pushing the nuns back into their seats. Ignoring the woman, the priest turned to his audience: "I promised you that you would witness a miracle, the likes of which you could only read about in the Bible..." The man caressed the baby's face, then approached the benches and gently placed the infant into one of the nun's hands. "But before that, let me tell you something. Before my journey to Damascus, doubts tormented me. I was afraid. I must confess to you that doubt tormented me because I saw so much horror in the world that it shook my faith in God. I prayed constantly. I asked God to show me His infinite grace and love, to bring mercy upon the world, or at least to allow me to show them the way to heaven! But no answer came." He lowered his head, then began to walk among the benches. "I didn't understand why. Would God disappear?" he asked. "After all, the Old Testament is full of His miracles, His appearances, the holy people who spoke with the Lord, to whom the Creator spoke!" he said with fanatical smile on his face. "Then why wouldn't the Lord speak to me? Perhaps I did something wrong? And here I must pause." Ramirez turned around, then his gaze swept around the small chapel. "I realized how much wrong I had done, and yet I never atoned for it. Neither God nor man punished me for the sins I committed. Oh!" he exclaimed. "My sins were countless even before I became a priest, and I did not completely abandon my sinful ways even when I devoted my life to the Lord. Because I only believed that I dedicated myself to the Lord!" He raised his index finger. "And then came the moment when I lifted my eyes to the sky, and I cried out all my sinful deeds to the heavens, I expelled every sinful thought from myself, and the miracle happened! I felt the presence of the Holy Spirit. For the first time in my life, I felt that God was with me! Not with the soldiers on the battlefield, but with me, then and there! And on my journey, I went into the wilderness, as Jesus did, and I placed my fate in God's hands. And the miracle happened." Ramirez excitedly stepped onto the podium, gesturing to the Indians. "And not only did it happen, but the divine miracle came to life before me! He looked at me with his beautiful eyes and said, "*Be a witness to the second coming!*"

A smile spread across his face, and he spread his arms, continuing: "Brides of Christ! See with your own eyes the true miracle! The herald of salvation, who leads everyone to paradise, who bears the sign of the Lord!"

Ramirez gestured with his arms towards the iron door at the back of the podium, and the Indians on either side opened it. A peculiar, smoke-like fog flowed out from behind the door, and Kassandra's heart immediately began to beat faster. The Indians retreated with their guns aimed forward, while Ramirez remained motionless. "*And he opened the bottomless pit, and smoke arose out of the pit like the smoke of a great furnace; and the sun and the air were darkened by reason of the smoke of the pit.*"

Evelyn's vision began to clear, and she looked towards the door. The smoke billowed, and the lights filtering in from the background cast strange, grotesque shapes onto the fog.

Kassandra stood up, her expression incredulous, and stepped towards the podium. No one paid attention to her; all eyes were fixed on the altar. Silence descended upon the chapel. The eerie quiet was shattered by a bone-chilling scream. The nuns gasped, trembled, or screamed, clutching their lips. The smoke continued to fill the small chapel, but Kassandra crept closer to the podium. She heard clicking, rattling sounds, as if beetles were swarming the floor. Then, she heard a sharp, insect-like screech, and she almost instantly froze at the sight before her. Through the billowing smoke, she briefly glimpsed a locust-like creature bending over the altar.

"And out of the smoke came forth locusts upon the earth; and power was given them, as the scorpions of the earth have power," Kassandra whispered in horror to herself. Paralyzed by shock, she couldn't move, unable to lift her gaze from what she saw. Her mind pleaded to shut her eyes, but she was incapable of making even the slightest movement. The locust-like creature wore a headpiece resembling a golden crown, its hair as long and strong as Samson's, its face smooth and youthful. It looked hungry. Several screams erupted from the benches. Kassandra heard several dull thuds and was certain that several had fainted.

"Behold the miracle!" Ramirez exclaimed, pointing towards the creature. "The angel of the Lord has come to us!" The man stepped to the edge of the podium.

The clicking and rattling sounds grew louder as Evelyn screamed. She tried to flee, but her exhausted body wouldn't allow it. She leaned to the side, then fell off the altar. She hit the ground hard, then crawled on all fours, trying to escape towards Ramirez.

The creature emerged from the smoke, eliciting more screams, and Kassandra involuntarily took a step back.

Evelyn reached out her hand towards the Mexican, but the creature spread its insect-like wings, lifted its head towards the sky, and pounced on the vulnerable nun. Fear engulfed her as she tried to push herself away, but her body was too weak. A pale light glinted off the creature's headpiece, its long hair falling onto Evelyn's face. It stank of death. The nun gagged, gasping for air.

The creature lifted its gaze to Kassandra. Alongside its animalistic hunger, deliberate cruelty emanated from its eyes, like that of a predator playing with its prey. It opened its mouth, revealing lion-like teeth. A high, metallic scream escaped it, then a stinger emerged from its throat, resembling a scorpion to Kassandra.

Evelyn tried to retreat, but the stinger pierced her neck. The woman's eyes widened, white foam flowing down her chin and chest.

Ramirez watched with reverence, then spoke with a smile: "*And they had tails like unto scorpions, and there were stings in their tails; and their power was to hurt men five months.*"

None could speak among the onlookers, only with eyes filled with fear and trembling limbs did they watch as the creature wrapped its front legs around the naked nun's body, and through its stinger, it drained the woman's fluids. Evelyn's face aged within seconds. Her skin whitened, shrank, and wrinkled. She opened her mouth, her eyes wide. The creature pulled her depleted body close, sucking the life out of her with loud sucking sounds.

"Enough of this blasphemy!" Kassandra shouted.

Ramirez looked at the woman, the only one standing among the benches. Her face was resolute, fearless. She made the sign of the cross and spoke: "You are not the servant of the Lord, Diego Ramirez! And this abomination here is not an angel of God!"

The creature continued to suck Evelyn's fluids, paying no attention to the events around it.

"I promised a miracle, and you received it," Ramirez whispered in a raspy voice. "But our Lord Jesus warned about the unbelievers, the betrayers, the Pharisees!" He looked at the Indians, who still aimed their guns at the creature. "Take it away from my sight, as you do with everyone else! In time, you will also be tested, to see if you bear the mark of the Lord or not." The Mexican cast one last glance at Sister Evelyn, then left the chapel amidst the benches.

The thick chain clanked uncomfortably in Jonathan Dalton's hand. The shackle cut into his skin; he could almost feel his fingers begging for the fresh, oxygen-rich blood. He was familiar with the chains that had held him captive for years. He closed his eyes and breathed in the fresh, salty sea air of the early morning. Despite being among the country's best shooters, he'd still ended up in chains. The sheriff's deputy made a simple offer: fight with them or hang. Although he had become a bandit, keeping his word meant something to him. He didn't want to die, not yet. Without hesitation, he said yes, and thus escaped the jaws of death. He knew the brothers thirsted for his blood, but he also knew that for Jeremiah, breaking his word and honor were unthinkable.

"How are your guts, Dalton?" the deputy sheriff asked.

Jonathan looked grimly at Fred, who chuckled and then stroked his horse's head. "Oh, come on, don't look at me like that!" he said. "I heard that in the war, you did worse things than feeding someone a little scorpion."

"Perhaps you could tell us the story of when you were expelled from the army and sentenced to death," Arisztid interjected. "I can't wrap my head around it! Why did you set fire to your own army's hospital?"

"I thought they were holding Confederates inside. That's what they told us," Jonathan replied in a flat tone.

"You're insane!" Fred exclaimed. "They told you that, too, to mislead Confederate spies!"

"Which didn't work," chuckled Wratiszlaw. "Oh, you're a real troublemaker, Dalton! Do you know that? You confused your own government. The nigger riots that broke out in Washington because of you even scared President Lincoln."

At the mention of the name, Fred wrinkled his nose and spat on the ground. "Damn that swine!" he cursed.

"One thing must be admitted, Captain Dalton, you're a damn good shot," continued the sheriff. "You sent many of my friends to the afterlife."

"Not enough," muttered Jonathan under his breath.

Aristede and Fred exchanged glances, then the sheriff spoke sternly over his shoulder: "Just because we're riding together doesn't mean we're friends! I suggest you watch your words once the White brothers arrive and steer clear of foolish deeds. With Fred here, we can't guarantee your safety."

Dalton rolled his eyes, then glanced over Arisztid's shoulder. In the harbor, he saw a smaller ship, with a Creole man standing on deck, waving frantically at the sheriff and his deputy. They exchanged a half-smile, then stopped their horses in front of the ship.

Pedro wore a straw hat and a tattered, yellowed shirt. First, joy crossed his face, then a moment later, disbelief. "A thousand devils and ten thousand hells! If this ain't Jonathan Dalton chained up!"

"Glad you recognized him right away, Pedro," replied Arisztid. "We didn't manage it on the first try."

The sailor scratched his chin, then hurried to the horses and led them both onto the deck. "Well, how could I not recognize the Vicksburg monster! But how did you manage to chain this man?" he asked incredulously.

"He tried to run, so I hit him over the head with my pistol."

Pedro flashed his yellowish-green teeth, then leaned in close to Dalton. "What's the matter now, nigger? Not so talkative, huh?" He laughed, then tried to turn to the sheriff, but Jonathan headbutted him hard.

The sailor lost his balance, then fell to the ground. Aristede pulled and tightened Jonathan's chain, causing him to fall to his knees. "I told you to watch out for foolish deeds!" Wratiszlaw said sternly. "Doesn't seem like you'd heed what I say!"

Fred approached the man kneeling on the ground, then, scanning the sea, spoke to him: "If you can't behave, Captain, you might get another sting from the scorpion. What do you say to that?"

Dalton's heart pounded fiercely, but he tried to calm down. He took deep breaths, then replied: "It won't happen again." "Great!" the deputy answered. "But I suppose you wouldn't mind if we left the chain and shackles on you, right? Your kind is accustomed to this, so it shouldn't feel strange."

The sheriff and his deputy laughed as they boarded the ship and settled in.

Jonathan sat down beside the railing, waiting for the White brothers to appear in the harbor. Arisztid adjusted his hat, then took out his flask and took big gulps from it. He offered it to Fred, but the deputy just shook his head.

"I don't drink before a mission" he declared. "And neither should you."

"Oh, come on, my friend," Arisztid said after he sighed. "A little liquid courage."

"You could try aiming without alcohol, maybe then you'd hit something!" retorted Fred.

"That was below the belt." Wratiszlaw pointed at his companion. "Even from you, Deputy!"

The sheriff turned around, then rummaged in his bag, checking his weapons, bullets, and knives. Despite the cheerful and light-hearted words, fear gnawed at him. He hated the taste of failure and bitterness, of which he had experienced plenty lately. A sad sigh escaped him, then he wiped his itchy eyes. *My whole life is a bitter torment,* he thought. He remembered his childhood illness, which had left him bedridden for years, spending those years weak, helpless, and lonely when he should have been playing and learning with his peers. The feeling of vulnerability returned; this time not a mysterious illness clouding his mind, but fear of the unknown. After the war of independence, he knew he had to survive and start a new life alone, and he did. As a peacekeeper, he knew exactly how to proceed, just as the frontlines were clear during the war. But now, as he headed towards Mexico, he was frightened by the thought that he didn't really know what he was looking for. He didn't know if he would be able to recover the kidnapped children and thus restore the city's future, nor did he know if he could find the missing nun. He looked towards the sea, then twirled his mustache. His hand began to tremble, which he attributed to the lack of opium. He feared that he might be leading his impromptu team to their deaths. He heard the sound of hooves approaching, and turned around. The two brothers had arrived at the port with their strange traveling companions. Anton and Jeremiah White rode proudly, heads held high, determined. Strength and self-confidence radiated from them. Arisztid reluctantly admitted to himself that despite their dubious reputation, he felt calmer facing the unknown by their side. His gaze lingered on Dalton; he grimaced, then looked at Fred. The deputy returned the gaze. Their eyes revealed everything. They knew perfectly well that there would be a serious conflict between Dalton and the brothers, and one of them would not return.

The two bounty hunters boarded the ship, throwing their heavy bags onto the benches, which landed with a dull thud.

"Welcome, Sheriff!" nodded Jeremiah.

Fred and Arisztid greeted them, then helped the priests to board and settle on the ship.

Agustíno scanned the sea, sweat drops trickled down his face, which the sheriff found peculiar at this early hour.

Cristofano looked around with curious eyes, a wide smile spreading across his face. "Gentlemen!" He spread his arms wide. "We are like the crusaders on a pilgrimage to the Holy Land! We are fulfilling the mission of the Lord! Let us feel honored!"

Arisztid chuckled at the priest's enthusiasm, then stepped beside him and patted his shoulder. "Well, Father... No one has ever called Mexico the Holy Land!" He smiled. "But rest assured, the sin you'll find there is almost divine!"

The others laughed, but Agustíno interjected sternly: "Do not dare to equate God with sin!" His gaze radiated anger. "Have you forgotten how serious this matter is? That children are suffering, and one of our sisters, while you talk about 'divine sins' here? If I were you, I would talk about what we will do when we reach Matamoros."

"Exactly!" Anton chimed in. "What's the plan? Where do we meet the Bear Hunter?"

Wratiszlaw cleared his throat and spoke up: "Once we dock at Matamoros, we'll scout the city. We'll ask around, rest, and assess the situation. I'll need you for this!" he gestured to Dalton and the deputy. "We know these hooded figures went there, so the locals must know something. Watch their eyes, see if their gaze reveals anything! If you see fear, excitement, or anything unusual compared to the question, back off! I repeat…" He raised his index finger. "This is not an official operation! While we're questioning in the city," he pointed to Dalton and himself, "Anton should hide on some high vantage point where he can overlook the inn and the main square, in case someone attacks us… Jeremiah and the two priests will go for Bruce, who lives on a farm at the outskirts of the town. I'll give you precise instructions."

The two brothers looked questioningly at the sheriff. "You and Dalton?" asked Jeremiah.

"I beg your pardon, Mr. White, but you two look like killers from afar! Please don't take offense… My foreign accent and Captain Dalton's skin tone can help blend in with the crowd. They won't suspect us. Do you understand what I mean?"

"Not entirely…" Anton replied uncertainly.

"Well… I'll be the 'moneyed European gentleman, ' and Captain Dalton will be my servant." Arisztid turned towards Jonathan and kicked his leg hard. "Did you hear that, Captain?"

Anger radiated from Dalton's gaze. He hated the feeling of humiliation. "I heard" he replied coldly.

"Excellent!" The sheriff clapped his hands together. "Now, everyone rest, and when we get there, I expect maximum discipline from everyone! I want this operation to succeed, and I want everyone to come back alive!"

They passed along a rocky coastline, very close to the mainland. The water crashed hard against the rocks, the sounds of seagulls echoed nearby. The sheriff leaned against the railing, staring ahead, thoughts swirling in his head. Thoughts he still couldn't decipher. *Who is doing this, and why? Why did they kidnap the children of my town?* He sighed and lit a cigarette. The noise of footsteps caught his ears.

Pedro appeared beside him, holding a canvas bag. "The clothes you requested for the nigger."

"Thank you," nodded the sheriff. "It will be great."

"Arisztid…" Pedro began in a hesitant voice. "I feel it's my duty to ask, are you sure about what you're doing?"

Wratiszlaw raised an eyebrow, then asked in surprise: "What do you mean, Pedro?"

"Based on what I've seen from the hooded figures, I think this is beyond your capabilities."

"Thank you for caring about my physical well-being." Arisztid smiled. "But we will handle the situation." The sheriff glanced at the other members of the group, who were already preparing for the landing. Prayers were uttered, knife blades flashed in the sunlight, bullets were loaded into chambers. A few funny remarks were made among the team members, followed by laughter. Smiling faces, brave souls risking their lives for different reasons, but all for a noble cause. Arisztid knew there would be sacrifices. There always were…

"We're docking!" Pedro yelled.

The sheriff approached Dalton and tossed the bag to him.

Jonathan looked up and asked: "What's this?"

"Your clothes, Captain. Change into them. And don't forget! You're now a servant to a European nobleman! Put on your best manners and do as I ask. If you survive, I promise you can leave freely."

Dalton snorted and muttered under his breath: "The attic's already full of white man's promises…"

Arisztid shrugged off the sharp remark and took a seat instead. He needed a few more minutes of silence before setting foot on Mexican soil. The team brought up the horses, saddled them, and checked their gear. Wratiszlaw pulled out a paper from his pocket and handed it to Jeremiah. "The map to Bear Hunter. Be so kind to hold onto it."

"I wouldn't dare to be anything else," said the elder White.

"Well then, let's get going, people! Towards Matamoros!"

The team set off towards the city. The heat was almost unbearable; the dried, barren earth burning the horses' hooves, making them march forward restlessly.

Jeremiah looked up at the sky, where he saw a white dove flying towards the city. *Unusual*, he thought to himself. As they progressed, they were surrounded only by the wild Mexican nature, with no trace of people. Silence dominated the landscape, only the gentle breeze caressing their faces, the sun's rays burning their skin.

Despite straining his ears, the sheriff heard not a single sound. Not a stray chirp, not a dog's bark, nor any other animal noise. He looked around anxiously, but everywhere was silence and tranquility. He glanced stealthily at his companions, seeing the same bewilderment and doubt in their eyes, but none of them dared to ask the obvious question yet. Arisztid spotted a farmhouse in the distance and gestured to the deputy, who nodded and rode ahead. "Anton, you stay here and protect the priests. We'll check out what's ahead."

"What are you so afraid of?" asked Father Cristofano. "It's just a farmhouse."

Arisztid turned back to the priest: "We've been on the road for a while, Father... Where are the people? The animals? Not a single bird in the sky... Didn't you notice?"

"Now that you mention it..." he pondered, then looked anxiously at his companion, who returned the look.

The sheriff looked at Jeremiah, who nodded, then rode after the deputy, and they approached the seemingly deserted farmhouse from three sides. "Keep your eyes open" said the sheriff.

Fred muttered something under his mustache, which Arisztid didn't understand. The deputy's eyebrow twitched, he sniffed, then spat on the ground. Curiosity mixed with fear reflected in his eyes.

Wratiszlaw looked at the elder White, who dismounted and headed towards the courtyard of the house. It was a simple straw-roofed house, the average dwelling of poor rural people. The vegetation on the dry ground had already worn off, leaving only dust, debris, and excrement spread out before them, nothing else. An old rocking chair stood empty in front of the door, the windows were closed, their curtains drawn.

"Careful, Mr. White!" Fred shouted. "Watch the ground! Footprints! And..." Bewilderment appeared on his face. "And something else... I don't recognize it." The deputy looked at the others, fear and horror radiating from his eyes.

Jeremiah and Wratiszlaw also observed the tracks, but apart from a few boot prints, they saw nothing

"I don't understand you..." whispered the bounty hunter. "Footprints and a few blurred spots. What's so special about it? Let's go in!" Jeremiah leaped over the fence with a sudden movement.

The deputy shouted after him: "Be careful!" Fred grew increasingly nervous. "I've never seen a track like this in my life, and I've been in the wilderness all my life! Are you really going to rush headlong into the unknown?"

"Enough bickering, gentlemen!" the sheriff burst out, still keeping his voice low. "I'll go straight ahead, you two from the sides. I'll kick the door in, and you enter through the window, got it?"

The two men nodded, then set off. Arisztid cocked the hammer of his revolver and aimed it in front of him. Slowly, step by step, he advanced in a straight line. He felt a tightening in his throat, sweat trickled down his temples, his fingers whitened on the revolver grip. The dry ground barely crunched beneath his feet. He glanced at the rocking chair, then at the once-green door. Most of the paint had peeled off, revealing the decaying wood beneath. He rested his hand on the door and took a deep breath. He grasped the handle, then tore the door open with a sudden movement and burst into the house. Immediately, a horrible stench hit his nose. He covered his mouth with his hand, and started to retch. The terrible smell penetrated his nose, his mouth, he felt as if his entire body was saturated with horror, something that he couldn't even describe with words. He turned on his heel and ran out of the house. His companions stood on either side of the house, their faces showing similar expressions, covering their noses, spitting. The sheriff straightened up, then gestured for the priests and Anton to come over. Arisztid took deep breaths, trying to drive away the hellish stench from his memories, but thanks to the open door, the smell kept spreading towards them. The sheriff didn't even notice as he kept backing away further and further.

"What in sulfur's arrow is in there?!" exclaimed the deputy.

"I've never smelled anything like this over mass graves or stinking wells," Jeremiah replied.

The two priests quickly dismounted their horses and headed towards the house. Father Agustíno watched the door of the house almost mesmerized, paying no attention to the stench, and entered. The sight of the priest's strong stomach surprised everyone, as did his investigation inside.

Arisztid took out a handkerchief from his pocket and covered his nose, headed towards the house while talking to Agustíno: "Father, come out of there! That place is not for you!" The sheriff felt his stomach becoming more and more unstable as he approached the house.

"Hold on!" replied the elder priest. "I thought you were men, not hysterical little girls. Look at this!"

The sheriff and his deputy followed Jeremiah into the house. The unbearable stench tortured them, but Agustíno seemed not to notice, focusing on the dead body lying on the ground. An elderly man's contorted body lay naked before them. His skin was loose and dry, skeletal, his bones almost piercing through his skin. His eyes stared blankly into nothingness, his face revealing horrific agonies and torment. A blackened stab wound protruded from his neck, from which a strange, pus-like discharge flowed.

Arisztid looked at the body in astonishment. He had never seen anything like it in his life, and he couldn't imagine what could have caused this.

Agustíno knelt beside the dead man, inserting his fingers into the wound. The pus-filled injury made a disgusting squelching sound. He withdrew his fingers, turned them towards the light, and examined the discharge. He smelled it, then cautiously licked it. His face twisted in disgust, and he spat on the ground. Wratiszlaw still stood there, stunned and unable to speak as the old priest wiped his fingers on his handkerchief and headed for the door.

Fred examined the corpse on his knees, but could only ask one question: "What in God's name...?"

Agustíno paused at the door and turned back. His black robe shimmered ominously in the light, and determination emanated from his eyes like never before. "Not exactly, my son... Not exactly." With that, he turned on his heel and hurried back to his horse.

Arisztid's stomach churned, the absence of alcohol and opium began to gnaw at his body. His hands began to tremble, his legs wobbled as he stepped back and fell. He hit the dry boards hard. His hat rolled away, his head fell back, his eyes fixed. White saliva poured from his mouth, he began to cough and choke.

"Sheriff!" the deputy exclaimed, rushing to his aid. "Jeremiah, help me!"

"The smell..." Wratiszlaw groaned. "Get me out of here. My head, it's splitting again! Just like... just like when I was a kid... I can't move... Fred, help me!"

The sheriff coughed as white saliva streamed down his face and neck. He tried to stay conscious, but his gaze became fixated on the dead body of the elderly man. The dead eyes no longer looked upward but straight at him, piercing him, bringing to the surface the diseased and tormented childhood, every fear and agony of his life.

Fred lifted Arisztid's head, who was trembling all over, thrashing wildly. Jeremiah rummaged through Wratiszlaw's pockets for the opium tincture, which he found with difficulty. He took out the bottle and pried open the sheriff's mouth, pouring its contents inside. The bounty hunter clenched Arisztid's mouth shut as he continued to thrash, but gradually, the movements subsided and then ceased altogether. His body went limp. Fred and Jeremiah sighed, momentarily forgetting the horrendous stench.

"This will be trouble" remarked the elder White. "He won't withstand the journey."

"He'll be fine." The deputy wiped Arisztid's forehead. "I'll take care of him. Just like in the war, I won't let him die here."

Jeremiah grimaced, then stood up and dusted himself off. "You know best, deputy! But if I were you, I'd cross myself for those kids already! Look at him! When we were at the convent, he had a similar seizure! But not this severe! This looks worse to me."

Fred knew the bounty hunter was right. The sheriff had never been seized by such a strong fit before. He himself was plagued by doubts about whether Arisztid would make it through or not. "Help me get him out into the fresh air! Then gather the priests and your brother, and go get the Bear Hunter!"

"And Dalton?" Jeremiah asked suspiciously. "That worm, if he even senses the slightest chance of escape, he'll come after you!"

"He's our concern now!" the deputy replied firmly. "Take your brother and go!"

The elder White turned away, refusing the help, and started towards the door, but Fred grabbed his arm. He turned back, and their eyes met.

"Learn as much as you can from Agustíno about what all this is! Did you see how he wasn't even surprised by the smell? How he examined the dead man as if he knew what had happened to him? And those tracks outside..."

Jeremiah nodded and headed towards the door. What he saw inside weighed heavily on him as well. Those eyes... He had seen many dead bodies, some hardly resembling humans anymore, but what he had seen inside the house instilled fear even in him. He looked at his brother, who sat on his horse with an unsuspecting but concerned expression, shading his eyes and watching what was happening. The elder White buried his face in his hands, allowing desperation, terror, and panic to momentarily overwhelm him before regaining control. He sighed, lifted his hat, ran his hand through his hair, then hurried to his horse and mounted. "We're heading for the Bear Hunter."

"Jer, what the hell happened in there?" the younger White asked curiously. "The priest came out as if he was going into battle, and you two were nowhere to be seen. What in God's name is going on here?"

"I'd like to know that myself, brother!" he retorted. "But we've stumbled into something we weren't assigned to handle!" His accusatory gaze fell on the two priests.

Cristofano and Agustíno were conversing under a distant tree, making sure not a single word was overheard by the brothers. The younger priest nervously covered his mouth with his hand and turned away from his companion. Agustíno didn't let it go, he stepped beside the younger one again and explained to his companion as passionately as if he were about to attack him.

Jeremiah had had enough. He spurred his horse forward, galloped over to them, then dismounted, grabbed the elder priest by the throat, and slammed him hard against the tree. Agustíno gasped for breath, struggling to get air, but the bounty hunter was much stronger than him.

"What are you doing?!" Cristofano exclaimed in shock. "Let him go immediately!" He attacked the bounty hunter, who delivered a massive slap with one hand, knocking the young priest down, then grabbed his face.

Anton arrived running and shouted at his brother: "Have you lost your mind? What are you doing?!"

Jeremiah looked back at his brother with fiery eyes. "I'm tired of these whispering, secretive wretches! Can't you see what they're doing?! They've convinced us to travel across states, God knows why! Then they whispered seductive things in our ears, persuading us to embark on a journey to Mexico with the family butcher! Enough! I want answers, priest! NOW!"

Agustíno tried to cough but couldn't catch his breath. His face turned red, he kicked the ground with his feet, trying unsuccessfully to push the bounty hunter away.

"Let him go! You're going to kill him!" Anton yelled.

The elder White released his grip, and the priest took a deep breath, coughing and gasping for air. As color returned to his face, the bounty hunter pressed him against the tree again, grabbed his face, and looked into his eyes. "Now you're going to answer, priest! What in God's name happened in there?!"

"As I said... It didn't exactly go as planned!"

Jeremiah slapped the old man hard across the face, who was momentarily surprised, then his face twisted into a grotesque smile. "I was a member of the last League of the Holy Inquisition! You can't do anything to me that I haven't done to others, or anything new to me! I know all the pains of the flesh, so believe me, son, you're just wasting your time!"

"Answer me!"

Agustíno leaned closer to the bounty hunter, fanatic rage emanating from his eyes. "Something happened in there that your sane mind couldn't even comprehend! And if I'm guessing correctly, this is just the beginning..."

A click sounded near Jeremiah's head, then another a few meters away. "Release Father Agustíno immediately! Or I'll shoot!"

The elder White smirked, then lifted his gaze to the sky. "Sheriff! Glad to see you're feeling better! It seems the opium worked. Do you really believe you could finish me off?"

"We're two against one," replied the deputy.

The bounty hunter glanced into the priest's eyes again for a moment, who held his ground firmly. Jeremiah winked, then with a sudden move, he jumped back and fired two shots. The sheriff and his deputy couldn't react, they only saw the flash and felt their hats flying off their heads. They both staggered and fell. Jeremiah rushed to the sheriff and stomped on his hand before he could reach for his dropped revolver. He pointed his gun at the man's face and turned to Frederick, who froze mid-motion: "Neither of you stand a chance against me! Remember that! Next time, I'll shoot you both dead! And you!" He pointed at Agustíno. "I'm not done with you yet! Now, dear brother! Let's go!" Jeremiah spun his pistol around his finger, then slid it back into its holster. He adjusted his hat, mounted his horse, and rode off. His brother just smiled and shook his head.

Chapter Five

*"His mouth is full of cursing and deceit and violence;
Under his tongue is mischief and wickedness."*

Psalm 10:7

"I'm starting to get seriously mad at your brother, dear Anton!" said the sheriff in an offended tone.

"As am I," Fred replied. "Next time he won't get away with it, that's for sure!"

"I'm sure next time it won't be their hats he's poking holes in," the younger bounty hunter chimed in. "It's time for them to get off their high horses, because if they mess with the wrong person, they might find themselves in trouble."

"Believe me, Mr. White," Dalton rasped, "there will soon be someone who settles his brother once and for all..."

Anton shot a furious glance at Jonathan riding beside him, then spurred his horse forward, positioning himself directly in front of the man. The sheriff and his deputy immediately stopped and turned around, but by then they were already locked in a stare-down. "Captain Dalton..." emphasized the younger White. "Don't push your luck, as you are unarmed."

"Just like not long ago up in the mountains I was unarmed... for a while. Then you ran off leaving your dead behind."

Anton seized Jonathan and with a determined motion pulled him off the horse, causing it to rear up in fear and gallop away. Fred cursed loudly and chased after it, while Arisztid angrily positioned himself between the two men on horseback. "May the good Lord bless you, enough is enough!" he shouted. "You!" He pointed at the younger bounty hunter. "Don't let a few sharp words get to you! And you, Captain, dare not sharpen your tongue at your comrades! We have a task at hand! Everyone came for different reasons, but our goal is the same. If we're unable to cooperate, it would be simpler to put a bullet through our own heads now! Perhaps we'd spare ourselves the torture! Are you willing to behave at least a little like men and focus on the task at hand, or shall we continue digging our own graves?"

Anton turned his gaze away; he knew the sheriff was right. He had behaved foolishly, letting his emotions get the best of him. He stroked his horse's head and silently continued towards the town.

Fred brought Dalton's horse back, and he mounted it, and they continued on in silence. The sheriff and his deputy exchanged meaningful glances; both knew how difficult it was to control the situation. Fred whispered to Arisztid: "Perhaps it was a mistake to bring them along."

"It may be..." sighed Wratiszlaw. "Perhaps this entire mission was a huge mistake. It's possible that, due to my immeasurable pride, I overestimated my own abilities."

"Nonsense!" Fred snapped. "I simply say that maybe we didn't think this through enough."

"Think it through?! The whole town turned upside down in just a few days! What was there to think through? We might have started too late as it is!" the sheriff snapped back.

"It will soon become clear, my friend... It will soon become clear," Fred reassured him.

They continued their journey towards Matamoros in silence, while Arisztid was lost in thought. Too much had happened to him in the past few days, events had unfolded too quickly. He was plagued by doubts, unable to control the events. He searched for his own responsibility, his own mistakes. He thought about how the cross of his tragic childhood still weighed heavily on him. The mysterious illness that had tormented him and confined him to bed for years, the mysterious and rapid recovery, the curious glances, suspicious looks, and his father's distant hostility still defined his personality to this day. The compulsion to conform, the constant need to prove himself, had trapped him in worse situations time and time again. Neither alcohol, nor women, nor opium could soothe the emptiness gaping in his soul. He sighed, then lifted his gaze. A radiant sky and a picturesque landscape surrounded him, which he would have enjoyed under different circumstances, but the silence was extremely unsettling. He took a flask from his vest pocket, took a big gulp, then put it back.

"You should quit it," Dalton interjected. "Alcohol has ruined many a man."

"You're right, Captain, but what would I have left if this pleasure were taken away from me?"

"Freedom," he replied. "Something to cherish! Not everyone is entitled to such things!"

"Oh, please! Don't play the martyr! Freedom is an illusion! We're all like chained dogs, the only question is how long the chain is and how tight the collar. You've cast off your shackles, appreciate it and stop whining!"

Dalton reluctantly shook his head, then trotted forward, straight to Anton's side. The younger White stared ahead blankly, the city of Matamoros already looming on the horizon.

"Anton," Dalton began. "I owe you an apology!"

The bounty hunter turned to the captain with a surprised glance. "Look out! What's Dalton up to?"

Jonathan shook his head, then replied:"Misunderstood! The sheriff is right! I didn't come here willingly, only the desire to live brought me here! But for that, we need to stick together, even if the conflicts between us seem insurmountable."

"The slaughter of my family seems pretty insurmountable to me too..." he grunted, then spat on the ground.

"Anton..." The captain lowered his head. "You may or may not believe it, but I didn't kill your family, I didn't take part in the looting or the arson."

"You're just saying that so I don't shoot you dead."

"No! I'm saying it because the truth is in everyone's interest. We'll all die if we don't move past this. Mourn your family, but please, Anton, let's set aside our hatred at least until we're here. I assume you also wish to leave here alive."

Anton pondered what he had heard. Perhaps the captain was right; if they wanted to live, unnecessary quarrels, vengefulness, and pride would only hold them back.

"Alright, Captain!" He nodded. "You need not fear from me anymore. I won't come after you, but I expect the same from you! I cannot make promises on behalf of my brother, but I suggest you speak with him as soon as possible. Look..." He pointed straight ahead. "There lies Matamoros. From here on, our paths diverge." The younger White turned around, then addressed the sheriff and his deputy behind them: "Gentlemen, Matamoros lies ahead of us. According to plan, I'll seek out a vantage point and keep an eye on you."

"Once it's dark and we find everything in order, I'll signal at the inn's entrance," replied Arisztid. "I'll tip my hat and touch my face twice. If we sense any danger, I'll just step out and light a cigarette. Stay vigilant, Anton!"

"Will do!" He nodded. "Good luck, gentlemen!" The bounty hunter spurred his horse and galloped towards a nearby hillside. The sheriff and his deputy headed towards the town, accompanied by Dalton. On the dusty dirt road leading to the city, weary carters urged their aging mules forward, pedestrians walked with hay bales slung over their shoulders, casting only sad and desperate glances at the strangers arriving in the city. The lively buzz of life had vanished from the streets, replaced only by soft whispers and eerie silence.

Arisztid observed the streets, the people, but saw no young men or women, only elderly women and tired men wandering aimlessly through the streets. "Where are the young people?" asked Wratiszlaw.

"That's a great question. Something is seriously wrong here," replied Fred. "What do you think, Dalton?"

"This place gives me the creeps... It's like happiness vanished in an instant."

"To the inn, gentlemen," declared the sheriff. "Carefully, but let's try to find out what happened here."

The three men dismounted, tethered their horses at the trough in front of the inn, then entered through the swinging door. Instead of the typical loud singing, guitar playing, and joy of life typical of Mexico, they were met with an uncomfortable silence. Behind the counter, a woman in her forties with chestnut brown hair wiped the glasses, curiosity reflecting in her eyes at the sight of the strangers. Setting the glass down, she approached the men already seated at the table. "¡Buenos días, señor. Habla Español?"

"Lo siento..." Arisztid spread his arms. "No. I came from Europe with my servant for a little adventure. This is Friday." He gestured to Dalton. "Just like in the famous novel! And my friend here is an English gentleman, Frederick William. Welcome, Señorita!"

The woman nodded politely and bowed. "Welcome to Matamoros! I'm sorry, but you didn't choose the best time to visit our wonderful little town for an adventure."

"Yes, I thought I saw it on the street. More precisely, I noticed its absence," he emphasized, "the absence of youth. Just as the absence of song and joy of life. Perhaps the area is not struck by war?"

"Something like that, dear sir... What can I get for you?"

"We'd like three tequilas, and a good beer, if possible!"

"Right away," the woman nodded cheerfully. "My name is Remedios."

The sheriff smiled and tipped his hat in greeting and watched as the woman turned her back on him and hurried towards the tap, seeming embarrassed by his attention. The sheriff was surprised by the woman's reaction, as he was sure that someone who worked in such a place wouldn't just receive an innocent smile.

"Friday...?"

Dalton stared. "Are you serious?"

"Have you read Robinson Crusoe?" asked Arisztid.

"I was raised in a wealthy family. They taught me to read..."

"An educated negro!" Fred slapped his shoulder. "Where is the world heading!" He laughed.

Jonathan gave the deputy a murderous look, but the sheriff calmed him down. "Stick to your role, Dalton! You're a servant now, not a duelist!"

The captain pursed his lips, then observed the people in the inn. He furrowed his brow as he saw nothing but suspicion, disappointment, fear, and sadness on the faces staring at him. "Something is not right here... Do they think it's the bandits?" asked Jonathan.

"They certainly keep the locals in terror," replied Arisztid. "But we must proceed very cautiously, we are already conspicuous. More than we should be."

The barmaid returned to the table with three tequilas and three tankards of beer, then distributed them among the men, who thanked her for the drinks and raised their tankards.

"Gentlemen!" began the sheriff. "Let's drink to success! Let's pledge that we will not return home until we bring back our children! Let's assist each other's cause with honor, respect, and loyalty, so that we can return home with a clear conscience!"

"So be it!" nodded Fred.

"So be it!" Dalton also nodded.

The three men took big sips of the beer, then sighed with satisfaction as they put down their tankards. The sheriff signaled to the barmaid, who hurried over to their table. "Tell me, señorita... Would you like to take a short walk around the town with me?"

The woman smiled reluctantly, then looked at the group sitting at a distant table.

Arisztid followed the woman's gaze. Two creole men were sitting there, drinking, and they were watching. They had graying beards, wore ponchos, and sombreros on their heads.

Wratiszlaw gently touched the woman's hand, who startled. "Excuse me, señorita, I didn't mean to be intrusive. Perhaps the gentlemen over there have something to say to me?"

The bartender took a step back, then replied in a colorless voice: "Leave the town as quickly as possible."

A desperate scream ripped from someone's throat. The sound bounced back and forth on the cold stone walls, straight into Kassandra's ears. She trembled all over, icy sweat running down her body. On Sister Judith's advice, she had abstained from opium, but she felt herself succumbing more and more. What she had seen in the chapel had shocked her. The locust-like creature haunted her every night in her nightmares. A sound echoed in her head, the sound it had emitted as it took Sister Evelyn's life. Months ago, the Holy Father had prepared her to see things beyond imagination, but like modern-day nuns, priests, and believers, she too believed that demons were mere metaphors, explanations for the illness of the human mind. The realization that she was wrong pushed her to the brink of madness. The awareness that everything the Bible wrote was true disturbed her deeply. *"Certainty comes at a price!"* the Holy Father had told her. But in her worst nightmares, she never thought she would have to pay for it with her sanity. She wished she had never pursued the thirst for knowledge, the unquenchable thirst for truth.

"Kassandra!" a voice sounded. "How are you?"

She turned towards the sound, then crawled on all fours to the corner of the cell. She cautiously moved one of the stones of the partition, and familiar eyes stared back at her. She was sure Sister Judith was suffering too. Many of them had perished in recent times. "I can't believe that several of our sisters have committed one of the gravest sins..."

A moment of painful silence ensued. Both of them knew that the souls of suicides could not be saved.

"Their flawed human nature prevailed over their faith. I sincerely hope that someday they may find redemption," Sister Judith replied.

"Why are they doing this to us?"

"Kassandra, only you know the answer to that! Tell me, my dear..."

"They didn't send me here to bring us to this point! But to find this monastery..."

"Then you've fulfilled your mission," declared Judith.

"The situation is, sister, that this place found me, not the other way around. I failed! The Holy Father won't..."

"The Holy Father?" Judith exclaimed in astonishment. "Is he here on papal orders? But... then you're not... Impossible!"

The sound of footsteps could be heard from outside, and Kassandra quickly put the stone back in place. She leaned her back against the dirty, damp wall, waiting for the next act of terror. She closed her eyes, then began murmuring a prayer softly.

The heavy door slammed open, and standing in the doorway was their cruel guardian. The man approached her, grabbed her by the shoulders, and pulled her up. The woman crossed her legs, trying to cover her body in shame, but the monk grabbed her firmly, pulled her close, and licked her face all over.

Kassandra felt the disgusting smell of the monk's sweat, the touch of his unkempt, greasy skin made her feel nauseous.

The man noticed the disgust on the woman's face, then pushed her away. "Just so you know... You're also very stinky!"

"But you're holding me captive! You're disgusting on your own!"

The monk stepped closer again, then spoke in a threatening tone: "Everyone here is a prisoner!" he said sternly. "No one came here willingly... But this is God's way! We follow Him on the path to salvation! And now, let's go! Father Ramirez wants to see you!"

The monk tried to grab her, but she stepped aside. "I can walk on my own feet," she stated.

She walked barefoot through the dimly lit, musty corridors. The rough ground cut her soles in several places, but she showed no sign of pain. She couldn't let them see her suffer. The opium took away her mind, her pride, but she, with the help of the Lord, would regain her dignity. The monk followed her, and Kassandra could feel his lustful, lecherous gaze on her. Under ideal circumstances, she enjoyed being stared at, even though she knew it was sinful. Upon reaching the spiral staircase, she found herself back in the chapel. The creature was gone, but the nauseating, dreadful smell still lingered in the air, emitted during its feeding. In front of the altar stood Corpus Christi altar boys, and Father Ramirez, stepping down from the podium, was marking crosses on their foreheads and feeding them wafers. Fear was evident on the children's faces, and Kassandra's heart ached painfully at the sight. She knew that if these children survived this hell, they would leave the church forever. She lowered her head, then approached Ramirez, as he gently caressed the children's heads along the way, hoping they would feel his care.

The priest placed a wafer in the mouth of one of the boys, then spoke: "Now let us pray together! Repeat after me! You came to me, Jesus, the King of heaven and earth!"

"You came to me, Jesus, the King of heaven and earth!" echoed the children in trembling voices.

"To the beggar's dwelling of Thy little child!"

"To the beggar's dwelling of Thy little child!"

"I bow in reverence at Thy feet!"

"I bow in reverence..."

"Stop!" Ramirez raised his hand, causing all the children to flinch and look down at the ground. He stepped onto the Mexican side, descended the stairs, and stopped next to a boy who hadn't repeated the lines, just stood silently, defiantly staring at him. The priest grabbed his shoulder and forcefully pushed him to the ground. "I bow in reverence at Thy feet, young man!" he yelled. "Will you not bow before the Lord? Will you not accept the Savior into your heart?"

The children continued to stare at the ground, most of them trembling all over, tears streaming down their faces.

"Answer, boy!" he snapped.

"Leave him alone!" Kassandra yelled. "These are just boys! What do you want from them, you filthy madman?!"

"They are the future," the priest replied, completely naturally. "And their education is vital! In today's world, where God has slipped down the hierarchy of importance, it is the duty of people like me to bring them back on the right path."

"Rot in hell along with your right path!" the boy retorted, then pulled out a small knife from the sleeve of his clothes.

The woman cried out in horror, and the children sought refuge behind the altar in terror.

"The sheriff gave me this!" the boy said, tossing it towards Ramirez, who calmly stepped aside so that the knife flew past him.

It landed hard on the chapel floor, and the man smiled at the boy, who, seeing the failure of his attack, began to back away. But Ramirez quickly lunged forward and grabbed his arms. The thin, weak little arms snapped, and the boy cried out in pain.

"Leave him alone!" Kassandra yelled, then lunged towards the priest.

The father struck the woman so hard across the face that she fell to the ground, blood spurting from her mouth onto the floor. Ramirez looked down at the trembling child, whom he still held firmly. "The Lord lives, and so does your soul, for it was the Lord who prevented you from committing murder, and from seeking revenge with your own hands. So, bow before the Lord in reverence!"

Then he forcefully pushed the boy to the ground, who groaned in pain. The priest knelt beside him and continued softly: "What better proof of the Lord's love is there than this, that even in such circumstances, He saves your soul? The sheriff... He gave you a weapon to kill, to damn yourself. But God guided your hand to miss the mark." Ramirez stroked the child's face. "Obey, and you shall receive testimony from me beyond your wildest dreams."

The chapel door suddenly burst open, and the priest lifted his head, turning towards the sound. A tall, black-haired Native American walked in, a cross hanging around his neck, a long-barreled hunting rifle slung over his shoulder. He looked down at Kassandra lying on the ground, then at the children hiding behind the altar. Confusion reflected in his eyes, but he didn't have much time to contemplate what he saw. "Forgive me, Father, for interrupting." He bowed his head. "I bring urgent news."

"Speak then."

"He has arrived in the town."

"Ah, excellent," nodded Ramirez. "Take Sister Gareth to my room and prepare her for the sacrifice. And you, Joseph, gather the team. We're going to Matamoros."

Jeremiah adjusted his black hat and rested his hand on the handle of his pistol. The touch of the weapon always comforted him, but it hadn't always been this way. He still remembered the days when he'd lived as a simple noble, attending balls, dinners, and auctions as an honored guest. He remembered his sister's laughter, the shine of her hair, the day they proudly marched off to war, and the day they lost everything. He felt like he could only regain his honor with a gun. On lonely evenings, when he was alone with his thoughts, his demons took hold; doubt and fear plagued him. He questioned himself. Was he on the right path? What would his parents and sister think of him now? Would they be proud of him? Would they be ashamed of him and his deeds? After the initial pain of the first days, everything seemed so simple to him. Easy money, shifting responsibility dulled his mind. But now, here in Mexico, the events of the past few days had confused him again. Fear crept back into his soul. He knew that if he wasn't careful, his only remaining sibling could meet his death. His own demise didn't really concern him, but he couldn't afford to die; who would then watch over his brother? He glanced over his shoulder. Father Agustíno was purposefully trailing behind him. He didn't like the priest. He hadn't from the beginning. He knew, he felt in every fiber of his being, that the man was lying. And he was right. He hadn't told them the whole truth, and Anton's mind was clouded with religious nonsense. Discipline had turned into chaos, he thought.

Father Cristofano rode up beside Jeremiah, and they silently rode together for a few minutes on the dirt road. Around them was nothing but forest. The young priest listened to the birds chirping, filling him with genuine joy. Life had returned... *Or have we just left death behind*? His thoughts focused on what he had seen earlier. He knew the journey would be dangerous, and he also knew he would see things that could shake his faith. A multitude of questions tormented him, for which he himself had no answers. But what happened to that unfortunate soul in the house? Why was Agustíno acting as if he knew what had happened? No matter how much he asked, he didn't get a straight answer; his companion only spoke of unwavering faith and their work for God, which tolerated no questions. Cristofano sighed and looked despairingly at the sky. *Help me understand the incomprehensible, Lord! I know you're there! Shed light on your servant, for he is lost in darkness!* he prayed silently.

Jeremiah glanced at the priest, then asked in a somewhat friendly tone: "Do doubts trouble you, Father?"

The young man looked at the bounty hunter, then after a moment of hesitation, he replied: "I must admit they do..."

"Don't be ashamed, I know the feeling well. It's human."

"My shame lies in my inability to grasp God's will and plan for us. And what happened between you and Agustíno... I never thought it would come to that."

"I'm sorry for attacking you," Jeremiah replied coldly. "It was a mistake. I lost my composure, which is unacceptable in my line of work. Hear that, Agustíno?" he called back. "I apologize!"

"It's nothing," the elder priest replied disdainfully. "You're not the first to question the will of the Lord, and you won't be the last."

Jeremiah chuckled, then looked back. "Father! I'm not questioning the will of the Lord, but your honor! The two are far from the same!"

"Honor or dignity don't matter, nothing matters except God."

The elder White rolled his eyes, anger flooding him again. He stopped, then turned to face the priests.

Father Cristofano was once again overcome with fear and desperation. "Gentlemen, please let's stop this quarrel! Our lives may depend on our ability to work together!" The young priest spoke with a conciliatory intention.

"Our lives mean nothing, Cristofano! Only God matters!" Agustíno replied.

"The Holy Father entrusted us with a mission! If we fail, we betray the Creator! So our lives do matter!" the younger priest shouted. "Mr. White has the right to know why we are here! It was a mistake to lie!"

Jeremiah patiently waited and watched as the two priests confronted each other. He knew that if there was a chance to gather more information, it was now. He didn't have to do anything but wait.

Anger flashed across Agustíno's face, his features contorted. "Cristofano! We're not talking about this!" he declared firmly, not allowing any contradiction, but the younger priest shook his head.

"Mr. White..." he began. "Promise not to leave us! In return, I will share something with you about our true mission. And when we return to the city, we will inform you about what we know."

"Cristofano... please don't!" Agustíno pleaded. "The Holy Father forbade it..."

"Don't we answer to God?" he asked back. "Mr. White is also a child of the Lord, he has the right to know why he is risking his life. Do you promise to stay with us?"

"I promise." Jeremiah nodded.

"Alright" the priest replied. "Well... Sister Gareth... Kassandra," Cristofano corrected himself, "is a sort of pilgrim. She has dedicated her life to the Lord and, at the behest of the Holy Father, visits places where miracles have occurred. You know... to make sure that they have indeed happened, and are not just the work of a fraudster. Well... The sister sent a rather disturbing letter to the papal residence."

"What kind of letter?" the bounty hunter inquired.

"About strange and extremely suspicious deaths," Agustíno replied. "At first, there were just signs... Dead animals: calves, horses, pigs. The locals thought it was some kind of disease. Then the local pastor or priest died. It's not just affecting Catholics... Protestants too. After their spiritual leader passed away, the children disappeared too..."

"Excuse me, gentlemen, but I don't understand. Whose spiritual leader disappeared?"

"Several small towns in succession."

"In the States?" Jeremiah asked.

"And in Mexico," Agustíno replied. "There have been significantly more mysterious cases than can be attributed to chance."

"And Kassandra figured this all out?"

"Truth be told, she saw the pattern in it, yes. Our belief in our own greatness blinded us..." Cristofano replied.

"Thank you, gentlemen," said the elder White. "I'm glad you shared this with me, now it's clear why the pope is so eager to reclaim this woman... Now I need your help. Who are those hooded figures? Who are we after?"

"We don't know" Cristofano replied.

"Who, or what, killed that poor soul in the house? What was that stench?"

"We don't know," Agustíno stated firmly. "If they knew we'd encounter something like that, they wouldn't have sent just two vulnerable priests, but the cavalry..."

Jeremiah paused for a moment, then nodded and turned forward. He took out the map drawn by the sheriff from his pocket, raised his gaze to the sky, then to the sun, and looked ahead again. "We're heading in the right direction, we'll be there soon."

They continued on silently, lost in their own thoughts. The bounty hunter still didn't trust the priests. He knew they were still keeping something from him, but he didn't want to push it further. He vowed to uncover the truth, but he also knew he wasn't the best at investigation. Although he had reservations about the sheriff as well, he knew the sheriff could help. In the distance, a small cabin appeared, and on its porch sat a small figure holding a rifle. Although Jeremiah had never met Bearslayer, he was renowned as a huge, fearsome warrior. The bounty hunter had a bad feeling about this. He signaled to halt, then turned to the priests.

"Gentlemen... We've arrived, but I don't think that guy over there is Bruce."

"How do you figure?" asked Cristofano.

"Do you think that guy looks like a bearslayer?"

The two priests exchanged glances, suspicion evident in their eyes.

Jeremiah put his hand on the grip of his revolver and headed towards the house. The man sitting on the porch wore a brown, worn-out hat, his greasy and unkempt red hair reaching his chin. His gray coat was patched in several places, and he held a long-barreled rifle which he was cleaning with relish. He glanced up at the newcomers but paid them no mind, continuing to clean his weapon. The elder White stopped several meters away from the stranger and greeted him. "Good day to you, sir!" He raised his hat. "We're looking for Bruce. I presume... he'll be around here somewhere."

The man looked up again, then smirked mockingly, not stopping his cleaning. "The Bearslayer?" he began contemptuously. "Well, you can only meet him if you challenge him to a duel and I send you to the afterlife. Is that what you desire?"

Jeremiah was taken aback by his insolence; he was accustomed to being instantly recognized and instilling fear in people. "My name is Je..."

"Jeremiah White!" he interrupted. "I know very well who you are. Tell me, Mr. White, are you also longing for the afterlife?"

The bounty hunter brushed off what he'd heard. He knew that if Bruce was dead, and this guy was capable of killing him, then maybe it would be worth taking him with them. Nevertheless, he had a bad feeling about it.

"Just tell me, Mister...?"

"Red," he said.

"Red... Please tell me, if it's not a secret, how did you finish off the Bearslayer? Just so I can learn from you!" Jeremiah leaned in theatrically.

Red laughed, then sighed heavily. He adjusted his coat, stood up, and approached him. He pointed the gun forward as if to show something. "You know, Mr. White... They still pay good money for the Bearslayer these days. I heard he lives alone here in Mexico. It's been a long time since they paid for Indian scalps. You see... Obtaining animal skins isn't such a challenge. I thought... Bruce was out of practice. And I was right!" he sighed dramatically and continued. "I watched him, his habits, where he goes and when. I noticed he often massages his right hand. The shooting hand... He must have had pains. I observed that when he hunts, he shoots wide. So I confronted him and challenged him to a duel. Oh! Crows were cawing around us and the sky was roaring with thunder! Lightning struck and the storm raged! And I shot him. A quick shot between his eyes and the mighty Bruce lay dead... Here it is!" He pointed to his gun. "This is his weapon. Should I keep it or sell it? A collector would pay good money for it..."

The bounty hunter looked at him in dismay. He was obviously lying, but Bruce was nowhere to be found. Perhaps he did end him somehow, and he was embellishing the events.

"You know, Red... We, my friends here," he gestured to the two priests, "came to offer a job to the Bear Hunter. Since he's out of the game, the question arises whether you would join us. We're going after a group of armed men who abducted a nun. We're headed to Matamoros."

Red scrutinized the two priests, scratched his chin, leaned his gun against his shoulder, and replied: "Well, based on my abilities and future reputation, I think fifteen thousand dollars would be a suitable reward for my services. Deal?"

Jeremiah glanced at the two priests, and Agustíno nodded. The bounty hunter rolled his eyes, knowing this guy would be a thorn in their side. "Alright" said the older White.

Red's smile stretched from ear to ear. "I'll pack up and be rea..."

The sharp sound of a swoosh filled the air, followed by a dull thud. Red's smile faded from his face, and his gun slipped from the hand resting on his shoulder. With his last strength, he placed his hand on his head, where he felt the handle of an axe protruding from it. The man gaped, trying to say something, but life left him as quickly as his reputation turned to nothingness. He fell to his knees, then collapsed dead.

Jeremiah froze in surprise, then looked towards the forest next to the house, from which a tall, broad-shouldered, powerful figure stumbled out.

He wore a half-open white shirt, his chest hair almost completely covering his skin. His beard, reaching down to his chest, was adorned with rings, and he wore a black bandana on his head. The burly guy cursed loudly as he hurried towards Red's lifeless body. He spotted Jeremiah and the two priests, but ignoring them, he limped towards the body. "Seven hundred!" he said incredulously. "I've been on his trail for three full days! Three full days!" The Bear Hunter leaned down for his axe, then, after stepping on Red's neck, he pulled the tool out of the man's head. With a loud crack, the axe came free "This miserable fool threw dynamite at me while I was meditating on the hillside! He stole my gun and my food! It took me three full days to catch up to him!" Bruce pitied the guy's body. "This fool thought he killed me with the explosion or the fall."

"One stick of dynamite would take out many" Jeremiah remarked.

"But not me!" he retorted. "What did he tell you?"

"That lightning was flashing, thunder was rumbling, and crows were circling when he shot you in a duel."

"Hah! Lightning and crows! This one never saw a duel in his life!"

"And won't see one again..." the bounty hunter noted. "Welcome, Bruce, my name is Jeremiah White."

The Bear Hunter took a step back at the name, then picked up his gun from the ground. "Did you come to kill me? Get out of here! I don't want bloodshed!"

"Calm down, Bruce! Wratiszlaw Arisztid sent me. He said you two are friends."

Bruce lowered his gun, genuine joy lighting up his eyes. "Arisztid?!" he exclaimed joyfully. "How's that drunken, perverted pig? I hope he hasn't gotten into some craziness again because last time I dealt with him, I was shitting scorpions for a week!"

"He's in Matamoros." Jeremiah smiled. "And we need your help."

The smile froze on Bear Hunter's face, his lips trembled, and his muscles tensed. "In Matamoros...?" he muttered quietly to himself. "No!" he snapped. "He needs to come out of there immediately! That place is cursed! I'll get my horse, we're leaving now!"

Bruce rushed into the house at a speed that belied his size and came back with a huge leather backpack. He saddled his horse, then wordlessly rode towards the town.

Jonathan Dalton let out a deep sigh. His sigh encompassed everything that had happened to him in the past days and weeks. He hadn't even had time to process the deaths of his friends and comrades. He looked down at his hands; they were shaking. He couldn't decide if it was from fear or excitement. Too much had happened to him, as it had to everyone around him. They had been preparing for a simple robbery of a small-town church, but it had unleashed chaos beyond imagination. "This is my luck." He smiled bitterly. He looked up at the now dark, clear sky and watched the stars. He sincerely regretted not knowing the constellations. In his youth, he had watched with envy as the two brothers and their little sister lay outdoors in the White family villa, telling stories of the old times and teaching their sister about the constellations. He was unable to learn even that. Fear and vulnerability had always held him too tightly and never truly let him go. *That's why I'm here now*, he pondered. He thought of his companion, his comrade, Nick. He was ashamed of what he had done to him. His name was feared nationwide, yet he had run away, leaving his friend behind. He didn't even understand why. Doubts plagued him regarding his own abilities. Maybe luck had brought him fame? No... he pushed the thought away. He was the best, he didn't allow himself any other possibility. If even one person were better than him, he would die, and that he couldn't allow. He had sworn to his parents that he would have children, live to old age, and live as a free man. His hands clenched into fists, then he looked at the deputy sheriff beside him. He knew he had to see this mission through to the end.

"How are you feeling, Dalton?" Fred interrupted his reverie. "You're not planning anything crazy, are you?"

"Isn't it crazy enough that we're here?" the captain snapped angrily.

"Oh, it definitely is," the deputy replied with a smile as he lit a cigarette. "Very much so. But duty calls!"

"Or the will to live..." Jonathan remarked.

Fred nodded in agreement. "Walk with me, Captain... There are a few things I'd like to show you." He turned his back on Jonathan and, crossing the dirt road, turned onto a side street. Rows of abandoned wooden houses were tightly packed together. No light or sound could be seen or heard from inside. Fred's first thought was that perhaps they were just sleeping, but his instincts told him otherwise. Fear and agony seemed to emanate from the entire town. The suspicious glances directed at them made him uneasy. He wasn't accustomed to this, but he also knew that he wasn't acting as a deputy now. Upon entering the town, he noticed that every door was marked, except for those on the main street. He took a long drag from his cigarette and exhaled the smoke slowly.

Dalton, walking beside him, had an expressionless face. "What do you want to show me, Deputy?" he asked. "Look at the doors! They've been marked."

Fred stepped closer to one of them, then ran his hand along the dry wood. It was rough, and it was clear that the owners had neglected their home.

Jonathan squinted, but in the darkness, he couldn't make out what was painted on the door. "What is this?" he asked, trying to examine it.

"Blood." declared the deputy. "All the doors, painted with blood."

"Maybe they fought. Perhaps the hooded figures attacked them."

"No!" Fred retorted. "Just look!" he pointed to the bloodstains. "They've been painted in one stroke. Think, Captain Dalton! Our priests have been killed, the sacristan and the altar boys were taken from the town, and a nun has gone missing. And the perpetrators most resemble monks. What does this tell you?"

"A religious reckoning?"

"And I think it has something to do with the Bible too. Remember what they painted on the wall in the convent? And with blood, no less..."

"Without the shedding of blood, there is no forgiveness of sins. Blood is a symbol in the Bible. The Jews in Egypt marked their doorposts with blood to keep evil away," Dalton said.

Frederick leaned against the door, smiled, then flicked his cigarette. "Captain... you're mistaken! The Jews didn't want to keep away evil, they wanted to ward off the wrath of the Lord!" The deputy stepped closer to him. "What kind of godless act do you think is happening here if they want to ward off the Lord's wrath?! I don't like any of this..."

Jonathan fell into thought, pursing his lips as he pondered what he had heard. Fred was right. What was happening within the walls of this town that they feared the wrath of the Lord? The very thought brought a smile to his face. "Do you really believe they want to keep God away?" asked Dalton. "Damn it, it's 1867! We live in the age of science and medicine! We traverse the country with steam locomotives, conquer the skies with hot air balloons!" Jonathan lowered his voice to a whisper, as if he were about to utter madness. "I read in the *New York Times* that they're developing a device, modeled after the telegraph, that will be able to transmit speech over several miles! And in such an age, they truly fear God?"

Frederick continued to smile. A mocking disbelief was written on his face as he patted Dalton's shoulder "Transmit speech over several miles? That's nonsense! Don't believe everything you read in the papers!"

Jonathan opened his mouth to respond, but rhythmic bird chirping caught his ears. He glanced back over his shoulder and scanned his surroundings, but saw nothing except the faint lights filtering from the main road.

Fred looked in the direction of the sound, but he saw nothing either, placing his hand on the grip of his pistol. Both of them listened in tense silence to the night. The deputy closed his eyes, trying to merge as much as possible with the nature around him, along with every sound it produced. Another chirping arose, this time from further away, as if in response. The two men looked at each other, and then Fred drew his revolver.

"Give me a weapon!" Dalton pleaded. "I can help!"

"Sssh!" The deputy put his finger to his lips.

The two men stepped onto the dusty dirt road, then slowly, crawling, made their way towards the main road. The Mexican night cast peculiar shadows in front of the pair. The cold air uncomfortably gnawed at Fred's throat, his heart beating faster and faster. Another chirping arose, this time closer, and the response came immediately. He was sure now that these were not birds. He turned to the side and spoke to Dalton: "We need to inform the sheriff immediately!"

The deputy was about to start running between the houses, but Jonathan grabbed his shoulder. "For God's sake, I'm the best gunslinger in the country, give me a pistol!" Dalton whispered softly.

The deputy brushed the man's hand off his shoulder, then replied quietly: "The best gunslinger in the country and a convicted murderer! You're not getting a weapon! Stay beside me and follow! If I die, you can take my gun!"

With that, Fred turned on his heel and started running. He ran with all his might, with Dalton close behind, when he heard a sharp, swooshing sound, followed by a dull thud.

They both stopped and listened intently. Shadows moved in the darkness, sneaking from house to house, carriage to carriage. Fred gestured, then they sought refuge by a wall of a house. The deputy pointed forward, and Dalton followed his gaze. One of the local residents lay dead in a side street, an arrow protruding from his chest. Fred couldn't see where the shots were coming from, only the moving shadows in the distance. He stepped out of his hiding spot, took aim, and fired. The murmuring from the inn was suddenly replaced by silence, as if life itself had stopped. The deputy looked around; no one moved. Dalton caught up with him and requested a weapon again. "God damn it! Not…"

Bone-chilling war cries filled the streets of Matamoros. The two men turned in fear towards the direction of the sound, where the previously hidden Indians emerged. Their long black hair flowed freely, their faces adorned with war paint, large crosses hanging around their necks. Fred was shocked for a moment, then he aimed and fired. "Run! To the inn!" he shouted.

They ran, arrows whizzing over their heads, past them. Jonathan helplessly watched the events unfold; the Indians emerging from the houses frightened him. Fanaticism emanated from their eyes, determination from every movement.

Fred fired shots while running, some hitting their mark. Painful groans filled the air as several Indians fell dead. As they reached the inn, the deputy pushed open the swinging door, but to his greatest surprise, determined men were not waiting inside. The townsfolk sought refuge under tables, behind the counter, while others rushed towards the back exit or jumped out of windows, hoping to escape.

Inside, the sheriff stared wide-eyed at his companion, clutching his revolver in his hand, then pressed his shoulder against the wall near the window and looked out. Outside, Indian warriors went from house to house, dispensing death without mercy. "What the hell is happening out there?" Arisztid asked.

"Indian attack," Dalton replied. "They have neither rifles nor pistols! Look!" He pointed towards one of the Indians, who was attacking an unarmed woman with a tomahawk. "Give me a gun, and we can easily deal with them!"

Fred looked disapprovingly at Wratiszlaw, who ignored Jonathan's request.

"Fred!" the sheriff called out. "I'll cover you; you run out to your horse, and we'll divide their attention! On three! One... Two... Three!"

The sheriff smashed the window with his elbow and fired six shots in succession. The Indians hesitated for a moment and sought cover behind the barrels, wagons, and the stagecoach on the street. Taking advantage of the tactical advantage, the deputy started running and disappeared into the small, unlit street next to the inn. From the street came cries for help, pleas, painful screams, and sobbing. Arisztid was familiar with these sounds; he often heard the pleas of the wounded in his dreams, those he couldn't help. He closed his eyes, feeling another wave of assault engulfing him. He felt dizzy, his head almost splitting from the pain, his eyes wide open, his heart pounding in his throat. He felt his fingers whitening around the pistol grip. He looked towards Dalton, who stepped beside him in alarm, then delivered a strong slap to the sheriff.

"Stay here! For God's sake, you're a warrior, not a cowardly piece of shit!"

Arisztid knew the captain was right. He couldn't let his attacks take hold of him again. He straightened up, took a deep breath, and pressed his spare pistol into Dalton's hand. He rummaged in his pockets, then handed the man two handfuls of ammunition. "And I don't want to regret it!" Wratiszlaw said with a choked voice.

Jonathan twirled the pistol in his hand. Its weight wasn't perfect, but he knew that such details didn't really matter to him. He looked at the sheriff. His face was pale, his lips white. He tried to reload his revolver, but his trembling hands hindered him, causing him to drop several rounds.

Arisztid cursed, then crouched down to retrieve the bullets.

Dalton pursed his lips, then took a deep breath. He saw the Indians emerging from their hiding places and heading towards the inn. He took another deep breath and charged.

With his shoulders, he pushed open the swinging door, then fired two shots on the run. Jonathan's attack caught them off-guard, so they didn't have time to flee. The shots hit their mark, and two Indians fell dead. Sweat beads ran down Dalton's forehead, adrenaline coursing through his body. The warriors on the ground writhed, emitting painful groans, then became motionless. The captain jumped off the inn's veranda and ran towards the house opposite, from which a warrior emerged, clutching a tomahawk. Their eyes met. Dalton was horrified by the Indian's determination as he raised his weapon, screamed, and charged at the captain. Jonathan didn't hesitate; he fired. The bullet tore through the man's chest, causing him to stagger mid-charge, his eyes bulging as he stared at the gaping wound. Blood flowed thickly down his body. He dropped his weapon, fell to his knees, glaring at Dalton with blood between his teeth. The captain stepped closer to the dying man, aimed at his head, and fired. He had two more rounds left in the chamber; he knew he had to find cover. From behind him, he heard the sound of hoofbeats and gunshots. Jonathan dashed to the side of a house, pulled out ammunition from his pockets, and reloaded. As he looked up, he saw the deputy riding into the midst of the attackers. The horse reared up and trampled an Indian on the ground. Bones cracked, agonizing screams filled the air, ending with a shot.

Fred looked at Dalton, who was hiding by the wall, his eyes burning with anger at being armed. The captain raised his pistol; the deputy had no time to react. The shot rang out, and Fred braced himself for the searing pain. He closed his eyes, curled up in the saddle as much as he could, but the pain didn't come. He heard a desperate groan and a dull thud. He opened his eyes, glanced back over his shoulder, and noticed a dead Indian sneaking up behind him. He looked at Dalton, then nodded.

The captain made a gesture of respect, then fired more shots. More painful screams filled the air. One of the Indians screamed, causing the others to stop.

The sheriff stepped out in front of the inn, watching the strange scene unfold. The warriors paused for a moment, all looking at the three men, then turned their backs and ran away. The previous chaos was replaced by silence. The three men looked at each other, bewildered. "Is everyone alright? What about Anton? Do you think they caught him?" Arisztid asked.

The deputy took a step towards the sheriff on his horse, but didn't take his eyes off the warriors moving away from them. "Even if they didn't catch him, Mr. White abandoned us."

"It's hard for me to believe that Anton would flee from a fight," Dalton retorted. "We should find him."

"I agree" nodded Arisztid. "Fred, ride to the hill and see what happened to him. Dalton! You come with me!"

Behind Wratiszlaw, the swinging door creaked loudly, and the frightened innkeeper, Remedios, rushed over to him. The woman was in a hysterical state, her hair disheveled, her eyes red, tears streaming down her face. She grabbed the sheriff's arm and fell to her knees. "What have you done?!" she screamed hysterically. "Do you have any idea what you've done?! We're all going to die because of you! We'll never see our children again!"

Arisztid was stunned by the woman's behavior. He gave his companion a puzzled look, who watched the events with concern. He took hold of the woman and helped her to her feet, then looked deeply into her eyes. "Remedios! We saved your town! Now we're going to go and free your children, just as we'll free ours! We came to help, do you understand?!"

"Help?!" she cried out anxiously. "If you wanted to help, you would have left when I told you to! It's all over! He's coming!"

"Who?" He shook the woman's shoulders. "Who's coming?"

Remedios tore herself away from the man's arms, then rushed back into the inn.

Wratiszlaw looked at his companion, who stared into the distance, revolver raised and aimed. Arisztid turned around, and in the distance, a figure appeared. He wore a dark hat, his black hair brushing his shoulders, his upper body covered by a gray poncho. He wore a belt around his waist, with two gun holsters hanging from it, containing a golden, elongated-barrel revolver. The sheriff was curious, took hesitant steps towards the stranger, who continued to walk towards them with his head bowed.

"Should I shoot him?" Fred asked, then cocked his gun.

"Not yet!" Arisztid raised his hand. "Let's negotiate instead. I suspect the Indians will come back armed with guns..."

The stranger continued to march forward, commanding respect, keeping his gaze on the ground, hands away from his pistols. The man stopped, looked up, and glanced at the sheriff.

Wratiszlaw found the eye contact peculiar. An intelligent gaze looked back at him... Yet... It seemed otherworldly.

The man smiled, theatrically tipped his hat, and bowed. He seemed like he was about to speak.:

"Enough! I'll shoot!" shouted Fred. The deputy aimed and was about to pull the trigger, but the stranger was much faster.

With a sudden movement, he drew both of his pistols and fired several shots towards Fred. The shots hit the deputy's horse, which neighed in pain, reared up, and fell onto its side.

Fred cried out as they hit the ground. Sharp pain shot through his entire body; he felt his leg shatter under the weight of the fallen horse. He tried with all his strength to push the dead animal away from him, but it proved too heavy, and the agony was unbearable. He screamed, and as he tried to move, his fractured bones ground together, ligaments tore, and muscles detached from the broken bones. Stars danced before his eyes, yet neither fainting nor merciful death came to him.

The sheriff reached for his pistol and returned fire, but all his shots missed the stranger, who calmly and measuredly walked towards the nearby wagon. Arisztid took cover at the entrance of the inn and watched his companion. The deputy cried out in agonizing pain, and Arisztid tried to leave his safe cover, but immediately bullets rained down on him. *Where's Anton*? he asked himself angrily, but he had no time to dwell on it.

From the opposite side of the alley in front of him emerged an Indian warrior. The floorboards of the inn creaked loudly under the sole of his leather boot as he stepped onto them. He held a tomahawk in his hand, and his face was painted black beneath the eyes. His long black hair reached almost to his waist, and his eyes radiated fanatical hatred as he looked at the sheriff crouching at the inn's door.

Arisztid took out a cartridge from his pocket and tried to load it into the cylinder.

The Indian's face twisted into a malicious grin as he approached closer and closer, ready to strike with his weapon still raised.

Wratiszlaw jumped up and cast a last glance at his suffering companion.

Fred looked towards the sheriff, reaching out his hands in supplication. The Indian raised his weapon, let out a war cry, and rushed towards the man. A shot rang out, tearing through the Indian's chest, and he fell dead instantly. The shots came from the hill next to the town in quick succession. The returning Indians were now able to return fire with rifles.

Captain Dalton, taking cover behind vegetable sacks and barrels, reloaded his revolver. He cautiously peeked out, searching for the stranger with his gaze, whom he found.

The man in the poncho holstered his weapons, then slowly, deliberately, almost calmly walked into town, where a fierce gunfight broke out between the sheriff and the Indians.

Dalton looked towards the hillside, from where the constant flashes of muzzle fire indicated that Anton was covering them. The captain knew what the bounty hunter was capable of. They had fought on opposite sides in several battles, and the young man had quickly become one of the Confederacy's best sharpshooters. He'd never thought that one day he would entrust his life to Anton White, but that day had come. He took a deep breath, exhaled, and ran forward again. Leaving his cover, he fired deadly shots in quick succession and ran across the road to join the sheriff.

Arisztid stepped out from beside the house, firing blindly to provide cover for the captain's path. The Indians sought cover.

"Thank you, Sheriff" nodded Dalton. "I'll cover, you go to the deputy, we need to get him out of there!"

Arisztid nodded, then stood ready to run at the base of the inn's wall.

Jonathan quickly checked his ammunition, then stepped out and fired.

Wratiszlaw started running. With each step, a dry, crackling sound answered from the decayed veranda. Bullets rained towards him, tearing up the side of the inn around him. Approaching Fred, he placed his pistol on the ground and crouched behind the dead horse. A spreading pool of blood was forming under the deputy's trapped leg, Fred's eyes were glazed, he seemed to be losing consciousness almost completely. "Fred, snap out of it!" He slapped him. "I'll move the animal, you pull out your leg, do you hear me?"

The deputy's gaze slowly wandered to Arisztid. He nodded, then replied in a fading voice. "Do it!"

The sheriff took a breath, then tried to move the animal enough for his partner to free himself.

Fred screamed again as he moved his leg, but the pain didn't relent. He grabbed his broken leg, then with a quick, decisive motion pushed it towards Arisztid.

The sheriff let go of the horse, then grabbed his partner. "We need to get to the inn. Fred, take my pistol and shoot with both yours and mine! I'll drag you in! Dalton and Anton will cover us."

The sheriff glanced back over his shoulder, and Jonathan nodded, providing covering fire.

Arisztid jumped up and grabbed his partner by the shoulders, starting to pull.

"Ah! Rather let me die here!" shouted the deputy as they moved.

The sheriff didn't let go, constantly pulling his friend towards the safety of the inn, leaving behind a long, thick bloodtrail.

In the distance, the stranger sat on the steps of a house watching the events unfold. He sighed, then dusted off his pants and retrieved his pistols. Standing up, he looked at Dalton just a few meters away. He whistled once, knowing that his comrades would all charge at once. They did not fear death. They all knew that the Kingdom of Christ awaited them if they fell. The man spun the revolver in his hand, then aimed at Dalton. He didn't want to injure, only to disarm, so he aimed at the man's pistol and fired.

The captain was completely caught off-guard. The bullet hit the barrel of his revolver, the force of the shot ripping the weapon from his hand. He cried out in pain, then looked towards the stranger.

The man aimed his unarmed hand at Dalton and fired at the sheriff with the pistol in his right hand. The captain tried to run into the side street, but the stranger fired another shot at him, hitting the ground right in front of his feet.

Jonathan stopped and raised his hands in surrender. The man gestured for him to step to the side of the house, then the Mexican took off running. Several more shots landed behind him, but all missed their mark. Once out of Anton's line of sight, he turned both of his guns towards Dalton.

"Welcome to Mexico!" he called. Curses were heard in the background, followed by more shots, then silence.

Jonathan closed his eyes in resignation. He knew that his comrades were either dead or captured. He clenched his fists, then addressed the stranger: "Better shoot me now, let's end the games!"

The man smiled, then holstered his weapons. He cautiously glanced beside the inn. Immediately, a shot rang out, but he managed to step back in time. "We've captured your companions," he said coldly. "Although one of them is in pretty bad shape..."

He winked at Dalton, then drove an uppercut into the man's jaw.

Dalton's head snapped back, and he collapsed unconscious.

"Kill the hunter!" the stranger shouted to the Indians.

Several immediately started running towards the hillside, while Anton fired more shots. Several warriors fell dead, but the rest, oblivious to their comrades' deaths, continued to charge towards him. Once he deemed it safe, the Mexican stepped onto the main road beside the inn and approached Arisztid near the swinging door. "Welcome, Sheriff!" He tipped his hat. "I've been waiting for you."

Chapter Six

"Stone him with stones, that he die; because he hath sought to thrust thee away from the Lord thy God, which brought thee out of the land of Egypt, from the house of bondage."
Deuteronomy 13:10, The Summary of the Law

Anton White watched the clear, cloudless night sky as he lay in the dry grass, hands under his head. It had been hours since the sheriff walked out of the inn, tipping his hat to signal all was well. He'd been keeping an eye on the landscape for a while now, but he couldn't detect any movement anywhere. He sat up, took out his flask, then slowly sipped his drink, reflecting on moments of his life, as he often did. His carefree childhood seemed like a distant memory now, as if it had happened in a completely different life. He adored, almost idolized, his brother, whom he followed everywhere. A wide smile spread across his face as he remembered the first night he and his beloved sister Zoey, along with his brother, had sneaked out of the family villa and wandered by the nearby lake. They all knew they would be punished if caught, but they didn't care. Zoey, the little one, loved to look at the stars, but as she grew older, the villa's workers and the servants of neighboring noble families began to look at her differently. Jeremiah would never have let Zoey out alone, so they'd had no choice but to follow the determined girl. They sneaked out, and for the first time in their lives, they could truly do as they pleased. They were not bound by any noble etiquette, rules, or customs. Anton pondered what would have happened to him if the war hadn't come, the war that changed everything in their lives. He never dared to admit to his brother that he didn't believe in the ideals of the Confederacy. He knew he wasn't the smartest person in the White family, but he also knew that their wealth and the family name would have been enough for him to attend university. A somber expression crossed his face as the shameful thought that had spurred him to fight a few years ago came to mind. He'd wanted to be a hero. He'd wanted to return home to the family villa adorned with medals, so that his father, mother, and sister would be proud of him. He rubbed his face as he felt the tears rolling down. He had been mistaken. He had made a huge and fatal mistake that had forever diverted him from the path he had imagined for himself. He knew he had acted selfishly, but the hope that he could return to the right path seemed to be taking shape again. It had become his conviction that if he selflessly did good now, then God would accept him back into his grace. He wanted to believe, sincerely and unconditionally, but so far doubt had prevailed. Money ruled. *He who pays the most lives, he who pays less dies,* he thought. He'd never dared to tell his brother about his feelings, but he found it increasingly difficult to stay by his side. Jeremiah had changed. He knew perfectly well that behind his own tough exterior and his bloodthirsty mentality was a man who longed for hope. He sincerely hoped that this journey would also change his brother, and that one day they could return to their estate, rebuild the family villa, and continue the family line. He took out a wooden pipe and tobacco from his pocket. He filled it, then searched for matches, which he lit on the sole of his boot. He took a deep puff from the pipe, then exhaled the smoke slowly. He looked towards the town, and noticed movement. He reached into his bag, searching for his spyglass. He observed the figures moving in the town's side streets, and as he recognized what he saw, his blood ran cold. Indians. He reached for his rifle, loaded the chamber, and took aim. He saw muzzle flashes, heard the blasts. His heart pounded in his throat; he knew he had once again made a mistake and spotted the attackers too late. *Damn it, damn it, damn it,* he cursed to himself. He aimed towards the inn, where he saw the sheriff, trembling as he tried to reload his revolver. A chill of horror ran through him as he spotted the armed Indian advancing towards Arisztid. He aimed and fired. The warrior fell dead. He fired again and again and again. His gun clicked, the barrel empty, and he reloaded. He felt the familiar rush of battle, his heart pounding wildly, his whole body bathed in sweat, yet he enjoyed it. Somewhere deep inside, he felt ashamed, but there was no time to dwell on it in the heat of battle. In the small alley beside the inn, he saw Captain Dalton talking with Arisztid. The sheriff took off running, and Anton followed him with his gaze. "My God, the deputy!" he gasped as he noticed the man pinned under the horse. Panic gripped Anton. If only he had noticed sooner... He opened fire again, taking out more attackers, when he saw movement out of the corner of his eye. He aimed with his rifle and fired. The poncho-wearing stranger returned fire with two revolvers, shooting frighteningly fast and accurately. The bounty hunter opened fire again, shot, again and again, but the stranger skillfully dodged the bullets and disarmed Dalton. Anton recoiled, then struck the rock beside him in frustration. His hand throbbed painfully from the blow, his skin torn open and bleeding. He took a deep breath, then aimed again, but was shocked by what he saw. The Indians were heading towards him. A tingling, icy fear ran through his body, a huge lump formed in his throat, and sweat trickled down his temples. He started shooting again, but despite taking out several attackers, they showed no sign of fear.

"Damn it!" he yelled and started to back away. He slung his rifle over his shoulder, grabbed dynamite from his bag, and reached for his revolver. Branches cracked beneath his feet. He held his weapon in front of him, waiting for his attackers. He looked around, but all he could see were the rocks of the hillside. He turned around and sought shelter behind one of them. He took a deep breath, trying to concentrate with all his might. A cool, nocturnal breeze brushed his face, sending shivers down his spine. He looked up at the starry sky, remembering the night when they'd returned disappointed yet hopeful to their burned-down villa. He closed his eyes and prayed that his journey wouldn't end here. He opened his eyes at the sound of footsteps, cautiously peering out from behind the rock.

Three Indians had reached the hilltop, their faces painted white with a black stripe under their eyes, and a cross hung around their necks. One of them crouched down and began examining the ground. He looked up, straight towards the rock. His long hair gently swayed in the wind, every muscle in his body tense. "He's nearby," he said to the others. "Search for him! When you find him, finish him!"

Anton felt uneasy. The bounty hunter took the dynamite in his hand and tore off the fuse, which ended up only a few centimeters long. He knew he was about to perform a dangerous stunt, but he felt it was better to explode than to be scalped. He lit a match on the sole of his boot and tossed the explosive over the rock. There were agonizing screams, painful cries. Anton's hat flew off his head, his eyes, nose, and mouth filled with dust. He blindly fired a shot while peeking out from his cover.

The explosion had sent one of the Indians flying several meters away, ripping off one of his legs. He screamed in pain, clutching the bloody stump where his leg used to be as blood poured out in thick streams from his body.

Taking advantage of the chaos, Anton discreetly propped himself up above the rock, closed one eye, and aimed at another attacker. He pulled the trigger. The gun thundered loudly, hitting the warrior on the top of his head.

The man emitted a wrenching, surprised groan, and pieces of his skull flew far away. He fell, dead.

Anton pulled back his head and waited for the right moment. Bullets rained down, hitting the rock or tearing up the ground around him. He leaned to the side and returned fire, but missed his target. The last living Indian cried out angrily and rushed at him. The younger White was taken by surprise by the attack; he fired, but once again missed his target. The man kicked the pistol out of his hand, then swung his rifle hard, hitting the bounty hunter in the face, causing him to stagger and fall. His attacker dropped his weapon and then knelt beside Anton, pinning him to the ground. Fanatical hatred emanated from the Indian's eyes, blood dripping from his face onto Anton, who thrashed wildly, trying vainly to break free from the grip. The assailant pulled out a knife and swung it towards the bounty hunter's chest, who tried to deflect the blow, but the warrior proved to be stronger.

Anton screamed, groaned, and struggled, but the blade advanced inch by inch towards his heart "No!" he screamed. He felt every ounce of strength leaving his body, waiting for the stabbing pain that would put an end to his life forever, his strength fading. But suddenly, he heard a dull sound, and the strong grip that had been pressing down on him ceased. He opened his eyes and saw a burly, tall man in an open white shirt, pulling his attacker off him with a lasso. He immediately knew that his brother, Bearslayer Bruce, had returned, along with his brother and the young priest. The Indian's face reflected astonishment.

Jeremiah stood beside him and lifted him from the ground. His face was angry as he handed Anton his pistol. "Don't lose this again!" he said. The elder White turned back and approached the now bound Indian. The warrior writhed and struggled to break free, but he had no chance.

Bearslayer sat the man up, leaning his back against a rock. He tossed a black leather pouch onto the ground, opened it, and let the snake inside it emerge.

"Christ in heaven, you keep something like that in your bag?" Father Cristofano crossed himself.

"When a man's married, he has to think about many things," Bruce retorted.

"I've never heard anything like this," the priest said, and turned around.

Bearslayer glanced for a moment at the writhing snake as it flicked its tongue, striking towards him several times. Bruce only hissed a few times and grabbed the snake's neck with a quick movement. The animal tried to escape, wriggling wildly. Bruce stepped towards the Indian and pushed the snake towards his face. "Listen! How many of you are there and where are you hiding? If you answer correctly, I might suck the poison out of you."

The warrior looked deep into Bearslayer's eyes, then spat in his face. "I'm not afraid of death! Christ died for me on the cross, so the kingdom of heaven awaits me!"

"So be it!" Bruce pressed the snake's jaws to open its mouth, revealing its huge venomous fangs. With a quick, decisive movement, he pressed it against the Indian's face, and the snake immediately bit into his eye. Its fangs pierced his eyeball, blood and clearish jelly running down the warrior's face, who screamed and kicked, but it was too late. The deadly poison spread through his veins, and his agonies were terrible.

Anton was still in shock, his heart pounding wildly in his chest, his hands trembling. He took hesitant steps towards the Bearslayer and watched as he finished off his attacker. "Heavens above! You really mean it!" he said, astonished.

"I hate redskins!" Bruce replied. "Do you think I collected their scalps for fun? Well… maybe a little."

Bear Hunter smiled as he threw away the animal. The injured Indian writhed on the ground, blood flowing from his eye, his whole face swollen from the effects of the poison, white foam coming from his mouth. Bruce watched the dying man for a while, then turned towards the distant screams. The sounds of battle cries echoed. "We have to go," he said. "More are coming."

Anton rushed for his bag, grabbed his gun, and with the others, began to run towards the valley.

The sheriff stared blankly ahead as he observed the desk filled with papers in front of him. His hands were handcuffed to the bars. He glanced at his restraints, then shook the chain. The cold metal clinked unpleasantly. He tugged on it a few times, but he knew the material wouldn't give in. He had handcuffed countless people before, always watching with pity as they attempted to break free. It was an instinctive human reaction, and he knew how pathetic he must look now. A fly buzzed around his head, landing and scurrying a few millimeters across his face before taking off again. It particularly bothered Arisztid, but given the events of the past few days, he felt he'd rather spend the rest of his life in the company of annoying insects than sit here in handcuffs. Painful screams and groans emanated from another room. He knew how severely his friend Fred was injured. Although he still had time to tighten the tourniquet around his leg, he had no other options. They had been ambushed and taken prisoner, and the situation was not unfolding as planned. He had no idea who the mysterious stranger could be. The man had addressed him as sheriff. *"I've been expecting you,"* he'd said. Thoughts raced through his mind, confusion washing over him. *How did he know we were coming? Why was he waiting for me? Who is this man?* A multitude of questions to which he had no answers. He took a deep breath, trying to calm his anxiety, leaned on the bars and stood up. The dry, dusty air scratched his throat, and the room's lamplight cast ominous shadows into the corners rather than filling the space with life. A bead of sweat trickled down his neck. He took a yellowed handkerchief from the pocket of his black vest and wiped away the unpleasantly salty moisture with shaking hands. He put his hat on, then took a hesitant step alongside the bars. His spurs clanged metallically on the creaking dry boards, sending an uncomfortable chill down his spine. He glanced towards the closed door, hoping to catch a glimpse through its window, but there was complete stillness outside. He felt like his heart was about to burst through his chest, it was hard to breathe. Though there was no one in the room, he felt surrounded by accusing glances, as if he were in a besieged city. He had to muster all his strength to appear resolute. There was movement outside, and he saw two Indians pushing a man in front of them, his hands in cuffs and a sack over his head.

The door opened, and the prisoner was pushed into the room. The man stumbled and fell to the ground, groaning in pain as he rolled onto his back. One of the warriors stopped beside him, kicked him hard in the head, then squatted next to him and pulled the sack from his head. Dalton spat bloody saliva into the man's face, who recoiled, then looked down at the fallen Jonathan with pitying disgust. They helped him to stand up, opened the cell, and pushed him inside.

"Where's Fred?" the sheriff asked anxiously. "What have they done to him?"

The Indian glanced back over his shoulder. His companion nodded, then they carried in the injured deputy, blood dripping from his leg, his trousers torn, his face pale, his whole body drenched in sweat. The warrior tossed Fred into a corner of the cell, and his face contorted in pain. Their captors didn't shackle or tie him up; they knew he would be incapable of escape or attack in this condition.

"Fred! Fred!" Arisztid called out. "Look at me!"

The deputy slowly lifted his head, fixing his gaze on Wratiszlaw. His face reflected terrible agony.

Despite the short chain, the sheriff tried to reach into his vest pocket. With difficulty, he managed to take the vial of opium out, but then he dropped it. With his foot, he nudged it towards Fred. "Pick it up and drink!" he instructed. "It will dull the pain."

The man did as his friend requested, quickly consuming the opium with a single gulp, then he tossed the vial aside, shattering it. He rolled onto his back, his gaze growing distant. "That filthy swine treated me badly," he remarked. "Arisztid... my friend... You know I won't survive this, don't you? I just want to ask..."

"Don't you dare say your goodbyes, deputy!" Arisztid shouted at him. "I won't let you die here!"

"That's enough!" shouted his companion, then started coughing. "I've lost a lot of blood, you know that. We went through the war together, we both know what this kind of break means. If I don't see a doctor, it will get infected, and I won't let them amputate my leg. I won't be a cripple. Listen to me, Sheriff!" The deputy, at terrible pains, sat up straight and looked his partner straight in the eye. "We came here to take our children home. At any cost! Do you understand? You and Dalton need to figure out how to get out of here! Leave me here, don't worry about me."

"Forget about it, Fred! Your fate will be the same as ours!"

"The deputy is right," Dalton interjected. "Look at him, Sheriff! He can't take a single step on his own, so how could he possibly fight out there?"

Arisztid banged on the bars in frustration and turned away. He knew the captain and his partner were right. His heart was breaking with pain, knowing that his only true friend wouldn't survive this night.

"But we can put an end to this, Sheriff," Fred said. "You just need to break free. Look at the beds and the bars!"

Wratiszlaw turned around and immediately understood what his partner meant. "Dalton, can you break free from here?"

"How could I?"

"Is the bed frame movable? Check it!" Fred said.

The captain turned around and pushed the bed, which moved.

"It is" he replied.

"Excellent. Then, when they sleep, take off the blanket, lift the bed frame, and push it against the bars. The hinges will move. Remember, Sheriff...? We replaced our bars last year."

"I remember."

"So, you should do the same. When they get out of here, I'll draw their attention to myself so you can make your move."

Dalton and Arisztid looked at each other. The sheriff lowered his head, a deep sigh of sadness escaping him as he responded: "We'll come back for you. We won't leave you to die here."

"I don't expect any less from you, either," Fred lied, thinking about the single-shot pistol hidden in his pocket.

The deputy slowly leaned back, his eyes becoming hazy, his eyelashes closing. The opium had finally knocked him out.

Arisztid rested his head against the cold metal, then sighed. He wiped his sweaty neck with his dirty shirt sleeve, then clasped his hands together in front of the bars. Despite the heat, his body was covered in cold sweat, his hair hanging damply in his eyes. His heart pumped blood into his weary limbs at a steady pace, but he knew he would soon have to work the worn ticker again. He looked up, then carefully examined the room. The simple writing desk, the orderly papers, the meticulously organized filing cabinet did not reflect the bloodshed that had recently raged outside. The noise of footsteps caught his ear, and he turned towards the sound. He heard the dull, metallic sound of spurred boots growing louder and closer, then he saw the man. His heart raced for a moment, an uncomfortable pressure forming in his head, but upon recognition, he was able to calm down again. This wasn't him.

The Indian wore black leather pants, his upper body covered only by a leather vest, his waist-length hair glistening in the light of the lanterns. His face was covered in bloodstains and white war paint. He held keys in his hand as he approached the sheriff "Show me your hand!"

Arisztid raised his arms as much as he could, and the man removed the handcuffs from him. The sheriff stretched his numb limbs, then addressed the Indian in a mocking tone: "Well... Just what we needed, another native! I suppose you also have some wise Indian name, like Cross-eyed Buffalo or Crooked Pipe..."

Anger flashed in the warrior's eyes as he approached the bars, lifted the golden cross hanging around his neck, and thrust it into Arisztid's face. "Do you see this here?" he asked in a hoarse, soft voice. "My name is Joseph, and I am reborn in our Lord Jesus Christ!"

Wratiszlaw snorted, then pushed the crucifix away from him. "Oh... I'm already relieved that you'll scalp me in the grace of the Lord."

The Indian growled furiously and grabbed him by the hair, slamming his head hard against the metal bars.

The sheriff groaned and slumped to the ground. Sharp pain seared through his face, as he felt his skin split and blood trickle down his cheek. He coughed, spitting bloody saliva onto the hard wooden planks. A smile crept onto his face as he grasped the edge of the bed and pulled himself up.

He pulled out a yellowed cloth from his pocket and pressed it against his bleeding nose.

"I won't allow a sinner like yourself to mock our Lord Jesus!"

"I'm not mocking our Lord Jesus, just you, you damn copper-skinned savage!" he retorted through his clenched teeth, muffled by the cloth.

The warrior stepped determinedly towards the bars, but a sharp, authoritative voice echoed from the doorway: "Enough!"

The sheriff's heartbeat quickened, exacerbating his nosebleed. A fit of coughing seized him, and he turned towards the wall. He dropped his dirty cloth from trembling hands, desperately trying to catch his breath, but his lungs failed him, and he collapsed onto the bed.

The Indian turned back in alarm, his gaze falling to the floor as he knelt down. "Forgive me, Holy Father!" he pleaded. "Anger overtook me."

The man approached the kneeling figure on the ground, then helped him up. The young warrior still avoided his gaze, refusing to meet his eyes. The stranger gently caressed Joseph's face, smoothed his hair behind his ear, and spoke to him in a soft, kind voice. "Son, are you so afraid of me that you avoid my gaze?"

"No, Holy Father!" he immediately retorted and looked at him.

The man leaned closer, almost whispering as he continued: "Good. Please tell me, why did you kneel before me?"

The young Indian tried to respond awkwardly, his gaze darting around, his hands beginning to tremble. "I... I didn't... Please."

"Shh..." The Mexican placed his finger to his lips. "You can only kneel before God, my son! Now go and pray with the others."

Joseph nodded, then hurriedly left.

Arisztid sat up on the bed, then stuffed the bloody cloth into his pants pocket. He had to gather all his strength to be able to stand up. His head throbbed, his palms were sweaty, his fingers whitened. He gasped for air, feeling like the tiny cell was crushing him. He lifted his gaze to the man standing before him. The Mexican wore black pants, a dark gray poncho, and a black hat. His black hair grazed his chin, a scar marred the right side of his face, his right eye gleamed glassy and white. The sheriff wanted to flee, to at least hide somewhere where he could never be found. But he had no choice. Alone, vulnerable, trapped, he had to face the kidnapper of the children who had disappeared from his town. His right hand started to tremble more violently. He clenched it into a fist, then put it in his pocket. The stranger stepped closer to the cell, and Arisztid instinctively moved back.

"Welcome, Sheriff! My name is Diego Ramirez" He tipped his hat. "It's good that we can finally meet in person. Are you enjoying the Mexican hospitality?"

"Oh, of course!" he replied, feigning determination. "Cheap tequila, beautiful girls, lively brothels. The cells are a bit moldy, and I haven't eaten yet, but well, nothing is perfect, right?"

"There's a discreet charm to the devil's servant seeking perfection. That's solely the privilege of the Lord. If you accept the Savior, grace will find you, and in heaven, everything is perfect, no one suffers lack. By the way, do you want a cigarette?" The Mexican pulled out a cigarette, then lit it and handed it over through the bars.

"Don't you smoke?" asked the sheriff.

Ramirez shook his head. "No. Disgusting habit."

A bitter scream echoed from the street, and the two men turned in its direction. Curses filtered in, followed by a gunshot. Silence ensued. Arisztid lowered his head, and a drop of blood dripped onto his boot. "I hear your Joseph is fervently praying, and grace has found yet another unfortunate soul. Tell me, Ramirez," he looked him in the eye, "how did a corn-eating Mexican, a rotten copper-skinned, become possessed by the devil to abduct children and murder innocents in the name of God?"

"Innocents?" The man raised his eyebrows, then leaned against the bars. "There are no innocents, my friend! Look around and tell me what you see. People trample upon everything that is holy and true. Children sell their bodies on the streets so their parents can get drunk again in the evening, men rob unsuspecting travelers just to find joy in violence. Women push away their husbands to spend a few more years with their secret lovers. In contrast, I saved the souls of pagans from damnation, I keep the souls of Christian children on the path of righteousness! I give them purpose and faith..." He smiled, then took a few steps back. "Allow me to ask you something! Do you consider yourself a man of the law, truly? Someone who rides into the wild and cruel Mexican wilderness after innocent children, isn't that right?"

"I didn't come to this cesspool for fun, believe me," replied the sheriff.

The Mexican's face twisted into an angry, contorted grimace, then he gripped the bars and yelled loudly: "If you represent justice, my friend, then tell me why you came to us with common criminals?! Who are the righteous heroes in your little gang? The black looter, the mercenary brothers, or the scalp hunter? Perhaps the wanton deputy? No, sheriff..." Ramirez shook his head. "You know exactly the kind of people you've surrounded yourself with, and you know that if any of them were to die, it would be true justice. But today, *you* can achieve justice. You can make a truly brave and responsible decision."

"You've lost your mind," Arisztid replied, bewildered. "I care about the lives of the children, nothing else. Give them back, and we'll be out of here."

"Alright," the Mexican replied calmly.

"Alright?" Wratiszlaw exclaimed in disbelief. "What do you mean, alright? Then open the damn cell and let us out."

A wicked smile spread across Ramirez's face as he scrutinized the sheriff. "Since the Lord has given us free will, I'll release one child. They will be free to run into the arms of the devil, but in return, you must do something. You must name someone from your group. You must sacrifice a sinner so that your soul may gain redemption. Are you ready for this, sheriff?"

"What? Excuse me?" he gasped, his face turning pale as a sheet. "Absolutely not!"

"Then one child chosen by me will die. Can you live with that?"

Arisztid made a sudden movement, reaching through the bars to grab the Mexican, but he stepped back just in time.

"Name someone from your group. I won't ask again."

Wratiszlaw began to see stars; he felt dizzy, and his stomach clenched. He sat down on the edge of the bed, staring blankly ahead with empty eyes. He buried his face in his hands, then whispered softly, barely audible: "You're a despicable worm..."

"What was that, please?" Ramirez asked. "I didn't quite catch that, my friend."

"You're a despicable worm!" the sheriff yelled. "What kind of game are you playing?!"

"Oh, I see." the Mexican smiled. "Think logically... Here are two people besides yourself. One is a healthy, ready-to-fight veteran," he gestured towards Dalton, "and there lies a severely injured, weakened man who will likely descend into hell by dawn."

Ramirez stepped closer to the cell, a sinister glint in his white, glassy eyes. "Think about it, my friend... The Lord sacrificed his only son to save your soul. So where is this sacrifice compared to Jesus'? And can you truly not decide whether to alleviate the suffering of a dying man or preserve the innocent life of a child?"

Arisztid's hand started trembling more strongly, tears welled up in his eyes, his lips dried out. With shaking hands, he rubbed his face, then looked at his companion, his friend. Fred lay with closed eyes, motionless. He knew he would never be the same person he was before. *Perhaps this is truly the best for him...* "If I do this... Do you promise to release the child? To ensure they safely return to Corpus Christi and can live their life freely?"

"I swear on the holy name of God, my friend!" Ramirez dramatically placed his hand on his heart with a smile.

The sheriff gripped the bars tightly with both hands, groaning in agony, then spoke softly, almost inaudibly: "I sacrifice Fred."

"What did you say?" The man brushed his hair from his ear. "I didn't hear."

"I sacrifice Fred," he said louder, still avoiding the gaze of the Mexican.

Ramirez angrily slammed the bars. "Say it aloud that you sacrifice your best friend! Say it!"

The sheriff, with fiery eyes and a voice filled with hatred, shouted as he stared into the eyes of the Mexican: "I sacrifice to the Lord Frederick William, Deputy Sheriff, so that he may depart freely in exchange for the child's life!"

Ramirez started laughing, sending shivers down Dalton and Wratiszlaw's spines. Ramirez clapped and then replied: "So I'm not only facing a living damnation, but also a coward. Fine." He spread his arms. "Then let it be your friend. I hope, sheriff, you know you could have given your own life for the child. I didn't expect a logical decision from you, but sincere repentance. But you didn't even consider the noblest sacrifice. Ponder upon this." He pointed his finger at Arisztid. "Now I'll send your friend to the afterlife."

The Mexican turned away from the bars and glanced towards Fred, who was now watching the events with open eyes, half-sitting. With all his strength, he concentrated, aiming his revolver at the man. "I'll send you to the afterlife, you vile scumbag!" the deputy said, then fired.

Ramirez, after a moment of shock, snapped out of it just in time to dodge the bullet, but it still grazed him. Sharp pain seared through his left shoulder, causing him to stagger and fall. The sheriff reached through the bars and grabbed hold of the Mexican. Ramirez desperately reached towards his assailant and successfully broke free from his grip. He cast a hateful glare at the sheriff. He wasn't accustomed to making mistakes. Ignoring the pain, he got up and approached the now unarmed deputy. Fred was unable to retreat or defend himself. Ramirez stomped on the open wound with the heel of his boot. Fred was overwhelmed by excruciating pain, his mouth gaping open, but he couldn't produce a sound, his eyes wide open. Ramirez sensed he was about to pass out. "Oh, no! Not that!" He squatted down, then repeatedly slapped the deputy forcefully. The man pulled Fred up from the ground, then forcefully pressed his head onto the desk. "You lied to me, sheriff!" Ramirez hissed. "You're sacrificing nothing to the Lord, only offering another sin to Satan's altar of lies! Consider our deal null and void!"

Arisztid leaped towards the bars, hitting them with all his might while screaming inarticulately.

Ramirez pressed the helpless deputy onto the table with his left hand, reached for the knife strapped to his belt, then triumphantly held it towards the sky. He pressed his knee against Fred's back, causing his head and shoulders to arch backward. The Mexican grabbed his hair, placed the blade of his knife against his forehead, and deeply cut into his skin.

Fred began to groan in agonizing pain as Ramirez meticulously peeled off strips of his scalp, inch by inch.

Dalton stepped back a few paces and turned away, covering his ears. He couldn't bear to see or hear what was happening.

Arisztid continued to scream, pounding his hands against the bars, all in vain.

The blade slowly but surely cut through the skin and veins. The bloody scalp separated from the skull, and Ramirez raised it high into the air. Blood dripped down, staining his clothes. The Mexican threw the peeled skin towards Arisztid, returned the knife to its sheath, and grabbed the head of the deputy who was suffering in agonizing torment. The man tried to resist, but against his opponent, he had no chance. Ramirez forcefully smashed Fred's head into the table with all his might. The skull resounded with a hard thud against the beautifully crafted, lacquered surface. He lifted his victim's head again and struck it against the desk forcefully, again and again, until the loud thud turned into a dull thump, then into a mushy squelch. The blood-soaked Mexican released the dead deputy, whose lifeless body slid down to the floor.

Arisztid no longer pounded the bars, no longer screamed, just stared in shock at the grotesque scene unfolding before him.

Ramirez panted like a wild animal, wiped his face with his hand, then took a deep breath and slowly, triumphantly approached the shocked sheriff. "Tomorrow... you and the nigger will die by hanging. Because you're a coward, a liar, and a blasphemer."

With a theatrical nod, he then seized Arisztid's arm and pulled the man towards him through the bars. From his pocket, he took out a small vial and used the knife to cut the sheriff's palm. Wratiszlaw hissed in pain, attempting to pull his arm away, but the Mexican was stronger. Ramirez filled the vial with his blood, sealed it shut, and hurriedly departed.

The sheriff's mind echoed with the footsteps and the words he had last heard. He was unable to move, unable to even blink. Losing his strength, he fell to his knees, burying his face in his hands, his eyes growing heavy. The familiar darkness from his childhood once again enveloped his mind, sucking him in. *What kind of man am I?*

Gunshots filled the valley. Younger White glanced back over his shoulder as he rode alongside the others. Muzzle flashes lit up, and he pulled his collar up, looking towards his brother. Jeremiah leaned forward on his horse, oblivious to the barrage of shots. Above them, only the clear sky and stars were visible, the cool air hitting Anton's face. They had managed to flee from the hill, but the Indians quickly found them. The young bounty hunter reached for his pistol and fired blindly, not knowing if he hit anyone. More muzzle flashes illuminated the scene, and bullets struck around them.

The horses whinnied in fear, and Jeremiah yelled: "Nobody shoot at them! Let's lure them into the gorge, come on!" Older White spurred his horse and galloped ahead, the others following. Riding towards the rocky mountainside, they heard the pursuing warriors shouting, firing shots as they prepared for the impending clash. They knew they would soon be in close combat. Taking advantage of the team's lead, they reached the gorge and dismounted from their horses.

Quickly grabbing their knives and ammunition, Anton drove the horses away, then turned to the others: "And now?" he asked.

Bruce rushed to a nearby tree, then climbed its trunk to see how far away their pursuers were.

Jeremiah approached the priests: "You!" He pointed to the two men. "Find shelter on the side of the mountain! We'll try to defend ourselves, but it won't be easy."

Agustíno showed his revolver. "Deal with the attackers. We can defend ourselves if necessary!"

Jeremiah stared at the old Italian-style pistol in astonishment, then nodded. "We'll keep an eye on you as best we can. Anton!" He turned to his younger brother. "Climb up to the tree where Bruce is! Let them get close, then unleash hell on them! Bruce! Get down from there! We'll split up and take them under fire from both sides. But be careful! Don't shoot me in the eyes!"

Bearslayer nodded, then replied with a smile: "Don't worry, Mr. White, my weapon is specialized for the colored ones!" He raised his head sharply at a piercing sound, then looked in the direction of the noise. He squinted, then spotted several human figures approaching. "They're coming" he whispered. "Time to work, boys!"

Bearslayer lay prone, his body completely disappearing among the tall grass. He raised his pistol in front of him, held his breath, and waited for the right moment.

The approaching Indians slowly crawled forward, holding rifles in their hands, and carefully searched for any small noise. Branches cracked under their feet, their rifles tightly gripped.

Bruce looked up and saw Anton targeting the warrior passing below him, waiting patiently. He glanced sideways, locking eyes with Jeremiah, who nodded. Bearslayer smiled, then aimed and fired. At the sound of the shot, birds fluttered into the air, the Indian groaned and fell dead. Anton whistled from the top of the tree; one of the warriors looked back and found himself facing the barrel of the bounty hunter's pistol. Another shot rang out.

Jeremiah stepped out of his hiding spot and fired a short burst. Their attackers became disoriented; they returned fire, but this time they had no chance, falling one by one. After the shots ceased, silence fell over the landscape. Everyone listened intently, but there was no movement. Jeremiah exhaled, then holstered his pistol.

Bruce also stood up and approached Anton, who was climbing down from the tree. "This was easier than I thought," he said, surprised.

"Almost disappointing," replied the younger White.

Jeremiah stood behind them, motionless, and watched intently, his instincts telling him it wasn't over yet. He closed his eyes and listened, shutting out all noise. He became aware of voices, coming from the mountainside.

"The priests!" He started running, followed by his brother and Bruce. They ran towards the mountainside, through dense vegetation, reaching a small clearing. The ground was barren, lifeless, filled with rocks and damp. His boots sank into the soggy earth. In front of the rocky mountainside stood Father Cristofano, one hand raised to the sky, the other holding a holy cross towards an Indian who, wielding a tomahawk, was poised for attack. Jeremiah looked around, but saw no sign of Father Agustíno.

The younger priest kept his gaze fixed on the figure before him, praying aloud. "Saint Michael the Archangel, defend us in battle; be our protection against the wickedness and snares of the devil! We humbly pray... Command him, God! And you, O prince of the heavenly host, by the power of God, thrust into hell Satan and all the evil spirits who prowl about the world seeking the ruin of souls."

The warrior raised his weapon high in response to the prayer and stepped closer to the priest.

Cristofano didn't flinch, but continued more determinedly. "For there is no holiness like Your holiness, no power like Your power, no goodness like Your goodness, and no wisdom like Your wisdom, Our Lord and King, Creator of men and angels, who with the blood of Your Son have redeemed us from the power of Satan and the evil spirits. Savior God, source of purity and peace, grant us victory through the resurrection of Jesus, through the power of Your Spirit, through the intervention of Your angels! Protect us from evil, so that united with the glorious host of angels, we may bless and praise you forever and ever."

A sinister smile spread across the Indian's face as he lowered his weapon and approached: "Angels?" A baleful gleam flashed in his eyes. "The angel of the Lord is already among us..." he hissed. "Look to the sky and see his wings, hear his voice, which..."

The sound of gunfire filled the air, causing Cristofano to flinch.

The Indian looked down in surprise at his bleeding chest. He took a few steps back and fell to his knees.

Father Agustíno emerged from the bushes, holding a smoking revolver in his hand. The warrior coughed up blood, which ran down his face, neck, and chest. He lifted his gaze to the elder priest and spoke with a smile. "The father warned..." He coughed. "Warned that the supreme..."

Another gunshot rang out, this time hitting the Indian in the head. The warrior fell onto his back and died instantly.

Father Agustíno tucked the pistol back into his pocket and approached his astonished companions: "Gentlemen! This is not the time for prayers, but for battle!"

Bruce, recovering from his surprise, took over: "The priest is right! There's a man who lives at the end of the valley... Rodrigo. Perhaps he'll help us. We must go, now!"

The others nodded and hastened to their horses. After just a few minutes of riding, a small, thatched-roof house appeared on the horizon. Bruce nodded, and the others quickened their pace. Around the small house at the end of the valley, there was nothing else but a well and a stable. Even in the moonlight, it was clear that life ruled this area. Upon reaching the house, Bearslayer dismounted his horse and cautioned the others to be cautious. Anton and Jeremiah, gripping their pistols, kept watch for any hostile movement.

Bearslayer approached the small wooden door of the house and knocked firmly. "Rodrigo! Are you in there?" There was a short silence. Bruce glanced back anxiously at his companions before knocking again. "Rodrigo! It's me, Bruce! We need your help! There are Indians..."

A faint light flickered inside, followed by the slow shuffle of footsteps. The door creaked open.

Rodrigo's face was marked with deep wrinkles, his elongated skin mottled and his patchy hair fully grayed. He held a lantern in his hand, which he raised. With his brown eyes, he scrutinized Bearslayer, then glanced past him at his strange companions. "Bruce..." he said. "What are you doing here? I thought you'd retired."

"An old friend asked for my help. I couldn't refuse." Bruce shrugged. "Will you let us in?"

"Come on in," the man replied, gesturing them forward. "What kind of trouble have you gotten into this time?"

"Indians..." Bruce began as he entered the house, followed by the others. "But you know, they're not like they used to be."

The old man gave the Bear Hunter a meaningful look. Sadness and deep pain were evident in his eyes. "I know." He sighed.

"Rest assured!" Anton said. "We've taken care of those who were after us. They don't know we're here."

"Oh, but they do," Rodrigo replied. "And they also knew that I'd let you in."

Anton stepped anxiously to the window, scanning around for any signs of enemies.

"Don't worry, ombre," the old man said. "They won't come here. They dare not."

Father Agustíno examined the painting on the wall, finding it particularly interesting and captivating. Without looking at the old man, he posed his question: "And why wouldn't these savages dare to come here?"

Rodrigo stepped beside the priest, ignoring the question as he looked at the painting, then addressed Agustíno. "It's an interesting painting, isn't it? Personally, I love it; it shows the true power of God. Do you know what you see?"

The older priest touched the painting. It depicted an angel preparing to strike with a raised sword. The mountain in the background seemed familiar to him. Lightning flashed, and falling angels were clearly visible in the night sky. The kneeling figure before the angel had long, golden hair adorned with a crown, but its wings were broken. Chains wrapped around its wrists and ankles, pulling it into the depths of the mountain.

"Fallen angels," Agustíno replied. "Where is this painting from?"

The old man chuckled pleasantly, as if he had just heard a child's question. "Of course, I brought it from the monastery, a long time ago."

The older priest turned to Rodrigo with interest. His voice deepened, becoming raspy.   "What monastery?" he asked again.

The old man chuckled again and didn't answer. Slowly, he turned around, approached his rocking chair, and sat down, stretching out in it for a long moment. His tired bones cracked, and he sighed contentedly. "You know, certain parts of the earth were once battlegrounds for heavenly hosts. I know!" He raised his voice, looking at Jeremiah. "Some of you might consider this all nonsense. Old beliefs. And perhaps you don't believe in angels and demons as much as you should." He gestured towards the priests. "But believe me, these are not just metaphors; they are very real! The painting you see is nothing but the Archangels' ultimate victory over the rebels."

"Referring to Lucifer and the rebel angels?" asked Cristofano.

"Oh, no!" Rodrigo shook his head. "Lucifer was not the only rebel angel, not the first, and not the last. The one in the picture... Kasbeel."

"The apostate," Cristofano replied. "This painting should be in the Vatican! Locked away! Not here... on a ranch," he said with disgust in his voice.

The old man chuckled again. "You're ignorant, my boy. Where better to hide it than here... on this ranch? Who would search for it around here?"

"Sorry to interrupt the storytelling, but we have very serious problems!" Jeremiah burst out. "We came after missing altar boys and a nun. In Matamoros, we were attacked, three of us got stuck there, one of them seriously injured."

"Mr. White is right! We don't have time to ponder on prehistoric human eras... Rodrigo, do you know where they'll take the prisoners?" Bruce asked.

The old man cleared his throat, then, keeping his gaze on Agustino, replied: "Ramirez always takes the resistors, rebels, and anyone who stands in his way to the fortress. He sets an example."

"The old Spanish fortress east from here?" Bruce asked.

The old man nodded. "But be cautious. Beyond the valley, the savages dominate the land."

Bearslayer approached the White brothers, then carefully assessed both of them. "It might sound crazy, but it would be best if we went into the fortress." He looked towards Rodrigo, then continued. "They'll hang them, right?"

"Yes."

"And will this Ramirez be there too?" Anton asked.

"I strongly doubt it. Diego hasn't shown his face in the light for a long time. They'll get in, there's no doubt about that. If they manage to free their friend, they'll come back here. I assume they also want to find the monastery."

Agustino grabbed the old man's arm, and their gazes locked. "Definitely."

The two men stared at each other for a long time, then Rodrigo smiled. "Rest now, you have a long and difficult journey ahead of you, you're safe here. They won't come here. And leave at dawn. May God protect your steps!"

A small drop of blood dripped onto the floor from the sheriff's nose. He had been unable to move for quite some time, only kneeling, gripping the bars, staring at the ground.

His mind echoed with the agonizing cries of his friend, Fred's torment burned into his eyes. His heart beat slowly, rhythmically in his chest, no longer concerned with his own fate. He looked up. The dim light cast ominous shadows in the corner of the room, broken only by the small pool of blood spread out beside the desk. His friend's blood slowly soaked into the dried wood. Arisztid heard Dalton lift the metal-framed bed and, following the deputy's advice, attempting to escape. He looked up again. He saw the man struggling, but he knew he was doing it wrong, yet he didn't care. He looked back down at the floor. Bitterness and pain tormented his heart. He had no idea if it was just his mind tormenting him or certain knowledge, but he believed Fred would have chosen differently. He wouldn't have sacrificed him like this, considering how many times he had saved his life, yet he was unable to reciprocate and brought him on a mission that cost him his life.

Jonathan exclaimed angrily, then, panting, pushed the bed back into place. "Sheriff, look at me!" he called out. "We need to get out of here!"

Arisztid didn't lift his head, continuing to stare at the ground.

"Hey! Hey!" Dalton clicked his tongue. "Sheriff, snap out of it! If we want to survive, we have to work together!"

Wratiszlaw grew angry at the words, then shouted angrily: "If you want to survive, don't count on me!"

Jonathan lowered his head, then sighed sadly. He knew the sheriff had suffered a wound to the soul that would never heal. He also knew that alone, unarmed, he stood no chance against Ramirez and his men. "Sheriff... Please, look at me."

Arisztid raised his gaze to Dalton. It held nothing but pain and profound sadness.

Dalton gripped the bars, then continued: "Look, I know what you've been through!"

"You know nothing..."

"But I do!" the captain retorted. "Remember the soldier whose body you found in the church? You do remember, right?"

Wratiszlaw nodded almost imperceptibly. "His name was Nick. He was my friend, I knew him since childhood. You see, among my kind, not every child made it to adulthood. If we got sick or severely injured, our owner didn't call a doctor unless it was cheaper than getting a new slave. Nick was a servant for the neighboring family, I knew all of his siblings. By the time the war broke out, he was the only one left; his sisters, brothers, younger and older, all dead. We were all each other had left. We escaped up north, where we thought we could live freely. You don't know, Sheriff, how wrong we were. I know people think I went to fight, but I didn't. I was tired of fighting, just like Nick. I didn't want anything else but a place of my own, a job to sustain myself and my future family. Nick and I built a house, then another. But then the Union soldiers showed up and forcefully took us, took our homes we'd barely lived in; they took everything. They said we'd get it back after we served our mandatory time, that we should be grateful they took the chains off our necks and let us breathe their air. So we fought. Day after day, year after year. Why did we start robbing? Not out of revenge, Sheriff... But because we had no money. No food, no drink. They said we should fend for ourselves. You know... While we're at it... I didn't tell the truth even when I claimed I tried to burn down the Southerners. I wanted my own captain, but they weren't in there... So we were left to fend for ourselves. Eventually, others with similar fates joined us. There were indeed deserters, bandits, and criminals among them, but that's what we got... Nick didn't want to do this for a long time, in fact! He protested vehemently before we raided your little church, and I left him behind..." Dalton turned his gaze away, tears welling in his eyes. "I let the man who was with me for most of my life, through thick and thin, die. You were led by coercion... And I was led by my cowardice." Jonathan withdrew his hands from the bars, then a deep sigh escaped him. He stepped back to the bed, sat down, and continued softly: "I beg you, Sheriff, don't let your friend die in vain! I can't make sense of Nick's death, but you can still do something!"

"Death has no meaning, just as life doesn't!" Arisztid said in a colorless voice. "There are people who have nothing but suffering."

"Oh, come on!" the captain scoffed. "What do you know about suffering? Everything about you, your behavior, your speech, screams that you're from a wealthy family!"

"What do I know about suffering?" He looked into Dalton's eyes. "Well, let me tell you something! The lives of the rich aren't much different from those of slaves. Are we whipped? No. At least not on our bodies, but on our souls, which never heal. From my childhood until this moment, I've been haunted by doubt, fear, and the knowledge that any moment could be my last. I was a sickly child. In an aristocratic house, such things mean one thing: family shame... You see, my father called a coffin maker to me when he was still alive. I was barely four years old! And that cursed man measured me as if I were just a simple tailor!" He chuckled bitterly. "It all started with a simple headache. I remember that day vividly. My mother thought that the sun drained my strength and burned my head, and that a little sleep would help me. But it didn't. By the next day, not only my head hurt, but also my hands and feet, my chest was tight, and all my energy had left me. I remember," he said in a trembling voice, "my father came into my room and looked at me as if I were the illness itself, a curse that stained our family's honor... He didn't come closer than two meters to me, he just watched my tiny body being consumed by the illness, scrutinized my eyes, I suppose searching for reason in them, fearing that my mind was slipping away too. Fear and panic raged inside me, but my body was so weak that I couldn't even shake. I wanted to reach out to him and beg,

188

'Father, help me,' but I couldn't. The effort only made my eyes bulge and foam started to form at my mouth. My father ran away. Since I was born into a noble family, my parents could afford to pay for the best doctors in Buda. Every time a new doctor arrived with his frightening instruments, there was suspicion, horror, and pity in their eyes. My father wouldn't let my sister and brother come near me. He moved them to the attic and hired a caregiver for me. A sweet little peasant girl. My father thought that I couldn't infect a trained nurse with my mysterious illness because his aristocratic friends were already meeting us with fear. And the death of an uneducated peasant girl meant nothing to him. I can't forget that stale, musty smell, the nights when the wind made the beams creak and groan. My brother, whom I loved and idolized, never sneaked into my room like my sister did. When my caregiver fell asleep in the chair next to me, dear Juli would sneak in and tell me about the happenings in the outside world. Those minutes were the most beautiful of my childhood. But after my father caught her, she never came again... Not because she didn't want to, but because my father locked her in the dark cellar with the rats for a whole day. Hungry, thirsty, without light or hope, a six-year-old girl... Yes, Mr. Dalton, that's my father! A free and wealthy man! And my illness wouldn't relent." He sighed. "It only tightened its grip on me even more. One doctor, after thoroughly examining me, determined that my blood was infected and needed to be drained. Covered from head to toe in leeches, I was powerless to resist. After they were removed from me days later, my headache intensified. Another doctor arrived, attempting to alleviate my pain by piercing my skull beside my temple." Arisztid turned his head to the side and showed the scar to Dalton. "And guess what happened? My condition only worsened... There was a fleeting moment afterward when my mind cleared and I gained enough strength to open my eyes and look up. Everyone stood beside my bed, surrounding me and staring at me. Pity, fear, horror, pain, and tears. Sometimes, when my parents argued, their voices echoed up to the attic. My father wanted to suffocate me with the small pillow my sister had sewn for me, to finally erase the family's shame from his accustomed noble life, but my mother wouldn't allow it. She begged him to try one more thing, just one. Eventually, my father agreed. To this day, I don't know who those people were. Two of them came to me. One had eyes a blue so brilliant I haven't seen since. He stroked my head with his ice-cold hand. And darkness engulfed me once again. And the next day... I felt well. For the first time in a long while, I was able to sit up in bed without assistance. Later, I could take a few steps on the attic floor under my own power. My mother believed it was a divine miracle and thanked the Lord every single day. And my father... Well, he never treated me as his son again. Then I burst with happiness when I could run again. I looked at my father, straight into his eyes. I didn't see pride or love in him, but hatred, contempt, and terror. He dreaded that his son had survived. Can you imagine this, Captain Dalton?"

Jonathan listened in astonishment to Arisztid's story. He understood that despite being born wealthy, the sheriff's life had been no easier than his own.

"I'm sorry, Sheriff... I never would have thought..."

"Don't worry about it, Captain," Wratiszlaw waved dismissively. "Believe me, I know suffering all too well! Whether by force or not, I betrayed the one person who didn't want to push me into the jaws of death, but instead reached out and pulled me from there. Frederick William was the first person I met in London at the end of 1849... You see, after my illness, I became so strong that when the revolution broke out, I went to fight alongside my brother... I won't bore you with the details, but we lost. My brother died. My father was completely shattered, and my mother disappeared without a trace. I never found out what happened to her. My father had enough honor left to smuggle
190

me and my dear sister to London. She quickly found a fiancé and started a family, and I came to America with Frederick, the young Texas lad. They took us in, gave us a home, loved us, and protected us. And I... I killed..."

Arisztid buried his face in his hands, and an inarticulate, painful scream escaped him.

"Sheriff! Look at me! Don't leave me!" Dalton called out. "Even if you're not able to, I swear I'll avenge Frederick and free the children! If nothing else... At least I can ease my conscience somewhat."

The noise of footsteps could be heard from outside. Boots clattered, voices reached their ears, and then the curtained door swung open. Joseph stood before them, accompanied by two Native Americans. White feathers adorned his head, his face covered with red and white war paint. A bloody cross was drawn on his forehead. He briefly observed the traces of the bloody reckoning, then smirked mockingly at Arisztid. He held a rope in his hand, then gestured to his companion, who opened the cell door. Joseph stepped in front of the sheriff and firmly seized his hands, tying them up. Arisztid didn't resist; he simply bowed his head in resignation. Dalton shook his head in defeat as Joseph moved to do the same to him. The Native American pushed the two men toward the door. "The Father has entrusted me to send you to the afterlife," Joseph said hoarsely. "And I'm happy to oblige."

Arisztid looked at Dalton, a wicked glint reflecting in his eyes this time, and Jonathan felt relieved to see that his words might have had a positive effect after all. "If this is the Lord's will... Who am I to contradict him?" he replied, then walked toward the door with his captors.

Outside, a covered wagon with bars awaited them. After they boarded, Arisztid spoke to Dalton once more: "I sincerely hope that Mr. White and the others are watching over us somewhere and will rescue us."

Chapter Seven

"For false messiahs and false prophets will appear and perform great signs and wonders to deceive, if possible, even the elect."

Matthew 24:24

Ramirez stood at the door of the chapel, listening to the screams. They had become increasingly rare lately, and he couldn't decide why. Perhaps they had grown accustomed to the cruelty, maybe a few more had perished, or perhaps their sane minds had ceased to exist. He loathed the screams. He leaned his shoulder against the hard stone wall and looked at his hands; hands that had taken so many lives already and would commit so much more horror, yet he felt no remorse. His life had gained meaning on the day he first saw the holy angel of the Lord. He thought of his father, who beat and humiliated him because of his ability to hear God's calling. No matter how he tried to convince him, explaining the angels' greetings, his father scorned him. He tortured him and locked him away in darkness. He sighed. He knew these days were coming to an end. Forever. The thought of the new children abducted from Corpus Christi came to his mind. A soft smile spread across his face as he thought about how these youths would also become messengers of the Lord. He turned around and hurried to the altar through the chapel. He paused for a moment, took a deep breath, and opened the massive metal door. The door creaked loudly as it opened, revealing a chamber behind it. His gaze rose to the three-meter-high, five-meter-wide thick steel cage. The being watched him. He could feel its blessed gaze on him. Its golden crown shimmered with a pale light in the faint glow, and the click of its insect-like legs echoed in the chamber. He knelt one meter away from the cage and made the sign of the cross. "Praised be Jesus Christ!" he said, causing the creature to hiss loudly.

He swallowed hard, sweat dripping down his temples, his gaze fixed on the ground, then continued: "Forgive my sins, O holy angel of God! Forgive my weaknesses, have mercy on me and my fellow monks, the warriors of faith. Their fear is too great, and their understanding is so little! They are but men who have completely severed themselves from God's love and true faith because of the Church's fault!"

The creature turned its head sideways, its long, golden hair cascading onto its chest, then slowly approached the bars. It reached its arm through them and caressed Ramirez's face. Its skin was cold, hard, and rough. It emanated the scent of death, yet the man eagerly absorbed it. The creature spoke in a deep, resonant, otherworldly voice: "Have you obtained it?"

Ramirez hastily reached into his pocket and pulled out the vial filled with the sheriff's blood, which he held up while still staring at the ground. The creature emitted a high-pitched, sharp sound, which reminded the father most of the sound of joy. "Two more, and your companions will be free," it said with reverence in its voice. "The Angelic Truth will shine through your guidance!" With a sudden movement, the creature seized Ramirez, and forcefully pressed his body against the bars. The man's hat fell to the ground, his eyes bulged as the air escaped from his lungs. He gasped for air, but the grip was too strong. He heard the creature's jaw loudly snap, and knew its fang had emerged. Saliva dripped onto his neck, burning his skin. The fang scratched, touched his face, got stuck in his nose, but didn't pierce it.

"And the girl?" echoed the voice in his head, sending a terrible pain through his head.

He choked, unable to speak due to the pressure; his face reddened, veins bulged on his neck and temples. Sensing the man's suffering, the creature relented its grip slightly but still didn't let go. "Not yet... I don't know the whole truth..." The Mexican man coughed, and the creature roughly pushed him away. Ramirez stumbled forward, then dropped to all fours, gasping for air. He turned towards the cage, pressed his forehead to the ground, and pleaded, "Have mercy on me! Soon my brethren will learn the full..."

"FINISH HIM!" The creature roared so loudly that the walls trembled.

Ramirez covered his ears with his hands and curled up in a fetal position on the ground. He whimpered, his mouth foaming, and the agonizing headache from his childhood overtook him. He felt his mind engulfed in darkness, his body weakening, and emptiness sucking him in. Rolling onto his back, he felt hot liquid dripping onto his skin, flowing onto his face and into his mouth. His mind returned from the darkness, and with great effort, he managed to open his eyes and saw the creature feeding on the vial of blood. Ramirez opened his mouth and greedily swallowed the fluid, which replenished him with new strength. He sat up, then turned towards the bars, and answered in a determined voice: "You will not be disappointed in me... Master!"

Kassandra took a deep breath, then slowly exhaled. Her whole body trembled. While the withdrawal symptoms had eased, the pain returned intermittently. Her captors hadn't attempted to force another dose down her throat, but she didn't wish to tempt her luck, so she didn't provoke them either. She remained silent, carrying out their vile, disgusting commands without a word. Guilt gnawed at her for bringing the sisters to this place. Her prayers fell on deaf ears. Ever since she saw the evil in the chapel, she had known with absolute certainty that God was real. If evil incarnates, then the Lord must exist somewhere. She wanted to pour her heart out to someone, to tell the whole truth, even if it meant defying the Holy Father's command. A bitter, wry smile played on her face. *If I've already broken all my vows, why would I keep this one*? She looked at herself, her gaze lingering on her own unkempt, sin-stained, dirty body. She had been warned in Rome that she would experience horrors, but she had never thought it would be like this... With her dirty fingers, she raked through her disheveled hair and plucked out a cockroach. She flicked the insect away, and it scurried frantically towards a tiny hole in the corner. She looked up, the dim candle barely illuminating the gray stone walls of the small cell, almost burnt to the stub. Her heartbeat quickened as the thought dawned on her... If it burned out, darkness would engulf her. She lowered her head, and tears streamed down her face. She heard the sound of crying, realizing that it wasn't just her own soul's pain torturing her. She crawled to the wall and removed the stone, looking for Sister Judith, but in vain.

"Sister Judith!" she called. "Sister Judith, please answer!"

The crying ceased, replaced only by sniffles and groans in response. Kassandra closed her eyes, filled with pain for her companion's suffering. She wanted to help her. "Speak to me, sister! You've always been so strong and steadfast! Please don't give up now!" she pleaded.

"Why shouldn't I give up?" came the choked response.

She didn't know what to say. She would have been ashamed to answer that God's ways were inscrutable, that the Creator had a purpose, that He tested their faith. She wiped her eyes, then replied: "What if I told you who I really am? Perhaps in that light, you might see the situation differently."

Sister Judith let out a bitter laugh. " Sister Gareth!" she said. "Although I'm not sure if I can even call you that... Can you say anything that would make this place less torturous? Do you believe that someone is attempting to rescue us?"

"I believe, sister, that the sheriff of Corpus Christi is coming after us... After all, it's not just us who have disappeared, but the altar boys too."

"He's just a drunken fool!" Judith replied. "He can only find his way to the brothel."

"He's much more than you think!" Kassandra replied. "I know he's coming for us, and he'll set us free. If not him... then the Holy Father will send someone, an entire army of rescuers!"

"What makes you so sure of this?"

"Because he entrusted me with something that is of utmost importance to him. If I fail, much stronger forces than me will come, and not alone, like me! "

"What is so important to the Holy Father?"

Kassandra sighed. Every part of her soul wished to speak, yet she didn't want to break her promise. Thoughts raced through her mind, and she decided to choose mercy. "Ecclesia veritatis angelicae..." she uttered aloud. "The Church of the Angelic Truth. Have you ever heard of it?"

"Never in my life."

"An extremist Christian group," Sister Gareth replied dryly. "A year and a half ago, when they attempted to kill the Holy Father..."

Judith gasped. "They tried to kill the Holy Father?" she asked in a trembling voice.

"Yes. That's when we learned about their existence. Pope Pius sent out the Vatican's best investigators around the world... including me."

Tense silence fell over the dungeon.

"The assailant was a member of the Swiss Guard; he took his own life before we could interrogate him. We found one of their correspondences while searching the barracks. After the assassination attempt, he was supposed to report to Castel Sant'Angelo. The Angel Castle in Rome. So we went there. While searching the catacombs, we found traces of blasphemous rituals that trample on God's teachings, which I couldn't have imagined before. They carved names, words I didn't understand, shadows, grotesque figures on the walls. Above their altars, however... Well, we saw that same evil painted on the wall that we saw with our own eyes in the chapel... Pope Pius personally inspected the scene. I will never forget his face. You know, the Holy Father is a very cheerful, kind, sincere, and lovable person. He cares for others, never prioritizes his own needs, but always those of the needy, the afflicted. He is not afraid of the people because he has nothing to fear. But there... I saw terror in him. Not like when we are startled by the unknown... But when an old fear manifests... The Holy Father knew exactly what it was, and he only said: 'We must find the Black Monastery, we must bring home the records of Edward Kelley and John Dee!'"

"But the Black Monastery is just a legend!" Judith interjected.

"Well, Sister, I believe we are there now."

"You think so?" she asked in astonishment. "But didn't the Holy Father tell you?"

"The truth is, he himself doesn't know exactly where it is. We searched the Vatican archives for days unsuccessfully, but we found a letter. Pope Leo X sent a letter to Hernan Cortés, the famous Spanish conquistador. He practically begged him to take apocryphal documents, scrolls, and records that should never fall into the hands of the Ottoman Empire. So Cortés made a deal with the Church, and for decades, the Spaniards brought to the new colony everything that the Vatican feared. Popes changed, but the agreement lived on until the monastery was completed, where they hid everything that the Church feared, didn't understand, or tried to conceal. The monks of the Black Monastery were chosen by Pope Leo X, members of knightly orders who swore to protect the secrets at all costs, even at the cost of their lives, they could never fall into the wrong hands. All the records about the monastery were destroyed, they didn't tell the Pope exactly where it was, so that he couldn't reveal it even under physical torture. But it seems that centuries have corrupted the monks. We believe that the headquarters of the Church of the Angelic Truth is the Black Monastery itself, so I came to Corpus Christi. The city has Mexican roots, the convent was built by the first Spanish conquerors. It quickly became clear that I was in the right place. I found traces of human trafficking, prostitution, séances. The pastors and priests of the surrounding villages all died, and their places were taken by those who are not Protestants, not Catholics, but their followers... Children disappeared, young nuns were transported in chains to Europe on Austrian ships... The threads reach much deeper than we ever dared to think."

A heavy silence fell, but Kassandra continued with all her strength: "I rushed to Corpus Christi as fast as I could. Once I realized who was behind it all, I sent a letter to the Holy Father. The letter left the United States, but Ramirez struck the city church just as he did the convent."

"So help is coming?" she asked hopefully.

"Yes, Sister!" said Kassandra firmly. "Don't give up! The Lord has not forgotten about you either!"

Father Cristofano stood in front of the house of old Rodrigo, gazing at the sky. He took in the cold night air and sighed. Sleep was elusive for him. Peering over his shoulder, he looked through the half-open door at the men lying on the ground. Though he was sure they were not sleeping peacefully, they were asleep nonetheless. Sadness settled in his soul at the realization that they had not been told the whole truth. Doubt plagued him. Their mission transcended the boundaries of honor, and they were priests who should have represented the truth. No mercy or grace could come from this falsehood. He needed to ease his conscience, but there was no one nearby with whom he could share his doubts. The painting he saw inside had shocked him. He pondered. What else could have leaked out of the monastery over the centuries? He rubbed his face and then looked straight ahead into the distance. He himself had not anticipated such difficult weeks as the ones they had just endured, despite being prepared for it. He doubted the honesty of the Vatican. *If we do not tell the whole truth, perhaps they are also keeping something from us?* he asked himself. He knew the answer. He laughed bitterly and kicked a stone aside. *Of course, they haven't told us everything...*

He heard footsteps approaching behind him, turned around and saw Father Agustino. His face, too, appeared troubled by doubts, yet his determination seemed unshakeable.

"Can't sleep, Father?" he asked, then amiably patted Cristofano's shoulder.

"Doubts torment me, Father Agustino," he replied, then looked at the sleepers. "We are unfair to them because they know nothing about the sect."

"Sect?" Agustíno asked. "Why do you call them a sect?"

"Because they kill people, extort, rape, commit adultery, and have strayed from the right path!"

"Perhaps we haven't killed anyone over the past centuries?" the old priest pondered. "Perhaps we haven't extorted, raped, or erased other cultures from the face of the earth? But we have..."

"But we live according to God's commandments! Our deeds are forgiven if we do the will of the Lord!"

"Was it God's will for us to slaughter priests and priestesses of other religions, desecrate their temples, and build our own in their place? The Lord never asked us to do such things. He didn't ask us to persecute scholars or go on crusades. This whole thing..." He sighed. "It's nothing but politics. The Catholic Church no longer represents God; it only pursues its own ambitions."

Cristofano couldn't believe his ears; the words of the older priest deeply shocked him. "How can you say such a thing? This is offensive to God!"

"Lies are an offense in the eyes of the Lord!" Agustíno said decisively, looking his companion in the eye. "The Church needs reform; you know this, too! Perhaps we should allow the Angelic Truth to unfold..."

The young priest stepped back incredulously, covering his mouth in horror. "How dare you suggest such a thing? The Angelic Truth is a cult playing with forces beyond comprehension! The Holy Father knew very well why those writings had to be hidden!" Cristofano stared deeply into his eyes, then continued suspiciously. "Father... What is your real intention, and what are you hiding from me?"

Agustíno stepped closer, and in a low, almost whispering voice, he continued: "The Holy Father entrusted us to immediately deliver the notes of John Dee and Edward Kelley back to the Vatican, along with Kassandra Gareth," he declared, and his companion nodded. "But I want to understand the Angelic Truth! What we saw on the farm, the corpse... I've seen such things before, years ago in Damascus. We went there because of an alleged angelic apparition. You know how this works!" He waved dismissively. "The Church now receives miracles and apparitions with skepticism, but there was a time when these were almost everyday occurrences! You know it yourself! But now there are investigation committees, bureaucracy, paperwork, gathering evidence, interrogating witnesses. Faith is lost! But I believe that what happened in Damascus is happening here now, too. The painting inside!" He pointed towards the house. "The people of Damascus unanimously confessed that an angel with a golden crown and blond hair emerged from the mountains! We searched for weeks! Months, we were on its trail, but we found nothing... Only the bodies. If it happens here too, if the Angelic Truth has found the sealed ones... Can you grasp, Father, what that would mean?"

"Kasbeel refused to betray his brethren! He remained loyal to his comrades, and for that, Michael locked him away in the mountain with more than twenty thousand other angels!"

"Even if he did escape in Damascus and somehow ended up here... He still killed people!"

"He was hungry!" Agustíno explained. "Don't forget... As punishment, they were forced into flesh-and-blood bodies that need sustenance! Think about it!" the old priest said excitedly. "If the Pope saw it, if the believers saw a real angel, we would eradicate Islam! The Jews! Every other religion! The unbelievers would bow down to us, and we could bring earthly paradise without bloodshed! Have you read the book of Revelation, Father? You know exactly what the second coming of Christ will look like... But no one should be damned if everyone were believers! Because they would see with their own eyes that we are the truth!"

Cristofano stepped back. Despite the cold, sweat covered his body, and his hands trembled. The words spoken had shocked him. "And what is your plan, Father?" he asked skeptically.

"Let us surrender ourselves to the Angelic Truth!" Agustíno wiped his face and continued. "Think about it! Whoever this Ramirez is, he doesn't stand a chance against our team! He will fail. However, we cannot allow Kasbeel to slip away from us!"

"And if our team fails?" Cristofano asked suspiciously.

"If we were to 'disappear' too," his companion went on, "then the Vatican would send greater forces here. We are believers, and that is important. We came from Rome, we carry a thousand secrets, so the Angelic Truth needs us. If they don't capture us by force, but we go there... then they will accept us. Let us lead this church and unite with the Vatican! This is how it should be!"

He stepped closer again and placed his hand on Cristofano's chest: "You are a true believer, my friend... Just like me. Think about it!" he said determinedly. "Would it have been a mere coincidence that we had to come to Corpus Christi? The body of Christ... and the fact that the White brothers said yes? That Jonathan Dalton, one of America's best shooters, happened to be there? That the sheriff knows the Bearslayer? We have a team of fearless warriors behind us, who can easily crush this sect... And I am sure we will find a way to present the angel as evidence to the Vatican..."

"What makes you so sure about this?" Cristofano asked.

"Because the Lord is with us! And we are bringing back not just the notes requested by His Holiness, but much more than that! We are bringing back certainty to the Church. We are restoring humanity's faith... Didn't you swear to this? So, what do you say, will you come with me, Cristofano?" he asked, then reached out his hand.

The young priest stared at Agustíno's outstretched hand for a brief moment, then grabbed it firmly, shaking hands. "I am with you, Father!"

The first rays of the sun appeared on the horizon, and Bearslayer almost immediately woke up. His body was covered in cold sweat, his hands trembling. Nightmares never left him alone; recurring memories had tortured him since childhood; he was just a little child when the Comanches raided his village. Bruce wiped his face and sighed. The scent of his mother's hair, his father's dry, tough, yet loving hands that he could almost feel on his face, flashed in his mind. Decades had passed, but the wound in his soul never truly healed. The Comanches, showing no mercy, had slaughtered everyone in the village, and he watched his loved ones' painful deaths as they lay hidden in the hay. He sat up and slowly stood up. He walked to the window, leaned on the sill, and gazed into the distance. Outside, Indians were killing again with impunity. The child had grown into a man, and he knew there was no justice, only interests. At barely thirteen, he had been taken in by a fur trader family who raised him as their own. As soon as he was old enough, he joined the army and fought in the Indian wars. A sound of movement caught his ear, he turned around and saw Jeremiah also sitting up.

"Is there coffee even in the middle of nowhere?" the bounty hunter asked.

Bruce smiled. "I doubt it."

Jeremiah kicked his brother's leg, waking him.

"What the...?" Anton rubbed his head, then looked at his brother. "What do you want?"

"Get up! We need to go!"

"I agree, Mr. White," Bearslayer said. "We need to reach the fort by this morning."

Anton got up, then took out his flask and took a big gulp from it before offering it to his brother.

Jeremiah shook his head. "We're heading into battle, I don't drink at times like this," he declared.

The young bounty hunter shrugged, then took another sip. The strong alcohol sent shivers down his spine; he shook himself, then slowly got up. "You know what this reminds me of, Jer?" he asked. "Those days when we waited for the dirty Yankees' attacks at dawn." He chuckled. "We kicked some northern ass, didn't we, bro?"

"As you say," Jeremiah replied, slinging his bag over his shoulder. "Sometimes we kicked their asses, and sometimes they kicked ours. Many good men fell in those days..."

Anton raised his flask again, then said respectfully, "To our fallen comrades!" He took more sips, then sighed. "And you, Bruce? Where did you fight?"

"I didn't participate."

The White brothers paused in their movements, then looked at him with surprise.

"Just you? How's that possible?" Jeremiah asked.

"I don't want to kill Americans. Only redskins. I fought in the Indian wars, but we Americans are all brothers."

"Those northern bastards are not my brothers!" Anton retorted.

"Where did your ancestors come from, Mr. White?" Bruce asked.

"Our family comes from the British Isles, from England," replied the elder bounty hunter.

"I'll tell you, most of the Northerners do too. Irish, Scots, English, Welsh... Of course, there are also French, Germans, Spaniards, Portuguese, and who knows who else, but I hope you understand that we almost all came from a common homeland. The redskins didn't."

"But this is their land," Jeremiah replied. "And we took it from them. We massacre their people, confine them to reservations, and call them natives. We treat them like animals. It's understandable that they don't like us very much..."

"Have you ever killed an Indian?" Bruce asked.

The elder White shook his head. "When I accept a contract, I never look at the color of their skin. If someone needs to be killed, they die. If they need to be brought in alive, we do it. If someone needs protection, we protect them. Ancestry doesn't matter."

"It's all about the money..." Bearslayer shook his head disapprovingly.

"Just the money," Jeremiah nodded. "But we should be going now."

Old Rodrigo cleared his throat as he tossed a huge sack among the men. "Gentlemen, put these on so you don't stick out immediately! They're just ponchos, but you can hide your weapons and clothes underneath them perfectly. Leave your horses behind and cover the last mile on foot. Don't worry, they won't hurt you because they're preparing for a spectacle."

"Are executions common in the fortress?" Bruce asked.

"Oh, yes!" the old man replied. "Far too common."

Bruce persisted, asking, "Are there still some who resist them?"

Rodrigo shook his head. "Most of them are already dead, the rest have fled or are hiding."

"Then we might catch them off-guard," Anton interjected. "If there's no resistance, perhaps we can surprise them. We did relatively well in Matamoros."

"That's exactly why they'll be prepared, brother!" Jeremiah cut in. "We only have one chance, if we mess it up, we all die." He looked up at the priests. "Are we ready to go?"

Both men nodded, but Rodrigo stepped in front of them. "What if the fathers stayed behind? What use would two lamb-hearted holy men be in battle? But I am old now, my body can't handle the strain like it used to. I'd appreciate it if you helped me around the house until you return."

The two priests reluctantly glanced at each other, then at the bounty hunter.

After a long, awkward moment, Jeremiah finally broke the silence: "Rodrigo is right! You would indeed be of no use in battle. And you have no objection to helping out here, do you?" Without waiting for an answer, he clapped his hands together and turned to the others. "Excellent! So be it! Everyone check your weapons and ammunition, and on the way, we'll discuss how to rescue the others!"

They conducted a final check on their weapons, on their ammunition belts. They filled their canteens, grabbed some food, and saddled their horses. The two priests stood in front of the small house, watching as they rode off into the distance, hoping it wouldn't be the last time they saw them.

Agustíno glanced back over his shoulder at the old man, Rodrigo. He saw a glint of deceit in the old man's eyes, but he couldn't decipher its meaning.

"Come inside, gentlemen, I wish to speak with you," the old man said.

The two priests exchanged glances once again, then followed the man into the house.

Rodrigo moved slowly, with tired steps, towards his worn armchair, and sat down heavily. He sighed deeply, keeping his gaze fixed on the priests. Agustíno and Cristofano sat opposite him, and an awkward silence filled the room. "I won't beat around the bush, Father," Rodrigo said. "I overheard you last night." The old man squinted disapprovingly, then leaned closer to them. "You have no idea what kind of game you're getting into."

"And what about you?" Agustíno asked. "How do you know about the monastery?" He gestured towards the painting. "You said you brought it from there. How did you get in?"

"I was once a monk," Rodrigo replied. "But that was many years ago! Things were different back then. In those years, when I was young and strong, I believed that the Lord had tasked me with guarding his secrets. I acted accordingly, but nobody guarded us, and that was the problem."

"What do you mean by that? How come nobody guarded you?"

"You see, the founding monks were warriors. Valiant soldiers of glorious knightly orders. They could face Indians, plunderers, thieves, and rapists. But as the years passed and they returned their souls to the Creator, it seemed their abilities for self-defense disappeared as well. They didn't take wives, didn't bear children, so all that was left for us, the monks who remained, was to accept and make monks out of the few weak wanderers who joined us. As the centuries passed, the Black Monastery became nothing more than a gathering place for old men, even forgotten by the Catholic Church itself. It was just a legend, known only to us. But the treasures we guarded... they hold immeasurable value for those who know how to use them. Thieves came, plunderers, not to mention Indian attacks. But they never took the real treasures, only the chalices, crosses, silver, and gold. Nothing we couldn't replace. But human lives..." He sighed. "If it wasn't the attackers who killed one of us, it was illness, old age, or accident. I still remember the day when the Indians appeared on the hill opposite the monastery. There were so many. And we, with trembling knees, fervently prayed to the Lord to protect us. And He did. To our greatest surprise, He did. That day, for the last time in my life, I felt that God was with me. When they stormed our temple, shots rang out. Only one man stood in front of the monastery door. We didn't see when he appeared, it was as if he had emerged from nowhere. His hands moved so quickly, as if he weren't human, and the Indians fell like flies." The old man crossed himself, then continued, "God forgive me, but I was terribly happy that those poor souls died. My fellow monks rejoiced and, as soon as the battle ended, they opened the gate. It was Diego. The others, of course, immediately welcomed him, they didn't ask anything. And that day... That day everything changed."

"What happened?" asked Cristofano.

"Diego was a good boy. Enthusiastic, well-educated. He was intelligent and brave. He immediately won over the monks. Many times, he knocked on the door of my bedroom at night; I had never seen him afraid, except on those nights. I remember his confusion, even shame, for what was happening to him. He confided in me that he heard voices. Believe me, gentlemen, among the monks, it's a very bad omen if someone hears voices. He confessed regularly, and what he confessed horrified even me, though I knew Diego better than anyone... As months went by, he asked more and more about our library. None of us wanted to talk about it at first. We had a rule, laid down by the founding knights, and it was never to be broken; it was forbidden to use, read, translate, or apply the writings of our secret library. They were kept in bolted chests, chained, buried, and hidden behind stone walls for centuries. But Diego brought more young men, with blind zeal and fanatical faith in their hearts. He trained them, turned them into warriors. The attacks ceased. By the time we realized we were much safer during the attacks, it was too late; we had become prisoners in God's house. They broke into the secret library, tore down the walls, and cut the chains. The monastery was no longer God's house but his madness, his evil. We became the temple of blasphemy, and Diego changed forever. He used the chapel for rituals that shouldn't exist. My companions who tried to oppose him died, the others submitted. Diego began to travel. You know those records left behind by our predecessors, they contain many references to other... how should I say? 'Apocryphal documents'. At the end of his travels, he always returned with more and more writings, objects, and relics, but once he brought something else... A huge chest, with engravings and inscriptions on the side that I had never seen before. It was a pale, golden chest, with a name on the side."

"Kasbeel," said Agustíno.

"Exactly," replied Rodrigo. "And I didn't hesitate; I left the monastery with the painting."

"Why did Diego allow this?" asked Cristofano.

"Even I don't know that. But you are about to meet him, aren't you? Ask him if you truly wish to, but believe me, you won't survive that."

Sweat beaded on Cristofano's forehead; he fidgeted in his seat, nervously. "But what is the purpose of all this?" he asked.

"I pondered on that for a long time myself," Rodrigo said grimly. "Diego showed serious interest in the Vigilantes. Many times... he made blasphemous statements, pushing the boundaries. He believed that the Lord had erred in judgment regarding them, that He had made a mistake. He began to seek them out, and I believe he found one."

"The Lord erred?!" the young priest burst out. "The Creator is infallible, perfect, and almighty! It's impossible for a Mexican vagabond, a murderer, to find and unleash..." His voice froze. His pupils dilated, his lips began to tremble. He raised his gaze to his companion, then continued slowly, almost whispering: "Unless the Lord has a purpose..."

"Diego believes that too, that he was placed in the monastery for a reason, and everything he does happens according to the plan and will of the Lord."

"Could it be possible?" asked Agustíno. "Do you think it's possible that Diego is truly moved by a divine plan?"

Rodrigo sighed and shook his head. "I strongly doubt that the Almighty would be capable of doing this. The Vigilantes were not imprisoned without reason."

"But if we could manage to get them to the Vatican and people saw, then we would triumph once and for all!" said the old priest.

"Do you think so? Believe me, Kasbeel is no longer what it once was, just a monster that seeks to feed."

"But if people were to see that a real angel walks among us..."

"Do not forget, Father," Rodrigo interjected, "when the Vigilantes last walked among people, the Creator destroyed humanity with the flood, leaving only Noah and his family alive! The world has since become much worse. Perhaps we wouldn't get another chance, and this time the Lord would finally destroy us."

Bruce casually held the reins and gazed into the distance, taking in the landscape spread out before him. He knew well where the fortress was located. He had heard about the executions and tortures, but so far, he had managed to steer clear of that place. He reached for his flask and poured some of the still cool water down his dry throat. Wiping his mouth, he then looked at the two brothers. He saw determination, firm will, and readiness in them. He had also heard about the exploits of the White brothers, knew their dubious reputation, and what he had seen from them so far had not disappointed him. "We'll reach the edge of the valley soon. It's time to put on the ponchos," he said.

"I agree," Jeremiah replied, "although I doubt it can hide us."

"They don't know our faces," Anton interjected. "If they don't see our weapons, there won't be a problem."

"Oh, don't worry!" Bearslayer grinned. "Getting in won't be a problem. Getting out... that's where the trouble lies."

"We've been in tight spots before," the elder White said. "We'll figure it out."

"I have no doubt about that, Mr. White!"

"What kind of fortress is this, anyway?" Anton asked.

Bruce looked at the men again, then spoke after a brief silence: "It's an old Spanish fortress, built by the first conquerors. I heard that after the invasion of Emperor Napoleon, it was taken over by soldiers of the Monarchy."

"Are they still there?" Jeremiah asked. "Do the soldiers collaborate with the indigenous people?"

"I heard Diego bribed the captain, who handed over the structure to him. Neither the French nor the Monarchy's men care about it; it's too remote. Juarez and the rebels are heading towards Mexico City. Here, everyone can do as they please."

"Sounds great," the elder bounty hunter said.

"European folks are different," replied Bearslayer calmly. "If you have money, you can get anything from them. They talk about honor, loyalty, and integrity, but as soon as the coins jingle, these values disappear instantly."

"So, you don't trust the sheriff either?" Anton asked.

Bruce raised his index finger, then answered decisively: "I'd entrust my life to him! But I hope it never comes down to his marksmanship in a duel!" He chuckled. "I'd surely end up six feet under then!"

The siblings chuckled too, then continued on their way. The dawn seemed to fade away, the biting cold giving way to the pleasant warmth of the morning. They advanced in silence until Jeremiah caught movement out of the corner of his eye. He looked up and immediately spotted a white dove soaring high above. Thoughts raced through his mind like lightning, and he didn't hesitate. He reached for his pistol and shot. The sound of the shot echoed through the valley, and the bird plummeted down. The others stopped and turned anxiously towards the direction of the shot, both reaching for their weapons, but they saw nothing. The elder White moved towards the dove, the others closely following in his footsteps. The elder bounty hunter found the bird. He dismounted and quickly approached it. It had been struck in the chest, with bloody feathers scattered around its body. Jeremiah reached for a paper attached to the bird's leg, took it off, unfolded the letter, read it, then looked at his brother.

"There's a traitor among us" he declared. *'They're heading towards the fort, finish them off*! ' That's all the letter says."

Bruce and Anton looked at each other incredulously.

"Well, who could it be?" asked his brother.

"The priests," Jeremiah replied without the slightest doubt. "This whole thing stank to me from the beginning! Let's go back!"

"What do you mean?" asked Bearslayer in surprise. "What makes you so sure about this, Mr. White? They wanted to come with us! Think about it! Why would they do such a thing?"

"Bruce is right," said Anton. "They paid us serious money, and we came here because of them. If they wanted us out of the way, they would've gotten rid of us long ago! They just had to ask! And we only just met the old man."

"I know Rodrigo, he wouldn't do this," said Bruce.

"Why not?" Anton shot back. "This is Mexico, these damn corn eaters would sell their children for a measly dollar!"

"I agree with Bruce," said Jeremiah. "I saw this dove at the port and towards Matamoros, too. It couldn't have been Rodrigo."

"So now I have to ask, who could it be then?" asked Bearslayer.

The elder White wiped his forehead, then pocketed the letter. He stood up, looked around. He surveyed the valley, observed every movement, every tiny motion, but saw no life other than themselves. "We were attacked on the road to Corpus Christi. In groups. They didn't seem like simple bandits. Their faces were covered with black scarves, just like their heads, like Arab warriors. Have you ever seen anything like this around here, Bruce?"

Bearslayer searched his memories, but only vague rumors came to mind. "I've only heard a rumor that spread rapidly when Napoleon's soldiers arrived."

"What kind of rumor?" Anton asked irritably.

"Allegedly, the Emperor is a very religious man and collects relics. I heard that he brought his treasure hunters from France. They attack under the cover of night, swiftly and lethally. They wrap their bodies in black rags, cover their faces, their names are shrouded in mystery, but I myself have never seen them. It just sounded like tavern gossip."

"The description fits them." Jeremiah nodded. "But they're not as deadly as you claim. They couldn't rob or injure us."

"But it seems they're on our trail." Anton grimaced. "Great! Crazy monks, bloodthirsty Indians, fanatical relic-hunting shadows! And if that wasn't enough, we left behind a bunch of angry bandits, frustrated whores, angry townsfolk in Matamoros; there's not a single doctor nearby, we could die from a moderate injury or be torn apart by hungry animals! And what do we have? A scalp hunter, the two of us, and a sheriff who can't aim!"

"Don't forget about the nun and the bastard deputy!" Bruce chuckled.

"And there's the nigger," added his brother.

"Now I feel much better!" Anton clapped his hands indignantly.

"Let's set aside our concerns and move forward!" Jeremiah said. "Let's watch for any suspicious signs. The traitor will try to strike again, but the element of surprise is on our side now; they won't be waiting for us in the fort!"

"Mr. White is right! This is the best and only chance we have to rescue them."

"That's right." Jer nodded. "Let's not waste any time."

They had barely been traveling for an hour when they reached an abandoned dirt road leading out of the valley. There were no signs of life here either, only a few footprints were visible in the dried dusty road. In the distance, they spotted the old, decrepit fortress. Indian warriors watched the landscape from its thick, high stone walls. Along the road leading to it, men and women walked on foot and on donkeys, heads bowed, fear in their eyes. Bruce, Anton, and Jeremiah dismounted and approached the structure on foot, leaving their horses behind, carefully surveying the surrounding area.

Anton pulled his hat over his face and watched the railway track next to the fortress. "Is there a railway here, Bruce?" he asked.

"They only transport military supplies. I have no idea exactly when."

Jeremiah took in what he had heard, then they headed towards the entrance of the fortress. Half-naked armed men stood on either side of the gate. Their faces were painted white, holy crosses hung around their necks, and their heads were adorned with black, red, and blue Native American feathers. Bearslayer's eyes radiated anger and disgust, and he had to gather all his strength to conceal his emotions. As they passed by the Indians, they only received insulting remarks, but they were able to enter without any trouble.

The younger bounty hunter separated from his companions at the stairs leading to the fortress wall and quietly disappeared. In the middle of the fortress, the gallows had already been set up with two ropes, waiting to take someone's life.

"You go left, I'll go right" Bruce whispered.

Jeremiah nodded. "I'll shoot the ropes, and you protect the sheriff, the deputy, and Dalton."

"There are only two ropes," the bounty hunter remarked. "According to Anton, the deputy is severely injured, perhaps already dead."

Bearslayer furrowed his brow with concern. "Then we'll save whoever we can," he declared.

They looked at each other once more, then headed in opposite directions, blending into the crowd.

Arisztid leaned against the cold, moldy stone wall with both hands. The dimly lit dungeon beneath the fortress was lit only by a small candle, barely illuminating the cramped space. The two men barely fit in the cell, which was at most two meters wide and three meters long. They had been transported under the cover of night, neither of them seeing exactly where from within the covered wagon. The sheriff's stomach growled from emptiness, his hands trembled from lack of alcohol, his mouth and throat completely dried from thirst. He felt nauseous, dizzy, but despite retching, nothing came up from his empty stomach.

Dalton sat beside him on the floor, leaning against the wall, doubt and fear emanating from his eyes. "Do you think they'll feed us?" Dalton asked. "I'm starving."

"Before the hanging? I doubt it," the sheriff replied resignedly. "Let's just be glad if they don't beat us again."

"Or scalp us," Jonathan said, immediately realizing what a mistake he had made.

Arisztid's hands clenched into fists, and he struck the wall hard, tears filling his eyes.

"I'm sorry, sheriff!" he said sincerely. "I didn't mean it that way... you know. I'm sorry."

Wratiszlaw's face twisted into a grimace, his heart pounding heavily, gritting his teeth as he responded: "You're right, captain. We should count ourselves lucky if they don't do to us what they did to Fred..." The sheriff's voice choked, then he covered his mouth with his hand. He stepped away from the wall, trying to wipe his face with his dirty sleeve, only managing to make it dirtier.

"Have you ever thought about what awaits us after death?" Dalton asked.

The sheriff looked at Jonathan, whose eyes radiated fear of death. It surprised him. He never would have thought that the dreaded marksman, the northern veteran, also feared death. *After all, he's only human,* he thought. "I believe, captain, that after death, nothing awaits us but emptiness."

"You said you were often sick as a child. Did you see something?"

"Don't be foolish!" Arisztid snapped. "I was sick, not dead. And when darkness engulfed me, I saw and felt nothing, I didn't even know about my own existence. I assume death isn't any better."

"And what if it's true?" Jonathan asked with faint hope in his voice. "What if what the Bible says is true?"

"Mr. Dalton, if it's true, then you and I will burn in the deepest pits of hell for eternity! Hope that nothing awaits you after death."

Dalton disappointedly lowered his gaze from the sheriff and stared ahead. He felt that neither in life nor in death could he have what he truly desired: peace and happiness. "It's unfair," the captain finally said. "We suffer, we endure, we fear and freeze in the trenches all our lives, only to have eternal fire as everyone's reward?"

"Not everyone's, just ours. You killed, plundered, robbed, murdered, and raped. What did you expect? Glory?"

"Or the seventy-two virgins," Jonathan smiled. "That would be something."

"I don't want to disappoint you, captain, but the Quran doesn't specify whether the seventy-two virgins awaiting us are male or female. I assume men aren't interested."

Disappointment and outrage spread across Dalton's face. He slapped his hands on the sheriff's legs. "To rob a person of even the slightest bit of hope and joy even at death's door! You're simply unbelievable! God damn you!" he burst out. "I don't want to die yet! There's so much I haven't done and so much..." His words faltered. "So much I've messed up, it's painful to admit even to myself. But I swear, sheriff, if we get out of here, everything will be different."

"I'm a sheriff, and I've sent countless people to the gallows," Arisztid began calmly. "And every one of them said exactly the same thing. And you know the terrible truth? If we ever let any of them go, they went right back to where they left off. And each one ended up in the grave, by rope or bullet."

"I'm not disappointed in you, sheriff. Not a single good word," Dalton retorted.

"I'm just sharing my experience, captain. Completely honestly. I don't believe that with your past, abilities, and experiences, you're capable of change. But God's ways are inscrutable, aren't they?"

Dalton chuckled, and Arisztid joined in.

They were in an impossible situation where both knew that death awaited them. The sheriff didn't want to die either, but he would never voice such fears. He had learned one thing well as a child; he had to conceal his fears and weaknesses, face them, and overcome them. Minutes passed in silence, then they heard footsteps from outside. Wratiszlaw knew what was coming. The noise of footsteps grew louder, and they stood up, exchanging glances. Arisztid reached out his hand to him. "Please accept my apology for feeding you a scorpion and trying to hang you," he said.

Jonathan returned the handshake, then replied: "I apologize for trying to rob your church. I'm sorry."

The sheriff nodded, and the door opened.

Joseph stood before them with a rifle in hand. "Move, you worthless scum!" he yelled. "It's time to send you before the Creator!"

They walked out the door, then through the dirty corridor to the stairs. They ascended and stepped into the sunlight, which blinded them both. Dalton tried to shade his eyes with his hands, while Arisztid turned his gaze away. Two Indians appeared in front of them, who grabbed their hands and tied them behind their backs. One of them pushed the two men forward, and they started towards the gallows. Arisztid looked up. Three steps led up to the wooden gallows. *Just like the one we built for Dalton*, the sheriff thought to himself. He surprised himself with how calm he remained. Death had been embracing him his whole life, and the moment seemed to have arrived to pull him in. He looked down, then stepped onto the stairs. The wood creaked under his weight as he climbed up. He stopped in front of the rope, examined it carefully, then bowed his head. His heart was pounding, yet somehow he managed to stay calm. Joseph grabbed him, then looped the noose around his neck. Tears streamed down Dalton's face as he stood beside him. Arisztid looked up, then began to scan the crowd. Elderly men and women stood before the gallows, fear and pity reflected in their faces. Arisztid was sure that deep down, they were glad not to be the ones in the executioner's hands this time. He looked to his left and caught a brief glimpse of a familiar face. Bruce.

Joseph slapped him across the face and stared deeply into his eyes. "Now you're going to die, bastard," he said with hate in his voice. "Do you wish for the last rites?"

"Oh, certainly!" the sheriff replied. "With another last rite, I'll almost become innocent."

Joseph slapped him again and then spat on him. "I despise your kind. You mock the power and strength of the Creator! The world is about to change, but you won't see it."

The warrior stepped back, then made the sign of the cross in front of Arisztid and spoke with reverence: "May the Lord, by His great mercy and grace, help you through this holy anointment; may He deliver you from your sins, save you, and strengthen you kindly!" This time, Joseph stepped closer to the sheriff and addressed him threateningly. "Would you like to say anything in your final words?"

"Yes," nodded Arisztid. "Do you wish for the last rites?"

The Indian's pupils dilated, then he stepped back in surprise. He looked around but didn't see anything suspicious. He snarled and pulled the lever. The floor beneath the sheriff opened up, and he began to fall. The rope around his neck tightened, cutting deeply into his flesh. The remaining air rushed out of his lungs, and he began to suffocate. His body convulsed involuntarily, his eyes bulged, saliva dripped from his mouth. His heart pounded fiercely in his chest, desperately trying to reach the life-giving air. He heard the sound of a gunshot, then suddenly continued to fall. He hit the ground hard. He started coughing. He struggled with the ropes tying his wrists and managed to get a hand free, then reached up and loosened the noose around his neck, slipping it back over his head. He rolled onto his side and looked for Dalton.

Jonathan was already sitting, not understanding what was happening around him. "What's going on here?!" he yelled amidst the chaos.

"The White brothers have arrived."

Chapter Eight

"For I will gather all the nations against Jerusalem to battle, and the city shall be taken and the houses plundered and the women raped. Half of the city shall go out into exile, but the rest of the people shall not be cut off from the city."

Zechariah 14:2

Entering the fortress, Anton nodded towards his brother before rushing up the stairs and finding himself in a corridor. The ancient stone walls were gray, adorned with moss and mold between the stones, while crates and barrels lined the base, providing ideal hiding spots. Stealthily moving along the wall, he heard voices. Crouching beside one of the crates, he tried to conceal himself and eavesdrop. Two Indians walked side by side, one clutching a rifle, the other holding a white dove and attaching a paper to its leg. Similar birds lined the ledges, each carrying a message or ready to have one attached to their leg. The younger White was astonished by the quantity of messages. He had never imagined such an extensive and coordinated armed group beyond the military. As the Indians conversed, they stopped. Anton took a knife from his pocket and aimed at the unarmed man. Gripping the knife tightly, his fingers almost whitening, he took a deep breath and grabbed the Indian's hair. The warrior was stunned, but before he could react, Anton jerked his head back and swiftly slit his throat. The Indian choked, spat blood, then grasped his throat and fell to his knees. Before the other could react, Anton plunged his knife between that man's ribs, forcing the blade in and up, into the lung. Younger White exerted his full weight on the warrior, covering his mouth as he removed the blade and thrust again, this time, into his heart. His body slackened, and Anton let him fall to the ground. He wiped the blade of his knife on the victim, then took his rifle. Looking around, he saw nothing else. He checked the cartridges, then approached the window and saw Arisztid and Dalton, as an Indian was placing a rope around each of their necks. The painted-faced warrior made the sign of the cross over the sheriff and said something to him. The sheriff replied with a half-smile, visibly annoying the man, who pulled a lever, and the floor opened. Anton felt he was too late and could only hope that Dalton and the sheriff's necks wouldn't break from the fall. He raised the rifle to his shoulder, then fired a shot, and another. Both ropes snapped, and Wratiszlaw and Jonathan fell to the ground. Younger White didn't have time to ensure their safety; he seized the brief advantage. He fired another shot, dispatching the confused Indian near the gallows. The crowd began to scream and flee in all directions. Chaos erupted among the Indians. Anton scanned the scene for Bearslayer and his brother, who were already at the fortress wall, firing from cover at the warriors. Younger bounty hunter fired another shot, killing another Indian. Screams echoed from the corridor, and he glanced up. Two men were running in his direction, but hadn't noticed him yet. He loaded his gun and stepped out from behind the crate, firing a shot. The bullet tore through one warrior's chest, causing him to scream in agony and collapse.

Anton didn't wait for his partner's reaction; he fired again. The shot ripped through the man's throat, and he grabbed at it, dropping his weapon and falling. Anton dashed forward. He ran down the stairs, into the fortress courtyard, to Dalton and the sheriff. "Let's go, let's go! There's no time, we have to go!" he said, reloading and firing again.

Arisztid was still coughing, as was Jonathan, but they both got to their feet and started running. Bullets rained down, tearing up the ground or slamming into the fortress walls. The crowd stampeded, screaming, toward the gate as the Indians opened fire on them. As injured people fell to the ground, the others trampled over them until their cries for help faded away.

Arisztid pushed the fleeing people aside and hurried to the entrance of the underground dungeon. When he reached it, he and Dalton leaned their backs against the wall, waiting for Anton, who was retreating.

Younger White took cover, then yelled over his shoulder to the pair. "Go down already, come on! We don't have time to wait!"

"And how am I supposed to go down without a weapon?!" Arisztid snapped. "Should I kindly ask them not to shoot us?!"

"Take my revolver out of my holster!" Anton said. "Do you know where their weapons are?"

"Yes," Dalton replied. "I saw where they put them. Sheriff, do you mind if I have the pistol?"

Wratiszlaw rolled his eyes angrily, then responded irritably: "But not to shoot me down!" He pointed his finger at Jonathan.

"I'll stick to my word, Sheriff."

"Let's go already!" Anton yelled.

Dalton took the bounty hunter's pistol, then glanced towards the staircase. Seeing no movement, he aimed his weapon ahead and started descending, with Arisztid following closely behind.

In the dimly lit corridor, the fierce battle above became increasingly muffled. Dalton burned with combat fever, determinedly advancing towards their former cell.

Meanwhile, the sheriff felt like the narrow corridors were closing in on him. The sight of the torch-lit narrow spaces, rusty bars, and moldy doors turned his stomach. He felt the onset of nausea once again. Leaning against the wall, his heart pounded wildly, stars danced before his eyes. His head spun, and terror immediately gripped him as a foreign voice echoed in his head. "Come to me!" it said. Arisztid's mouth gaped open, ready to vomit.

Jonathan opened the chest in front of the cell, removed the pistols, ammunition, and clothes, and without even looking at the sheriff, threw his belongings aside. "Pick them up and let's go!" he said.

Wratiszlaw reached for his gear with trembling legs. He felt like his head was splitting from the pain, almost all strength leaving his body. He strapped his bandolier around his waist and put on his vest, where a flask was hidden in the pocket. He opened it and drank its contents in one go. He looked up and watched Jonathan as he checked his weapons, loaded his revolver, and prepared his single stick of dynamite. "Finish him," the voice whispered, and the sheriff raised his pistol with trembling hands. He stared at the weapon, which gleamed silver in the pale light of the flickering torch. Taking hesitant steps, he circled around Dalton, who still hadn't noticed the sheriff's condition.

"Let's go, come on!" Jonathan started to run.

"Wait! " the sheriff called after him and raised his weapon. "Kill him!" the voice screamed in his head, and Arisztid grabbed his head with his free hand.

Dalton turned around and saw in astonishment that the sheriff was pointing his gun straight at him. "What the hell..."

The gun went off, muzzle flash flickering, and Jonathan couldn't react. He expected sharp, stabbing pain, but instead, he only heard a painful groan, followed by a dull thud. He turned around and saw an Indian emerging from one of the cells, collapsing lifeless. He turned back to the sheriff and nodded. "Nice shot," he said approvingly.

"It was just luck," Arisztid tried to joke, the voice in his head terrifying him to death. The compulsion had required all his strength to resist. He couldn't even tell exactly whom he had shot. Straightening up, he took a deep breath. Ignoring his suffering, he headed towards the stairs. They ran up to Anton, who was still firing. Meanwhile, Bruce and Jeremiah joined him.

Bruce looked at the sheriff, then greeted him with a wide smile, while firing several shots in rapid succession. "Sheriff! You still look like crap! Where's Fred?"

"He's dead," he declared coldly.

Bearslayer lowered his head, then looked back at the Indians and fired again.

Dalton ran across to the other side of the gate behind the others, seeking cover, and started shooting. He took out several fighters, then spoke to the others: "Run! I'll hold them off and follow you!"

Anton, Arisztid, and Bearslayer nodded and stepped out from their cover. The Indians who had taken cover in the emptied fort's yard continued to shoot and slowly, disciplinedly advanced closer to the group. Bruce and Arisztid fired a few shots as they reached the gate, then started running.

Anton stood at the gate, firing shots to cover them. "Run, Jer, we have to go!"

Jeremiah heard his brother, but the Indians kept them under constant fire and were dangerously close to them.

Dalton lowered his weapon, then took out his last stick of dynamite from his boot. He lit the match and quickly tore the fuse short. He leaned out of his cover and threw it. "Boom!" he yelled, then threw himself to the ground.

It landed among the Indians, who screamed and started running, but it was too late. An explosion shook the fort. Rocks, earth, and pieces of wood flew in every direction. Dust covered the two men, who stood up coughing. Many of the warriors died instantly, but some lay on the ground with serious injuries, screaming loudly in pain. Some were in shock, mumbling prayers under their breath, with severed limbs.

"Dalton, come on!" Jeremiah called out, then started running, but stopped at the gate. He looked back; Jonathan was still taking cover. "Goddamn it, what is he doing?! We need to go now!"

Dalton shook his head. "There are too many of them. Our horses are far away. They're coming after us and they'll hunt us down. I'll stay. Go, I'll hold them off as long as I can."

Jeremiah nervously kicked a barrel, then approached Jonathan. "Don't mess with me! We don't have time for foolishness! Come while you still can!"

"No!" Dalton yelled, then moved closer to Jeremiah, grabbed both of his shoulders, and looked deep into his eyes. "I sincerely regret what happened to your family!"

The older bounty hunter was shocked at the mention of his family. He hadn't expected it, especially not in this situation.

"There's no point in lying, Mr. White..." he continued. "Please believe that I didn't kill them. I truly regret it and ask for your forgiveness for everything that happened between us in the past years. I hope you'll find your peace in the future, too."

Jeremiah couldn't get a word in. He didn't have time to react because Dalton pushed him away and yelled at him: "Go!"

Bullets whizzed past them. The warriors screamed and left their cover.

"Go already, you idiot!" Jonathan yelled and jumped back behind cover. He engaged with the Indians, forcing them to halt.

The elder White cast one last glance at Dalton, then took off running. He ran through the gate, across the dirt road in front of the fortress, straight into the forest. The others were waiting there. He gasped for air.

Bruce glanced back at the fortress. "Where's Dalton?" he asked.

"He stayed behind to buy us time" Jeremiah replied.

Anton nervously wiped his face, then ran towards their horses. "Maybe this way we'll make it out. They outnumber us. Captain Dalton dies a hero."

"Indeed..." Arisztid replied, then remembered what Dalton said to him in the cell: *If I get out of here, everything will change*. It seemed to him that Dalton truly was the exception. "Rest in peace," he finally said and took off running.

Jeremiah watched as the sheriff ran off, but he was unable to follow. Jonathan Dalton symbolized for him the fulfillment of revenge. He blamed him for everything he had lost. It gave him strength to start anew and to begin a new life with his brother. The emptiness he felt almost instantly consumed him. He cursed loudly, kicking the tree next to him with all his might. "Damn Dalton to hell!" he shouted.

He turned around and took off running. Gathering all his strength, he ran to find him still alive. Arriving at the fortress, he saw Dalton retreating continuously, now without cover, standing in front of the gate, shooting aimlessly. Jeremiah raised his pistol and fired several shots in rapid succession at the Indians near the gate. He hit several of them, who slumped dead.

Jonathan looked back. Surprise and incomprehension radiated from his eyes. "What are you doing?!" he yelled. "I told you to go, you fool!"

"Not a chance!" he replied and fired again. "I told you already, Dalton! Only I can finish you off! And the White brothers never run away!"

"You're insane!" Jonathan shot back.

The two men fired off their deadly shots in succession, and the warriors fell one by one. They slowly retreated towards the forest, then, reaching the cover of the trees, they reloaded their revolvers.

"The others ran to the horses. I suggest we run now too" Jeremiah said.

"Where are we going?"

"There's an old man living in the valley, we'll head there. It's safe. We'll figure out the rest there." The elder bounty hunter peeked out from behind the trees, no longer seeing attackers. He rubbed his face and spoke to Dalton: "I want you to know, Captain, that I regret what happened up in the mountains with your friends. I regret chasing you all these years."

Ramirez leaned against the wall, gazing at the crucifix hanging on it. The crucified Christ stared at the sky with a painful expression, bloody tears falling from his eyes. His suffering seemed boundless, yet Diego knew what sacrifice the child of God had made for the spiritual salvation of all mankind. He admired with reverence as fresh blood dripped down and splattered onto the floor. The holy blood had been flowing incessantly ever since the angel arrived at the monastery. Ramirez consecrated his warriors with the blood of the statues. He was proud that the tribe had renounced their pagan faith and sworn allegiance to the holy name of Christ. A satisfied smile spread across his face as he recalled the glorious deeds he had accomplished in recent years.

After a bitter, painful childhood, he had found the path of the righteous. He had long considered the violence experienced in the army as punishment, but eventually realized that the Lord intended this task for him. He'd had to become the best warrior, and he had. He felt there was no opponent for him. He scratched his chin, then stood up and walked across his room. Kasbeel's words weighed heavily on him. He knew he could not fail now. A seemingly impossible path lay behind him, yet he had successfully overcome the obstacles in his way. Only one small element was missing for the ritual. He smiled and sighed contentedly. He envisioned the world he was about to create. A perfect world where unbelievers vanished, and angels and humans together would create earthly paradise in complete harmony. He hated the thought, but he had entertained the idea more than once that the Lord had erred. *Could it be possible?* he asked himself. *It's impossible for God to be wrong. He tested us, and we failed. But I will bring justice.* The door creaked open, and Ramirez turned toward the sound. One of his loyal monks entered, followed by Sister Judith. The woman stood with a lowered head, her face dirty. Despite her dirty, torn clothes, her beauty was evident. Sinful thoughts crossed Diego's mind, but he had long ceased to be troubled by guilt. The violence and pain he inflicted on people had killed his belief in his own goodness. He stood up and nodded to his monk, who returned the gesture and left. The Mexican took slow, measured steps toward the nun. "Praised be Jesus Christ," he said.

"Praised be, Father," the woman replied timidly.

Sensing her fear, Ramirez approached her, caressed her face, and kindly continued, "Do not fear, Sister. I do not intend to harm you."

"But you already have," she said with a hateful tone. "You have harmed me and not just me, but my sisters as well. What do you want from me? Do you intend to cast me into damnation, too?"

Diego smiled and took a step back, spreading his hands. "Far from it, my lady. The Holy Angel of the Lord currently has no need for sustenance. However, I would bestow upon you... freedom."

Sister Judith's eyes welled up with tears at the word. Every part of her body and soul longed for freedom, for safety. Yet she knew this was not the Lord's way. "And what would you ask for in exchange for this freedom?"

Ramirez smiled again, approached the crucifix hanging on the wall, and caressed it. "I ask only this, Sister, that you tell me what you know about Miss Gareth. If you do so, I promise you will come to no harm." Diego approached her again, caressed her face, neck, and untangled her matted hair behind her ear, but the nun averted her gaze. "Think about it, Judith," he whispered in her ear. "You will no longer endure violence. No impure hands will touch you where none should. All you need to do is tell me what I ask."

The nun pushed him away. "If I tell you, I'll go to hell. I'll be no better than Judas."

"Miss," Diego said emphatically, "you are bound for hell regardless. It's only up to you how painful the journey there will be. If you tell me what I want, I will grant you a reward, and then you may leave freely."

"And Kassandra?"

"Kassandra Gareth will come to no harm. You have my word."

"Will she also be allowed to leave freely?"

"In time," Ramirez said, nodding. "But first, she must fulfill the Lord's task."

"What task?"

"That is not your concern. Your task will be fulfilled once you start talking."

Judith turned her back to Ramirez, but she felt his gaze upon her. Thoughts raced through her mind. If she could truly leave freely, she could send help, free her sisters, and notify the Vatican. "Kassandra won't be harmed, right?"

Diego approached the woman, embraced her, and pulled her close "You know the answer, for I have already spoken it."

A tear ran down Judith's cheek, she sighed, and gently pushed away from the Mexican. "Sister Gareth is not a nun," she said matter-of-factly.

Interest reflected in Ramirez's eyes. "Continue."

"She recently arrived at St. Lucia's. The Vatican sent her on a papal mission. She's an investigator. She came to acquire the records of Edward Kelley and John Dee. She's looking for the Black Monastery."

"And she found it," Diego replied. "Are others coming?"

"She believes so."

"Two priests arrived from Rome," Ramirez stated coldly. "The sheriff of Corpus Christi with his deputy and a bandit came to Matamoros. We heard that a marksman is assisting them. They were captured in the city. The marksman is still on the run, but we'll find him soon. They won't leave, I can assure you of that."

"She also spoke of a new church," Judith said fearfully. "She mentioned the Church of Angelic Justice, that they attempted to kill the Holy Father in Rome and took refuge in the Angel's Castle."

"Rome is corrupt. Everyone knows this," Diego replied passionately. "While others suffer, they feast on their divine banquets from golden thrones, drink their expensive wines from silver goblets, surround themselves with idols and treasures. God and his angels exist only in books for them. They've become politicians hungry for power, but we'll put an end to this." Ramirez turned to Judith. "Thank you for sharing with me, Sister. I appreciate what you've done. Please accept our church's gift from me."

The Mexican stepped to the door, knocked, and then the monk entered with a warrior at his side. "Sister... I gift you with the holy seed of Kasbeel," Ramirez said.

Confusion, then fear, spread across Judith's face. Her pupils dilated, she tried to step back, but the Indian seized her shoulders.

Ramirez approached closer and continued in an ecstatic tone: "It is your honor, Sister, to bear a Nephilim! The children of the Watchers will walk among us again. Once you have borne it, you may leave freely."

The woman screamed, trying to break free, but the monk and the Indian pinned her to the ground. They bound her hands together and lifted her up. "Offer her to the angel!" Diego commanded them. "After you have made it hers, take her to the catacombs with the others!"

Judith sobbed, her body writhing wildly as the two men carried her away.

The Mexican listened to the sound of her suffering for a while, filled with blissful joy. He knew that this time he pleased the angel, and his reward would be immense. He stepped before the crucifix, fell to his knees, and began to pray. He clasped his hands together and murmured softly in Latin. The noise of footsteps interrupted his prayer. He opened his eyes and turned with an irritated expression. One of his warriors stood before him, panting, his body drenched in sweat, his face covered in blood. Diego rose with curiosity, then approached the Indian with slow steps. Their eyes met, and the warrior fearfully turned his head away. Finally, Diego broke the awkward silence between them. "What happened?"

The Indian began to speak but stopped himself mid-sentence. He knew well how carefully he had to choose his words if he wanted to survive. Taking a deep breath, he looked into Ramirez's eyes and began: "We were ambushed. We suffered heavy losses in the fortress. The sheriff and the nigger fled. We followed their trail, which led to the valley. Following the father's orders, we did not enter."

He would have continued, but Ramirez grabbed the man's chin. The warrior's pupils dilated, he opened his mouth in fear. Hatred and contempt emanated from Ramirez's eyes. "To the valley?" he hissed. "The old man..."

The Mexican pushed the Indian away, who grabbed his chin.

"Should we pursue them, Father?"

"Absolutely not!" he snapped. "As darkness falls, I myself will visit Rodrigo!"

The sheriff watched his own trembling hands as he sat by his horse in the grass. The afternoon sun was still scorching enough to burn his skin. He had lived in Texas for many years, which was almost like Mexico, but he couldn't get used to the heat. Dull and powerful waves of pain washed through his head, and he needed all his strength to suppress the sound. A numb terror crept into his soul; the fear of losing control over his own mind. During the war, he had heard similar stories of soldiers losing their minds, hallucinating people, but he had never truly believed in them. Until now. He reached for his flask, which was empty. In his anger, he slammed it to the ground and cursed. He buried his face in his hands and angrily blew off steam. He looked up and watched the others as he took a cigarette out of his pocket. The smoke had the power to calm him, but he also knew it would only last for a very short time. "Bruce!" he finally called in a weak voice.

Bearslayer was rummaging through his saddlebag for something when he heard Arisztid's voice. He looked at the man with a friendly gaze and half-smiled. He took out a bottle of whiskey from his bag and threw it to him.

The sheriff caught the bottle, uncorked it, and took big gulps from it. "Thanks, friend!" he said.

Bruce sat down beside him on the ground, then pulled out a cigar and lit it. For a while, they simply sat beside each other, watching the peaceful landscape around them. "My condolences for your friend," Bearslayer said empathetically. "Fred was a good and honest man. Were the Indians responsible?"

"Diego," Arisztid replied in a trembling voice. "They... they scalped him."

"Sweet Lord," Bruce placed his hand on his friend's shoulder. "Don't worry, my friend! We'll avenge his death. That damn Mexican and his Indian gang will pay for all of this."

"They will pay," said Arisztid with a snort. "It's ironic that we have to meet again like this." He looked at Bruce, then continued, "but I'm glad to see you alive, my friend!"

"It's not so easy to get rid of me..." Bearslayer grinned. "I think you know that very well."

"Oh, yes!" the sheriff grinned. "I'll never forget when in Panama, because of you, we were almost eaten by cannibals! Poor Pedro still hasn't recovered... And of course, he blames me."

Bruce laughed. "We were only almost eaten, just almost! Truth be told, I've never seen so many arrows stuck in a ship before."

"But Pedro brought us home on a sinking ship, injured and terribly drunk."

"Seasoned," added Bearslayer. "I couldn't get rid of the smell of spices for weeks, and my dogs were clinging to me all day."

"We would have been a tasty bite for sure, but let's skip that in the future."

"Agreed," he laughed, then patted Arisztid's back. "Have something to eat, my friend, you must be hungry. I have some dried horse meat in my bag."

Bruce struggled to stand up and approached his horse. He stroked the restless animal's head, then pulled out a piece of dried meat from the saddlebag. He handed it to the sheriff, who ate slowly, tearing small bites.

He couldn't remember the last time he had eaten something decent. He looked at the meat, grimaced, then stuffed it into his pocket.

"Sorry to interrupt your meal, but it's time to move on," Jeremiah interjected, "we have no idea if the Indians are following us or not."

"Oh, you can be sure they're following, we just can't see them, but they're here," Bearslayer replied, then lowered his voice. "Have you thought about what you'll tell the priests?"

Jeremiah shook his head. "This isn't the best time. We're out in the open, and if things go south..."

"What could go wrong?" Dalton asked.

Bruce and Jeremiah looked at each other, then the tracker sighed and answered: "There's a traitor among us." He pulled out the message from his pocket and handed it to the captain. "Do you recognize the handwriting?"

Jonathan read it, a look of shock and horror spreading across his face. With trembling hands, he passed the letter to the sheriff, who had joined them in the meantime.

Arisztid read the short message with an expressionless face and handed it back to Jeremiah. "Did you know about this, Bruce? Did you know there was a traitor among us but didn't say anything?"

"It wasn't the right time" he apologized. "And there's no guarantee the person is one of us. Think about it! Why would the two priests hire the White brothers if they wanted to harm us? Why would they beg for our help if they had malicious intentions? And I'm sure Rodrigo wouldn't betray us, either. This is an external threat. Like I said... They're watching us. Not just the Indians."

"Who else is watching us?" the sheriff inquired.

"The Emperor's men," Anton said. "They attacked us on the road leading to Corpus Christi."

"I remember you saying that." Arisztid nodded. "But not that they were the Emperor's soldiers."

"We only suspect that," Jeremiah interjected.

"But it makes sense" Anton suggested. "My brother heard them speaking French to us."

The elder White brother furrowed his brow, sweat dripping down his face. It was obvious he was struggling with the long journey and its challenges. "The question is, what do they want from us?"

Anton chuckled, then gave him a firm pat on the back. "Well, we'll find out soon enough! Whoever watches also attacks sooner or later."

"I agree," Jeremiah said. "And it wouldn't be good if they caught us off-guard under the open sky again! Let's go!"

The members of the group nodded in agreement. They all mounted their horses and headed towards the valley.

Jeremiah looked at his younger brother. He felt a constant concern for his only remaining sibling, but he knew that the man riding beside him was not just his little brother anymore; he was a seasoned warrior. Their comradeship in battle and their honest confessions had eased the pain of the wounds burning in his soul. He sighed with relief and rode up next to his brother. "How are you, bro?" he asked with a grin as he slapped his brother across the face.

Anton was taken aback, then answered unusually honestly: "I felt like shit froze in me when the Indians attacked us back in Matamoros." He grimaced, spat to the side, and continued: "I'm telling you, brother, these guys are crazy. We've seen plenty of killers, looters, and rapists. Disgraceful people who knew they were nothing but lowlife scum... But these ones here... They truly believe they're doing the right thing..."

"So I guess you haven't found God after all, the one you've been searching for so desperately," his brother mocked.

"This isn't funny! Why can't you accept that I'm not your little shit of a brother anymore, who has to follow you around in everything?"

"Watch your mouth! Just because you're my brother doesn't mean you can talk to me however you want."

"Maybe you'll shoot me? Come on! And what about Dalton? He killed our family, and you're hugging him close after a tight spot?"

"Maybe we were wrong about him... Believe me, when you see enough dying men, or someone who wants to ease his conscience because he knows he's going to die, they don't lie. He swore he didn't do it. For some reason, I believe him."

"Well, I don't!" Anton averted his gaze. "If it wasn't him, it means we have no idea who killed our little sister and our parents, who burned down the family estate. It means we have no chance for revenge! They died in vain..."

"Yes!" Jeremiah yelled, drawing everyone's attention towards them. "They died in vain! There was no point to their deaths, and revenge won't change that! It's time to let go of the past and look towards the future. This is my last mission as a bounty hunter. I've had enough."

"Finally, we agree on something," Anton retorted angrily. "If we're done here, I don't want to see you for years!"

"Cut the bickering, you two!" the sheriff intervened. "This isn't a New York tea party to squabble at! One mistake could cost us our lives! And I won't let any of them end up like Fr..."

Arisztid's voice faltered, then he averted his gaze. The death of his partner and friend had inflicted such a deep wound in his soul that the mere thought shattered his heart into a thousand pieces again and again. The group rode on in awkward and uncomfortable silence towards the valley.

Lost in thought, Dalton stared into the distance, pondering over his conversation with Jeremiah. He couldn't decide whether to believe him or if it was just another trick of the bounty hunter. The experiences of the past years whispered to him that trust kills and to be vigilant, but this mission revealed new nuances of life. Perhaps it was time for him to look at it differently too. Although he thought the differences between them were irreconcilable, he hoped that this time luck, fate would be on his side.

"Here we are," Bearslayer said.

The silhouette of a distant farmhouse filled Jonathan with calm. Though he had never met old Rodrigo before, this time he trusted his companions' words. For the first time in a long while, he felt genuine willingness to help. Though it had all started with bargaining, he had a strong conviction that if there was fate, then it was guiding each of their steps now.

The old man opened the door at the sight of the newcomers, then slowly, with tired, slow, elderly steps, he stepped out in front of his house. Time had bent his back and lined his skin with deep wrinkles, yet his gaze retained its strength. He smiled and waved to the riders who entered his yard. However, as they dismounted, they saw tired, injured, and pained looks. The old man sighed, then invited them in. "I hoped you would all return safely. The soup is still hot, please, come in!"

Upon entering the house, everyone took a seat wherever they could find one. Exhausted, hungry, and worn out, they sat on the floor amid painful sighs.

Rodrigo handed each of them a plate of hot soup, which the men devoured eagerly. "I see not everyone has returned," he remarked quietly.

The others ate in silence, their sad gazes giving the old man the answer.

Rodrigo pursed his lips and asked in a shameful, faltering voice: "Was it Diego?"

"Yes" answered the sheriff. "And he intends a similar fate for all of us."

The gazes of the two priests met, and they listened to the conversation suspiciously.

The old man didn't let it go and continued to interrogate the silent sheriff: "How do you mean he intends a similar fate for all of you? Have you spoken with him?"

"I have. He sentenced Dalton and me to death. He cut my hand and collected my blood in a vial."

"We took them down from the gallows," Anton interjected while slurping his soup. "I tell you, this Diego is a real bastard."

"He forced me to sacrifice Fred..." The sheriff took back the word.

"And did they try to ambush you?"

"Yes," said Dalton. "The deputy injured him, the sheriff almost caught him, but he escaped."

"I'm sorry about what happened to your friend, sheriff. Diego is no longer who he once was. However, the fact that they targeted his life means one thing. Either he dies or you. He won't stop, and he will find you."

"Not if we find him first," replied Arisztid with a distorted voice from anger.

"The sheriff is right," Jeremiah said. "We'll finish the bastard, bring back the nun and the children. There's no other option." Jeremiah looked at the two priests, then pulled out a small piece of paper from his pocket. "However, there's something else here..." He handed the short message to Cristofano, who quickly read it. Fear and shock spread across his face as he passed the paper to his companion.

Agustino looked at the message with an emotionless face and responded: "What do they expect from us? Shall we prove with a handwritten letter that we didn't write this?"

"We expect an explanation. We've already done much more for you than could be expected," Jeremiah replied, then stood up and approached the priests. He looked deeply into their eyes and continued: "If it turns out you were involved, I'll shoot both of you dead along with Diego. I won't ask questions or hesitate. Is that clear?"

"As crystal," Cristofano immediately replied. "But it won't be necessary. It wasn't us."

"I share this opinion as well," added Bearslayer. "There's no logical explanation for it."

238

Arisztid felt the excruciating pain taking hold of him again. He set down his plate and stood up. He walked to the window, opened it, tried to take deep breaths, but the terrible pain overwhelmed him. It felt as though a blade had sliced through his left temple, the agony coursing through him. He yelled out and slumped onto the windowsill. His plate crashed down, making a loud noise as it hit the ground.

The others watched in silence, only Bruce stepping closer to him. "What's happening?" he asked.

"It's that strange seizure again" Dalton said.

The old Rodrigo got up and rummaged through his drawer. Muttering under his breath, he glanced back and forth at the increasingly sweaty, suffering sheriff. The old man found the vial he was looking for and quickly pocketed it before anyone could notice. "Help me," he pleaded to the others, as Jeremiah and Bruce took Arisztid by the arm and led him into the only small room where Rodrigo's bed was.

They laid him down, and the old man waved them off, signaling for them to leave them alone. "I know a bit about medicine. Let him rest."

The two men nodded, and Rodrigo closed the door behind him. He cast a nervous, excited glance at the suffering sheriff. From his pocket, he pulled out the vial and sat on the bed. "Open your mouth and drink this!"

Arisztid looked at the little bottle, which contained a deep red liquid. The pain became increasingly unbearable; his eyes glazed over, and darkness began to consume him. He had to muster all his strength to be able to respond: "I need... opium."

The old man brought the vial to his mouth and poured its contents inside. He coughed up the salty liquid a bit, but Rodrigo covered his mouth, ensuring he swallowed the peculiar drink. "If this doesn't help, you'll get opium."

The sheriff's headache immediately eased. He could swear he could almost feel the medicine coursing through his veins, filling him with energy, life. He coughed and then sat up in bed. The headache was gone, something he couldn't believe himself. He felt as if he were suddenly a child again, who had miraculously recovered. "What did you give me?"

The old man didn't answer, just watched the events unfold in amazement. His eyelids twitched, sweat dripped down his face. "Did you suffer from the disease in your childhood?" he finally asked curiously.

"Yes," Arisztid replied, surprised.

"Strange. What did the voices tell you?"

Arisztid turned his gaze away; he hadn't even told his parents about the mysterious voices in his head that had spoken to him again after many years. He had thought it was just childish imagination, a side effect of his serious illness, but what he had experienced recently seemed real to him. "They called out to me. But after I recovered, I never heard them again until today. The headaches returned only a few months ago."

"Only a few months ago..." Rodrigo muttered to himself. "You claim someone was able to drive the sickness out of you? Who was it? Tell me!"

"I have no idea," the sheriff replied. "I was a child, and my mother never revealed it, then she disappeared without a trace. But you know this... You've seen it! Tell me what's wrong with me!"

Rodrigo hung his head, answering in a voice filled with sorrow and pain: "I've seen it before, but I didn't know what it was. However, I never thought anyone could drive out this curse. I've seen what it does to a child, how it corrupts and takes away their sanity until they become a monster. Whatever your ailment is, Mister, I'm sorry, but it doesn't bode well. The fact that it's returned is even worse."

The sheriff looked puzzled at the old man, then asked back in astonishment: "Diego...? Have you known Diego since childhood? How is this possible?"

"He's my son," declared Rodrigo, looking Arisztid in the eye. "And I've seen what this disease has done to him." He sighed, stood up, and began to pace slowly back and forth in the room. "You see, I was a monk for most of my life. I renounced marriage and fatherhood. But, like every man, love found me too. I knew I was breaking my vows, and I knew the danger I was putting Diego in, but love cannot be commanded or restrained. He was born, and I was never happier than I was then. My wife lived here in this house, and I visited them often. Years passed without any trouble... But when Diego turned four, he suddenly fell ill. He was tormented by terrible headaches, shivered with cold, and sweated profusely. His strength left his body. As a monk, I understood something about healing."

"But you only achieved a few days of success," Arisztid interjected.

"At first, yes. Then he only got better for hours, later for minutes, and finally not at all. We even had a doctor visit us from Matamoros. We tried all the suggested therapies, but nothing helped him. Little Diego's mind returned only for shorter periods day by day, and when it did return... he spoke of voices echoing in his head. You see," said Rodrigo with teary eyes, "I never told Diego about the monastery. Yet he knew what kind of writings surrounded it. And when my son came to, I knew, I felt it in my bones, that something else was speaking to me. His gaze, his voice, his movements, everything changed. He said if I wanted him to be healed, I should bring something from the monastery. I doubted, how could he know? He told me where to look, exactly. The shock and fear I felt then were indescribable, for they were exactly where my four-year-old son said they would be. They wrote down the recipe for making a potion in a language no man could know, hidden centuries ago. One whose existence I myself was unaware of. After reading the notes written in ancient Aramaic, I decided to kill Diego because evil had taken over his body, and if I did as he asked, I would condemn his soul to eternal damnation. But I couldn't do it. Could you kill your child, sheriff? As I watched his tiny, trembling, fear-ridden body... I decided that if this was the Lord's wish, so be it. So I did everything to make the potion. It required such dreadful ingredients that I won't detail here, but I can tell you this much, sheriff, the first innocent child Diego did not abduct..." The old man closed his eyes, a tear ran down his face, and he continued sobbing with a broken voice: "The potion was made, and as best as I could, I forced it down Diego's throat..."

"And he got better" nodded the sheriff.

"Within hours, he regained his full strength, and even more. At first, I thought my eyes were deceiving me, but my wife confirmed my belief. Compared to Diego's age, he looked much older, stronger, smarter, and more cunning. Later, cruelty and the inclination to evil also emerged in him... At first, he tortured insects, then came the cats, dogs. Until one day, the children disappeared from a nearby farm. I found the remains of the little boy near our house, only the Creator knows what he did to the little girl. That day I sent a letter to the army. Days later, an officer came for him and took him away, I never thought I would see him again. When he appeared at the monastery years later, I felt that the Creator sent him back as punishment for me. Of course, I couldn't tell my comrades who he really was, just as he didn't reveal it either." He laughed awkwardly. "He was always good at lying and deceiving. At first, I thought it was okay. But as it turned out, his condition was much worse than I could have ever imagined; Diego bore no resemblance to my son. I woke up at night. Strange noises filled the corridors of the monastery, and I followed the sounds. Diego regularly went to the nearby forest."

Rodrigo turned away, confusion and shame in his voice. He wiped his face, not knowing how to put into words everything he had experienced. "When Diego left the monastery at night, he completely lost his humanity. He ate the flesh of animals from the nearby forest and drank their blood. It was only then that I realized he was showing himself less and less in the daylight, and eventually he even skipped the daytime prayers. He could only be seen within the monastery walls during the day, in places protected from the light. After he took over the power... He not only killed the monks who opposed him, but he also devoured them and forced those who sided with him to follow his example... to feed, because as he said, 'The body is true food, the blood is true drink.' They did. And shortly after, I escaped."

"I suppose Diego allowed it," said Arisztid. "He never pursued you?"

Rodrigo shook his head. "Not once. Neither his warriors nor his monks came down into the valley."

The sheriff pondered what he had heard. The words cut like knives into his mind and heart. Perhaps he, too, would become a monster? He couldn't know, but the strange voice in his head didn't bode well, he was sure of that. "What did you give me?" he asked curiously. "The same potion that you gave to your son?"

"God protect us from it!" Rodrigo crossed himself. "No, Señor, you received animal blood. And visibly, it has done you good. I'm particularly glad about that." The old man nodded. "But at the same time, it's terrifying."

"But what could all this mean? Why did the illness find Diego, and why did it find me?"

"I wish I could answer." The old man lowered his head. "I wish I could help my son... But my knowledge is insufficient for this." Rodrigo grabbed Arisztid's hand in a sudden movement, determination reflected in his gaze. "Stop him! Stop my son, because if you don't, he will unleash something upon the world that will only bring suffering and destruction! I was unable to do it, but you... I see the determination and strength in you!"

The old man let go of Arisztid's hand, then stood up and approached his small cabinet, from the single drawer of which he retrieved a yellowed map and a faded key. He carefully examined both, then handed them to the sheriff.

"Take it. The map will lead you to the entrance of the catacomb system beneath the monastery. And the key will reveal the terrible truth to you. But be cautious! The map will take you to the Valley of the Outcasts, where, once you enter, there will be no turning back! Whatever you see there, I beg you, do not turn back!"

The sheriff nervously wiped his face, his hands trembling, his heart pounding fiercely. He nodded, took the key and the map, then stood up and went back to his companions. The suspicious, nervous glances that were directed at him weighed heavily, but he knew the feeling well. He felt like every nightmare from his childhood was returning to him, and the familiar darkness was burying him once again, this time forever. With a forced smile, he looked at his friend and nodded.

Bearslayer slapped his own thighs, then jumped up and patted Arisztid's shoulder. "That's my friend! I knew you just needed a little rest!" Bruce looked at the others, then continued loudly: "Nothing can kill this man, only alcohol and opium!" He chuckled, and the others laughed along.

Arisztid felt like the world was spinning around him. Thoughts were swirling in his head. He had no idea if he was actually human, and if not, then what? He couldn't know if there was redemption for him, but he was sure that after this mission, nothing would be the same as before. For the first time in many years, he felt like a stranger. Nostalgia filled his heart, and he resolved that if he survived this, he would visit his father and uncover the terrible truth about himself. He looked up, cleared his throat, and then told his companions where they needed to go.

"The Valley of the Outcasts?" Jeremiah snorted skeptically. "What is this, some kind of poetry?"

"Never underestimate the occult power, Mr. White!" Rodrigo said. "Over the centuries, many monks have fallen into the sin of blasphemy and devil worship. Their bodies were buried in unholy ground, their souls will never find

244

rest, so you will face an enemy that cannot simply be shot down," the old man said disdainfully.

"But if the place is so dangerous, why should we go there? Surely there must be another way!" Dalton suggested.

"What's the matter, Captain, scared?" Anton mocked. "The great Jonathan Dalton, the terror of Vicksburg, tucking his tail and running! He could have done that in the mountains too..."

"Enough!" Jeremiah interjected. "The captain is right! Is there another way?"

"The monastery is also a fortress. With the right warriors, it can be defended very well. The only path is directly in front of the monastery—they would simply massacre you, no matter how skilled you are as fighters, you wouldn't stand a chance!"

"But if we go through the catacombs, through narrow corridors, we'll still be an easy target," the sheriff pointed out.

"Even Diego doesn't dare to enter the catacombs, let alone the Valley of the Outcasts," Rodrigo replied. "You can ambush them there."

"Great!" Dalton exclaimed. "Let's go where even the most hardened robber-murderer sect leader dares not go! Come on! After all, what could go wrong?"

"Could it really work?" Bearslayer asked with keen curiosity.

"I believe so. Through the catacombs, they will reach the City of the Dead. They will find the graves of the deceased monks there. From there, they can enter the lower levels of the monastery, which has functioned as a prison for quite some time. There they will find those they are looking for."

"If they're still alive" Arisztid interjected.

"Diego didn't kidnap the children to kill them, but to re-educate them and send them out into the world. They will be alive, you can be sure of that."

"And Sister Gareth?" Cristofano asked. "What was his goal in kidnapping the nuns?"

"You'll have to find that out for yourselves, my son" the old man said, and nodded. "Now rest, eat, and prepare for the journey." Rodrigo paused in his speech, then cautiously asked his question. "Does anyone wish to be baptized before the journey?"

The members of the team rewarded the old monk's words with mocking smiles, their eyes met, and they reached for their boots or weapons instead, to clean them.

Anton fixed his gaze on the ground, then responded: "I do."

Jeremiah lifted his head, then incredulously questioned his brother. "Are you joking?! Have you lost your mind?! What sense is there in such a superstition?"

Anton straightened up, then answered decisively: "For the first time in my life, I want to decide my own fate! And if I die now, I want to stand before the Creator with a clear conscience when he passes judgment on me!"

Jeremiah stepped towards his brother, reaching out his arm to grab him. "I won't let a wretched..." He didn't finish the sentence.

He knew his brother was right. He never let him assert himself, never allowed him to make independent decisions. He bowed his head, wiped his forehead, then spoke softly: "It's time for you to start your own life, brother, without my protection."

Anton grasped his brother's hand. "You'll always be my brother, and you know I'd kill for you. But as you said before... We have to let go of our family. Our pointless vendetta, causing only more suffering and pain to ourselves and others. I wish you find peace!"

Anton released his brother's hand, then approached Rodrigo. He knelt before him, arms outstretched, and spoke. "I am ready, Father!"

The old man nodded, then traced the sign of the cross with his thumb on Anton's forehead. "Almighty, eternal God, Father of our Lord Jesus Christ! We pray for this brother of ours, who seeks the gift of baptism and desires your eternal grace through spiritual rebirth. Have mercy on him, Lord, and as you have said: ask and you shall receive, seek and you shall find, knock and it shall be opened unto you. Grant now goodness to him who asks, open the door to him who knocks, that he may receive the eternal blessing of baptism and enter into your kingdom of grace, which you promised through our Lord Jesus Christ. Amen."

Rodrigo helped Anton to his feet, then patted his shoulders. "I wish you a long and happy life, my child! But when the time comes, may you stand before the Lord with a clear heart and soul!"

Chapter Nine

"Then Jesus said unto them, Verily, verily, I say unto you, Except ye eat the flesh of the Son of man, and drink his blood, ye have no life in you."

John 6:53

Kassandra lifted her gaze to the cold stone walls, from which the lime had long peeled away. The barren walls absorbed the sounds of suffering, radiating them as the sun radiates life-giving light. She knelt before the almost burnt-out candle, her tears washing her face, while her soul was tormented by guilt, pain, and doubts. Though it hadn't been long since they took Sister Judith away, her absence already gnawed at her heart. The knowledge that she had revealed her identity to her, thus endangering her, tortured her. With hands folded in prayer, leaning towards the warmth of the flame, she whispered her prayers. "From the depths of my heart, I repent, oh, my sweet God, for having offended You so often and so deeply, thus rendering myself unworthy of Your grace, falling out of Your favor, and deserving both temporal and eternal punishment.

Especially do I regret my sins because I have offended You, the supreme good, my most loving Father, and greatest benefactor. I am guilty because I have fallen into the sin of weakness. In the hour of darkness, I did not call upon You for help, I ignored Your teachings, and due to the weakness of my soul and spirit, I committed betrayal against my sisters and endangered Your earthly representative, the Church, which proclaims Your glory. Forgive me, Father, for I have sinned! Absolve me from my sins and have mercy on my soul, grant grace to my mortal body, protect me from the torment and pain that have been plaguing me, I know not for how long! Deliver me from evil and temptation, for the absence of good that You have granted to this world gnaws at my soul, I long for Your kingdom and I can no longer bear the pain."

She began to sob painfully, and in her anger, she swept the candle, the only source of light, to the ground. The candle made a dull thud as it hit the hard stone and rolled away. She buried her face in her hands and let her emotions overwhelm her. From outside, she heard the sound of footsteps, but she didn't bother hiding her weakness anymore. The door opened, and Ramirez's silhouette appeared in the light. She watched the Mexican for a while, then he entered the cell and sat down on the stone opposite her, leaning his back against the wall. She observed his face; the weak light illuminating his blind eyes cast grotesque shadows on his face. Diego smiled, sending chills down Kassandra's spine.

He watched her for a while before speaking. "I'm glad you're finally praying. It was about time you called upon the Creator for help. Frankly, I'm surprised you haven't done it before. After all, you are a nun, my dear..."

The woman averted her gaze and reached for the candle. She placed it back in its place and then asked: "What do you want from me?"

"The truth," declared Ramirez. "There's no point in lying anymore; Judith has already spilled everything. I know you're not a nun, and I also know that the Vatican is after me." Diego leaned forward in his seat and continued emphatically, in a hoarse voice, "But did the Church really think you would be able to get those records? I must admit, you've come further than I thought! I commend you, for you realized what the Church did not; that this is no longer about the records or a rival church. You figured out how far we've come, how many royal courts we've infiltrated, and..." Their eyes met. "You figured out who's behind it all. My compliments, miss, sincerely! It's a marvelous achievement! After all, you even managed to send a letter to His Holiness about what's going on here, and they sent help."

"His Holiness sent help?" Kassandra asked hopefully. "Then it's over for you, Ramirez!"

"Oh, I highly doubt that. They only sent two priests, accompanied by a few armed men. I've already taken care of one of them. But tell me, miss... Why did you conceal from His Holiness who's behind all this? Why? After all, you burned the letter! Oh, if only the old man knew! He would immediately excommunicate you, as you're endangering the existence of the Church," he said with a wicked smile on his face. "God is watching you, Kassandra!"

"If God is watching me, then He sees you too. And the Lord would vomit you out!"

Diego grabbed the woman's chin and then pushed her away.

Kassandra's head hit the hard wall as she fell, stars dancing before her eyes.

"I am fulfilling God's will because the Lord has chosen me!" Diego crawled on all fours, their faces almost touching. "I am the one who will bring earthly paradise! Salvation and true faith."

The woman spat in Ramirez's face, then replied angrily: "You will rot in hell because you are a murderer!"

Diego recoiled in surprise. He wiped the saliva from his face. "Am I a murderer? Yes, indeed. But remember Moses!

He also killed, was violent, and hot-headed. And yet he led his people to the promised land."

"Where he couldn't enter," Kassandra added finally.

"So you understand, miss, what my task is. It's not to live in wealth, luxury, and comfort, surrounded by idols and jewels. The Creator intended for me to bring salvation to people. My personal fate doesn't matter. If I have to go to hell to redeem and cleanse this world, so be it! I am willing to make that sacrifice!"

"Are you sure, Ramirez, that the Lord intended this task for you? Look at yourself! Look at what you've become! Your deeds have literally plunged you into darkness!" Kassandra slowly rose, her legs trembling, a surprising determination in her eyes as she confronted Diego. "You hunger and thirst, your body is tormented by agonies that no real human could bear. The power you crave has turned you into a servant."

Taking further steps toward Ramirez, her tousled brown hair falling into her face, her torn, dirt-stained clothes slipping off her shoulders, Kassandra seized both of his shoulders. "Tell me, Father, when you began, did you truly desire to be a servant to a bloodthirsty monster? I hear the monks talking. The seizures that torment you... The headaches, the glazed look in your eyes, the frothing at the mouth, the convulsions on the ground like a dying dog. They say it's the demon feeding off of you, because without it, you would have died..."

Diego's pupils dilated in surprise, but he quickly regained his composure. He angrily grabbed the woman and shouted in her face: "Enough!" Pushing her away forcefully, he continued, "Well done! You've cornered me very cleverly, but I assure you, I will find out why you kept our father's identity a secret."

Diego took a few steps back as the door of the dungeon opened. Stepping through it was the monk whom Kassandra hadn't seen in a long time. A menacing and sinister smile appeared on the man's filthy face as he held a small vial in his hand.

The woman immediately recognized the opium. Her heartbeat quickened, and icy fear ran through her body. "No!" she said in a trembling voice.

Diego smirked and replied, "You'll soon need it to dull your pain. You'll be grateful for it." Turning to the monk, Ramirez instructed, "Once you've knocked her out, do as you please with her!"

The man grinned, nodded, and menacingly approached the trembling woman as Diego turned his back and left the dungeon.

Ramirez walked through the monastery corridors lost in thought, heading towards the sacristy. He stopped, closed his eyes, wanting to feel the presence of the Lord. While others might have felt something dark and mysterious haunting this place, he knew that the presence of the Creator and His angels always instilled fear in people. Between the walls, it felt like some ancient force was tightening its grip on him and his companions. Sometimes, he thought he could hear echoes of past times, with visions of the deeds of the founding knights unfolding before his eyes. The dim corridors of the building seemed narrow and dark, with only sparse beams of light coming through the high windows.

Looking around, he noticed that a part of the monastery wall was covered in dried blood. He stopped and ran his fingers over the bloody handprints. The night of reckoning against the unbelievers came to mind. He shuddered as he recalled the smell of fear from the monks and the taste of their blood.

The corridors were illuminated by the light of candles, and as he passed by the statues of saints, his boots loudly echoed on the hard stone floor. He stopped in front of a statue depicting Christ and stared at the Savior. A tingling sensation filled his head. He hissed as the sensation turned into sharp pain, and he clutched his temple. The strength left his body, and he collapsed to his knees. He cried out in pain, knowing that the darkness had returned. He retched, but with an empty stomach, there was nothing to expel. As he looked up, instead of the gilded statue, he saw bloody bodies piled on top of each other, and above them, Kasbeel held his flaming sword high with a trance-like expression. "The holy angel of God has sent a sign..." he whispered weakly.

The angel looked at him, radiating mercy and love from his gaze. He reached out his arm towards Ramirez, who grabbed the angel's hand with trembling fingers. Kasbeel stepped towards the man through the corpses, helped him up from the ground, and placed his sword in his hand. The angel nodded.

Diego lowered his head and replied: "I will carry out your command. The children are ready for your task." He closed his eyes, then opened them again, finding himself once more in the dimly lit corridor.

As he progressed further into the interior of the building, the tension in his soul grew stronger. He was within arm's reach of his goal, and he couldn't allow anything to ruin it. Bloody traces adorned both the walls and the floor, and the breath of death was palpable. Finally, he reached the chapel and observed the massive cross in front of the altar. The children knelt side by side, praying aloud. Pride filled him as he saw more young and strong lives dedicating themselves to the service of the Creator, to bring salvation to sinful souls.

Behind the cross, he saw a shadow, whose shape and form resembled nothing else. The shadow loomed over the praying children, enveloping them and becoming one with them. He drew closer, but suddenly felt as if something touched his shoulder. He turned around and was astonished to see the figure of a woman standing before him.

The woman wore black attire, her sky-blue eyes shone in an otherworldly hue, her skin was as white as snow. Deep sadness reflected on her face, tears washing it.

Diego felt a chill of terror running through his veins. He immediately recognized his mother, who had disappeared without a trace many years ago. He had no strength to move or speak, he stood frozen, paralyzed, while the shadow behind his mother slowly advanced towards him.

As she came close, the woman spoke in a soft, hoarse voice: "My son... You can still save your soul, but if you continue, everything that remains of you will be lost."

Ramirez halted, and sudden sorrow overwhelmed him. His mother, who had always been by his side as a child, nurturing him, now looked at him filled with shame. Diego reached out his hand to feel the soft touch of his mother's skin again. The warmth that could soothe his tormented soul even in its darkest hours. He touched her, but immediately withdrew his hand. His mother's skin was cold, like that of the dead. "Why did you leave us?"

The woman, who seemed to embody the night itself, slowly turned around and looked at the praying boys. Her face was filled with hatred and anger. "Look what you've done, my son..."

The Mexican looked at the children, who were praying fervently while the dark shadow enveloped them.

"Fear guides them, not love."

"You wouldn't understand, Mother," he whispered softly. "The Lord has chosen me, and I will execute His will. You cannot stop me. Why have you come back?"

"I am here because I must be here. And you must be here too, but not for the reasons you think," the woman said. "If you continue on this path, son, your fate is sealed."

Ramirez's heart pounded wildly in his chest, and he felt suffocated. The shadow by the altar began to grow, and he saw his mother holding something in her hands. "Why are you here?" he asked in a trembling voice. "If you haven't shown yourself until now, then leave and don't come back! We don't need you!"

The woman laughed and extended the object she was holding towards the man. "I am the hope, and you are the sacrifice."

Ramirez recoiled, but he hit a wall, horrified to see that only he and his mother remained in the chapel. Everything around them had vanished, leaving only darkness. His mother pressed a silver crucifix into her son's hand. Diego cried out in pain as the cross seemed to cut into his skin like blades. He could smell the scent of burnt flesh in his nostrils. He tried to scream, but no sound came out of his throat.

"Look into your heart, my son!" the woman said angrily.

Diego, suppressing his pain, pushed the cross away and grabbed his mother. He looked deep into her eyes and replied resolutely, "You cannot stop me either!" He felt the grip loosen, and the strange vision faded away. Sweat dripped down his forehead, and his heart slowly returned to its normal rhythm. He glanced towards the altar, where he saw nothing but the praying youths. He sighed and then, with a smile and newfound confidence, he started walking towards them.

The lonely chapel was filled with the rhythmic chanting of prayers. The filtering light cast dark shadows on the young ministrants kneeling around the altar, their hands clasped together, eyes fixed on the ground as they prayed. Diego, who walked softly, almost soundlessly on the hard stone floor, observed the youths who obeyed his every command.

Their prayers, whispered almost inaudibly, barely pierced the oppressive silence. Ramirez felt as though something dangerous and mysterious lurked in the darkness of the chapel. Anger rose within his soul. The sacred prayers dedicated to the Lord must be strong! "Louder, my children!" he said firmly. "Are we to be like whispering demons in the darkness, fearing the wrath of the Lord?!"

The boys trembled. "No, Father!" they chorused, then continued their prayers louder and more confidently.

The Mexican's heart beat faster with joy as the children prayed louder and more confidently. Diego approached the altar of the chapel, then stopped as the boys continued to pray. Sweat streamed down his face, his hands trembled slightly as his mother's face flashed before him. He felt tempted by the devil. He turned his gaze back to the boys. He saw them dim, blurred, as if veiled by something invisible. He took a deep breath, and immediately felt filled with the fullness of divine presence. He felt the strength and righteousness of the angels within him, knowing that he stood with them in battle against the forces of darkness. He firmly believed that the power of their prayers was too weak to free the boys from the clutches of evil. They needed something else, something that would break through the shadows and lead them back to the light of truth. He stepped behind the altar, holding the Bible to his chest, deeply moved. "My children, listen to me!" he said firmly. "The power of prayer is just the first step in overcoming darkness. However, you must know that angels are messengers of righteousness and grace. They are the ones who reveal divine truth in the Scriptures and help us in times of need. The power of angels is fearsome, as the Scriptures say: 'The angel of the Lord encamps around those who fear him, and delivers them.'"

His words radiated strength, his determination filled the chapel, and the youths stood up.

"Do you fear the Creator?"

"Yes!" they replied.

"Will you carry out His will and swear to shepherd His scattered flock onto His paths?"

"Yes, Father!" they chorused.

He smiled, arms outstretched as if to embrace each one. "The time will soon come, my children. My task is finished because I was able to show you the way of the righteous! Today, some of my warriors will take you away."

He listened to the uncomfortable, tense silence, scrutinizing the faces of the youths. He was now completely sure that the apparition of his mother, the temptation of the devil, was nothing but a lie. He didn't see fear in them, but determination. It was as if he saw himself, many years ago.

"Where are they taking us, Father?" asked one.

"You will serve in the temples of the great cities of Europe: Paris, London, Budapest, Moscow. But!" He raised his index finger. "Until our time comes, you must not speak of what you have seen and experienced here. Soon, however, the Church will disappear, and there will be nothing else... Only the Angelic Truth," he emphasized. "Rest, eat, and drink! Prepare yourselves for the long journey, for a lifetime of service! Always be ready for battle, for you will know when our time has come!"

The youths nodded, then turned their backs to Ramirez and walked out of the chapel. Diego still heard the fading sound of their footsteps, but his thoughts were elsewhere. He sighed, then ran his hand over his chin. He knew he was about to face a meeting that should have taken place long ago. He thought of his father. The traitor who withheld the truth from his fellow monks, who fled like a coward to live the life of an outcast.

"When the sun sets, we shall meet again..."

The riders slowly made their way along the winding dirt road. The sight of the lush green fields and forests in the golden sunlight had a soothing effect on both the horses and the riders. Arisztid took a deep breath and, for the first time in a long while, was able to enjoy the scents. He looked up and saw the gentle touch of the northwestern wind caressing the treetops, its whisper accompanying the travelers' journey. The medley of scents from the blooming meadows and the shadows of the woods blended into the fresh air, creating a pleasant sensation for everyone. The sheriff pondered the old man's words. Was his illness, which seemed to be returning, truly from the afterlife, or just a foolish superstition, and would the ailment that plagued him today not pose a problem for medical science? He couldn't know the answer, but he felt in his gut that he needed to get to the bottom of it. Shame washed over his soul for relying on animal blood. He avoided the gaze of the others. Embarrassment and fear crept into his heart, but he had to concentrate with all his might. He couldn't afford to let his attention wane. He felt that the liberation of the children and Kassandra was the only remaining goal. He dared not even think about the possibility of failure...

In the distance, a village appeared. Bearslayer gestured, Jeremiah and Anton nodded, preparing their weapons. The sheriff took out his map, then spoke hesitantly. "There shouldn't be a village here."

"Perhaps the map is too old," Bruce replied.

"Proceed with caution. We don't know what awaits us. Stay vigilant!"

The dirt road leading to the village was desolate. Apart from the ancient, dried-up trees, there was no sign of life. The landscape had completely changed. The air grew heavy, with a pungent stench lingering. As they passed through the abandoned wooden houses, they encountered no one.

"Like a ghost town," Dalton said. "I've heard of such, but never laid eyes on one."

"We've all seen deserted villages, abandoned by those fleeing war," Jeremiah replied. "But this is something else..."

"Look at the doors!" Dalton pointed out. "Each one marked with blood. We found similar houses in Matamoros; abandoned, blood-marked houses. We thought they were meant to ward off the wrath of the Lord."

"What does this mean, Father?" the sheriff asked, turning to the priests.

Agustíno pondered, then answered: "During the ten plagues in Egypt, the Jews were instructed to paint lamb's blood on their doorposts, distinguishing themselves from the Egyptians. The Lord took the firstborn of every creature in Egypt, but those behind blood-marked doors were spared. I believe the logic is sound, but not replicable. Perhaps that's why this place is empty..."

"I don't like this," said Dalton. "The old man's leading us to our deaths! Why should we trust some unknown old man, who was a monk in the same monastery as that madman Ramirez?"

"Because he's our only chance," the sheriff replied. "And I trust Rodrigo."

"As do I. I vouch for him," Bearslayer said.

"Let's not waste time idling," Jeremiah interjected as he surveyed the dead town. "Let's proceed and hope the town truly is empty."

"And that nothing stirs with the onset of darkness," added Father Cristofano.

"They should have hanged us instead..." Dalton sighed.

The group pressed on. With each step of the horses' hooves, the dry branches and leaves crackled, echoing through the deserted streets of the abandoned town. From the dusty, faded buildings, even the faintest sign of life was lost, as if it had never existed. The only sound breaking the silence was the whistle of the wind as it swept through the dusty streets.

The lifeless settlement was dark and grim, with only the roots of the trees visible in the dried dead grass, struggling to reach for the last bit of nourishment.

"We're close now." Arisztid pointed out the valley spreading out at the edge of the town to the others. A sign awaited passersby beneath a lonely tree. The sheriff squinted, then loudly read what was written on it: "Ubi potestas Dei non est."

"Where God has no power," Cristofano muttered to himself in disbelief.

"Wonderful!" Jonathan exclaimed, increasingly agitated. "I won't be going in there!"

Jeremiah, losing his patience, turned to the captain: "You've been swearing up until now that you've changed and turned to the right path! Jonathan Dalton, since when are you terrified of a valley?"

"Jonathan Dalton fears spirits!" he retorted irritably.

"There are no spirits!" the older bounty hunter yelled back. "Just people who believe in things they can't see because they're afraid of death! Now everyone move forward!"

The riders proceeded slowly and deliberately through the valley. They watched their surroundings closely, keeping their weapons at the ready.

Arisztid glanced at the trees, and a chill ran down his spine. "Look!" He pointed upward.

"Good Lord!" Anton crossed himself.

Crosses of various sizes hung from every branch of every tree around them, from the smallest to the largest.

"There are crosses in the ground as well," Bruce said as they moved forward slowly.

"Watch for any movement," the sheriff whispered over his shoulder.

As they delved deeper into the valley, the natural light of the sun seemed to vanish, replaced by darkness. The ground felt damp, and with every step of their horses, a disgusting squelch echoed, obscured by the swirling fog; they couldn't see what they were stepping on. The sheriff's heart pounded wildly in his chest as he caught glimpses of moving shadows from the corner of his eye. He looked around and saw in his companions the same uneasy fear that he felt. The shadows took on grotesque forms in the darkness, shapeless manifestations of the unexplainable. The forest felt as if something terrible and fateful had occurred in the past, and the crosses were meant to cleanse it, unsuccessfully. The fog that engulfed the valley seemed to move as if it had a will of its own.

Dalton lifted his head and noticed someone standing among the trees, watching them. His eyes seemed to glow red. The stranger's figure blurred in the fog, then disappeared, but the riders felt its presence.

Forming a circle, the group continued, protecting each other, their nerves stretched to the breaking point as they ventured deeper into the valley.

From the unnatural silence of the darkness, they heard a deep, resonant voice that seemed to speak to them, but none of them understood what it said. The members of the group looked around anxiously, searching for the source of the strange sound, but they saw nothing, only the thickening fog, which made it difficult to even see each other.

"There's no one here," Arisztid said.

"Are you sure about that?" Bruce asked. "Something is watching us."

"What in God's name is in this miserable forest?!" Jonathan asked in a trembling voice, holding his weapon in front of him.

"Certainly not God," Anton replied. "How will we know if we're in the right place? What does that damned map say?"

Arisztid trembled as he looked at the paper. He was unable to orient himself and could only hope that they were still heading in the right direction.

"You haven't lost your way, have you?" Jeremiah asked nervously, then snatched the map from the sheriff's hand.

"I haven't lost my way! Although, a tracker like Fred would come in handy... Now, give me back the map!" Wratiszlaw tried to pull the map from the bounty hunter's hand, but he wouldn't let go. A heated exchange ensued between the two men, when Cristofano noticed a figure in the shadow of the tree in front of them.

The younger priest spoke with a trembling voice: "Gentlemen..." he began. "You should see this." He pointed towards the figure.

The two men looked over and immediately fell silent. They watched the unknown figure in front of them with astonishment. In the swirling fog, they couldn't see clearly, but its red eyes were discernible even through the mist.

As the others turned towards it, they all reached for their weapons, but the sheriff intervened: "No, no, no, don't shoot!" he hushed. "If it wanted to harm us, it would have already done so!"

Arisztid turned towards the stranger, dismounted from his horse, and with his hands spread out, almost humbly approached. "Greetings! Perhaps you could help us; I believe we might have gotten a little lost in this... not-so-pleasant valley."

The stranger stood motionless before them, his coal-black clothes occasionally revealed by the dispersing fog. The sheriff continued to approach cautiously, slowly. The shadow didn't respond, only watched the man standing before him with its red eyes.

"Calm down! We won't hurt you. If you want, we can take you away from this damn place, although the road might be a bit bumpy." The sheriff didn't have time to finish his sentence.

From the unknown figure, a bone-chilling, high-pitched scream erupted, then it grabbed Arisztid and lifted him up as if he were a rag doll. With a single swift motion, it pulled him behind the tree and pinned him to the ground. From its reddish eyes, a familiar gaze stared back at him. With its unnaturally white hand, it gripped the sheriff's face and drew it close, as if about to give him a kiss.

Their eyes met, and Arisztid felt the darkness engulfing him once again...

A short moment later, with a huge sigh, he regained consciousness. Gasping for air, he sat up. As he looked around, he couldn't find words to express his surprise; there was no trace left of the foggy, dark, oppressive place. He immediately recognized where he was: in the attic where he had suffered as a child. He looked around, touching the beams with fear and trembling. Standing up, he took a deep breath, and he could almost smell the beautiful forests of Buda, envisioning the mountain he had climbed so many times in his youth. "This is impossible," he said.

He heard a child's cough and startled. Slowly, he turned towards the sound. As he saw the source, his hands began to tremble. He took a few steps back until he hit the wall. Before him, he saw his childhood self, with wide eyes, lying covered in his tiny bed. The child's body was soaked in sweat, tormented by spasms, emitting painful moans. Arisztid took a hesitant step towards him when the noise of footsteps caught his ear.

The door opened, and an elegantly dressed man entered. He wore black leather boots, fashionable trousers, and a black silk shirt. His head was covered with a hood, but his jet-black hair was still visible. The stranger lifted his gaze and looked straight at Arisztid. His eyes gleamed in a radiant blue color like nothing Arisztid had ever seen before. The hooded stranger smiled, sending shivers down Arisztid's spine. The man sat down beside the child on the bed and gently stroked his trembling body. "You'll get better soon," he said. "This will heal you."

Wratiszlaw took tentative steps towards him. The mysterious stranger began to chant while cutting his own skin with a blade. He poured his thick, flowing blood into a bowl containing unknown ingredients to Arisztid. After finishing the chant, he lifted the bowl to the child's mouth and made him drink from it. The boy coughed, then began to convulse. His eyes opened wide.

Wratiszlaw recoiled at the sight. The child's eyes were pure white. He sat up in bed, arms spread wide, resembling Christ on the cross. He tilted his head to the side, smiled, then suddenly his fragile body relaxed and he fell back onto the bed. The man adjusted the boy's blanket, kissed his forehead, then slowly stood up and turned away from the bed. At that moment, a familiar voice from the doorway caught Arisztid's ear. "Will my son recover?" asked a trembling female voice.

The sheriff turned towards the voice. "Mother!" he reached out his arms.

The mysterious stranger glanced up, then walked towards the woman. With each step, the floor creaked uncomfortably. "Now, I demand my payment."

The woman turned her gaze away in alarm, as the stranger approached even closer.

"You knew well what I asked for. First you, then the child."

"But will he survive?" the woman asked, still staring at the ground.

"He will be stronger and healthier than ever before" replied the man. "Until the time comes, he will remember almost nothing of this. We'll be expecting you at the agreed place and time, miss. And remember..." he said in a threatening tone. "If you decide to deceive us, I can make your son sick again at any time."

The woman looked up, hatred and determination shining in her eyes. "I'll be there."

"Excellent." He smiled, then walked past the woman and left.

His mother immediately burst into tears as the door slammed shut downstairs. She approached her son's bed, pulling the unconscious boy close to her. She hugged him so tightly that Arisztid thought she might suffocate him.

"What's all this about?" asked the sheriff in panic. "Just a moment ago, I was in some Mexican nightmare valley with a gang of bandits, and now I'm here on the other side of the world? Can anyone hear me?!"

"You know the way," said the woman, turning halfway towards him.

Arisztid was shocked. "Excuse me?"

The woman suddenly and unnaturally stood up from the bed, catching the sheriff off-guard. His mother grabbed both of his shoulders, her eyes turning burning red, her skin pale. Arisztid tried to scream, but his mother's icy hands covered his mouth. "You know the way!"

She pushed him away, and Arisztid felt like he was waking up from a nightmare as hands grabbed him. He tried to fight back, but he was restrained.

"Calm down!" Bruce shouted.

His voice calmed the sheriff down, and he looked up, finding himself back in the misty valley, surrounded by countless crosses, lying on the ground. "What the hell is happening to me?! What? I don't understand anything! I want to get out of here, I don't want to be here!" he screamed.

"Calm down! Something attacked you, but it's gone now! It's gone!" Bruce reassured him.

"What the hell was that red-eyed thing?!" Arisztid asked hysterically.

"I don't know, but next time, it might be wiser not to make friends with such things," his friend replied.

"Next time, let's just all shoot" replied the sheriff. "Where did it go?"

"As it lunged at us, we tried to take it down, but it was as strong as an ox... It threw Jeremiah aside as if he were just a sack of straw. Dalton, Anton, and I opened fire, and then it ran away."

"Jesus, what if they had hit you?"

"Well, sheriff, that's why we're the best, because we don't hit you, just the target," Anton said proudly.

"How long was I out?"

"Only a few seconds," Bruce replied.

Arisztid rubbed his face, then remembered his vision. "You know the way," his mother had told him. He had no idea what had happened to him, whether what he had seen had really happened, or if his sane mind was slowly collapsing. He looked around, and the confusion he had felt earlier vanished. He became convinced that he really knew where to go. He stood up, brushed himself off, then purposefully turned to the side and started walking. "Follow me, gentlemen!" he said, surprising the others, who then followed the swiftly departing sheriff.

"Stop!" Bearslayer shouted after him. "Where are you going?"

"I don't even know myself," Arisztid replied uncertainly, "but I will find what we're looking for."

The dense canopy of trees barely allowed any light to penetrate, and the eerie silence was only broken by the distant sound of water trickling. Wratiszlaw fervently searched for his destination, paying no mind to the difficult terrain surrounding him. He couldn't exactly tell which way he was going, and he no longer paid attention to his map. He stopped, looked around, but in every direction, all he saw was thick trees. Squinting into the distance, he noticed something. "That way!" He pointed.

The sheriff almost ran, with the others following closely behind. Arisztid felt his lungs betraying him, he gasped for breath, his heart pounding. His feet slipped on the wet rocks. As he looked ahead, he could clearly see their target. "There it is!"

The others also noticed the crypt standing alone beside the swamp, covered by dense vegetation. Its façade had once radiated grandeur, but now only ruins remained. The moss-covered stone walls were marred by huge cracks, worn away by years of rain and decay. The heavy wrought iron gate lay broken and rusted on the ground. Arisztid entered and looked around. He saw nothing but an empty crypt. There was nothing else, only the cold stone walls adorned with some kind of relief. The others caught up with him and also entered.

Arisztid looked at his companions. "What kind of crypt is this, where no one rests?"

"Are we sure we're in the right place?" Jeremiah asked. "I thought we were heading to the catacombs."

The sheriff examined the walls and tried to decipher the relief. He touched the cold stone, which depicted a river. His gaze followed the river, and at its mouth, he saw the entrance to a cave, with two travelers standing in front of it.

"I believe we are in the right place" Wratiszlaw replied. "Father, look! Above the cave, there's a Latin inscription. Do you know what it means?"

Agustíno and his companion approached the relief and examined the inscription. "Ego cum nulla creatura coaeterna sum, sed tantum aeterna; et in aeternum permaneo" the old priest said.

"And what does that mean? Tell us!" urged the sheriff.

"I am not coeternal with any creature, only with the eternal; and I remain in eternity," said Cristofano.

Confusion spread across the faces of the others.

"But we don't have to solve a riddle, do we?" asked Jeremiah irritably.

"No," replied Arisztid. "This is a line from the Divine Comedy..."

"Indeed," nodded Father Cristofano. "Specifically, the beginning of the third canto."

"The gate of hell..." said Arisztid, then buried his face in his hands. "That doesn't help us either. We don't need an empty crypt with a vague quote, we need a miserable entrance! I thought we would find a door where we could just walk in... It was a naive thought of mine."

"Not so sure about that!" said Agustíno as he held his hand against the relief. "Can you feel it? The air is moving."

The sheriff stepped forward and checked with his hand, feeling the cold gentle breeze on his skin. "You're right!" he said. "Let's find the seam and take it off!"

Bruce stepped beside the sheriff, and they searched for the seam with their hands, finding it after a few minutes. Arisztid took out his pistol and shot into the stone. The sound echoed in the crypt, making his head throb. He looked at the stone, which had cracked. Wratiszlaw reached under the stone slab, and together with Bruce, they took it off the wall. A musty smell of decay and mold hit their noses. Arisztid stepped back, trying to get some fresh air into his lungs, then turned around. On the wall, he didn't see a door, just a hole that even a crouching person couldn't fit into. Immediately above the hole, he noticed another Latin inscription written in red. A grimace formed on his face.

"Oh, come on! Why does there always have to be something written on the wall?"

The sheriff, ignoring the message, peered into the hole. "This leads somewhere" he said. "I'll go ahead, you follow."

He pushed forward and climbed into the opening, but before he could proceed, Agustíno grabbed his leg. Arisztid struggled to look back.

"Et ventre reptantes ingrediantur in regnum tenebrarum," Agustíno said. "And they shall enter the kingdom of darkness crawling on their bellies. That's what it says on the wall."

Arisztid shivered as he realized he would have to crawl on his belly to enter the monastery. "Great! This is what they mean when they say God's ways are inscrutable, right?" he said, looking ahead and starting to crawl. "Although these ways could sometimes take me to a place I might enjoy even a little..."

The night was quiet, only the branches of the trees whispered as the wind blew. The shining light of the moon illuminated the path. Diego rode slowly on his horse, lost in his thoughts. As he pondered, memories came flooding back to him. He could never forget the terrified look on his father's face on the day he was able to stand again. Joy filled his soul as he could run and play like a child after a long time. However, the fear and hatred he felt towards his father unsettled him and filled him with doubts. Even as a child, he considered his sudden recovery a miracle of the Lord, which his beloved mother reaffirmed every day in her faith. A pleasant smile spread across his face as he remembered his mother. She was the only person he truly loved. The sorrow he'd felt when she disappeared was indescribable. His father refused to answer, no matter how much he asked. And one day, even his own father gave up on him. The memory of the soldiers appearing in front of their house and taking him away was vivid in his mind. He'd never thought he would return one day. In the distance, he could already see his father's house. He immediately recognized the rickety fence they had built around the house with Rodrigo. Those days were the happiest of his childhood. Like other boys, he worked hard with his father, while his mother awaited them with delicious food in the small house. But all that was long gone. He observed the old, dilapidated fence. It was just like his relationship with his father; torn apart by storms. The lamp was still burning in the house. He knew his father was awake, just as he knew that the sheriff and his team had been here. As he approached, he saw his father sitting outside the house. Ramirez smiled. The old man was waiting... He rode through the gate, then stopped in front of Rodrigo. He tipped his hat and dismounted from his horse. "Good evening, Father. I have returned."

The old Rodrigo slowly, painfully, got up and stepped in front of his son. Tears welled up in his eyes, his lips trembled, he embraced his son and kissed him on the cheek.

Ramirez gently pushed himself away. "What are you doing?" he asked, confused.

The old man smiled and stroked Diego's face. "I'm just glad to see you again after so many years, my dear son."

"I didn't come back to be your son again."

"I know." Rodrigo lowered his head.

"Do you know what happened to my mother, truly?"

The old man looked into his son's eyes, which reflected only sadness. "Did you see her?"

Confusion spread across Ramirez's face. "How did you...?"

"How did I know? I saw her too. She warned me that you would come and finish me. Panic and fear used to control my actions, but not this time. I face you, son, because I am the reason you have become like this."

Diego leaned menacingly close to his father, their faces almost touching. "What kind of?" he asked with a voice filled with hatred.

"A monster," Rodrigo said with a trembling voice. "If I hadn't done what the entity that captured you wanted, you would be in the kingdom of heaven today, and your body would rest in peace. But I condemned you to damnation. Forgive me!"

The old man grabbed his son's arm, but Ramirez shook his father's hand off. "You have no idea what you've truly done! Just as you were unable to serve God with all your heart and soul throughout your life, you still cannot understand His will! I am the Lord's incarnate fist, bringing certainty to the people! I found Kasbeel, which no one was able to do before, and I found a way to set the others free too! The ritual will be performed tonight! The Holy angels of the Lord will walk the earth again to take wives and create the perfect race! Without sin, living for the Lord, without sickness, pain, and death!"

Upon hearing this, the elderly Rodrigo burst into tears, once again grabbed Ramirez's hand, and begged him: "Stop this! STOP IT! Look at what those angels have done to you! Just look at yourself! You can't bear to live in the light, you skulk in the darkness and consume human flesh, drinking their blood too!"

"Just as Jesus told the apostles..."

"No!" his father yelled at him. "Jesus didn't teach them cannibalism, but that He is the only way to salvation! Him, not you!"

"Then how do you explain my accomplishments?!" Diego snapped back. "They follow me faithfully because I showed them the truth!"

"That's not faithfulness if you destroy everything they love and they stick by you out of fear! That's not God's way! It's evil's!"

Diego stepped closer to his father, then whispered softly in his ear: "Would God be evil, too, for destroying humanity with the flood? No... The Creator's ways may seem cruel and violent, but He has always been right. Just like now. He led me to the angel, I owe my abilities to Him, and you can't change that!"

Rodrigo stepped back with a sad look, lowered his head, and wiped his tears from his face. "Then, my son, you will perish. Tonight."

"You mean the sheriff and his useless team? Come on!" He waved it off. "They won't even make it to the monastery gate! Unless..." Ramirez was surprised. "The valley... You sent them to the valley!"

"It's too late, Diego. By the time you return, they will have freed those you kidnapped. Just so you know: the sheriff is just like you. Afflicted with the same sickness, yet he didn't turn into a monster."

Ramirez's eyes reflected curiosity and surprise. "Really?" he asked. "During my travels, I've only heard of one child like me. And he already serves our church. But for you, Father, you don't have to worry about that anymore... Just tell me one thing! Is my mother still alive?"

"Your mother still exists, but she's no longer alive," said Rodrigo, then he took out a vial from his sleeve.

"She exists, but she's not alive...?" Ramirez asked confusedly when he saw the vial.

The old man raised the small bottle to his mouth and drank its contents. His hand trembled, his knees weakened, and he fell. Diego knelt beside his dying father, reached out his hand under his head, and gently lifted it. Rodrigo coughed up blood, then spoke in a choking voice: "Tonight, my son, we stand before the judgment seat of the Lord... Repent your sins so your soul may be cleansed. If you don't, you'll meet the same fate as your mother..."

Rodrigo coughed up blood again, his eyes glazed over, his body trembled, and he convulsed wildly.

"What do you mean she exists, but she's not alive?!" Diego shook the dying man. "Answer me!"

His father stared blankly into nothingness, his body becoming motionless.

Diego released his father's lifeless body and stood up. He brushed himself off, glanced at his horse. He'd died as he lived... meaninglessly and in suffering. He stepped towards his mount, mounted it, and galloped away. He knew he would find the team at the monastery, and he also knew that the hour of reckoning had come.

"Come, give me your hand!" Arisztid said, grabbing Father Agustíno's hand.

The priest groaned in pain, then fell out of the gaping hole in the wall. The sheriff helped him up, dusted him off. Agustíno looked around, sighed, then spoke: "Damn it, I hate narrow passages!"

"No one likes them," Dalton called out as he examined the room with his lantern. "This is a crypt. Look!"

The walls of the burial chamber were damp and moldy. The air was heavy, humid. Arisztid couldn't identify the pervasive smell. He examined the walls, on which there were more reliefs, but he didn't recognize the story. He stepped towards one of the tombs. The heavy stone lid depicted a warrior, resting for eternity with his sword clutched to his chest. "Knightly tombs?" he asked.

"It seems so," Cristofano replied. "These could be the founders. It's incredible! Templars, Teutons, Knights of Saint Lazarus..."

"Then look at this," Jeremiah called out.

The sheriff and the two priests approached the arched entrance of the crypt, above which there was a clearly readable inscription.

"Here rest the holy warriors of God, who gave their souls for the protection of faith," Arisztid read aloud. "Lovely... Where could the captives be?"

"There's only one way, I assume we won't be able to avoid them," Jeremiah said.

"I'll go ahead," the sheriff said. "Jeremiah, Bruce, you come with me. Captain! You and Anton guard our backs. We need to be cautious... We don't know what awaits us."

They proceeded deep into the dark catacombs, the light of torches hanging on the walls illuminating the corridor. Their footsteps echoed with each step. Arisztid held his weapon in front of him, sweat dripping down his temples. Fear swept through his mind again. He tried to push the thoughts away, but they kept coming back. He had no idea about himself anymore. He felt like he was reaching the limits of his endurance, that his mind was about to collapse, and he would perish here in the darkness, alone, consumed by fear.

"Are you okay?" Jeremiah asked.

"I'm fine," he replied. "Do you hear that sound too?" Arisztid stopped, placing his hand on the boarded-up door next to him. A murmuring-like sound filled the space.

"It's as if..." Bruce said. "Someone's speaking."

Jeremiah pressed his ear against another door. "I hear the voices of children and women. Let's set them free!"

The bounty hunter reached for the boards, but Father Agustíno grabbed his arm. "Do you remember what we saw up there? They depicted the story of Virgil and Dante on the relief!"

"So what?" Jeremiah asked back.

"Whatever is inside, I wouldn't open that door."

The two men looked at each other. They stared at each other with angry glances, but Arisztid intervened: "The priest is right! We have to keep going... Whatever is in there, it will stay there."

Elder White let go of the board, pushed Agustíno aside, and caught up with the sheriff.

"I don't like this," Captain Dalton said. "This place gives me the creeps."

"Was the valley perhaps better?" the sheriff retorted. "We'll be out of here soon, and you'll leave Texas."

"Believe me, sheriff... I won't go anywhere near Texas or Mexico." He glanced back at the priests over his shoulder. "And I promise not to break into any more churches! Just look at what became of that."

A half-smile appeared on Cristofano's face, but fear gnawed at his heart too. A greenish light could be seen at the end of the corridor. "Look over there!" He pointed ahead.

Jeremiah grabbed his revolver and started forward, followed by Dalton and the sheriff. The greenish light surrounded them more and more, then they entered the next room, which had once served as a crypt.

As Arisztid realized what he was seeing, he lowered his weapon. His pupils dilated, and a sense of horror swept through his entire body. "Christ in heaven..."

Upon seeing the sight, Cristofano immediately fell to his knees, made the sign of the cross, and began to pray.

Agustíno stood rooted to the spot, staring blankly at the three-meter-high tanks in front of him, filled with a watery liquid. The bodies of the nuns from the Saint Lucia nunnery were immersed in the peculiar liquid, held tightly by grotesque, insect-like creatures. Their probosces protruded from their mouths, piercing the necks of their victims.

Wratiszlaw approached the tanks with trembling steps. "What is this?" he asked incredulously, looking at Agustíno. "What is this? What am I seeing?!"

The priest still looked stunned. He approached one of the tanks and began to examine the creature inside. "It's impossible" he said. "Astounding."

"What the hell is this?" Anton asked.

"These, gentlemen..." he said, and pointed at the tanks. "They are Nephilim."

"What are they?!" the sheriff asked.

"Nephilim," Cristofano repeated. "Angel-human hybrids. The Bible speaks of them."

"This is living proof of God!" Agustíno exclaimed with reverence. "Isn't it marvelous? Just look..." He gestured towards the nuns' thighs. "These holy women gave birth to them and continue to nourish them with their bodies."

Arisztid covered his mouth, feeling his stomach churn. The creatures, once they emerged from their mother's body, didn't detach from her; they clung to her, slowly and gradually sucking in their bodily fluids and innards.

"Dynamite," declared Jeremiah. "I've had enough of this. We'll blow this godforsaken place to pieces."

"I doubt dynamite will achieve anything, Mr. White," replied Agustíno. "And if you blow up this monastery, we'll go down with it."

"Not if we do it smartly," he retorted. "The sheriff and I will stay here with Anton and ensure this place is destroyed. You go on, find the children and the woman. Clear the way for us so we can get out of here."

"I support Mr. White," said Arisztid

"Then let's go!" Bruce shouted.

Bearslayer raised his pistol, with Dalton and the two priests following closely behind. Leaving the crypt, they found themselves once again in a dimly lit corridor. As they passed by stone statues depicting saints, the echoes of faint screams, cries for help, and weeping reverberated around them, but they paid them no mind, pressing forward, not really knowing where to go. The noise of footsteps from the end of the corridor caught Bruce's ear. He raised his fist, then stopped, dropping to one knee and aiming ahead. A monk emerged from behind one of the doors. He muttered curses under his breath, then locked the door with a heavy iron key and headed in the opposite direction to Bruce. Bearslayer signaled to Dalton, who reached for his knife, and they silently followed the monk. The man didn't notice the approaching figures behind him, and by the time he sensed their presence, it was too late. Bearslayer grabbed him, pinned him to the ground, pressed his pistol against his face. The monk cried out in fear, and Bruce covered his mouth. The man trembled, tears welling up in his eyes.

"If you stay quiet, you'll survive" Bruce said. "I'll let you go now, but if you scream, you die. Clear?"

The monk nodded, and Bruce removed his hand from his mouth. The man coughed, trying cautiously to free himself from Bearslayer's grip.

"Don't try anything" Bruce tightened his hold. "Where are the children?"

"Th-the children?" he asked with a trembling voice.

"Yes! The children! The ones Ramirez kidnapped and brought here! Where are they?"

"Th-they're not... they're not here..." he stammered, confused. "The priest took them. They've already repented!"

"Where did he take them?! Answer me!"

"To... all corners of the world," he replied, then smiled.

"Damn it..." Dalton cursed, then rubbed his face. "The nun! Where is the nun?"

The monk glanced towards the door he'd come through.

"Dalton, you go in! We, Agustíno, and Father Cristofano will go ahead and clear the path. Father, do you have your gun?"

"Indeed I do," Agustíno replied, then pulled out his weapon.

"Get ready to use it! Dalton, take the key!"

Bruce tossed the key to the captain, who caught it, then approached the door. Bearslayer's gaze turned back to the monk." And now you die!" he said.

"No!" he cried out. "You said..."

Bruce grabbed the man's head and snapped his neck with a single motion.

"There was no need for that!" Father Cristofano said.

"I just sent him to the Creator! Now let's move forward!" Bruce started walking again, with Cristofano and Agustíno following suit.

Jonathan Dalton opened the door and slowly entered. The cell was illuminated by a single candle, burnt almost to the end. The stench of excrement, urine, and other bodily fluids hit the captain's nose immediately. He covered his nose with his hand as he cautiously stepped forward. In the corner of the cell, he noticed a woman slumped against the wall. Her head tilted to the side, eyes wide open. Her clothes were dirty, smelly, and torn. Her hair was messy and greasy. Dalton took another cautious step towards her, then addressed her: "Miss!"

Kassandra stirred almost imperceptibly, and a glimmer of awareness returned to her eyes. She looked at the man and replied in a lifeless tone: "Did you come to defile me?"

"No, miss," he replied. "I came to free you. Corpus Christi's sheriff is with me, the White brothers, a guy named Bruce, and two priests, straight from the Vatican. Maybe you know them. Fathers Agustíno and Cristofano."

Doubt reflected in the woman's eyes. She reached out towards Dalton, but due to her weakness, it seemed more like a wave. "You're lying" she said. "This is just another of Ramirez's tricks to torture me."

Jonathan knelt beside the now trembling Kassandra, took off his cavalry cloak, and draped it over her. "No, please believe me. We came to rescue you. Can you walk?"

The woman only shook her head.

Dalton sighed, glanced towards the door, then back at the woman. *Damn, I really hope they're actually clearing the way.* "Alright miss, I'll lift you up and take you out of here. Do you know which way the corridor leads from here to the right?"

The woman's gaze became clearer, and her speech more coherent. "To a spiral staircase, which, if you climb, will lead you to the chapel."

"Do they turn off anywhere?"

"Not that I know of."

"Alright. Then I'll take you out of here nicely." Dalton embraced her, then slowly lifted her. Her weight was barely noticeable to Jonathan. He was sure they'd starved and tortured her. He knew exactly what she must have been through. The woman's gaze wandered to the man who looked back at her, and for the first time in his life, he felt that someone was not looking at him with hatred and contempt. Dalton smiled at her, and Kassandra smiled back.

"Thank you" the woman said. "I knew you would come for me."

"Let's get out of here" Jonathan replied.

"You mentioned that Fathers Agustíno and Cristofano are here too? How did Father Guasparre handle the journey? It's surprising for someone of his age to undertake such a long trip."

"Guasparre?" Dalton asked confusedly as he saw the spiral staircase.

"Agustíno."

"Oh, I see! Well... Sometimes we had to rest, but it was no problem. Agustíno handled it well."

"Please stop."

Dalton was surprised but stopped. Kassandra moved, and Jonathan carefully helped her to stand up. "Are you sure you can walk?"

"I'll manage," the woman replied determinedly. "I'll leave this unholy place on my own two feet."

The captain nodded, then took out his revolver, and they started up the stairs.

Bruce cautiously opened the door, holding his weapon in front of him. He peeked inside. He saw a chapel ahead of him, standing empty. He stepped behind the altar and observed the empty rows of benches. The heavy silence that settled upon them disturbed him. He found it too empty, too quiet. "Where are the Indians? The monks? Where is everyone?"

"Perhaps they suffered such heavy losses at the fort that they decided to flee."

Bearslayer shook his head. "Impossible... They still had the upper hand in the end; we had to flee. And the children? Where could they have taken them?"

"To all corners of the world..." replied Cristofano. "At least that's what the monk claimed. If this is an extensive sect, perhaps we can believe him."

"The children are not here..." Bruce replied. "But will we ever be able to find them?"

"Perhaps, if we inquire at the Austro-Hungarian ports or with the French..." Cristofano mused.

"Oh, come on!" interjected Agustíno. "And what would you ask? "Excuse me, do you happen to have a few kidnapped and tortured Texas altar boys?"" he mocked. "You could be smarter than that, Father. The children are already gone."

"Shall we just give up on them, then?" asked Bruce.

"The sheriff will decide whether to continue the investigation," replied Agustíno. "But the townsfolk won't be happy."

"You wouldn't be happy either if your child was kidnapped and sold..."

"My child is already free, walking in the path of God."

He raised his eyebrows and stepped closer to the priest. "Your child? I thought you lived a holy life and took a vow of celibacy."

"I wasn't always a priest," replied Agustíno. "I once lived the life of sinners. I frequented card games, took part in showdowns. It was then that my dear daughter was born, whom I gave to the church. Later, I became a priest."

"That's an interesting story," replied Bruce, noticing out of the corner of his eye that Captain Dalton had also arrived.

Jonathan led Kassandra, who was still trembling, by the arm. Her hair hung in her face, and she stared at the ground with each step.

"Is everyone all right?" asked Dalton without looking

"It's too quiet," replied Bruce. "I don't like it."

"Let's get the lady out and move on. The others will catch up," said Jonathan.

Struggling to maintain her balance, Kassandra stepped towards the altar, cautiously glancing up. Fear etched her face, quickly turning into shock and terror. She grew dizzy and collapsed to the ground.

Dalton reached out, kneeling beside her. He observed the gasping, hysterical woman. "What's wrong?" he asked.

Kassandra lifted her arm and pointed her finger at Agustíno. "He's not Father Guasparre!" she said in a trembling voice.

Dalton frowned, staring at Kassandra.

Agustíno reached for his gun and aimed it at Bruce, who had turned towards him. The sound of the gunshot filled the small chapel.

Jonathan turned towards the sound and saw Bearslayer dropping his weapon and clutching his side. The man staggered, a painful grimace on his face.

Agustíno fired again, hitting the man in the chest this time.

Dalton grabbed the woman and pulled her towards the pews, seeking cover. "What are you doing?!"

The young priest reached for Agustíno's hand, but the old man, with his pistol's handle, struck him across the face. Cristofano fell, clutching his nose. He looked at his bloody hand and heard his companion firing into the pews. He glanced at Bruce, who lay against the wall, pressing his hands against his bleeding wounds. The young priest reached for Bearslayer's gun, but the turning priest stepped on his hand. Sharp pain shot through him, feeling several bones break.

"Don't even try, you filthy scoundrel!" Agustíno shouted. The older priest turned towards Dalton and fired another shot at them.

"Kassandra!" he shouted. "Don't you even greet your dear father anymore?"

"Her father?" Jonathan asked in astonishment.

The woman lowered her head, murmuring a prayer softly. "They struck the convent afterward, once I figured out who controls their church…"

Dalton blew a frustrated breath and checked his ammunition. He cautiously peered out from behind the pew and immediately opened fire on Agustíno. "Stay calm! The sheriff and the White brothers will be here soon!"

The door opposite Dalton swung open, revealing several armed Indians entering, followed by Ramirez. The captain's heart rate quickened as he realized they had fallen into a trap. He closed his eyes, sighed, then leaned out from beside the pew and fired at the Indians. One warrior cried out in pain as the fatal shot struck his chest. His body thudded heavily on the hard stone.

"It's over!" Ramirez yelled. "Drop your weapons and surrender!"

"Go to hell!" Dalton replied, then fired again.

Ramirez crouched behind the pew, but did not return fire. The warriors took cover, assumed firing positions, and waited. A heavy silence fell over the chapel, broken only by the sound of footsteps; the White brothers and the sheriff had arrived.

They all took cover behind shots, while Arisztid, crawling along the wall towards the retreating Agustíno, called out: "Father! Come back to cover!"

The priest aimed his gun straight at the sheriff and fired. Arisztid exclaimed in surprise. He sought cover behind the altar when he saw the severely injured Bruce, whose wounds Cristofano was trying to staunch. "My God! What happened?"

"Agustíno lied to us!" Cristofano said. "He's not who he claims to be, he's with them!"

Anton and Jeremiah White kept the Indians under constant fire as the elder bounty hunter tried to reach Dalton.

Ramirez stood up and confidently advanced, firing several shots towards the brothers. "You won't get out of here!"

Jonathan grabbed Kassandra by the shoulders, looked deep into her eyes, and said, "Run to the sheriff, I'll cover you! Get out of here and finish this bastard!"

The woman nodded, then kissed the captain on the cheek. "Please come with us!"

Dalton winked, then stood up and opened fire.

Kassandra bolted, bullets whizzing and slamming around her.

The sheriff grabbed Sister Gareth and pulled her behind the door for cover. "We can't stay here! Everything down there is rigged with dynamite! We have to break out. Jeremiah!" he shouted. "The dynamite!"

The elder White brother nodded, took out two sticks of dynamite, and tossed them to the sheriff.

Arisztid looked up, watching Dalton as the Indians closed in on him. He lit a match on the sole of his boot, then the dynamite.

"Surrender!" Ramirez yelled. "There's no way out! If you drop your weapons, I promise your death will be painless!"

The sheriff smiled, then discreetly dropped the dynamite behind him through the door, lighting the other one as well. "You know, Diego... You just forgot one thing. And that's what's going to cause your end."

Ramirez grinned. "And what would that be, señor?"

"I'm the damn sheriff!" Arisztid grinned, then tossed the dynamite towards Ramirez. "Dalton, get down!" Arisztid shouted.

A blast shook the chapel, followed by flying wood splinters and smoke. As the dust settled, Wratiszlaw jumped to Bearslayer. "Let's go, buddy, we need to go!"

A series of successive explosions shook the chapel from below. Windows cracked and shattered, statues toppled over.

Bruce looked at his friend with misty eyes. "Go. I'll stay." he said, coughing up blood. "I'll make sure this bastard dies for sure."

"Not happening!" Arisztid shook his head. "You're coming with me! Get up!" The sheriff tried to help his friend stand up, who cried out in pain.

"We have to go!" Jeremiah yelled and grabbed Arisztid. "We have to go, this damn monastery is collapsing! Let's go!"

Bruce pushed his friend away.

The sheriff yelled, Jeremiah held him firmly, pulling him through the chapel. "Do you want to die?! Run, run!"

The stones of the monastery trembled more and more beneath them as the members of the group started running. They raced through the collapsing building's corridor toward the exit.

"There's the gate! Open it, let's go!" the bounty hunter shouted to Dalton.

The captain pushed with all his might and opened the double door. A foul, stale air hit his nostrils, as if dead, decaying plants surrounded them. Once they reached a safe distance, they continued running until they felt they were far enough.

Arisztid turned back and watched as a long crack ran down the tower of the monastery, then it collapsed right where they had just rushed out. He held his head and fell to his knees. "Bruce..."

Dalton stepped beside him, then reassuringly placed his hand on his shoulder. "We need to go."

The sheriff didn't respond, he just stood up and pushed the man away. He approached Cristofano, grabbed him by his clothes, and pressed him against a tree. The air rushed out of the priest's lungs, his eyes bulging. "Give me one good reason why I shouldn't break your damn neck!"

"I didn't... I didn't... I didn't know! Please!"

"Who is the man inside?!"

"I don't know! We first met in Rome, he said he was Agustíno Guasparre!"

"I know who he is..." Kassandra interrupted. "His name is Harry Gareth, and he's my father."

Arisztid released the priest, then stared at the woman. His thoughts raced wildly in his mind, and the memory he had seen in the convent flashed back. "This is unholy betrayal, stemming from my own blood..."

Kassandra nodded. "Once I figured out who was behind it all, I sent a message to the Holy Father."

"But that letter was burned! You kept silent because you feared the consequences! But look around at what it led to!" he shouted.

"I'm sorry!" the woman retorted.

"Enough of this, we don't have time for this!" Anton interjected. "But look over there! Horses... they could belong to the Indians."

Arisztid turned away from the others toward the horses. Anger boiled within him, pain tainted his soul. But he didn't have time to dwell. A strange noise caught his ears, as if something was moving among the ruins of the monastery. The others also turned toward the sound. "What in God's...?" the sheriff whispered.

Emerging from the ruins, a creature unknown to them soared into the sky, then hovered in the air. The wind tousled its golden hair, it spread its insect-like wings, and it looked at the group with glowing red eyes.

"This... this..." Arisztid stammered.

"This is Kasbeel" Cristofano uttered.

The creature spread its arms, then a bone-chilling scream erupted from it.

"Run," the sheriff said softly, never taking his eyes off the creature. "RUN!"

Chapter Ten

"...And without the shedding of blood, there is no forgiveness of sins."

Hebrews 9:22

The pale light of the moon bathed the meadow spread out before them. The sheriff and his team galloped wildly across the landscape, the horses' hooves thundering loudly beneath them. Arisztid glanced back at the sky, scanning it. The peculiar creature continued to fly above them, never losing sight of them for a moment. The sheriff spurred his horse, trying to ride faster as he headed towards the fortress. He knew their only chance of survival was to confront this creature in a covered place.

"What is this?" he asked Kassandra, who was holding onto him tightly.

"Kasbeel. A fallen angel. A Watcher, imprisoned in the mountain by the Creator until Judgment Day!" the woman replied.

"Well, it doesn't seem to me like he's locked in a mountain!" retorted the sheriff. "Do you know how to kill it?"

"I doubt there's a way!"

"Great!" Arisztid sighed. "That's all we needed!"

The creature above them screeched, then launched an attack. With almost blinding speed, it crashed into the ground in front of the riders. A cloud of dust enveloped them. The horses reared up and neighed in terror. The sheriff tried to calm the animal, while also searching for Kasbeel. The thick cloud of dust around him seemed almost unnatural. "Where is he?" he shouted.

"I can't see him!" Dalton replied.

Laughter echoed from the thick dust cloud, then the sheriff suddenly screamed and clutched his head.

"So, you've returned to me, Arisztid. I've been waiting for you."

A gunshot rang out, and the sheriff fell from his saddle. Images flashed before his eyes, of him as a child being watched by a shadow. A golden crown. Glowing eyes. A fang touching his childish face. Another shot echoed, followed by a painful, otherworldly scream.

Arisztid sat up, and Kassandra looked deeply into his eyes. "Don't let it creep into your mind!"

The sheriff shook his head, then stood up. He drew his revolver and waited for the creature to appear. A pair of red eyes emerged in the darkness, and the sheriff opened fire. Kasbeel stepped forward in its full form. The members of the team backed away as they continued to shoot. The angel hissed, then lunged towards Anton. The younger White didn't have time to react. The creature grabbed him, its scorpion-like stinger emerging from its mouth, and plunged it into the man's neck.

Anton screamed in pain. He tried to push it away, but it wouldn't let go.

"Anton!" Jeremiah shouted, then started shooting at the creature.

Kasbeel pulled the bounty hunter towards itself, sucking the life out of him. Bullets rained down on it, hitting its body, but it seemed unaffected by their force.

Captain Dalton frantically reached for his bag, then took out his oil lamp. He lit it and threw it towards the creature. The glass shattered, and the fire spread across its insect-like body. Kasbeel screamed in pain as it released Anton. The younger brother's body fell limply to the ground.

"Keep shooting, let's go!" Dalton yelled.

The creature screamed in agony as its entire body burned. A nauseating, pungent odor filled the air. Kasbeel glanced towards Dalton. Their eyes met, and the captain froze. The creature spread its wings and attacked Dalton. It whistled through the air, then lifted the man into the air. The others kept shooting as they heard a cracking sound. The creature tensed Jonathan's body. The man screamed in agony as he felt his bones shatter. Kasbeel threw him aside, then turned towards the team. With its glowing eyes, it watched them for a moment, then flew up into the sky, disappearing from their sight.

Arisztid ran towards the fallen captain who had fallen further away from him. "Dalton!" he shouted.

He reached the man's lifeless body and knelt beside him. Jonathan Dalton's body lay in an unnatural pose, his skin torn, his muscles ripped apart. His officer's uniform was soaked in red blood, and terror was etched into his gaze. Arisztid closed Dalton's eyelids. "I'm sorry, Captain," he said quietly. Behind him, he heard painful groans. *Anton..* He turned around, then ran to Jeremiah White, who was kneeling beside his brother on the ground. He saw a red wound on Anton's neck, surrounded by greenish, decaying skin.

The younger brother screamed in agony as he clutched his neck. "IT BURNS! MY SKIN IS ON FIRE!" he screamed.

"Sheriff! Opium, now!" Jeremiah shouted.

Wratiszlaw tremblingly took out his last dose of opium and handed it to the man.

The older White brother pried open his brother's mouth and poured the liquid down his throat. Anton's body trembled, his eyes reflected agony.

"I doubt this will help..." Arisztid intervened. "We need to get to the fortress and burn the wound! But we can't stay out in the open sky!"

"We have to help him!" Jeremiah retorted.

"We won't leave your brother behind, but we need to get out of here! That damnation could come back at any moment!" Arisztid shouted.

Jeremiah nodded, then helped his suffering brother sit up.

Anton coughed, the wound on his neck blistered, black blood oozing from it. His skin turned pale, his gaze cloudy.

Jeremiah touched his brother's face. "He's burning up with fever" he said. "Help me get him on a horse!"

The sheriff and the bounty hunter lifted Anton and helped him into the saddle. The older White brother turned to Dalton's body: "That fool..."

"We can't leave him here" Arisztid said. "He doesn't deserve this."

Jeremiah grabbed the sheriff's arm. "We'll come back for him and for Bruce. We'll bury them properly, but we need to reach the fortress!"

The man nodded, and everyone mounted their horses. Arisztid glanced up at the sky, but all he saw was the clear Mexican sky adorned by the moon's glow. Under different circumstances, he might have admired the scenery, but now it only exuded the color of death. He lowered his head and cast one last glance at the field behind them. Spurring his horse, they continued towards the fortress.

Sharp pain shot through Agustíno's back as he crawled out from under the fallen rocks. His eyes burned, filled with dust that scratched his throat. He coughed, sneezed, trying to stand up, leaning against the wall. He wiped his face and looked around. The collapsed monastery wall still stood, but it was no longer safe. He noticed movement from the corner of his eye. Turning, he saw two Indians standing opposite him, their rifles aimed straight at him.

Agustíno nodded as he raised his hands. "Peace, my brothers in the Lord! Father Diego has already spoken of my arrival."

The warriors looked at each other in confusion, then lowered their weapons. "We were waiting for you, Father!" one of them replied.

"Where is Diego?"

The Indians looked at the priest with fear, then one of them replied in a trembling voice: "We dug him out from the ruins earlier. Father Diego... he's dead."

"No!" Agustíno snapped. "Show me where he is!"

The two warriors turned around and hurried towards the former entrance of the monastery. The priest followed them. He was so close to his goal that nothing else mattered. His heart pounded fiercely in his chest as he passed among the collapsed, shattered statues of saints. Stepping through the former arched gate, he saw Diego's motionless body lying on the ground. With slow steps, panting, he approached Ramirez. He knelt down and touched the man's face. His skin was cold. Unnaturally cold.

"Wake up, my friend!" he said. "The Lord still needs you."

Diego lay on the ground with open eyes, every fiber of his motionless body exuding death.

Agustíno leaned in close to the man's nose. He concentrated with every nerve, but he was sure Ramirez wasn't breathing. He looked at the Indian standing beside him with a frightened expression, then gripped his knife. "Are you willing to sacrifice even your life for the Redeemer?"

"Anything!" the warrior replied proudly.

"Lean closer!"

The Indian laid down his weapon and leaned in towards the priest. The man didn't hesitate. He grabbed the warrior by the hair and slit his throat. Gurgling sounds escaped him, his blood sprayed thickly from the long cut. The priest pressed the dying man's face against Diego's and waited.

The Indian choked, his hands twitched spasmodically, his eyes bulged as life left his body.

"Let's go, my friend... Let's go!" Agustíno growled.

Diego's fingers twitched, and the priest, relieved, almost joyfully exclaimed. Life slowly returned to Ramirez's eyes. Hunger, anger, and hatred emanated from his gaze. He seized the Indian and brought him close. With squelching sounds, he drank his victim's blood, then released him. He pushed the lifeless body away and sat up. His face was covered in blood, a wicked smile on his lips. He sighed as he tried to move his limbs. His bones cracked as strength returned to his body.

"So he does live after all!" the priest said relieved.

Ramirez slowly turned his head towards the man. His eyes glowed with unearthly shades, which frightened Agustíno. "May the Lord guide my steps," he replied in a raspy voice. "And I will fulfill His will."

"That's the spirit, my friend!" smiled the old man, then extended his hand and helped Diego up.

The two men stood facing each other under the clear sky, illuminated only by the moonlight. They gazed at each other intently, with admiration, and finally, the priest broke the silence. "I will never forget the day we first met!"

"Damascus," nodded Ramirez. "Your letter changed my life. I found it..." he said reverently. "I found Kasbeel thanks to your guidance! And the others will soon be free again!"

"And together we will change the lives of all people!" Agustíno grabbed Ramirez's shoulders and looked deeply into his eyes. "Do you have the blood?"

Diego took out two small vials from his pocket. "Of course, Father! The blood of the broken and the warrior."

He handed the vials to the priest, who took them and replied: "And I have brought the holy blood. Everything is ready for the ritual!" His gaze darkened, then he continued in an ominous tone: "We must deal with the remnants of the group. I was unable to get rid of them on our journey... I persuaded that senile old man that we didn't need armed escort, but the Pope insisted. He doesn't trust me. He couldn't prove it, but he suspected that I am not who I claim to be. But believe me, my friend, the Vatican has long lost this battle. We are already everywhere!"

Ramirez smiled. "If the Lord is with us..."

"Who can be against us?" Agustíno finished.

"Just leave the sheriff and his team to me. I'll deal with them easily," he scoffed. "They thought they could destroy Kasbeel's children with a few sticks of dynamite... If they only knew how wrong they were!" Ramirez perked up at the sound of chains.

Bruce cursed loudly as two Indians dragged him, chained, out of the rubble. His shirt was soaked in blood, his face contorted in pain. The warrior leading him jerked the chain, and Bearslayer fell to his knees. He wheezed, each exhale accompanied by a high, whistling sound from his lungs.

Ramirez stepped forward, then grabbed his face and looked into his eyes. "And they shall go forth, and look upon the corpses of those who have transgressed against me, for their worm shall not die, neither shall their fire be quenched; and they shall be an abhorring unto all flesh!"

Confusion reflected in Bruce's pained gaze. "What the hell are you talking about?" Bearslayer coughed up blood, some of which splattered on Diego's face, who merely smiled.

"You will burn! Your scream will be the symphony of their return! Oh, how joyfully I will listen to your suffering, and see how life fades from you in bitter agony! And from the flames, the rejected ones shall rise!"

Upon hearing the words, Bruce closed his eyes. He knew it was over. He would soon die, and only the faint hope comforted him that perhaps he would bleed out before they burned him alive. "It doesn't matter, you rotten corn-eater! The sheriff is long gone... We won!"

"Oh, really?" Diego asked. "I believe they went to the fortress." He pointed to his temple, then continued, "You see, dear Bearslayer, my connection with the holy angel of the Lord is much deeper than one of your kind can understand. He speaks to me; I hear his voice in my head. One of them is finished. And we will deal with the rest."

Bruce coughed again, blood streaming down his chin. "I wouldn't brag about voices talking to me in my head. But don't worry... It's not your fault. You Mexicans are like dogs. If there's something wrong with the bitch, the puppy will be worthless, too."

As he uttered the words, Ramirez hissed, then struck Bearslayer across the face with his fist. The man laughed. "What are you going to do? Beat me to death before you burn me?"

The Mexican squatted beside him, a wicked smile on his face, as he took out his knife and handed it to the Indian next to him. "Heat up the blade!"

The warrior nodded, then took the knife and made a fire. He struck two stones together several times until the pile of branches on the ground caught fire. The Indian dipped the blade into the flames and waited.

"You don't need every body part or limb for the ritual, señor... I've heard enough about you, Bearslayer Bruce... the scalp hunter. Oh, what a reputation you have! These here behind me," he gestured to the Indians, "used to frighten their children with your stories. 'If you don't come home before dark, Bearslayer will take you! ' they used to say. Though, I have no idea why they call you that. Have you ever killed a bear? But it doesn't matter... Not at all. But one thing matters a lot, Bruce! Do you believe in God?"

"Well, certainly not yours!"

"There is only one God, my friend! Just one! But you won't see Him with your own eyes in this earthly existence."

The Indian stepped beside Diego, bowed as he handed over the knife. The Mexican grabbed Bruce's hair, pressing the hot blade against his eye.

Bearslayer was overwhelmed by pain, crying out as he felt his skin sizzle, burn, and his eyeball burst in its socket.

The Mexican held onto the bound man tightly as he kicked, trying to escape, but he was unable. Ramirez let go, and he fell to the ground. The smell of burnt flesh filled the air, but Diego wasn't done yet. He straddled Bearslayer's prone body, knelt on his chest, and stopped the knife in front of his other eye. Contempt radiated from Bruce's eye. "So, even with your last glance, you still scorn me?"

"For all eternity!"

Ramirez didn't hesitate. He pressed the hot blade against the eyelid, filled with joy as he listened to the screams. It was music to him, always empowering. The feeling of power. He took the knife away, then stood up. He took a deep breath and looked up at the sky. He was filled with reverence as he saw the angel soaring in the sky. This was his moment, the happiest moment of his life, because he felt like victory was his. "Gather the survivors! All of them! We're heading to the fortress!"

Arisztid was hit by the wind; he lowered his head and spurred his horse on again. The horse galloped as fast as it could. He didn't know the animal, so he could only hope it wouldn't get scared and throw them off. He glanced back over his shoulder and watched Anton. The younger White brother was barely conscious. His head tilted to the side, his eyes almost closed, his arms hanging limply by his side. The sheriff was seriously concerned that he could fall out of the saddle at any moment. His brother, protective, closed ranks beside his younger brother, watching his every move. Wratiszlaw looked ahead, from the cover of the trees he could already see the fortress. They could only hope that the Indians had already left, but they had no choice. When they reached the clearing, they rode straight toward the main gate, bullets not raining down on them. They went in through the open gate, then dismounted from their horses. Arisztid approached Anton. The man just whimpered, emitting painful sounds.

Jeremiah and Arisztid took him off the saddle.

"That way!" Cristofano said, pointing towards the office of the fort.

The bounty hunter grabbed his brother, then tried to lift him up, but the sheriff intervened: "No! I'll bring him! You're better at shooting than I am, and they could attack us at any moment!"

Jeremiah shot Arisztid an angry glance for wasting time, then nodded a moment later. He took out his gun, ready to fire, and headed for the stairs leading up, closely followed by the others.

Wratiszlaw's stomach churned, tears welled up in his eyes as he got a closer whiff of Anton's rotting skin. The younger White's eyes widened, frothy saliva spilled from his mouth, and he began to choke. "Faster!" Arisztid shouted. "He's dying!"

Reaching the top of the stairs, Jeremiah gathered his strength and kicked the wooden door open with a single motion. He rushed in, looked around, found no one there. He looked toward the bed and yelled: "Lay him down! Let's go!"

The sheriff stepped to the side of the bed and gently laid the helpless man down. He took his gun, then tore open his shirt with a quick motion. He recoiled at the sight before him and covered his mouth in horror. "Oh my God!"

Ulcerated sores appeared on Anton's body, his skin had turned deep red, interspersed with black veins. He turned his head to the side, the gaping wound on his neck completely festering, from which tiny, worm-like creatures emerged.

Jeremiah watched his brother's agony in shock and disbelief. He couldn't move, his words caught in his throat. He glanced at Father Cristofano, whose expression mirrored the same horror as everyone else's.

"What is this?!" the sheriff asked angrily.

"I... I don't know!" the priest stammered. "I couldn't even imagine this, I've never seen anything like it!"

"Enough of your lies!" Arisztid grabbed the priest, pressing him against the wall, drawing his revolver and pressing it to the man's temple. "Speak, or I'll kill you!"

"Okay!" Cristofano surrendered. "I'll tell you! I'll tell you everything!"

"I'm listening," said the sheriff, cocking the hammer.

"The Holy Father sent us to retrieve the notes of John Dee and Edward Kelley along with Kassandra Gareth!" Cristofano exclaimed.

"What?" Arisztid asked angrily.

"The notes of John Dee and Edward Kelley about the angels," Kassandra interjected.

"These two scholars were obsessed with angels," Cristofano continued. "They studied them and allegedly developed a method with the tools of science at the time to find them. The Vatican began to investigate the matter and seized all their notes."

"Because John and Edward didn't find the heavenly angels," the woman said, "they found the ones buried in the

296

earth. The outcasts, the fallen, and the traitors. The notes proved so dangerous that they were never kept in their entirety in one place. Part of them was hidden in Damascus, part in the St. Lucia nunnery, and part in the Black Monastery. However, Ramirez seems to have been able to communicate with one of them without knowing the full text."

"And what can he do with the complete text?" asked the sheriff.

"I believe he can free all the fallen ones, whom the Lord imprisoned in the mountains as punishment until Judgment Day."

"He needed blood for that," Kassandra said. "And if I'm guessing correctly, he got it. Definitely from me."

"He got some from me too," Arisztid nodded.

"Agustíno cut me back at the monastery," Cristofano said, lowering his head.

"What happens if he manages to release those abominable beings?"

"If we take the Holy Scriptures as a reference," the priest said, "we can state that a fully empowered angel can destroy thousands in a moment."

"But since these are not fully empowered angels, it's hard to say exactly what will happen, but we can't expect anything good."

"Do we even know how many of them there are?" asked the sheriff irritably.

"In the Vatican, we know of twenty thousand... If they're even remotely as powerful as Kasbeel, then thousands, if not millions, will fall victim... And if they can reproduce..."

Arisztid closed his eyes, trying to digest what he'd heard. Behind him, Anton suffered in pain, his anguished groans piercing his soul. "How can we stop it?"

"We don't know..." Cristofano replied. "There is no written record of a human ever triumphing over an angel."

"Our only chance is to stop Ramirez," Kassandra said. "If the Watchers are freed, humanity is lost."

"But you won't be the ones to stop him," Arisztid declared. "You need to leave Mexico and alert the Pope."

Kassandra started to protest, but the sheriff raised his hand, silencing her.

"This is not up for debate!" he said firmly. "Mr. White and I will hold off Ramirez at the main gate. Meanwhile, you will sneak out through the tunnel and head to the port. Pedro is still waiting for us."

"What tunnel?" Cristofano asked, surprised.

"This is an old Spanish fort, Father!" Arisztid spread his arms. "The officers and important people always had an escape route. It will be near the dungeons, I'm sure of it. Take the horses and escape."

The priest and Kassandra exchanged fearful glances, both reflecting shame in their eyes.

"You can't stay here," Kassandra said. "You came for me, you freed me! I don't want more people to die because of me!"

"If we go, we'll all die," Jeremiah interjected, kneeling beside his unconscious brother. "This way, at least, we buy you time to get out of here." The bounty hunter stood up, anger, pain, and hatred burning in his eyes. He stepped to the window, looked out, and then spoke. "Not too long ago, you suggested, Sheriff, that I do something noble and selfless for free. I thought about your words... Now, I give my life to save two people and perhaps all of humanity as we know it."

The sheriff stepped up to the bounty hunter and placed a friendly hand on his shoulder, but the man stepped aside and continued:

"We need to set traps before the gate and find firing positions along the fort walls."

The sheriff nodded, then looked at Anton. "What about your brother? Perhaps it would be better... to end his suffering."

Jeremiah pondered the words, then stepped back to the window. Tears welled up in his eyes, and he wiped his face with his hand. He knew the sheriff was right, and he also knew that under different circumstances, he would do the same. If he were the one lying in that bed, he would expect his brother to do the same for him... He lowered his head, his face contorted in a painful grimace, then he struck the hard stone wall with all his might. A desperate cry erupted from him, a mix of pain and grief. "Leave the room," Jeremiah said quietly. "But the nun and the priest should stay."

"Why?" Arisztid was stunned.

"Ramirez needs to see them; otherwise, he'll send a team after them. If he thinks they're here, he'll only fight us."

"Smart thinking, Mr. White," replied the sheriff.

"Now, please leave us alone."

Wratiszlaw nodded, then took Kassandra by the arm, and they left the officer's office.

Father Cristofano knelt beside the dying Anton. His eyes were bloodshot, his skin swollen, and the gaping wound on his neck had turned black. The festering pus emitted a nauseating stench, crawling with tiny worms. The priest made the sign of the cross and administered the last rites.

Anton, summoning all his strength, looked at the priest. "Thank you, Father," he said weakly.

The priest nodded and then hurried out.

Jeremiah sighed, burying his face in his hands, then turned and stepped towards his brother. His heart ached as he looked at his brother lying on the bed, suffering in pain and dying. He felt like he had failed again, unable to protect him, just as he couldn't save his family. He sat down beside Anton, avoiding his gaze, staring ahead. Finally, he broke the heavy silence: "I'm sorry, little brother," he said in a choked voice. "I knew we shouldn't have come, just as I knew those damned priests were hiding something."

"Jer..."

"I can't believe that just a few years ago, our whole family was dining together, happy and safe. And today, the last White is dying."

"Jer..." Anton said louder.

Jeremiah looked at his brother.

Anton mustered all his strength to overcome the pain and speak to his brother one last time. He reached out and grabbed Jeremiah's arm. "Listen to me, Jer. You are a good man! I know because I've known you since I was born. I couldn't have asked for a better brother. But bad things happened to us that sealed our fate. My journey ends today..."

Jeremiah bowed his head, his tears flowing like Anton had never seen before.

"Sis would be proud of you, just like Mom and Dad. I am too. But promise me something!"

"Anything, Anton!"

"Survive this day and start a new life! Leave your pain behind. Please..."

Jeremiah squeezed his brother's hand and stroked his head. He was shocked to see a whole handful of Anton's hair come away in his hand. He looked into his brother's eyes and then answered: "I promise."

"Release me from my torment, please!" Anton groaned. "I feel decay and rot in every part of my body. Send me to be with our family!"

Jeremiah averted his gaze and let go of his brother's hand. He stood up and slowly drew his revolver. He cocked the hammer. The cold metal's click echoed off the room's stone walls. He sighed and aimed the gun at his brother. The two men looked into each other's eyes.

Anton smiled and closed his eyes. "Thank you."

A gunshot filled the room. Jeremiah dropped the gun. His heart pounded in his chest, and his inner turmoil choked him. He fell to his knees and began to sob. His last family member was gone, and he felt a loneliness he had never imagined.

Summoning all his strength, he stood up and covered Anton's body. "I will bury you, brother," he said in a choked voice. "I'll take you back to the family estate, and everyone will rest together. I promise!"

Arisztid stood by one of the fort's windows, staring into the distance. He saw no movement. The moon cast strange shadows on the trees, making him unsure whether he truly saw them or if his mind was playing tricks on him. He sighed. His voice was filled with pain, grief, and bitterness. He thought of the deceased. He lifted his gaze to the sky, and another thought crossed his mind. Today, he would die. He knew and felt it. He had no idea who or what would kill him, but he knew it was over. He didn't mind. He felt no fear and had no desire to cling to life with tooth and nail. Maybe because death had already embraced him in his childhood. Perhaps the wars he had fought had eradicated the instinctual will to live. He accepted his fate. What he had seen in the monastery was so shocking that he didn't dare to think about it. Whenever Kasbeel came to mind, every part of his mind protested and feverishly denied the fact that they were being hunted by a supernatural being. He searched his pocket for a cigarette, then lit it. He smiled and exhaled the smoke. *It would be simpler to be insane than to comprehend all this*, he thought.

Out of the corner of his eye, he saw Cristofano approaching, but he didn't turn toward the priest. He didn't know what to feel about him. Perhaps the priest was a victim too, perhaps not. Nevertheless, he and Jeremiah had decided to let him go with Kassandra. The priest stopped beside him and cleared his throat. The sheriff looked at him. Shame radiated from the man's every movement. "What do you want, Father?" he asked.

The priest stood with his arms folded, his words barely audible. "Sister Gareth and I found the way out. We also took the liberty of preparing the horses."

"Great!" Arisztid replied indifferently. "But you can't leave yet. Ramirez needs to see that you're still here, or else every damned Indian will hunt you down. Hopefully, we can hold them off long enough for you and Kassandra to get a safe distance away."

"I... I'm sorry, Sheriff," the priest said with genuine sorrow in his voice.

"Don't be. Just escape, and we'll handle the rest."

"I will pray for you, Arisztid! I hope we meet again!"

"Don't bet on it..."

The sound of a gunshot echoed in their ears. They both turned toward the noise, and a moment later, the sheriff reached for his pistol and started running. Sprinting through the hallway, he headed for the officers' quarters, where Jeremiah was already standing by the door. Arisztid knew what had happened. The two men watched each other, then Arisztid holstered his revolver, took off his hat, and nodded. "I'm sorry, Mr. White. Your brother was a fine man and an exceptional marksman."

Jeremiah didn't respond. Filled with rage, he pushed the sheriff aside and stormed off. Arisztid followed, catching up to him. "What are you planning?"

"This is a fort, isn't it?" Jeremiah asked irritably. "There have to be mines, cannons, and if we're lucky, maybe even dynamite. Let's set traps for these bastards!"

Wratiszlaw nodded and took off running. He headed towards the armory while Jeremiah went to the courtyard.

Arisztid opened the armory, looked around, and finally felt a stroke of luck. Dynamite sticks, ammunition, repeating rifles, and pistols were lined up against the wall. He stepped to the wall, took a belt, and started filling it with ammunition. He also put some in his pockets and hid dynamite in his boots.

"Sheriff, look at this!" Jeremiah shouted.

Arisztid stepped out of the armory and saw White leaning against a massive cannon, smoking a cigarette.

The man patted the weapon. "With this, we can give them a real roasting!"

"That's for sure, Mr. White!" Arisztid smiled. "We won't give ourselves up easily to these scum!"

"I see movement!" Cristofano shouted. "They're coming!"

The sheriff and the bounty hunter exchanged a glance, then both ran to the window. Torchlight illuminated the trees. Smoke billowed from the forest, and then Indians and monks emerged. They marched in military order, led by Diego Ramirez, with Father Agustíno closely beside him.

"Get the rifles!" Jeremiah ordered. "When they're in range, we shoot."

They stopped in the distance, out of range, so they couldn't be reached. Diego was brought a horse, mounted it, and began to gallop towards them.

Arisztid's heart raced as he saw him. "What the hell is he doing?" he asked.

"Look!" Jeremiah pointed. "He's got a white flag. He wants to negotiate."

"Whatever happens, shoot that bastard, understood?"

"I think we should hear him out," the bounty hunter retorted. "Let him see that we have the girl. While he's talking to us, Kassandra and Cristofano can show themselves and then sneak out through the tunnel. When we get tired of talking, then we shoot..."

Arisztid grimaced, but he understood what Jeremiah meant. "I'll talk to him."

The bounty hunter nodded.

Ramirez, holding a white flag high, slowly trotted towards the fort gate. A wicked smile spread across his face, his eyes glinting with an otherworldly light. He stopped and looked directly at the two men, as if he knew exactly where they were standing. "Good evening, gentlemen." He nodded. "Sheriff, please come down. I wish to speak with you."

"And what do you want to talk about, Diego?" Arisztid asked. "Say it from there, you stinking Mexican dog!"

Diego laughed and replied: "I thought you were better brought up than that, señor! Don't disappoint me! I do not wish to take your life; I only want the girl and the priest! If you hand them over, you and the two bounty hunters can leave freely!"

"I trusted you once before, and you killed my friend in return!" Arisztid shouted. "Kiss my hairy European ass, you corn-eating Mexican dog!"

Kassandra stepped up beside the sheriff, along with Cristofano. Both of them watched Diego intently.

"What more do you want from me, Ramirez?" Kassandra asked. "Is there anything left that you haven't taken from me?"

"Your father needs you, señorita!"

"Go," Arisztid whispered to the woman. "I'll go down and stall him for a bit longer."

Kassandra gave a barely perceptible nod, then stepped back from the window and headed towards the courtyard.

"You know what, Ramirez?" the sheriff called out. "I'm coming down! Just tell me what you want! And don't skimp on the details!"

Wratiszlaw turned his back on Ramirez, then hurried down the steps to the fort gate, which he opened, standing face to face with the Mexican. A shiver ran through him as he looked into those otherworldly red eyes. "How the hell do you do that? One eye completely white and the other brown during the day, but red at night?" he asked mockingly.

"Don't push your luck, sheriff," Diego said coldly. "I'm not here for small talk. Hand over the girl and the priest, and I will spare your lives."

"And if I don't?" Arisztid asked.

"Then I'll kill you all, including them," Ramirez replied.

"So if I hand them over, you'll only kill them? Do you really think I'd hand over an innocent woman and a defenseless priest to a Mexican killer? I'm a man of the law! No matter how much you ask, I won't do it!"

"If you won't, then maybe the White brothers will persuade you..." Diego glanced at Jeremiah, then back at Arisztid. "Where is Anton? Could it be he succumbed to Kasbeel's kiss?"

A shot rang out, then another. The sheriff threw himself to the ground and rolled aside. Looking up, he saw Ramirez's horse collapse, dead. At the last moment, the Mexican had leapt from the saddle, returning fire as he fell.

"The only reason I didn't shoot you between the eyes is because you're hiding behind that white flag!" Jeremiah shouted. "But if you don't get back to your redskin gang, the next one's for you!"

Diego stood up and dusted himself off.

Jeremiah continued: "Run back to your rabble! Let's see you move! Now!"

The bounty hunter fired more shots, which landed near Diego's feet. The Mexican retreated, turned his back, and started to run.

Arisztid gestured for Jeremiah to stop, but he ignored him. The sheriff knew that humiliating the Mexican would have serious repercussions. He sprang to his feet, ran back through the gate into the fort, and locked it behind him.

Ramirez ran back to his monks with a face twisted in anger. He hated being humiliated and couldn't let these infidels mock him.

As he drew nearer, Father Agustíno stepped in front of him and asked anxiously: "Are you alright, my child? Where is the girl? The ritual is pointless without her!"

Diego didn't answer, merely gesturing to one of the monks, who nodded and ran into the trees. "These bastards will learn that they can't mess with the warriors of the Lord! We'll offer a burnt sacrifice! There's no way out of the fort anyway! They're trapped!"

Agustíno noticed the sound of chains, followed by Bearslayer's agonized screams. The man was tied to a tree, cursing loudly. Bruce's burned eyes were covered with a black cloth. His open white shirt was soaked with sweat, and fever burned his body. He panted, tormented by pain. The ropes around his wrists tightened, cutting into his flesh. The priest's eyebrows raised at the mention of a sacrifice, and he stepped closer to Diego. "A burnt sacrifice?" he exclaimed. "But the Lord Himself forbids it!"

Ramirez turned to the priest and replied angrily: "You will do what the Creator commands, and I will do what He desires!" he hissed. "We will show our dedication to the Lord and teach them to fear our church!"

Diego turned away and signaled to the Native Americans. The warriors poured kerosene around Bearslayer's feet, on his clothes, and on the tree to which he was tied. After they finished, they stepped back, knelt down, and made the sign of the cross. They whispered confessions of their sins, seeking forgiveness.

Ramirez approached Bruce and spoke to the suffering man: "Your little friends will now see what happens when they defy the almighty will."

"You'll die!" Bearslayer responded, spitting in Ramirez's face.

The Mexican was taken aback, wiping the sticky saliva from his face. He pulled a match from his pocket, struck it, and spoke to Bruce again: "Save your breath for screaming! May the Lord have mercy on you!"

The Mexican flicked the match, igniting the kerosene. Flames shot up, momentarily blinding Ramirez. He shaded his eyes with his hand and watched Bruce being consumed by the flames. The man's face contorted in agony, choking and coughing from the smoke. Diego turned and faced the kneeling Native Americans. The warriors were entranced by the flames, the pale light casting eerie shadows on them. The Mexican spread his arms and began to speak: "Behold, my brethren, and see with your own eyes what we are! Behold, we are dust and ashes!" He pointed to Bearslayer, who lifted his head to the sky and screamed. "This man yielded to the devil's temptation and ate of that forbidden fruit called sin. And in that fruit, he ate death, not just for himself, but for his entire race. God was wrathful and thus cast him into the fiery pit of death and hell! Look! Behold!"

The Native Americans looked at Bruce, who screamed in agony, his face blistering and his clothes catching fire. The smell of burning flesh filled the air.

Ramirez clasped his hands in prayer and continued: "Deliver us from the devil's pursuit and the torment of hell! And lead us to the peace of paradise, and grant us the path to heaven and participation in all that is good!"

The painful screams almost drowned out the Mexican's voice.

Agustíno watched Bearslayer, then turned his gaze away. He couldn't bear to see the man's agony.

Ramirez fell to his knees, raised his arms to the sky, and continued in an enraptured voice: "And cry out to our Lord three times! Lord, have mercy!"

"Have mercy!" the Native Americans shouted in chorus. "Have mercy!" they all pleaded together.

Ramirez closed his eyes and deeply inhaled the smoky air. The symphony of suffering filled him with a perverse joy. He opened his eyes and saw terrified, astonished faces. He knew the time for the final assault had come.

"You've lost your mind!" Arisztid shouted when he saw Jeremiah. "What gave you the nerve to shoot at him?! We were supposed to buy time, not play cowboy!"

"We should have finished him off!" the bounty hunter retorted.

"All that would have done is get us overrun and killed! Then it would be for nothing, they'd catch Cristofano and Kassandra!"

"We're going to die anyway!" Jeremiah shouted. "At least we could have killed that Mexican bastard!"

Arisztid angrily punched the wall, then cursed as he leaped to the railing overlooking the fort's interior. He scanned for Kassandra and Cristofano, who were leading their horses to the cellar entrance. "You need to escape!" the sheriff shouted, tossing dynamite to the priest. "Once you're out of the tunnel, blow it up! They can't catch you!"

The priest caught the explosive and examined it carefully. Pain and sorrow were reflected in his eyes. He looked up at Arisztid and replied: "God bless you all!" he said. "I will pray for you!"

The sheriff smirked and replied sarcastically: "Just blow up that tunnel, Father. Take care of yourselves!"

Kassandra waved at him, and then both disappeared down the cellar entrance.

Wratiszlaw sighed and checked his bullets. The smell of smoke and burning flesh filled the air.

"You have to see this!" Jeremiah said.

The sheriff ran to the window and saw a human figure tied to a tree in the distance, surrounded by thick flames. He squinted to see more clearly. His pupils dilated, and his heartbeat quickened as he recognized his friend. "Bruce..."

The bounty hunter pressed his brother's rifle to his shoulder and took aim. "The wind is in our favor... Anton could take out that bastard, but I can only hope." The wind carried the sound of screams and the smell of burning flesh.

Arisztid felt his stomach churn. "Shoot Bruce!" he yelled. "Show him mercy! No one deserves to die like that!"

"I'm sorry, but the Mexican can't stay alive," the bounty hunter replied.

Wratiszlaw reached for his pistol and pressed it to Jeremiah's temple. "Shoot Bruce, or I'll end you!"

"We're dead already, Sheriff..."

"Shoot Bruce!" he shouted. "If it were Anton there, would he hesitate for a second?"

A shot rang out, then Jeremiah lowered the rifle. He tossed the gun to the sheriff and walked away, calling over his shoulder: "Your friend is dead. Now let's load that cannon!"

Arisztid glanced out at the field in front of the fort. He saw a wave of charging Indians, running toward the fort walls with reckless bravery. "I'm staying here. I've got plenty of dynamite and ammo. I'll hit them from here, but if they break through, you give them hell!"

"You don't have to tell me twice, Sheriff!"

Wratiszlaw prepared short-fused sticks of dynamite and took up a firing position. He pressed his rifle to his shoulder and focused all his attention on the approaching Indians. He recalled his first battle against the Austrian troops. He had been only fourteen when he took his first life. He was surprised at how easy it had been, but he saw no glory in war—only death, pain, and suffering. A dishonorable end, celebrated only by politicians, kings, and emperors within the safety of their palaces. The warriors screamed as the first shots were fired. Bullets struck around him, embedding in the walls, tearing through barrels, or whizzing through the fort. The sheriff aimed and fired, again and again. He knew his aim was terrible, so he didn't expect to hit anyone. He set the rifle down and reached for the dynamite. The match struck with a hiss against the sole of his boot, igniting the fuse. He threw the explosive, covered his ears, and took shelter behind the stone wall. An explosion filled the air, followed by cries. He reached for another stick of dynamite and tossed it out the window. More followed, one after another. Thick black smoke enveloped the landscape, obscuring everything from view. The screams had died away, leaving only an eerie silence and the harsh, grating buzz in his ears. Cautiously, he peered out the window. Through the dissipating smoke, he thought he saw a human figure with glowing red eyes piercing through the smoky veil like a predator sizing up its prey before striking. Although he couldn't see clearly, he instinctively knew the man was smiling. A sharp, whistling sound filled the air. He looked up in horror and saw the winged creature.

Kasbeel spread its wings wide and flew with full force at the old gates of the fort. The ancient double doors exploded into splinters as the angel passed through them. The ground shook beneath the sheriff, causing ammunition boxes and barrels of gunpowder to topple over. Arisztid lost his balance and fell. Summoning all his strength, he got up and rushed to the railing, looking for Jeremiah. The man was hiding behind the cannon, lighting it with a torch. Arisztid glanced toward the gate. The angel was kneeling, its golden-blond hair obscuring its face, and its pale golden crown glinted ominously in the smoke.

"Damn you!" the bounty hunter yelled, lighting the fuse.

With a deafening roar, the cannon fired and struck Kasbeel. The angel was hit in the chest, lifted off the ground, and hurled out of the fort.

Arisztid shouted in triumph and rushed to the stairs, searching for Diego. Jeremiah stepped out from behind the cannon, his weapon ready. From the thick smoke, Ramirez emerged and fired shots. The bounty hunter returned fire. The Mexican, advancing resolutely without cover, broke into the fort. The elder White brother, inching forward behind the crates, tried to flank the Mexican. Stepping out from the crates to take aim, he was shot before he could fire.

Jeremiah cried out in pain, his revolver slipping from his hand as he clutched his chest. Blood soaked through his shirt.

Diego fired again, and the bounty hunter collapsed to his knees, unmoving.

A wave of icy terror swept over the sheriff. He froze. Every nerve in his body was on edge; he wanted to run but couldn't move. It was as if his body had given up the fight, awaiting the release of death. His lips began to tremble, and he couldn't take his eyes off the motionless White. *I'm alone.*

Ramirez watched the bounty hunter for a brief moment, then slowly, deliberately, turned toward the sheriff. His red eyes bore the lascivious, murderous gaze of a predator, leaving Arisztid with no doubt that the Mexican was relishing every second.

"Where is the girl?" he asked. "It's over, sheriff. Hand her over, and you'll be spared! If you want to survive, do as I say!"

Arisztid stood motionless on the landing, his heart pounding in his chest. He had no idea what to do. He knew he had no chance against Diego. Gathering all his strength, he broke into a run, sprinting down the stairs and across the fort's inner courtyard. He tried to reach the cannon, but he wasn't fast enough. Bullets hit the ground in quick succession at his feet, driving him towards the fort's storage areas. He backed away until he stepped into the armory. Closing the door behind him, he leaned against it, panting, his body drenched in sweat. The acrid, foul air burned his lungs. His throat was completely dry, and his hands began to tremble. He felt the darkness engulfing him again. Grasping his head, he let out a painful scream, a mixture of grief, torment, and agony. He was not in control of his mind. Hatred flared within him, and he punched the wall with all his might. His skin tore immediately, leaving a bloody mark on the wall. "Get out of my head!" he screamed. He punched the hard stone wall again and again until the pain became unbearable. His mind cleared. He looked up and around. The rifles propped against the walls were all empty. The ammunition had been used up, and he had only a few bullets left. With trembling hands, he took the remaining rounds out of his pocket. He counted four. "Damn it," he cursed. Carefully peering out the window, he saw an Indian warrior joining Ramirez. Perhaps he was the only one left alive. Arisztid couldn't know for sure, but he sincerely hoped so. He sighed, mustering all his strength as he stepped towards the open window, aiming at Ramirez. His shot missed its mark, the bullet flying off into nothingness. He didn't have time to fire again before a barrage of gunfire rained down on him from the two men. He threw himself to the ground. Bullets pounded into the walls through the small window, knocking rifles off their hooks or ricocheting back. It was only thanks to his luck that none of the stray bullets hit him. The gunfire ceased, leaving an eerie silence in the small storage room. His head was spinning, he felt dizzy, and nausea washed over him. Carefully, he crawled towards the window again and peered out. The two men stood with their weapons aimed, waiting. Clearing his throat, he addressed Ramirez: "You know, Diego... I've been thinking about your offer."

"I'm glad to hear that, sheriff. Hand over the girl and the priest. You can go free."

"Sounds good," he replied.

"The decision is yours."

"That's the problem, you know... They're not here anymore."

A heavy silence followed. Arisztid didn't dare move, only concentrating, hoping to hear something. No one spoke, so he continued: "You see, in these old Spanish forts, there's always a secret exit. I suppose you didn't know that."

"You and the bounty hunter kept us occupied and distracted. Very clever, señor, I tip my hat to you. This changes my offer somewhat."

"Oh, I know this attitude well, Diego! You never disappoint!"

"We are who we are, señor. I'm leaving now. I'm going after Kassandra. If, by chance, you defeat my friend and come after me, you'll be a dead man. Don't forget that."

"But I can't allow that," said Arisztid. "Stand with me for a duel!"

Diego laughed mockingly, and the Indian did the same. "You can't be serious about this!"

Wratiszlaw cursed silently, knowing full well that this was his one and best chance. "Let's make a deal," he proposed.

"I'm listening attentively, Sheriff."

"If I defeat you, your friend and all your remaining men are let me go! I can gather our dead and bury them! If you win... Well, I think we don't need to say it out loud."

Diego pondered for a moment, then replied: "So be it! I accept the challenge! Come forward with your hands up! My associate will oversee our duel! His shot will be the signal."

"Agreed!" The sheriff slid his revolver back into its holster, then approached the door and carefully opened it. The old door creaked painfully, and Arisztid stepped out with raised hands. Ramirez also raised his hands, indicating that he wasn't going to strike. The sheriff walked towards the center of the area, surrounded by debris, rubble, and spent bullet casings. The Indian eyed him with hatred and disdain. Arisztid stopped in front of the Mexican, and the two men locked eyes for a moment. Their gazes intertwined tightly.

Diego theatrically bowed, tipping his hat. "Come on, Sheriff! You're an aristocrat, if I'm not mistaken... Don't offend me!"

Arisztid spat to the side. "Respect must be earned."

The Mexican laughed, then straightened up and looked at the Indian. The warrior nodded, took a few steps back, and aimed his rifle at the sky.

Diego held his hand ready to fire, as did the sheriff.

Arisztid felt time slow down, sweat dripping down his forehead, fear coursing through his entire body. He felt his stomach churn, his heart ready to give out. A gentle breeze brushed his face, feeling like a cold shower this time. He moved his fingers, waiting for the shot that would decide everything. His heart burned with anger, hatred, desire for revenge, and a sense of justice. Fred's death throes flashed before him, Dalton's martyrdom, the sacrifice of the White brothers, the smell of Bruce's burning flesh... And the hope that perhaps it wasn't all in vain. Kassandra and Cristofano had escaped, and he could only hope that Ramirez would never catch up to them. He closed his eyes and focused on the sounds. His sickly childhood flashed before him, he saw his sister's face, he almost heard his mother's gentle voice in his ear. Every muscle tensed. The silence was almost maddening, he felt like trembling, like the aspen leaf, as if all eyes were on him again, judgmental glances passing over him. Just like before.

The sound of gunfire echoed, and he immediately reached for his pistol. He grabbed the handle, but another shot rang out. He was too late. Slow. He waited for the overwhelming death, the final pain that slowly spread through his body, but the burning agony did not come. He cautiously opened his eyes. Another pistol shot rang out, followed by a dull thud. He looked to the side.

The Indian lay dead on the ground, surrounded by a pool of blood. He didn't understand what was happening. Everything was murky, and he was swept along with the events. Motionless, with his revolver half-drawn, he stood and waited. He glanced at Diego.

The man, with dilated pupils, in a state of shock, looked at the sheriff in disbelief. Thick sweat ran down his face. He opened his mouth, trying to say something, but all he could do was cough up blood. He dropped his revolver, which landed with a loud thud on the ground. With trembling hands, he reached for his neck. A stream of red blood gushed from his throat. The Mexican fell to his knees. He wheezed, gasped... he was dying.

From the corner of his eye, Arisztid noticed movement. Slowly, very slowly, he turned in that direction. For a brief moment, he couldn't comprehend what he saw, as if a ghost had returned from the afterlife to seek revenge for the wrongs done to him, to bring justice and fulfill his destiny.

Jeremiah White, with trembling legs, barely standing, his shirt completely soaked in blood, still held his revolver ready to fire. His face was completely pale. The man was tormented by terrible physical pain.

The sheriff spoke almost inaudibly: "Mr. White..." he whispered.

Jeremiah coughed, and his revolver slipped from his hand. He collapsed to his knees and fell over.

The sheriff hesitated for a moment, then rushed over, knelt beside the bounty hunter, and lifted his head. "Jeremiah! It's okay, it's over! Hang in there, I'll take you home!"

The bounty hunter's face twisted into a grimace. He had lost too much blood, with at least four bullets tearing through his upper body. Arisztid saw that the bullets hadn't exited the man's body, indicating the excruciating pain he must have been enduring.

Jeremiah grabbed the sheriff's collar and pulled him closer. "Do something for me, sheriff!"

"Anything!" said Arisztid.

"Bury me next to my brother! I want to be where he is..."

Wratiszlaw bowed his head and replied: "Of course, Mr. White."

In the distance, more gunshots rang out. The sounds of horse hooves and battle cries echoed. The sheriff looked up but saw nothing. He turned back to the bounty hunter.

Jeremiah White stared into nothingness with glassy eyes. His body went limp, and he breathed no more.

Arisztid rested his head on the man's bloody chest. "I'm sorry..."

He heard footsteps approaching from behind and the familiar metallic click of a revolver's hammer. A moment later, he felt the barrel of the gun against the back of his head.

"For this, I'll kill you," Agustíno said. "You denied humanity salvation! Angelic justice! The ritual... was not completed! And this is your fault!"

The sheriff sighed as he continued to hold Jeremiah's lifeless body. He no longer cared about his own fate; he could peacefully move on to the afterlife. The escape of Kassandra and Cristofano was all that mattered now. "Do it," he said.

A gunshot rang out, and Arisztid flinched. He heard the priest behind him collapse. Nothing surprised him anymore. He looked up.

A man dressed in black approached him. His face and head were covered with a cloth, revealing only his green eyes. The man pointed his weapon at him. "Stand up!"

Arisztid didn't let go of Jeremiah. He remained kneeling, as if he hadn't heard.

"I said stand up!" the stranger shouted.

He grabbed the sheriff and helped him to his feet.

Arisztid didn't resist; he raised his hands in submission. "Your name?"

"I'm Arisztid Wratiszlaw. Sheriff of Corpus Christi."

The stranger lowered his weapon, his tone softened. "We've been tracking them for a while," he said, looking at Jeremiah's body. "I'm sorry we didn't arrive sooner. And I'm sorry for the loss of your comrades."

"Who are you?" the sheriff asked, confused.

"It doesn't matter. What matters is who you are. Go home, Arisztid. Talk to your father and take over your family's legacy. You must continue the path you've started. This is not where you belong."

"How do you mean? What...? I don't understand!"

The stranger grabbed him by the shoulders, his mesmerizing green eyes penetrating deep into his soul. "Bury your friends and return to the Monarchy! They need you there!"

"And what about the angel? It's unleashed... How do you plan to stop it? No one has ever successfully fought an angel!"

"Do you think so?" he asked cryptically. "Kasbeel is not your concern. We'll handle it. Now go! Bury your companions, mourn them, and return home to the Monarchy!"

The stranger turned and walked away.

Arisztid, lost in thought, watched the departing figure in a state of shock. From above, the sharp, otherworldly sound of a scream echoed. The flapping of wings. Screams and hisses. The sheriff stood paralyzed, motionless. All that remained for him was solitude. He looked around. Corpses, ruins, and chaos surrounded him. He had no idea what was happening to him and around him. He closed his eyes. *I need to go home.*

Epilogue

"Lord, Lord, did we not prophesy in your name and in your name drive out demons and in your name perform many miracles?" Then I will tell them plainly, 'I never knew you. Away from me, you evildoers!'"

Matthew 7:21-27

Crosses. Standing closely together in the freshly dug earth. Wratiszlaw Arisztid dug the graves one by one. Alone. Thoughts raced through his mind, to which he himself couldn't find answers. He had no idea who the stranger was who had saved his life. "Only who you are matters!" echoed in his mind. As he smoothed the soil over the last grave, he stopped and looked over them.

Jeremiah and Anton White's final resting places were side by side, as per their last wish. Jonathan Dalton, Bearslayer Bruce, and Frederick William. He knelt beside his friend's grave and ran his hand over the marker. "My friend... You were always a loyal, devoted, and true friend. Rest in peace!"

He stood up, casting one last glance at the deceased. He tipped his hat and bowed.

Turning to his horse, he stroked the animal's head. He mounted up and set off towards Corpus Christi. It was a week's ride from the town, and he didn't want to take a ship. He longed for solitude. He wanted to traverse the road, which was a kind of pilgrimage for him. He wanted to clarify his thoughts and plans, knowing that he had no future in this country. He had to return home, to search for his family, to find out who he really was. He dreaded the thought of meeting his father again. He had no idea what awaited him in Hungary; he was a deserter who had fled the country. Perhaps they would hang him. He couldn't know, but he was sure that fate had other plans for him. He watched the setting sun as it dipped below the horizon. He whistled, and his horse set off towards their destination at a slow, measured pace.

The road leading to Corpus Christi felt foreign to Arisztid. The everyday problems of the people walking up and down seemed almost insignificant. Not long ago, he had been one of them, but everything had changed now. Surprised faces glanced at him. Arriving at the main street of the town, he saw Solomon's inn. The black-haired, mustached man was smoking on the veranda.

As he caught sight of the sheriff, Solomon lowered his arm in surprise, looked back over his shoulder, and whistled.

From the inn emerged old Anthony, the deputy sheriff. The old man hadn't changed a bit. He flashed his yellowish teeth, adjusted his glasses, and slowly shuffled towards Arisztid.

The elderly man with the hunched back waved at him. "Well, you are alive!" he said joyfully. "Thank God you're alive! I knew the angels were watching over you, sheriff!"

Arisztid's heartbeat quickened immediately upon hearing the words, sweat trickled down his neck, and suddenly he craved alcohol.

The innkeeper stepped up beside the deputy sheriff, who carefully moved aside and handed Arisztid a bottle of whisky.

The sheriff dismounted his horse and took a big gulp of the drink. It burned his throat, but undeniably felt good. The two men watched each other for a moment, then Arisztid broke the silence: "Kassandra and Cristofano?" he asked hopefully.

The innkeeper nodded. "That damn Pedro brought them back in one piece; they're on their way to New York. The priest said you were dead. Glad to see that's not the case!"

"I'm not sure if I'm glad. A part of me died in Mexico."

Solomon didn't reply, he remained silent. He immediately understood that the sheriff had gone through something no one should. He didn't pry or ask questions. "Follow me," said the innkeeper. "There's something I want to give you. A letter arrived from the Monarchy."

Arisztid was surprised. He had never received a letter before. "I assume you've read it."

"I did indeed, but I couldn't understand a word of it. It's in Hungarian..."

Entering the inn, he felt like he hadn't even left. People drank, ate, enjoyed themselves. They danced and reveled as if their children were not missing. Anger and bewilderment swept over him. "Did Cristofano tell you what happened to the children?"

"Yes," replied Solomon. "We symbolically buried them. People are trying to move on. Another tragedy in our town, which only time will heal."

Arriving at Solomon's office, Arisztid took a seat without being asked. The once beloved place meant nothing to him anymore, as if everything he loved had happened in another life. Nothing else remained for him, only the tormenting awareness of the truth, which he could never tell anyone. Once again, he felt like an outsider, someone who could never be a useful member of society again.

From the drawer of the innkeeper's desk, Solomon retrieved his badge and tossed it into Arisztid's lap.

The man didn't reach for it, just let it roll down his thigh and fall to the floor. It clinked metallically on the wooden floor.

"Take the damn thing, Sheriff!" Solomon cursed. "You're no goddamn sheriff anymore!"

"Not anymore."

An awkward silence fell over the room. Solomon scrutinized Arisztid. He seemed troubled, tortured, and broken. "What happened in Mexico?" Solomon finally asked.

"You wouldn't believe me anyway."

"I don't really care," the innkeeper said. "What matters to me is for you to pick up your badge and get back to work! For me..."

The sheriff shook his head. "It's over, Solomon. All of this around us... Your inn, the whores, the alcohol, the opium... It means nothing! Nothing at all! And I don't belong here. I'm going home."

Solomon didn't reply. He sighed. He knew Arisztid was serious. "Fine!" The innkeeper took the letter from his vest pocket and handed it to him. "Read this, while I check on my daughters, then take a rest. You could use it! Tonight, you can eat and drink on my tab, and the girls are half-price! Tomorrow, we'll talk again about who's the sheriff and who's not..."

"I've already made up my mind. As soon as I can, I'll head to New York and return to the Monarchy."

Solomon gave one last glance at Arisztid, blew a frustrated breath, and replied: "As you wish!"

The door slammed shut hard behind the man. Arisztid's ears rang for a moment. He held the letter in his hands, turning it over, unfolding and refolding it. It wasn't his father's handwriting; he recognized it immediately as the old Albert's. He had served his family since birth, and it seemed he still did. He unfolded the paper again and began to read.

"My Lord! Count Wratiszlaw!

With deep regret and sincere sorrow, I must inform you that your father, Elder Lajos Wratiszlaw, has departed from this earthly world after a short and painless illness. Please forgive my rudeness in not inquiring about your well-being in this letter, but time is pressing. The family estate, your father's investments, painting and antiquities collection are in jeopardy. Perhaps you remember from your youth how the Budapest hyenas, also known as aristocrats, can viciously fight for the carcass. Count Markovits, that scoundrel, has set his eyes on the family villa and your father's entire fortune! Posthumously, I must apologize, but—as you know—according to royal laws, I am responsible for your family's wealth until you or your dear sister return, so I bluntly rejected the Count's offer, not too politely, but firmly. Or as you say in the wild and barbaric West, 'I kicked his ass!' Please forgive the language.

Please return to Budapest and take up your family duties, enhance the Wratiszlaw countship as your predecessors did! If you do not respond to my letter by the end of May, we will be forced to officially bury you in a grand ceremony, and all of the family's assets will officially pass to your sister. I beg you, my Lord, please return home!

With respect and eternal loyalty to you and your family: Albert Kemenes"

The sheriff placed the letter on Solomon's desk, staring ahead with an empty gaze. His father had passed away... The family fortune was in jeopardy... Count Markovits, the aristocracy, the nobility of Buda... His head throbbed, he needed rest. Memories flooded back and relentlessly besieged his mind. This was the strange twist of fate, he had no doubt about it. He sighed, then stood up and walked out of the inn. Walking through the dusty dirt road, he entered his office one last time. He observed the empty cell where Captain Dalton had been tortured. He turned towards the deputy's desk. The aging desk stood lonely in the empty office. A thin layer of dust covered the neatly arranged documents. "Frederick William - Deputy Sheriff" stood on the small plaque at the edge of the table. He approached, then dusted it off, sorrow gnawing at his soul. He glanced at his own desk, adorned with a framed photograph. He lifted the picture and smiled. Fred, with his rifle slung over his shoulder, smiled back at him. Carefully, he took out the picture and pocketed it. From his pocket, he retrieved his badge and placed it on the table. "I won't be needing this anymore."

He turned around and headed towards the exit, his footsteps echoing on the dried-out boards, a sound he was now familiar with. He would miss the small town, the people, and Texas, but for him, this adventure had come to an end.

Two weeks of long and exhausting travel lay behind Arisztid. He had bid farewell to Solomon, Anthony, and the townsfolk one last time. He apologized for letting them down and promised that if he stumbled upon any of the children during his European journey, he would do whatever it took, even break the laws, to bring them home. The residents of Corpus Christi bid farewell to the sheriff, thanking him for his long and loyal service.

A brisk wind stung Arisztid's face as ship horns sounded. He looked up. An ocean liner was docked in the harbor, spewing thick black smoke from its chimneys. He hoisted his luggage and stepped onto the ship, presenting his ticket to Dublin. He cast one last glance at the ship. "Angel" adorned its side.

"Typical," he muttered to himself. He boarded and sought out his cabin. Passing through the ornate dining room and into the first-class quarters. He was an aristocrat, and he needed to readjust to the lifestyle they represented. He loathed the glitz, the extravagance, and the hypocritical chatter. After stowing his luggage on deck, he leaned against the railing, smoking with the other passengers, who waved their hats to those staying ashore. For the first time in a long time, he smiled and waved. He hoped that a better life awaited him in his homeland than what he had experienced so far. "I just don't want to see any damn angels..."

THE END

About the Author

Ferenc K. Zoltán is a Hungarian author currently residing in Oban, Scotland. His debut novel, *The Color of Death Is Red*, was published in 2019, exploring the 1944-45 siege of Budapest through the eyes of the soldiers defending the city.

This was followed in 2021 by *The Gospel of the Devil*, which portrays a series of ritual murders on the streets of Budapest. In 2023, the Hungarian edition of *The Black Monastery* was released, earning recognition from both *Creepyshake* and *Cinegore* magazines as one of the best books of the year.

Additionally, the *Horrorscope* podcast named it one of the year's top books. All of Ferenc K. Zoltán's published books have been nominated for the András Dugonics Literary Award, making it onto the final shortlist.

In 2024, his short story *The Soul of Paintings* was published in the June issue of the American magazine *The Chamber*, and four of his short stories were featured in *The Damned* anthology by *Dragon Soul Press*.

OTHER HELLBOUND BOOKS
www.hellboundbooks.com

Satan Rides Your Daughter Again

Welcome to the second volume of HellBound's satanic-themed anthology, our homage to all things Old Nick and those who worship him and his demonic underlings!

From a poor woman suffering at the hands of witch finders, the building of an infamous Bunny Ranch and absolute living Hell that is high school, to encounters with angels, Hades' pit, the quest for a hellishly good chilli, and so much more in between, Satan Rides Your Daughter Again is packed with devilishly good tales to torment your soul with a taste of the fire and brimstone underworld that roils below us…

Featuring some of the very best independent horror authors committing words to paper today: R.D. Tyler, Dan Bolden, K A Douglas, Dylan Bosworth, Conor O'Brian Barnes, Dan Muenzer, Josh Darling, Barend Nieuwstraten III, Matthew Fryer, Kevin L. Kennel, J Louis Messina, Terry Grimwood, James Musgrave, Donn L. Hess, Shannon Lawrence, Chase Hughes, KT Bartlett, Sarah Goodman, Mariah Southworth, and Terry Campbell.

Notes of Discord

These Squatters Are Going To Rot!

In the late eighties, the Lower East Side of New York City rippled with turmoil. It was the city against the poor and destitute, it was punk versus skin versus hippy.

All of it had a soundtrack, call it drunk punk, call it what you would, the LES throbbed with a new generation of punkers pushing the boundaries. Underneath it lay an evil that even the headline writers of the Post could never have imagined.

An unearthly evil that twists the will, an evil that an up and coming punk band will never forget.

An evil that will never forget them. *Notes of Discord*, part coming of age story, part personal memoir, and all horror novel. A book with lots of punk rock, and even more full-on bloody bits.

Anthology of Horror

hor·ror
/ˈhôrər/

A literary or film genre concerned with arousing feelings of horror.

Rest assured, HellBound Books knows what scares you!

Skulking around in the deepest, thickest, darkest shadows of our authors' imaginations lies a whole host of terrifying tales to scare you witless and stir your greatest fears and, dear reader, we have compiled twenty-one such short stories for that specific purpose within the beautifully crafted pages of this very tome!

So, dig in – we dare you – and do remember to leave a light on…

Featuring short tales of terror from: Cory Andrews, Kathrin Classen, William Presley, John Schlimm. K.L. Lord, Jane Nightshade, K. John O'Leary, Dante Bilec, D. H. Parish, Whitney McShan, Keiran Meeks, Josh Darling, Paul Lonardo, Martyn Lawrence, Eric J. Juneau, Terry Campbell, Brett King, Sophia Cauduro, Christina Meeks, Kody Greene, and HellBound Books' very own James H Longmore.

The First Time I Saw Her

Heart-stopping folk horror to keep you out of the woods!

Anna and her mother are on the run after a tragedy shatters their world. A stranger has offered them protection in a private community hidden deep in the woods, and Anna and her mother have no choice but to abandon their life and belongings to take refuge until they can figure out their next move.

But the woman who helped them may not be what she seems, and the safe-haven community has its own secrets ... and its own dangers.

Anna is no ordinary girl, though. She can perceive things others cannot, impossible things. Now thrust into an unfamiliar setting with horrors unfolding all around her, Anna must figure out what she is and what she is capable of before she loses what little she has left of her life.

A HellBound Books Publishing LLC Publication

www.hellboundbookspublishing.com

9 781966 296027